ART TO DIE FOR

A NOVEL

BY

JT HINE

BOOK 3 OF THE *LOCKHART* SERIES

CONTENTS

Acknowledgments

Without generous friends, no author could write a book worth reading. I am especially indebted to the beta readers: Renata Celin, Captain William J. Laz, U.S. Navy, Joy Phillips, Commander Renée P. Reedy, U.S. Navy, and an anonymous colleague of Sisters in Crime. Anne Carley gave me the name Trent Braxton for a villain as well as valued counsel along the way. The musical selections in the book came from Daniel Hine.

Kerry Genova has now edited six of my novels, and Kim Olson has proofread them all.

I have been delighted to work with the folks at ebooklaunch.com: Alisha designed the cover; John formatted the book.

None of these wonderful people had anything to do with any errors you may notice. Those are all mine. I would not mind knowing about them: jt@jthine.com.

Titles by JT Hine

Fiction

Lockhart

Enemies

Art to Die for

Emily & Hilda

Rule Number One

Emily Is Hard to Kill

Nonfiction

I Am Worth It!

Are You Bilingual?

Translator Education in the U.S.A.

Translations

Combat Aircraft by Riccardo Niccoli

Beyond the Age of Oil by Leonardo Maugeri

Schio: Industrial Archeology by Bernadetta Ricci

Man is Different by Don Zeno (with Emily Adkins)

The Fight against Blindness by Luciano Moretti

The Retirement correspondence of Thomas Jefferson

CHAPTER 1

ROME TO RICHMOND

NANCY LOCKHART AND SANDRA BILLINGSLEY stood under the portico of the Cavalieri Hilton hotel in Rome. Despite the heat, Nancy wanted to stand outside to wait for the Smithson Italia driver. She stared across the street as they talked. Sandra followed her gaze to the yellow and white five-story apartment building. The splintered hole still showed in the door to the lobby, reminding them of the assassination attempt on the Smithson Italia executive a month ago. She saw Nancy shiver briefly as if echoing her own thoughts.

"It feels so strange to stay in this hotel and look at the building that was my home for twelve years," said Nancy. "Joe grew up there."

"Too bad he couldn't come with us." Sandra felt the usual pleasant frisson when she thought of Nancy's son.

"He had orders to report to Naples. With his priority, he'll probably get back two weeks after we do."

"That building has so many memories," Sandra said, "and I only got involved in the last two years."

"Here's hoping the excitement is behind us for a while." They thought about that.

A hateful campaign against Nancy as an American executive had been exposed as a misinformation project by the leader of the neofascist party trying to frame the left-wing parties. The frequent car bombings around the country and two assassination attempts on Nancy had kept both women on top alert for far too long. Sandra had hardly been able to worry about her older brother Walter, deployed to Vietnam with the Third Marine Division. She tried to imagine what could happen next.

"Does anyone here have your address in Richmond?"

"No. Smithson forwards our personal mail."

"We're leaving some very angry people here. I won't relax until you are safe at home."

"Sandra, I owe you my life. Whatever the future holds for you and Joe, I hope we'll always be friends."

"Me too." She tilted her head toward the street. "There's Adriano."

They watched as the black sedan paused. The chauffeur looked around, then drove to the hotel entrance. He loaded their bags into the trunk while Sandra held the door for Nancy.

Soon they were heading out the Via Aurelia to pick up the Grande Raccordo Anulare, the ring road that would take them around the Eternal City to the Via Ostiense. Farmland stretched away from them on either side. Apartment buildings under construction shimmered in the heat between the highway and Rome.

Nancy and Joe had both watched the city grow outward along the ancient Roman roads, and Sandra had ridden past the job sites replacing the cane breaks and fields. *How long before this highway becomes a downtown boulevard?* she wondered.

As they turned toward the coast and the Fiumicino International Airport, Sandra asked Adriano, "*Sono come questa tutte le macchine con autista?*" Are all the chauffeured cars similar to this one? They continued in Italian.

"Most of them. Black, heavy, and fast. Why, *signorina?*"

"Just thinking ahead. There are usually two or three lined up to deliver passengers at the departures terminal, aren't there?"

"Yes."

"You're making me nervous," said Nancy, also in Italian.

"Adriano, leave us off short of the entrance and let the others take the spaces by the door."

"I understand, miss." He met her gaze in the rearview mirror. "Brava."

"What's that all about, Sandra?" She had developed a healthy respect for the young FBI employee's instincts.

"It will be their last chance to try something on you, and I'm not off duty yet."

Four black sedans came off the Via Ostiense with them. Adriano let them pass. At the terminal, he took a spot well back from the entrance. Sandra held the door for Nancy again, scanning the delivery zone and the surrounding buildings as the former Smithson Italia vice president got out.

"Don't come in with us," said Nancy. "We'll take the luggage, and you can take the car back."

He placed their suitcases on the sidewalk. Each woman had only one. They had shipped everything else to Richmond.

"So long, Adriano. I will miss you."

"Come back to us, signora," he said, choking slightly. He gasped as Nancy gave him a hug.

"*Arrivederci, allora.*" So long, then.

Sandra and Nancy picked up their luggage and walked toward the entrance.

"This way, Nancy." She motioned to the side door.

Just as they stepped into the vestibule, a flash outside triggered an instinctive reaction. Sandra whirled to the right and dove on top of Nancy, pushing them to the floor.

Glass exploded into the terminal, followed by the sound of the explosion, then the pieces of debris. Passersby screamed, and the hot blast from the limousine blew over the two women.

From her position on top of Nancy, Sandra looked around. People were running away from the scene while police and Carabinieri ran toward it. The burning sedan cast a frightening light over the three bodies crumpled against the frame of the entrance and the sidewalk.

"Are you okay?" She stood and helped Nancy to her feet. Both women could feel their hands shaking, but this was not the time to deal with that.

"A little sore where my chest fell on the suitcase."

"Let's get out of here."

They walked quickly into the frigid air conditioning of the terminal and found the check-in counter for Trans World Airlines. It was far enough away that the personnel were only beginning to react. As soon as they had checked their bags and collected their boarding passes, police appeared to order the staff to close.

At the gate, they were ushered immediately to the aircraft. As Sandra sat in her seat, she felt a sharp pain in her back.

"Do I have something in my back?" She leaned forward.

"Oh my God. It's a shard of glass. Hold still." Nancy pushed the call button for the attendant, then undid her belt so she could twist toward Sandra. She pulled Sandra's blouse up behind her head. Using a handkerchief, she extracted the six-inch long fragment, which had slid up Sandra's back, slicing her blouse and lodging under her bra strap. For all the damage to Sandra's clothing, it was a shallow cut. Nancy held the bloody piece of cloth on the wound.

"Please fasten your seat belt, ma'am – what?"

"Would you get a first aid kit, please?" Nancy said to the shocked attendant. "I need to disinfect a small area on her back. I'm a doctor, and this is not an emergency."

More than the words, the authority in Nancy's voice made the attendant hurry to the galley and come back with the kit.

Nancy cleaned and bandaged the wound created by Sandra's sitting back on the shard. "Another half inch and that bra would be doing you no good at all." She buckled up and returned the kit to the attendant with thanks. "Let's worry about your bloody wardrobe in the States, shall we?"

"Yes, Doctor." Each woman felt the adrenaline drain away as the aircraft lifted off from the runway.

ରରର

Midshipman Third Class Jason Joseph Lockhart, Jr., US Navy, approached the passenger service counter at the US Naval Air Facility Capodichino in Naples, Italy. His khaki shirt stuck to his undershirt and skin, and the damp summer heat pressed more moisture on him.

The yeoman third class on duty scanned his orders.

"Priority Three, sir. We have one flight each to Naval Station Rota and McGuire Air Force Base. The stateside plane is full. Would you prefer to take the C-130 to Rota and wait there?"

"Are the chances better there?"

"Yes, sir. Two flights a day to McGuire. You should come up with a seat in a few days. They also have a bigger barracks."

"I came through Rota on the way in but didn't get to see anything. Let's do it."

An hour later, he nestled into the webbing on the lumbering cargo plane and dozed off for three hours.

ଞଞଞ

"Nancy! Sandra!" The tall couple standing outside the crowd to the left waved. Sandra took both suitcases, so Nancy could hug her parents long and hard.

Sandra had enjoyed getting to know Brigadier General Matthew Ardwood and his Parisian wife, Annabelle Dampierre, last year when they invited her to Richmond, Virginia, for Thanksgiving and spring break. She had also been an awestruck fan of Nancy Ardwood Lockhart since before she met the trailblazing executive in Rome. Seeing the Ardwoods gathered in a loving family reunion made the emotion swell in her throat. She blinked hard to stem the tears. She had never pictured her hero as a tender daughter herself, hugging her parents as if they might vanish on her.

After a short while, the three stood back to savor the reality that Nancy was not home for a holiday visit. The other passengers on the *Silver Meteor* flowed past them to the exits of the Broad Street Station.

Soon, Matthew was driving them to the West End of Richmond, Virginia, to the antebellum house in which Nancy had grown up. Adele, the housekeeper, and François, the gardener, were waiting when they drove up. Nancy hugged the two Dampierre retainers before everyone moved indoors.

"How do you feel about having Joe's old room?" asked her father. "I cleared out of the study downstairs to free it up for you. The master bedroom is big enough for my small desk."

"Anything you want to do is fine, Dad. His room is bigger than my room in Rome."

"Good then. Sandra, you'll be across the hall. When do you have to go back to Washington?"

"Next weekend."

"Any word on Joe?"

"He took the train to Naples. He'll probably call from McGuire when he gets in."

"Until then, no news is good news." He motioned to the stairs. "Meet us on the veranda after you move in and freshen up."

ଷଷଷ

Nancy pulled the new white Alfa Romeo 1750 into the space marked "Dr. Lockhart" near the main door. She suppressed a momentary panic at the sight of her name so prominently displayed.

Inside, she headed for the elevators, stopped, and turned to the Facilities Management office on the ground floor.

The receptionist beamed at her. Brunette, maybe Joe's age, fresh with the enthusiasm of her first job. Nancy looked at the nameplate, "M. Berkeley."

"Hello, Miss Berkeley. Is Jerry Leake still the director of Facilities Management?"

"No, ma'am. Mr. Leake retired. Mr. Berken took over."

"Dale Berken from MCV?" The Medical College of Virginia.

"Yes, ma'am. He arrived over the summer."

"Is he in?"

"Whom may I say is here?"

"Nancy Lockhart."

Miss Berkeley punched a button on her phone. "There's a Mrs. Nancy Lockhart here to see Mr. Berken." She pulled the handset from her ear when the secretary in the director's office shouted something. Nancy smiled; it had been a long time since a new employee had not recognized her. "She said to come on back. Do you know the way?"

"If they haven't moved since last year, yes. Thank you, Miss Berkeley."

As she walked around the desk, the door to the rest of the department flew open. Dale Berken held it.

"Nancy – Doctor Lockhart. What a pleasure! Have you been back long?"

"Just a week, Dale. How are you doing?"

"Great. I'm sorry our new receptionist didn't recognize you."

"She was very professional and welcoming. Don't scare her off." Nancy smiled to reassure the terrified young employee, then shook hands with Dale's secretary. "Good to see you again, Margaret."

"Welcome back, Doctor Lockhart."

"Thanks." They went into his office.

"Can I get you anything?"

"No thanks, Dale. I'm on my way upstairs, but I have a request. Could you arrange a meeting with security? Is that still Pete Wembly?"

"Major Pete is still our head cop. What's up?"

"Let me walk around for a couple of days before we meet, but I have one item for you now. My parking place."

"What's wrong?"

"I need not to be so easily identified and targeted. Could we give me a spot farther from the door and without my name and job on it? I don't mind a few extra steps."

"You're home now, Nancy."

"But still a target, apparently." She explained the car bombing at the airport.

"Consider it done. I read about the way you dodged the shotgun attack." He paused. "Do you prefer to dive to the right or the left? I'll pick a spot that puts the flower beds on your favorite side."

"Right side, then, wise guy." She turned to the door. "I hope not to make a lot of changes, but that one worried me."

"Welcome home, Nancy. Pete and I have your back."

"Thanks."

ଧଧଧ

Joe Lockhart paused only a second before descending from the southbound *Silver Meteor*. He wasn't sure who to expect, but his mother's auburn hair shone over the crowd.

"Thanks for picking me up, Mom." He gave her a hard hug. "You're easy to spot."

"So is a naval uniform." Servicemen in uniform paid half price for train tickets. "Welcome home, Joe."

They joined the people moving toward Broad Street outside.

"It really is home now, isn't it?" he said.

"It is. Sometimes, I feel as if I've only been on a long business trip, then some big change surprises me."

"I can imagine – wow! That's one change!"

"It took no time to confirm that I needed a car." She opened the driver's door of the Alfa Romeo. "I wanted something that doesn't handle like Noah's Ark."

He tossed his seabag in the back and got in the passenger's side.

"Is this Berlina as zippy as the GT model?"

"I don't know, but it has all the pep I need." She downshifted and passed four cars before taking a smooth left turn into the neighborhood. "Aunt Mary will be here for the weekend too."

"Are the courts ready for us?"

"Your grandfather warned them, and RLTA threw a party when I showed up." Richmond Lawn Tennis Association. She parked behind a racing-green MG.

The delegation on the porch included Joe's grandparents, Matthew and Annabelle Ardwood, and Matthew's sister Mary. Joe paused to relish the unfamiliar pleasure of seeing them together.

Only his grandfather and great-aunt Mary had some distinguished gray in their hair. His mother's rich auburn hair and Annabelle's pale blond drew the eye away from the maturity of their faces, which were clear and smooth. The whole family was tall, with the slim, athletic grace of superior tennis players.

After long hugs, they moved to the veranda at the back of the house. Matthew poured Moselle for everyone as they admired the sunset. They could smell the *coq au vin* in the oven.

"You have mail, Joe." His grandfather went into the house and came back with a small stack of envelopes. "Already two from Sandra, who only left last week, and one from Diego." Joe's roommate at the University of Virginia. "The others seem to be business."

"Thanks, Grandpa." He put Sandra's letters in his pocket to read alone. He opened the letter from Midn. 4/c D. de la Torre, USN, Sixth Company, Bancroft Hall, US Naval Academy, Annapolis, Maryland. "I still can't believe Diego went to Annapolis."

"How did that work out?" asked Nancy. "We have his things in the attic."

"I thought my orders to the Mediterranean were a surprise, but Diego's appointment arrived the day he was to board the bus to Norfolk." Joe took a sip of his wine. "He always said his plan was to make a career, but he never expected to win an appointment to the Naval Academy. The principal was the son of a political friend of his congressman."

"What happened?" asked Matthew.

"The principal crashed his car the day before graduation. Diego was first alternate, so the congressman offered him the spot."

"I hope he's happy. Starting over means he is really serious." The Naval Academy required everyone to start as plebes, so Diego would be commissioned a year later than their UVA class.

Joe read the letter quickly. "He says now that Plebe Summer is over, things are less crazy. He is one of the older plebes, and the upperclassmen have more fun with the high school graduates." He laughed and looked up. "You know he takes a lot of grief for his dark complexion, don't you?"

"You took your share of grief being his friend," said Matthew. "Stupid people. Diego's family was farming the Central Valley of California before the Puritans arrived on the *Mayflower*." Sergeant Carlos de la Torre had fought at Guadalcanal in Matthew's regiment and earned a battlefield commission there. The Californian lieutenant and the Virginian colonel had bonded in that crucible of fire.

"But he looks Moorish," said Annabelle, "not African at all."

Joe said, "Apparently, an upperclassman called him a nigger. They were in the hall outside the company officer's office. Diego locked the other guy's arms behind him, marched him into the office, and asked the lieutenant if he heard that. He had, and no one harasses Diego anymore."

Matthew chuckled. "I love that guy. I'll write to him myself to remind him that we will still be his East Coast base."

"Do that, Dad," said Nancy. "I'm sorry I missed meeting him." She asked Joe, "Weren't you two going to get a place off Grounds this year?"

"Mrs. Page called," his grandfather said. Sandra had stayed at Mrs. Page's guesthouse when visiting Joe last year. "She said that she has a vacancy in a one-man room. She knows that you would prefer a place where Sandra could spend the night, but it would be easier to house-hunt from her place."

"I'd much rather stay there than in the residence halls. May I call her tonight?"

"It's your home, Joe. You can use the phone and anything else here. Just let me know if you call overseas, so I'm not surprised by the bill."

Aunt Mary asked Nancy, "Can he afford a place off Grounds?"

"Converting to regular NROTC made the college budget much easier." Naval Reserve Officers Training Corps. She tipped her glass toward her son. "Just don't make a habit of earning it the way you did last summer."

"Tell us about that," asked Mary, "or is that classified?"

"Most of it isn't. Mom told you about the midshipman cruise in USS *Point Defiance* in the Mediterranean, and you knew about the hate campaign against her in Italy. Remember the historic haul of stolen and forged paintings that was in the news?" The others nodded. "One of the men arrested in Rome ordered the hate campaign and the attacks on me and Mom. He is behind bars now awaiting trial, and his political career is finished."

"So, are you safe now?" she asked Nancy.

"Maybe, but General Arcibaldo has his base of supporters. We don't know if the bomb at the airport was intended for me, but—" Nancy shrugged.

"Not very comforting," said Annabelle.

"You are right, *Grandmaman*," said Joe, "but with the extra training in Tony Madison's martial arts studio in Charlottesville, I hope I can keep safe." He asked his mother, "What about Smithson?"

"We moved the obvious signs around the campus, and I had a walk-through with Pete Wembly, our security chief. He'll contact the local FBI and police, so they can be alert for threats to me or the company. That's as much as we can do right now."

"Would they attack Smithson headquarters?" asked Matthew.

"I don't know, Dad. Pete has implemented several changes."

The oven timer dinged. Leaving their wine on the dining table, they gathered in the kitchen and put supper out while Joe called Mrs. Page back. He would move on Sunday.

"How's the new job, Mom?" Joe passed the roasted potatoes.

"I like it. More business management, more research and development, and more frequent contact with investors and the Board than I had in Italy."

"Luke works for you now?" He grinned.

Luke Arland had been a colleague in Rome but now worked in the New York office. The family knew that he had helped Nancy finally grow past her grief, years after Joe's father died of an unknown virus. For that, they were all grateful.

"Not really. He is still vice president for Strategy and Investment. Headquarters would have brought him to Richmond long ago, except that travel is easier from New York, and our major investors are there."

Dinner and post-prandial conversation lasted until midnight. Saturday, they played tennis hard and fast on the courts at the University of Richmond. Sunday after church, Mary drove home to Amherst, Virginia, where she taught at Sweet Briar College. Matthew took the others to Charlottesville, so Joe could move in, and the family could treat their friend to dinner. Eleanor Page had been a guest of the Ardwoods in Paris and Berlin during her opera tours as a soprano before the war.

ଛଛଛ

Monday morning, Joe rode his bicycle to the University of Virginia. He stopped at the NROTC Unit and the Department of Italian, Spanish, and Portuguese to let the respective secretaries know he was in town and to give them Mrs. Page's address and phone number. He made an appointment to call on Captain Norwood, the commanding officer of the unit, on Tuesday. The following Saturday, the incoming first-year midshipmen would take the oath. Check-in for the academic year would start on the Wednesday after that.

CHAPTER 2

CHARLOTTESVILLE, VIRGINIA

TUESDAY MORNING, Joe donned his khaki uniform and walked to Maury Hall, one of two buildings used by the NROTC Unit. Mrs. Blankenship welcomed him warmly and told him to go in.

"Midshipman Lockhart, sir." Joe stood at attention at the door. Captain L. Michael Norwood rose and came from behind his desk. His appearance always impressed Joe: average height but solid and strong, with broad shoulders and kind eyes that seemed out of place in his chiseled face. The five rows of "fruit salad" on his chest spoke of service in three wars and combat missions on as many continents. The Purple Heart ribbon with three stars tended to catch Joe's eye because the senior officer did not show the effects of his wounds.

"At ease, Mr. Lockhart. Close the door, please, and join me." He motioned to a pair of armchairs and a coffee table to the side of the office. Joe had never seen anyone use that furniture. "First of all, thanks for reporting early. Once school starts, we won't get a chance to chat this way." He poured coffee from a carafe into two mugs.

"I thought you'd want a report on my summer cruise since it was different from the others." Joe had been sent to the Mediterranean with a contingent from the Naval Academy. His classmates had gone on an NROTC training cruise in the Caribbean.

"And some other things. I heard that you left the cruise."

"Yes, sir, as you suspected. I was pulled off and assigned to COMSIXTHFLT as a translator." Commander US Sixth Fleet. "While I was there, I prepared a daily briefing of the European press. It turned out to be quite popular."

"BUPERS has asked the units to look for multilingual midshipmen," the Bureau of Naval Personnel "so they can be flagged as CARS officers." Country, Area, Regional Specialists. "I'll bet you had something to do with that."

"Maybe, sir. Admiral Portague did not want me to leave when I got orders ashore in July."

"Where to?"

"Rome, sir. Events triggered the operation for which I was sent to the Med."

"Can you tell me about it?"

"A little. Do you remember the hate campaign against my mother?" The captain nodded. "I was the target, so when the first attempt to stop the perpetrator failed, they called me in to be a decoy."

"Sounds dangerous."

"I ended up in the hospital with a cracked rib, but the man was arrested."

"Why were you a target?"

"Something that happened two years ago." He shrugged and looked down with a frown.

"Classified?"

"Yes, sir. It's over now, but it will stay classified for a long time."

"I don't want to know. I'm just happy to have you back and well. I'm sorry we lost Mister de la Torre. You two were quite a team."

The older man took a sip of his coffee and put it down.

"Joe, I want to tell you something that I have concealed since you reported aboard." He had never used Joe's first name. "*Ti ho visto per la prima volta quando avevi sei anni, ai funerali per tuo padre.*" I saw you for the first time when you were six years old. At your father's funeral.

Joe gasped and paled. The memory of reaching up to slide his hand along the casket exploded in his chest.

"I'm sorry," said the captain. "I did not want to add to your grief. That was a sad day for me too."

Joe shook his head in disbelief: his commanding officer was speaking Italian with a distinct northeastern accent.

He answered in Italian, "I think I have accepted the grief, sir. It's just that my mother and I have not talked about that with anyone since we left Richmond. I'm stunned." He took a drink, straining to keep his hand from shaking. "How did you know my father?"

Captain Norwood put his finger on the Purple Heart ribbon. "The second star. Inchon. He sewed me up after my ship was hit. I was in a coma for two weeks after that. We spent a lot of time together while I healed enough to return to my ship."

"The right side of the church was filled with men in uniform. Were you there?"

"Yes. Remember what General Puller said?"

"Something about bringing them back from the deep. It was from the psalm *De Profundis.*"

"Your father saved every man there. That's why so many of us came."

"I never knew. I hardly remember him coming back from Korea."

"He was quite a hero. Imagine my surprise when I saw his – your – name on the list of incoming midshipmen."

"Why are you telling me now, sir?"

"A couple of reasons. Not revealing my connection to your father bothered me. And I have always hoped to meet your mother, especially after watching you. Do you think she would mind letting my wife and me have you two to dinner when she comes to town?"

"Now that she is in Richmond, that's doable, sir. I'll let her know."

"Thank you. You have so much of your father in you that it drove me nuts. You won't notice any difference in my treatment of you this year, but I'm glad to have this out."

"Me too, sir."

They stood. Captain Norwood shook hands with Joe.

"Carry on, Mr. Lockhart," he said in English.

"Yes, sir."

ଧ୧ଧ୧ଧ୧

Joe knocked on the door to Professor Giraldi's office in Cabell Hall, then opened it slowly.

"*Permesso?*" May I come in?

"*Signor Lockhart! Che piacere!*" What a pleasure. The tall, slender academic pumped Joe's hand enthusiastically while smiling with his deep black eyes. "I am so excited about your paper for the Italian Cultural Center in New York. That's a great honor!"

"Thank you, sir. It was a surprise to me. I only sent it in because I had it written, and it seemed to fit their requirements. It took three weeks for their letter to reach me, forwarded all over the Mediterranean and then to my mother's office in Rome."

"How is your mother? She is back now, no?"

"Yes. She is well. Executive vice president at Smithson Global in Richmond. Different work, but she is home with my grandparents and glad to be back."

"I should like to meet her."

"Richmond is not far."

"The faculty in the department wants to organize a dinner next month. Would you be willing to read your paper?"

"Of course, sir. I'd be honored. Do you want to invite my mother?"

"Yes. Please make sure that Signora Chavez has her address on your way out."

After a pause, Joe asked, "Has the Academic Committee considered my suggestion yet?"

"They met before dispersing for the summer and before the letter from the cultural center arrived. You will be allowed to complete the general requirements for the BA this semester. They thought fifteen credits was an overload until I explained the other work you do at the graduate level for us."

"That's great, sir. I'll be able to concentrate on the Italian courses in the spring semester then?"

"Yes. I think it will be a lighter load than you have subjected yourself to already, so you should enjoy it."

"If nothing else, I could take in more translation work. I hated having to turn down so many requests last semester."

"That will be a boon to us all." He went back around his desk and extracted a paper from the drawer. "I drew up a list of the graduate courses you should take. If you fit them in, you could complete the coursework for your master's degree by Christmas of next year."

"Then I could submit my thesis? Doesn't someone have to give me a bachelor's degree first?"

"That has not been brought up in committee yet, but all your teachers are aware that you will have met those requirements by next spring. More later on that, I think." He smiled and shook Joe's hand again. "See you Monday in class?"

"*Sì. Arrivederci, Professore.*"

CHAPTER 3

WASHINGTON, DC

AFTER LOCKING HER BICYCLE to the inside of the fence, Sandra walked toward the guard station. Something made her pause and walk back to the Ninth Street entrance. Concealed by the trees near the driveway, she observed two men across the road. One stood at the bus stop; the other pretended to look in a store window. When she had their features fixed in her mind, she returned to the inner courtyard of FBI Headquarters and cleared security.

"Thanks for coming, Sandra." Special Agent Redwood appeared while she was clipping the visitor's badge to her blouse. "He's upstairs."

Special Agent David Vasari was waiting in the conference room. Even after a year, she was still taken aback by his resemblance to the Renaissance art critic Giorgio, his many times removed grandfather. Though the famous Vasari had no heirs, he did father at least three boys and two girls. According to David, Giorgio recognized Beniamino, son of a Jewish merchant's daughter, but the records were lost in a fire in the synagogue in 1634.

David's grinned broadly. "Hi, Sandra. You're almost the only reason I would want to come to this building. Coffee?"

"Yes, please." She took the mug and sat. "Would you give me a moment? I have something for Agent Redwood, but I need to do this right away."

The two FBI agents poured their coffees while Sandra took a sketchbook from her bag and a box of pencils. They watched her in amazement as the pencils flew over the paper so fast that her hand seemed to disappear.

Five minutes later, she stopped, took a final look at the two sketches, and tore them out.

"These two men have been outside on Ninth Street the last three times I have come here. If they were yours, I would have expected a rotation of some sort, not the same two."

Redwood's eyes got wider. "I saw them, too, but I didn't think them unusual. What made you notice?"

"Like noticing where the rocks are when stepping over a stream. The people come and go, but those two are always there."

"Thanks. We'll check into it. You two get started while I give these to the right people." He left. Sandra turned to the other agent.

"David, it's great to see you again. You have something for me?"

"Yes." For the next hour, he showed her photographs of paintings and forgeries. Redwood joined them for most of the session and seemed happy to watch them work. His smile resembled that of an old master who had discovered a prodigy in his class. Sandra had come to him as a seventeen-year-old intern in Rome, Italy. She had stayed on full-time for a year after his secretary was injured in a serious auto collision. While at the George Washington University, she had applied for a secret program at the FBI Academy in Quantico, Virginia. Now she was the only female graduate of the program and the only one without a badge.

After graduation from the Academy, she was assigned to the New York Field Office, ostensibly as a GS-5 typist. She was in her last year at GWU, expecting to earn degrees in art history and accounting. She had continued to help the FBI with art crimes by examining potential forgeries and stolen paintings.

When she finished suggesting which paintings were done by the same person and how each picture differed from the others, David put the lot back in his briefcase with his copious notes.

"Thank you, Sandra. I wish you could come to New York again. But our friend here says that we may not even meet here soon."

"I'm sorry about that." She turned to Redwood. "Is something wrong?"

"Only that we have to tighten security. Agent Vasari has been here three times in two months. The people who watch us may notice."

"Do I need to do something?"

"Maybe. I'll let you know. By the way, the two guys outside are not ours. We're finding out who they are. There are interesting people in this building, so they may have nothing to do with us."

"I'm amazed – again," said Vasari. "I didn't know you were a sketch artist."

Sandra blushed. "Something I picked up in high school civics class."

"You're kidding. That's professional-quality courtroom sketching."

"Well, the local paper did hire me when their regular artist took ill during my last semester. It gave me practice."

"Goes with that attention to detail we admire," said Redwood.

Vasari nodded. "I wish I could stay, but I want to catch the four o'clock train to New York."

"Be safe, David."

"Call me when you get in," Jim said, shaking hands with his colleague.

Vasari left them.

"Time for another cup?"

"Sure."

They took the tray back to his "office," a corner cubicle on the next floor up.

When they were seated with their mugs. Redwood looked at her for a while. She wondered if she had done something wrong.

"Sorry about calling him by his first name."

"It's okay, Sandra. We're Jim and Dave outside this building too. Are you two friendly?"

"No more than what you saw. It's the shared fascination with art and forgeries that is the passion." She set down her coffee. "It's exciting to see him grasp what I'm seeing, and it is a high for me to be affirmed by someone with his expertise."

"I understand. Even with Joe around, I expected you two to hit it off when we detailed you to New York and Rome for your field office assignment."

"How long can we keep up this arrangement? Right now, it's ideal for me, with a full schedule at the university. Won't someone in Personnel wonder where the GS-5 typist is?"

"I had forgotten about the sketch artist thing. We could hire you for that after graduation this spring. It would pay better than typing, and we would not have to hide you."

"I can live with that. I may be the only art history graduate at GWU making a living in my major. You should hear my classmates."

"I can imagine. Artists and their biographers rarely make the big bucks, do they?"

ଓଓଓ

The next day, the phone rang as Sandra closed the door to her apartment.

"Could you meet me in the coffee shop in an hour?" The urgency in Redwood's voice unsettled her.

"Sure."

Darlene, the sassy Jamaican waitress who had supported Sandra since the young student had moved to the neighborhood, had just poured her some coffee when Redwood walked in. He hung his dripping coat and joined Sandra in a booth at the far wall. Darlene filled the other mug on the table.

"Thanks," he said. Darlene left them. He patted the booth on his side. "Move over here, so they can't see our faces." With his eyebrows, he directed her attention to the mirror, where she could see two men standing at the picture window, pretending to huddle out of the rain against the building. If they were really sheltering, they would be looking out at the street.

"Do you know them?" she asked.

"No, but I was followed on the way here. That's not happened to me before, that I know of."

"Since Rome, I've tried to watch out too."

"Maybe following your bicycle frustrates them."

"I look anyway. What is this about?"

"David was attacked getting off the train yesterday."

"Oh no! How is he?"

"The knife missed his heart, but he has a punctured lung. He'll be in the hospital for at least a week, then recuperating."

"Who? Why?"

"Nobody we ever heard of. Pippo Rizzuoli was a low-level punk from Brooklyn. He said he was paid by some strangers to take David out. No one told him he was up against an experienced FBI agent. David twisted and dislocated the man's arm in falling. He hung on to Rizzuoli long enough for the Port Authority police to converge on them before he passed out."

"I can't go see him, I guess."

"Absolutely not. David is known as an art crime expert in the New York office, especially after the operation in Europe last year. It doesn't mean that they also know about you. We don't want them to find out."

They sat silently, occasionally checking in the mirror on the two men outside.

"His briefcase?" she asked.

"The police caught a man trying to pick it up. A different assignment. Pablo Rincon was a hood from the Heights, hired to shadow David and steal the briefcase if possible."

"Any chance the same person hired both?"

"That would make sense. But we have no idea who. We're not even sure why. Revenge for the raids? An attempt to block the current investigation? Something else?"

"The people he puts away don't go in for revenge, do they?"

"Not typically. But hundreds of men were arrested. Have you been following the fallout from those raids?"

"Not after the initial press coverage died off. I was relieved not to see my name or photo in any of it."

"So were we. We're trying to profile who would want to kill David." He sipped his coffee. "Did you study the list of people arrested?"

"As many as were in the papers, especially the four groups in Rome. Why?"

"Would you be willing to help in the investigation?"

"Of course."

"Here is something that will keep you out of sight but which I think you could do better than anyone at headquarters. Connect the dots."

"Sir?"

"I'll bring you a list of everyone arrested in all five countries, the art they had, and other details, such as citizenship, hometown, business interests, et cetera. You trace those out and tell me what you find."

"Anything?"

"Anything. At first, it may not seem connected to the art, but art – collecting, forging, and dealing – is the one thing we know that they all have in common, isn't it?"

"What am I looking for?"

"I don't know. For this, we need an observant person with no preconceived ideas. I remember how you spotted those mafiosi in the audience at the trial in Rome."

"How do we do this? Shall I come to HQ?"

"No. Do you fancy dinner and some chamber music?"

"Did Arlene tell you to date me now?" Jim had escorted Sandra to some diplomatic dinners that his wife was loath to attend. Sandra had sketched individuals at the parties, so the FBI and CIA could determine their real identities.

"Not this time." They both grinned. "Selena Menendez is home from New York with her violin." Sandra had lived with Selena's family her freshman year at GWU. "Dinner and music at our house."

"I'd love to!"

"Let's do it Thursday night like we did in Rome."

"I have class until five, but I could help with supper if I come straight to your house."

"I wish we had Vittoria," the Redwoods' maid and cook in Rome, "but I'll be home. Just come hungry and bring your viola. Arlene or I will call with some ideas for music tomorrow."

"How big a backpack do I need?"

"The file is probably the size of a ream of paper."

"See you Thursday then. Looking forward to it."

ରୟର

The papers consisted of tightly typed columns of names, charges, the art involved, and details: date and place of birth, hometown, education, corporate connections, careers, spouses, mistresses, and children. More data than Sandra could have ever accumulated in the stacks of the library.

This is the FBI, she thought. *Why didn't they include shoe sizes?*

After paging through the stack, she knew she needed a plan to look at the material and still finish her degrees in art history and accounting at GWU. She did some counting and checked the course outlines for the semester against her calendar.

There were more than three hundred names in the file. Almost immediately, she noticed that more of the collectors were in North America than in Europe. Most of the dealers were in Western Europe, which made sense. However, some of the "dealers" were curators or directors of museums in a dozen countries, including Argentina and South Africa.

She decided to devote no more than five hours during the week and five on weekends to this project. She called Redwood at home and proposed that she brief him on Thursday nights. They agreed on a "cover name" in case she needed to call him at the office but otherwise to communicate through Arlene.

Reconnecting with Selena, however briefly, was a pleasure. She had been Sandra's best friend before seventh grade and during her freshman year at GWU. After Selena went back to New York, Arlene invited her advanced violin students to fill the spot. It was fun for all concerned, as was the tradition of fixing supper together.

The briefings took place after the violinist left. By meeting regularly, there was less to discuss each time.

🕱🕱🕱

"Federal Bureau of Investigation. How may I direct your call?"

"Message for Special Agent Redwood, please."

"From whom?"

"Miss Bari. He should call me back at his convenience."

Two minutes later, the phone rang in her apartment.

"Do you need a meeting?"

"Yes. Someplace where I can spread papers out for you."

"My house after the dojo?"

"That would work. See you about five."

ଧଧଧ

Arlene had a student in her studio when Sandra arrived. Jim took her to the dining room and closed the doors. He poured water for them from a pitcher on the sideboard and joined her at the table.

"Let's see it."

Sandra opened her backpack and spread out about fifty sheets of paper in a half dozen piles. Then she took out some large pages from her sketchbook. Those had diagrams with arrows leading to circles.

"At some point, I knew I had to lay this out for you. Too much is coming together to talk about it for a few minutes on Thursday nights."

Jim nodded and rolled his hand. Sandra took a deep breath.

"First, I have no idea if any of this will be relevant, but I found some interesting connections.

"This pile consists of museum personnel and art dealers or gallery owners. The next group is independently wealthy individuals."

"Not many."

"No. Most of the others are busy making more money. The thickest stack contains investment managers."

"Playing with other peoples' money."

"And these three piles are millionaires – and a few billionaires – who head up different companies. This is oil, minerals, and other extractive industries. Next to it are tobacco and drug company magnates. And these are what I call global investors, who own controlling stakes in multinational corporations without filling an executive position."

"This is *very* interesting. You have been busy. You may want to work in the RICO squad." The Racketeer-Influenced and Corrupt Organization unit of the Department of Justice.

"It's not boring, but I don't want a career in it. Let me stay with art crime."

Jim pointed at the diagrams.

"These drawings are how I am pulling the co-incidences together. Every node on the left edge represents the date of the raids last summer. Then companies related to the suspects begin to show up in the news. I used the *Wall Street Journal, Washington Post, New York Times,* and *Financial Times* to find articles. The library at GWU has them all."

"Sounds very tedious. True police work."

"Yes, sir, which is why I still have many issues to go. I started from July, but the number of articles with hits began increasing after just a month."

"What are you seeing?"

"Two different things: our suspects triggering a scandal and the stock losing value as the shareholders head for the doors, and more recently, entire corporations going bankrupt, especially investment managers who may have been using their clients' money for their purchases."

"Amazing. RICO has not alerted us to any of this yet."

"My work is only up to October and only includes the firms mentioned in your list. Also, no money laundering is involved. Not the sort of crimes that RICO was set up for."

"But they have the staff and the expertise to pick this up or turn it over to the SEC." The Securities and Exchange Commission. "What else have you noticed?"

"I'm not a stockbroker or anything, but the sheer number of companies in trouble frightens me. On these pages alone"—she pointed to the diagrams—"I counted four hundred losing value or going under."

Jim gave a low whistle. "That is a major impact. All from one art bust?"

"I don't know, sir. I'm still looking for connections. But there are suddenly a lot of very wealthy, scared men out there.

"So far, none of the financial newspapers has run an analysis pointing this out, and they have speculated other reasons for the gentle slipping of the Dow Jones index since August. If some correspondent notices what I have, there may be a panic at the stock exchange."

"Are the companies just in these industries?"

"No. There are smaller sectors that you would not call an 'industry.' For example, defense contractors and arms manufacturers."

Jim stood quietly and pored over the nodes in the diagrams.

"You looked worried, Sandra. What is it?"

"What happens when one or more of them realizes that they are not alone. I'm afraid, sir. Very afraid."

CHAPTER 4

MADISON COUNTY, VIRGINIA

A COLD RAIN LASHED THE WINDOWS as Sandra studied for her midterm exams. She enjoyed studying on rainy days. The steady noise outside soothed her and rinsed away the fears that filled her quiet moments. She pictured faceless men in fancy hotel suites meeting to plot her death or, worse, Joe's or Nancy's. One with a face, retired General Ettore Arcibaldo, had already rocked their lives for two years. How much more could a cabal of men threaten them if they got together?

Just as the principles of inventory audit came into focus on the page and she relaxed, the phone rang. After inserting a souvenir bookmark from the Vatican, she went to the living room, where the instrument sat on a small table near the front door.

"Hello?"

"Oh, Sandra!" Marcia Billingsley cried into the handset. "Walter – oh, Walter—"

Her father's voice came on. "She was hoping to hold on to tell you. Your brother did not come back from a mission last month. He's been declared MIA." Missing-in-action. Staff Sergeant Walter Billingsley was stationed with the Third Marine Division in the Khe Sahn Valley, Vietnam. The fighting in Khe Sahn appeared often in the newspapers Sandra scanned every day.

Suddenly, inventory audit, the FBI, and everything in her life collapsed and vanished. Sandra stopped breathing until she realized that she was about to faint.

"Sandra, are you there?"

"Yes, Dad. Do we mean MIA as in 'presumed dead'?"

"That's right."

"How are the others taking it?"

"We're all pretty bad off. James and Arnie went back to school after coming home today. Marty's been notified." Her eldest brother was on board the Sixth Fleet flagship in the Mediterranean. "Your mother is tough stuff. She is an Army wife, after all."

"Should I come home?"

"I don't think so. At least not until we know more." He said something off the receiver. "Here's your mother."

"Hello, Sandra?"

"Yes, Mom. I'm here."

"Suddenly I feel like a fool, worrying about you all the time when you're fine, and Walter is out there—" Marcia sobbed into the phone, then took a deep breath. "I'll be okay, dear. We always knew this might happen someday. It doesn't make the initial shock any less, though."

"Want me to come home?"

Marcia was silent for a while. "No, dear. It's not even sure yet. You focus on your studies. We'll keep in touch."

"I can afford to call. Shall I check in, say, on Sunday evening?"

"Yes. Maybe we'll know more by then. Be careful, dear."

"Always, Mom. I love you."

Her father came back on the line. Sandra promised that she would call on Sunday nights, so no need to run up the phone bill unless there was news. They hung up.

Her gaze went to the family photo on the dresser that served as the sideboard in her living room-dining room. Was it just last Christmas that she and her mother noticed that it was the first time in six years that everyone had been home? Walter stood taller than his older brother; both men wore their uniforms for the picture.

She dropped into a chair at the dining table and cried into her arms. When no more tears would come out, she wiped her face with a napkin and went back to her desk…

The following Sunday, there was no news, and Marcia was dealing with her grief. Her father suggested that they not call unless either side had something to report.

During fall break, she went to Richmond by train. In her room, before they went down to dinner, Joe had taken the news about Walter quietly. She knew it made him think of his father. He took her in his arms and held her while she had another cry. That allowed her to share the news with Nancy and the Ardwoods with less drama.

ধ ধ ধ

The phone rang as Sandra let herself into the apartment. She stood in her mackintosh and rain boots.

"Miss Barry?"

"Yes?"

"Would you please call Mr. Redwood at his office?"

"Of course. Give me ten minutes."

"Thank you. I'll tell him."

Her cover name alerted Sandra to use a pay phone and the secure phone number that they used for confidential conversations. She walked to the coffee shop at Dupont Circle.

"Hello?"

She recognized Redwood's voice.

"You wanted to talk to me, sir?"

"Where did you learn about PERT charts?"

"Never heard of them, sir."

"What were those bubbles connected by arrows?"

"Just my way of visualizing the connections."

"Well, I just saw something similar on a different project, completely unrelated to what you are doing."

"They have a name, PERT? What's that?"

"The P is for program, but I forget the rest. Something the Navy invented to manage the Polaris program. Could I introduce you to the mathematician who showed me? She'll be here Thursday."

"Exams start on Monday. I could do that. Your office?"

"No. We still can't risk that. I'll invite her to dinner. She might enjoy some chamber music too. Would an audience bother you?"

"My father would have thrown us out of the house if we couldn't handle public concerts."

"Good. No need to do anything exceptional, then. See you Thursday."

"Just a minute, sir. How's David?"

"He goes back to work tomorrow. Fit as a fiddle."

"Would you let him know that I wanted to come see him?"

"I already told him. And that I nixed it. You are still assigned to the New York office on the books, but we can't risk having you near there now."

"I didn't know that New York is my assignment."

"Devious arts I learned while assigned to Rome and the Vatican. It keeps the local honchos from wondering about you."

"Oh. But you're still my boss?"

"Bob Worthman is your SAC, but I write the evaluation reports that he signs." Special Agent in Charge.

"Maybe when I graduate, I'll move to New York."

"A reasonable prospect for an art historian, don't you think? Even without a badge, we could maintain a solid cover for you there."

"See you Thursday, then. Thanks."

ৡৡৡ

The rain stopped the next day. Wednesday, Sandra figured that she had studied as much accounting as she was ever going to learn and treated herself to a Roman dinner. But first, she phoned Charlottesville. Joe was out looking at two apartments. Mrs. Page would let him know that Sandra called.

Over her *bucatini in padella,* she scanned the classified and sports sections of the *Washington Post* for deals on a car. Maybe she and Joe could buy one together since she could not get her own car loan. Asking her father to cosign would expose her work for the Bureau to the family.

❧❧❧

Thursday stayed sunny and cool. Sandra hardly noticed as she finished revising the art history paper that would serve as her midterm exam. By four p.m., she dropped it off in the department office and walked home to prepare for dinner and music with her non-boss in Georgetown. Arlene had asked her to bring the Dvořák quartet that they had played last month. She carried the music and the FBI file in her backpack and her viola in its case.

Jim Redwood answered the door. "Come in, Sandra."

She touched his arm and motioned to the curb outside.

"Is that your mathematician's car?"

"Why, yes. Do you recognize it?"

"A 1954 MG is a rare car, and that one is impeccable. Is she here?"

"In the living room."

She walked alongside him and stepped into the room first.

"Hello, Aunt Mary."

"Sandra!" Mary Ardwood sprang from the armchair and crossed the room to hug the young woman. "What a surprise! You are the viola in the quartet, I take it."

"Yes."

"Your aunt?" Jim's surprise was obvious.

"No, Joe's."

"Great-aunt, really," said Mary. "Nancy is my niece."

"I heard that." Arlene Redwood came into the room. "Is that Nancy Lockhart? She's amazing."

"We're very proud of her."

"We?"

"Her mother, Annabelle, and I were friends in Paris before the war. I introduced her to my brother Matthew."

"In addition to the other business we have, I think we want a full introduction to the family tree, Mary," he said.

"Let's do that over supper," said Arlene. "Everybody to the kitchen and help yourselves. Jim, would you pour the wine?"

The doorbell rang. Jim went to the door and brought in a young woman.

"Friends, this is Amanda Curtis, the newest member of the NSO and an alumna of Arlene's studio." National Symphony Orchestra. Handshakes all around. "We were just starting to load our plates, Amanda. Join us."

&&&

Dinner and the music were delightful, but Sandra needed more than the usual effort to focus, knowing the conversation that lay ahead. She also could not figure out how to tell Aunt Mary and her non-boss about her brother. *That will have to wait.*

Amanda left shortly after they finished playing. Arlene insisted on cleaning up so they could meet in the dining room.

"This counts as mixing business with pleasure," he said.

"Just a minute, Jim," said Mary. "Sandra, what's wrong?"

Sandra stared at Joe's great-aunt. "Is it that obvious?"

"Yes. Let's deal with it."

Sandra explained the phone calls about Walter being MIA and where his unit had been fighting. "It's hanging over our heads now. Thank God I'm too busy to dwell on it."

"Good for us to know. I'm terribly sorry for you, but I can tell that most of the rest of the world can't tell."

"I didn't notice, for which I am embarrassed, and I apologize," said Jim.

"Then let's keep me busy, sir."

Jim gestured to her backpack on the sideboard. She brought it to the table.

"Sandra, what do you know about Mary here besides her relation to Nancy?"

"Only that she earned her PhD in mathematics at MIT, worked at the War Department on something classified, and at NASA before going to Sweet Briar to teach."

"That's enough for now. It should not surprise you that she works on some of our projects."

"Nothing in your department surprises me, sir."

"Would you show Mary your diagrams?" To Mary, he said, "We'll show you her data, too, but if Sandra is ever connected with this information, her life would be in jeopardy."

"Then it won't come from me, Jim. What do you have, Sandra?"

They gathered around the dining room table as Sandra laid out the sketchbook pages with her diagrams.

"These do resemble PERT charts, except for lacking legends, but I suspect that you know what everything means on them."

"Right. I use the drawings to make note of the relationships between groups of data that I have observed."

Mary looked closely at the contents of the bubbles and the notes on the arrows. "It is fascinating to see the thought process of a mind as bright as yours displayed graphically."

Sandra blushed, unable to think of anything to say.

Mary continued. "This isn't a PERT chart, but is it a coincidence that the arrows all have units of time?"

"Arbitrary on my part. I had a hunch that how long it took for each event in a bubble to happen compared to the others might be relevant."

"This isn't complete either, is it?"

"No. I have data only to October. I can see trends already, but I can't measure or predict yet."

Mary drew her finger along a line of arrows and bubbles. "Jim, if this were a project, this would be the critical path. Most of the bubbles describe the same steps, but this one has shorter times to each step. What is this data trying to show – or may I not know that?"

"You're cleared, Mary, and now you have a need to know. Tell her, Sandra. You might as well show her how you're working from the files I gave you."

For the next twenty minutes, Sandra explained the data and how she was collecting common data points as bubbles, the suspects who were associated with each, and noting the time each was taking to get to the various bubbles.

"So, I am worried that these men – yes, they're all men – might discover their common cause. They would be very dangerous."

"You are doing all this with paper and a pencil on your dining table?"

"Yes."

"Oh, Jim, shame on you! She needs computer support, and you need what she is finding out too fast for this medieval manipulation."

"I was thinking RICO or the SEC could tackle this based on what she has discovered."

"What have you discovered, Sandra?"

"Nothing. I've only started to notice trends that worry me." She explained the scandals and the downward trend of the companies' stocks.

Mary glared at Jim, who looked like a student with a failing paper.

"Jim, our machines could crunch this data much better and faster. My project isn't nearly as urgent. Let me work with her on this. She'll probably pick up the programming faster than my current crew. What's her clearance, by the way?"

"Top Secret, Codeword, SCI." Sensitive Compartmented Information.

"I thought that was just in Rome, sir."

"Just because we debriefed you doesn't mean we can't brief you back in. I kept your clearances active."

"Sandra, how much time have you been putting into this?" asked Mary.

"Five hours a week and five hours on weekends. I have to be strict about that or fall behind in my schoolwork."

"As a teacher, let me thank you for keeping your priorities in order. I think we can work with this."

"What do I have to do?"

"Do you have a job after school?"

"Only the consulting I do for the Bureau."

"You have one now. Let's go over your schedule and figure out when you could come to our location to work."

"Where is this?"

"Hidden on a farm in Madison County," Sandra started. Her family farm was in Madison County. "Virginia, Sandra, not Ohio."

"I'd need a car for that, Aunt Mary."

"Better start calling me Mary or Professor Ardwood. We shouldn't advertise our connection. As for the car – Jim?"

"We'll give her one. Where could you park it, Sandra? I don't want you near FBI facilities here in town."

"I'll find a lot or a garage."

"File a travel claim every week. The mileage should pay for the gas, and you can include the parking—"

"I filed yours for a year, sir. I can handle that part." They grinned at each other. "Can I use the car for personal transportation if I don't put it on the claim forms?"

"Wherever it has to take you between sessions on the farm is authorized."

"Come to Sweet Briar and Richmond, then." She winked. "Charlottesville is on the way to both."

Sandra opened her planning calendar. They determined that she would come to the farm on Wednesday and Friday afternoons. Mary thought that would be enough time to accelerate the data crunching.

As Sandra packed up the pages, Mary put her hand on Sandra's shoulder and arched an eyebrow at Jim.

"Remember what I called the critical path?" She drew her finger along that series of arrows again. The others nodded. "In the context of what you told me, this is the party that may become desperate first if he isn't already there. We should do well to be alert for others whose arrows get shorter."

The bubbles belonged to All Saints Investments, an asset management firm in New York with offices in

Rome, Zurich, and the Cayman Islands. The associated art collector was an Italian citizen, Sandro Santis.

❧❧❧

Sandra backed off the accelerator for the sixth time since leaving Washington. The Ford Interceptor engine sped up quickly with the slightest pressure from her foot.

She had expected a civilian car of some sort, maybe a small sedan. *Of course, the FBI would operate unmarked police cars.* She left the radio off after checking the frequencies and the scanner. The microphone hung out of sight under the console, and the holders for shotguns and rifles did not attract attention when empty. The trunk had a complete outfit of emergency equipment: first aid kit, towing ropes, defibrillator, emergency blankets, flares, etc. While looking for the hazard lights, she had turned on the flashing blue lights concealed by the grille and the rear window deck. That made her find the switch for the siren before she accidentally turned that on.

The cars on which she had learned evasive driving at the FBI Academy had not been police cars, but they had been full-sized Fords. She was grateful for that experience because the cars she drove in Italy were half the size and weight of this monster.

Coming off the ramp at Gainesville from the new Interstate 66, she settled into the more sedate pace of US-29. On either side, horses of many hues stared at the passing traffic. Corn, soybeans, and wheat separated the horse farms. Except for the rolling topography, the scenery reminded her of her home in Ohio.

Mary's directions were easy to follow. After the Methodist church on Main Street in Madison, Sandra turned right on County Road 657 and found herself in a secluded valley. The farmhouse was on a hill to the right, hidden by a stand of evergreens.

The dirt parking lot held a collection of old sedans and muddy pickup trucks.

As Sandra parked the car in a free spot, Mary came out onto the porch. With her hair pulled back in a kerchief, and her faded coveralls, the distinguished mathematics professor resembled nothing so much as a rugged farm wife. She smiled and waved Sandra inside.

Sandra was surprised by the cold.

"Air-conditioning in a farmhouse?"

"The AC is for the computers, not us."

"Did I overdress?" Sandra moved her hand over her skirt and blouse.

"Not really, but it helps not to have city-looking folks hanging around outside."

"Got any pigs to slop? I'll wear my coveralls from home next time."

"We do, but our landlord's family takes care of that." She indicated the window at the back of the house. Sandra saw another farmhouse surrounded by the usual sties, barns, and corrals. "It's a real farm. We modified the inside of this one building."

"The farmer knows about this?"

"He set it up. He bought this farm after retiring from the CIA. Our rent helped him get it started until he could break even."

"What an interesting collection of people."

"Indeed. Come."

She led Sandra upstairs. Across from a bedroom that was obviously an office now, another bedroom had become a conference room, with a long table, a blackboard on one wall, and a sideboard with a coffee mess on the other. In the corner was a photocopier, a newer model than the Xerox 660 that Sandra had learned to maintain but still familiar.

"I'll bet you need a copy of my data."

"Yes. We'll let Linda do that while we get started." A dark-haired woman two or three years older than Sandra came in behind them. "This is Linda Martinez. Linda, this is Sandra Bari. Linda is a graduate student at James Madison University and a former student of mine."

While Mary poured coffee, Sandra took out her sheets of data and gave them to Linda.

Mary came back with the coffee. "Make two copies of the lot, please."

"Right away, ma'am – sorry, Mary." She gave the professor a sheepish grin. "I need to get more copy paper." She left.

Sandra arched an eyebrow at Mary. "Bari?"

"Jim told me your cover name. I'm the only one here who goes by their real name."

"So, no Martinez at JMU?"

"There is a Lonnie Martinez in the History Department." She waved at the pile of papers. "Let's spread these out. We'll feed them to Linda as we work."

Linda came back and started copying on the slow machine. Mary pored closely over the pages, taking notes. After ten minutes, she straightened.

"No surprises here. These data will go in easily." She refilled her coffee mug. "You already surprised me with your non-PERT chart, Sandra. What do you know about Relational Database Management?"

"Nothing. What is it?"

"A way of rearranging data quickly, so we can examine different relationships within the database. Each datum in these sheets occupies a single location, doesn't it?"

"Yes."

"Each cell in the database is identified by the sheet"—she waved a page—"the row and the column. Makes sense?"

"I see why you just about chewed Jim out. A computer could search the collection quickly and arrange these cells any way we want."

"Brava. We have an RDBM system downstairs, which we can use to examine the data. First, of course, we enter each datum into a file. Mistakes in data entry are the bane of our existence. We have an acronym for that: GIGO. Garbage In, Garbage Out."

Linda stacked the last set of copies on the table. "Anything else, ma'– Mary?"

"Yes. Would you show Sandra how we input data? You or Mac can check her input. Give her the full tour. She's a quick study. Afterwards, you can tell me how she's doing."

Sandra followed Linda down to the basement, which was a single, brightly lit room. Floor-to-ceiling cabinets held computers with blinking lights behind spinning tapes. She counted a dozen cabinets. The cold air from the AC barely kept up with the machines, so the room felt comfortable.

"Let me guess, Linda. You graduated last spring, and Mary asked you to work here."

"Yes. I keep forgetting to call her Mary because she was a goddess at Sweet Briar. She hired me over the summer and taught me these machines. They're way more powerful than the ones at Sweet Briar – or at JMU."

"I can picture that. I'm an accounting major, but I don't have any deep training in math."

"No problem. If you can keep a checkbook, you can do this."

For the next three hours, Linda and Sandra worked with the RDBMS, setting up the sheets, rows, and columns, then typing in the values from the paper. Sandra did the initial entry, and Linda checked the entries against her copy. The work went so quickly that they spent an hour testing different queries.

"It would have taken me months to look at all these cells for connections."

"It's fun once you get the hang of it, no?"

A computer technician came out of the office. "Linda, Professor Ardwood asked if you are about done." He extended his hand to Sandra. "I'm Mac. You must be Miss Bari."

"Sandra." They shook hands.

"Thanks, Mac," said Linda. "Let's pack this up, Sandra."

Mac took a Sharpie marker and wrote some numbers on one of the tape spools, then removed it and gave it to Linda. They went into the office, where Linda showed Sandra how to set a personal combination on a small wall safe. "Only you and I will have this combination, so your data will be safe while you're away."

"Not Mary?"

"No. If something happens to both of us, the FBI will have to wreck the safe or reconstitute the data from scratch."

They walked upstairs to the office. It contained two government-issue metal desks and a pair of filing cabinets, with visitor chairs in front of each desk.

"It's spartan," said Mary, motioning for the two young women to sit, "because it serves several different people. We have our regular offices elsewhere."

"Sweet Briar?" asked Sandra.

"In my case, yes." Mary looked at Linda. "How far did you get?"

"We designed the database, keyed in the data on one hundred names, then we spent the last hour structuring queries with what we had."

"What do you think, Sandra?"

"I might have majored in math or computer science if I had known about this program."

"I'm glad you like it." Mary frowned. "Remember that this particular program is much more powerful than what is available commercially. This whole facility is classified, and the program itself is Top Secret."

"I haven't been briefed."

"I know. Here." She took some sheets from a file folder on the desk. "Read, ask questions, and sign."

Sandra had seen most of the briefing sheets in Rome, but the codeword clearances for the computer farm and the RDBMS were new.

While she read, Mary asked Linda how quickly she thought they might have the database ready for full use.

"As you said, she's a quick study. We could have finished the input today, but I thought showing her what we could do with the data would be useful. We can start working with it next time."

"Excellent."

Sandra returned the signed forms to Mary and put away her pen. "It's almost quitting time. Will this be the routine Friday and later?"

"Pretty much," said Mary. "Because of the sensitivity of the software, Agent Redwood will come here for periodic briefings, so you can enjoy your musical soirées without thinking about this."

"Any particular schedule?"

"I'll call him when we want to show him something."

ದದದ

Friday, Linda and Sandra finished keying in the data from the paper sheets. Building on the playing around they did on Wednesday, Sandra learned how to create original queries and extract answers from the database.

"I am going to enjoy working with this," she said.

"Partly why I'm in this field. I know how you feel."

"I have a general question. Can we work on it?" Sandra and Linda spent the rest of the day practicing different presentations of the data and considering how to integrate what she was learning from the newspapers into the database.

By the following Friday, Sandra could be left alone to structure queries, though Mary or Linda checked them before Mac ran them through the computers.

"Sandra?" Mac appeared at the door to the office. Sandra looked up. "Professor Ardwood asked for you to come to the conference room."

"Okay. Thanks, Mac." She made some notes on the printouts so she could pick up where she left off in her thinking, then returned her work to the safe.

Upstairs, she found Mary sitting with two men. Redwood stood and smiled. The wiry, gray-haired man next to him also rose.

"Hello, Sandra. I am hearing great things about your work."

"I don't have anything to report yet. Linda and I are designing a format to add large text fields to the database, so we can at least record the newspaper information and associate it with the subjects."

"So, you are still poring over newspapers?"

"Yes, and they are in the GWU library, so I can't do that here."

"Why not?" Jim frowned at Mary. She scowled back at him.

"Set it up, Jim. Sandra can get you the list." He broke into a grin.

"Consider it done. We'll have the papers delivered here. That way, she won't have to use her non-FBI time to scan the papers."

"It will make good reading around here for everyone," said Mary.

Sandra looked at the man standing next to Jim.

"Our friend here is on a different operation, which you worked on before," Jim said. "Have you finished up for today? You may be going home after this."

Sandra looked at Mary and Linda. "I made notes on the printouts, so I can pick up Wednesday, but the tape is still on the machine."

"I'll put it away," said Linda.

"Nice meeting you," Mary said to the stranger. "Let's go, Linda." She closed the door behind them.

Sandra felt a little sad and confused as if Mary had been dismissed.

Jim noticed her expression. "Linda is not cleared. Mary is an old hand at this, so she can tell when to extricate herself.

"Sandra, this is Special Agent Marty MacKenzie." They shook hands. "Show each other your ID."

Sandra removed her driver's license from her wallet and handed it to Marty. He gave her his credential pack.

"Naval Investigative Service?" She returned it. "Is the NIS doing art recovery now?"

Marty laughed. "No, but maybe soon. Jim and I collaborated on another operation. Last year I was the special agent afloat for the Sixth Fleet, and I shared my stateroom with a very interesting midshipman for a few weeks. He told me about his awesome girlfriend."

"Joe?"

"The same. I figured he was just starstruck. I was briefed into the program to stop General Arcibaldo and sent Joe off to Rome. I came to visit Jim after I reported for duty at our headquarters in DC, and I learned that Joe did not know half the story. Jim explained your curious situation of being the top of your cohort at the Academy without a badge. And he also told me about the art thieves you busted."

"Not I, sir. Interpol and the national police forces did that."

"Don't be modest," said Jim. "You were crucial to that whole operation.

"So, the NIS wants to make you an offer."

"Sir?"

"Recruit you as a Special Agent in the Naval Investigative Service."

"You mean a badge and a commission?"

"Exactly. You would be a federal law enforcement officer. NIS doesn't have the same hang-ups that the FBI has. Your record at the Academy and in the field qualify you. NIS has a precedent for working with the FBI and other agencies on art crime, counterespionage, smuggling, and other cases."

"The Bureau would ask for your services and assign you to the New York office," said Jim.

Sandra pushed her jaw back in place and stared at the two men, who grinned at her and each other.

"Let me see that cred pack again." She held out her hand. Opening Marty's wallet, she looked at the badge. "You know, as an artist, I have to say that the Navy has a cuter badge than the Bureau. I accept." The men laughed at that. "What do we do now?"

"Marty just took over detailing and recruitment for the NIS, so we can do it all here. Let's sit down." They brought mugs from the coffee mess and sat at that end of the table.

Jim said, "Before we get started, I want to share two things with you and ask you to make a fast but important choice.

"Just this morning, I learned from Mark Pietrowicz in Rome that the explosive at the airport was from the same lot as the bomb in Aprilia the year before. It was almost certainly the work of Arcibaldo's people, even though he's in jail now."

"Oh my God! Does Nancy know?"

"Not yet. I'll break it to her this weekend. I may involve the Richmond Field Office and some others in arranging protection for her."

"Who was in that car?"

"An executive for British Petroleum and his personal assistant. The driver was killed too. Speculation in the press points to left-wing animosity towards multinational oil companies, but no one in the know thinks they were the targets."

"Except that they arrived in one of four nearly identical cars."

"Yes. You saved Nancy's life again. And going in the side door kept you both out of the papers."

Sandra sat in silence for a while, taking in the terror of how close she and Nancy had come to dying just as they were about to escape from the dangers of the summer in Italy. As discreetly as she could, she took a slow, deep breath, then focused on Jim.

"Is the second thing related?"

"In a way, yes. Whoever was after Nancy knows about you as her bodyguard, driver, and housemate. We were able to keep your association with Vasari's investigation secret, but we can expect that Sandra Billingsley is a target."

"But who?"

"Obviously, Arcibaldo fans. Anyone who noticed that you were directly responsible for Nancy's dodging three assassination attempts. And, of course, the headhunters." He and Marty exchanged a smirk.

"Sir?"

"Any idea how much money you could make in the personal protection business? There are firms looking for your kind of talent, and they pay very well."

"You're kidding!"

"It's funny to think about it, but you would be a great bodyguard for a celebrity or millionaire."

"But I don't want to do that—"

"Good because we need you. And Joe would be heartbroken never to see you again." Jim chuckled. "Anyway, we have an idea for the new NIS agent."

"We'd like to bring you aboard as Alessandra Bari," said Marty. "What do you think?"

"Is that some kind of modified Witness Protection Program?"

"The name was my idea. With your Italian, we could give you a cover as an Italian or an American with documentation that would be easy to produce and easy to live with."

Jim said, "We have an opportunity here to bury your tracks by creating a completely new identity for you, which you would use in your NIS work. Anyone tracking Billingsley should lose the trail, or at least draw the conclusion that the undergraduate at GWU is not the NIS agent – if they ever find out about that."

"The name works, and I can still answer to Sandra." She pronounced the name in Italian.

"And we can let all the cases of 'Barry' add to the confusion."

"Is there a backstory for Alessandra?"

"We're working on that now," said Marty, "because your service record will be at NIS. It will be in a classified file while you are working on this project. I'll meet with you to pick a hometown and a history that is realistic. Then we'll produce the birth certificate, transcripts, travel history, etc., to back it up. Bari will even have the same Social Security credits as Billingsley."

"Let's do it."

Marty and Jim pulled forms from their respective briefcases, and Sandra signed another two dozen pieces of paper. The papers included NIS orders to report to the Federal Bureau of Investigation for "duties as directed" and temporary assignment to the FBI Field Office in New York City.

Marty administered the oath of office to her, gave her a credential pack and her commission, and shook her hand. "Welcome aboard, Special Agent Bari."

Sandra looked at Jim. "Joe and the Ardwoods?"

"You can explain the new identity to them. Everyone involved in the Arcibaldo affair should understand the stakes. I trust them to help you reinforce it. But keep your agent status hidden from everyone except Joe and Mary until Billingsley graduates. Of course, she can show up in London, Ohio, but no one there can know about Sandra Bari."

"I understand, sir. Thanks."

CHAPTER 5

RICHMOND, VIRGINIA

THE TELEPHONE RANG as Sandra hung her rain jacket above the beach towel she kept on the floor by the door. She rubbed her hands briskly before picking up the handset.

"*Ciao, bella, come stai?*"

"*Joe, che piacere!*" They continued in Italian, which they enjoyed.

"Fancy coming to the Marine Corps Birthday Ball again this year?"

"Counting on it. And I don't have to stay with Mrs. Page this time, do I?"

"No. Wait till you see this place. Could you come a little earlier? I can meet the train any day except Wednesday."

"I have a surprise for you – several surprises, actually. The first is that I have a car, so I can be there whenever. Let me come down Friday. We have a lot to discuss."

"I can't wait. I love you."

"I love you too. Ciao."

She took her books to her desk, then started supper.

ℜℜℜ

Friday, Sandra changed out of her coveralls and boots at the farm before driving to Charlottesville. Finding the house on Wertland Street was easy, and there was an open parking place out front.

Joe opened the door to her knock. He embraced her with a loving hug. Stepping back, he looked past her shoulder. "Where did you get the limo? You said you had a car, but that's not what I expected."

"More surprises inside." She picked up her suitcase and went in with him. They paused behind the closed door for a long kiss. "Where do I put this?"

He showed her his bedroom. "You can use either one, but I'm in this one."

"I didn't expect you to have a two-bedroom place."

"Neither did I, but Mrs. Page knows the owner. She convinced Mrs. Garland to charge me the same amount as a room on-Grounds instead of the going rate in town. I think she was thinking of Diego, but even without a roommate, I could afford it, so I jumped at it."

"You can have other company – or a roommate if you need one later."

"Mom used that room when she came to help me move in."

"That's a lot of books. And is that an IBM Selectric?" She ran her hand over the latest electric typewriter.

"Yes. I have typing balls for all my languages. It's fantastic to type as fast as possible without having the letters jam."

"What are you working on now?"

"Quarterly financial reports from Smithson Italia and Gucci."

"It does look cozy." Sandra put her suitcase in his room. "Any plans for supper?"

"You know the places on the Corner, but I was thinking of fixing something here."

"Let's see what you have."

They went into the kitchen. Joe had a refrigerator full of vegetables and fish in the freezer. They assembled a salad and put some salmon fillets to bake with potatoes and corn. When the food was ready, they carried it into the front of the apartment, which was furnished as both a living room and a dining room.

He came out with a bottle of Montepulciano d'Abruzzo and stopped at the door. Sandra turned and asked, "What?"

"Why do you look so – what it is? – detective-ish?"

She looked in the mirror at her white blouse, dark gray slacks, and sensible shoes. She had chosen a dark blazer for the cold weather and put her blond hair in a ponytail. She donned her mirrored sunglasses.

"Is this what you mean?" They laughed. She took off the sunglasses. "I never was the sweatshirt and jeans type off the farm, you know."

"It goes well with the car."

"That's not a limo out there." She reached into her blazer pocket and clipped her badge to her belt.

"Wow! You *are* an FBI agent."

"No, I'm not." She gave him the badge.

"NIS?"

"Yes. Your old roommate Marty Mackenzie arranged it with Jim Redwood. The NIS can recruit female agents. At least at first, I'm on loan to the FBI New York Field Office. Same work, same classified projects, but now I have agent status." She sat while he poured the wine. "Let's eat. I have more to tell you, and most of it will remain between us."

Supper demanded the first few minutes of attention. Joe was bursting with curiosity, but Sandra had skipped lunch to pack after class.

With half her fish and some salad accounted for, she took a sip of wine.

"Marty had some very high praise for you."

"He was great. He whisked me off *Point Defiance* and again off the flagship so fast that no one knew I was gone until long afterward."

"Well, he is one of only two people outside the Bureau cleared to know about my work. You're the other one."

"Just what are you doing? It probably has to do with art and forgeries."

"I'm working on a new request from Interpol. Most of the cases are in Europe, but the US is the biggest market."

"Sounds exciting."

"It's rather too exciting. David Vasari was attacked in New York, and we don't know if it was because he headed up the case last summer or if someone wants to stop the new investigation."

"Is he okay?"

"He is now, but he got a punctured lung from a knife that missed his heart."

"I'm sorry. He seems like a great guy – even I can't help being jealous of him."

"No need for that, dear. I'm seeing even less of him now. In fact, it's a top priority now to conceal my connection with the FBI, so I never go near headquarters or see anyone from New York."

"How can you examine the pictures?"

"That has stopped for now. I am working on a different project, using computers in a secret location in the country."

"That's why the car?"

"Yes. Also, remember the car bomb at Fiumicino when Nancy and I came back?"

"It was meant for you?"

"Probably. Same explosive lot as the bomb at the Aprilia plant."

"But Arcibaldo is in jail."

"Two problems: he has lots of friends who are angry that he was arrested. And they know who Nancy's driver, bodyguard, and roommate was."

She ate some more while Joe considered what she had said.

"They'll be after you too."

"They'll be after Sandra Billingsley, who went back to school at GWU. No one knows about my association with the art crime investigation. The Bureau does not want Billingsley connected with that other work, so I am changing my name and separating the undergraduate at GWU from the rest of my life. After I graduate in May, the only time I'll be Sandra Billingsley is on the farm in Ohio."

"The suspense is killing me," said Joe. "Who am I in love with?"

"Alessandra Bari." She pronounced it in Italian as she showed him her credential pack.

"*Mi piace,*" said Joe. I like it. "*Da dove sei?*" Where are you from?

"Brooklyn, but the hospital I was born in, the house I grew up in, and the elementary school I attended burned down."

"Is there a backstory I should know?"

"My parents died in the house fire, and I lived with my aunt to finish high school. She's dead too. You can ask questions, and I'll answer them until you are comfortable with it."

"Anyone with basic research skills could crack this."

"Yes, but by the time I graduate, the cover will be very deep: academic records at GWU, high school transcript, and vital documents on my family in New York and in Italy."

"Italy?"

"Of course. With that name, NIS can easily set up a cover for an Italian or an American. Is my Italian good enough?"

Joe laughed. "Sure. Just don't get drunk in Trastevere. *Sei troppo educata.*" You're too well-bred. "What about Diego, Tony, and my other friends?"

"Don't mention my surname. They all know me as Sandra anyway. And don't tell Diego until we can do it in person, whenever that will be."

"That should work. So, what do we put on your place card at the Marine Corps Ball?"

"Alessandra B. and run out of room when you get to the surname. Will that work?"

"I can fix that tomorrow."

ଙଙଙ

Sandra and Mary leaned over the printouts on the conference table. Linda and Mary had modified the engineering software provided by the Navy to identify the individuals along the side at the start of each path of bubbles and to label the duration value along the arrows.

"This display shows the lengthening and shortening of the paths, but there is one thing that keeps this from being a proper PERT diagram," said Mary.

"No endpoint?"

"You've been reading up, young lady."

"Yes. PERT is aimed at planning the steps to a known outcome, usually the delivery of the project."

"Right. What would make this more useful?"

"Well, for one, if we could define an event and a date for it, we could drive these nodes toward it and see what needs to happen to reach the event."

"What event?"

"I can think of two, at least. One would be an attack on us, with the assumed nodes of the participants recognizing their shared state and collaborating. The other would be if none of them ever figure this out and never look for us."

"And then there is the real unknown. Only one gets desperate and tries to do something alone."

"The way Arcibaldo did."

"Yes. With three hundred potential actors, a single enemy is very probable."

"How about one endpoint being our discovering a conspiracy and successfully preventing a crime?"

"That's good too." Mary looked at her watch. "You're coming to Richmond for Thanksgiving, aren't you?"

"Yes."

"See you there, then. Let the endpoints cogitate this weekend."

They locked up the printouts. Mary drove one of the pickup trucks. Sandra admired the way the professor maintained her cover all the way to Amherst.

ಬಬಬ

Thanksgiving at the Ardwood home checked all the boxes required by the cultural mythology of the American holiday. The family worked in the morning to prepare the feast, and the table would soon groan under turkey, sweet potatoes, corn, beans, pies, and two different kinds of bread. The aromas were not quite what one would expect if Norman Rockwell's paintings had an olfactory element: the clever use of herbs and sauces betrayed the influence of Annabelle's Parisian heritage and Nancy's long residence in Rome.

The darkening skies went unnoticed. The forecast was for sunny weather after the front blew through on Thursday.

About ten a.m., a knock on the front door caused the hubbub in the kitchen to stop. The door opened before anyone moved.

"*Permesso?*" May I come in? The voice called from the hall.

"Luke!" Nancy dropped the meringue she was assembling and ran. When the others arrived, the two lovers were locked in a tight embrace and clearly unaware of anyone else. Finally, they disengaged. "I thought you couldn't make it."

"I said I would try. We closed the merger talks in Toronto late last night. I flew down this morning and rented a car."

"I'm delighted. Here, meet the family." Nancy introduced her parents, Aunt Mary, and Sandra.

"Joe needs no introduction." Luke shook hands with everyone. To Joe, he said, "Congratulations on making the varsity team. Will we see some of that this weekend?"

"Maybe tomorrow. I don't think anyone will be able to lift a racket today," said Joe with a quick glance at his grandfather. "If the car is open, let me take your luggage upstairs while you use the restroom and join the others in the kitchen." Luke held out the keys.

General Ardwood closed his mouth. He nodded to the midshipman to carry on.

ଷଷଷ

By early afternoon, the prep work was done. While the turkey and fixings baked in the oven, the family relaxed in various ways. Luke went up to shower and change, accompanied by Nancy, which made Sandra and Joe giggle quietly.

"Do you think she's afraid he'll disappear if she lets him out of her sight?" said Sandra. They went out to the veranda to watch the thunderstorm pummel the duck pond into a frothy maelstrom.

"I don't blame her," said Joe. "He's the best thing to happen to her – to us – since my father died."

"You explained that, but it's cute to see it play out live. They are so darling together. He's never married?"

"No. It's first love for him."

"Kind of romantic, isn't it?"

"It didn't hurt that they met in Rome."

Sandra squeezed his arm. "Yeah. We did that, too, didn't we?"

ଷଷଷ

The thunderstorms rolled on, and the sun came out in time to light up the backyard as the family gathered on the veranda with glasses of pinot grigio.

Nancy briefed them on her work at Smithson Global.

"Is it still as patriarchal as ever?" asked Mary.

"It feels different – and good – not to be the only woman in the building or at management meetings. Not many of us, but the men are discarding their assumptions about what the women can do. Having Madeleine there before she went to Rome helped."

"How is Doctor Grimaldi doing in your old job?" Joe asked.

"Great. I talked to Maria Grazia the last time I called. For the rest of you, she was my secretary in Rome. I expected that my leaving would be a hand coming out of a bucket of water."

"Completely forgot you, eh?"

"That's what I said, but Maria Grazia corrected me. She said that occasionally someone still asks for *dottoressa* Lockhart or calls Madeleine Nancy."

"Gone but not forgotten," said Matthew.

"It's been three months, Dad!" He saluted her with his glass. "Anyway, that's the news at Smithson." She looked slowly around the room. "But I have other news that I have been saving because the fewer times I repeat it, the safer everyone will be. *Sandra, vuoi continuare la presentazione?*" Would you take over the briefing?

Sandra stood. She held her breath as she contemplated these people, the closest friends she had outside her family. Joe sat back. Luke and the Ardwoods looked curious.

"First of all, let me say that what I am about to share is highly classified. Luke, when you showed up, I called DC, so you don't have to leave. One way or another, you are all cleared for it, being familiar with the hate mail campaign against Nancy in Italy." She paused to see the understanding in their eyes. "Only Joe knows the whole story because we concluded two operations together in Rome, but everyone can guess the stakes."

She took out her driver's license and passed it around.

"Say goodbye to Sandra Billingsley. You will never hear me use that name outside London, Ohio."

"Witness Protection Program?" asked Matthew.

"Kind of, but what I do is codeword-classified. Is there anyone who does not remember the art bust in Rome and four other cities?"

"That was a record recovery," said Luke. "You were involved in that?"

"Yes. And there are hundreds of wealthy men who would order me killed yesterday if they knew."

"Hence the new identity."

"That's only part of the story. One of the men arrested in the art recovery was behind the hate campaign, which was intended to hurt Joe. While the investigation was coming to a head, I happened to be guarding Nancy because of the hate campaign. Just when we thought we were past all that, a bomb went off at Fiumicino as we were going to our plane. Apparently, it was intended for Nancy but destroyed a similar car."

"But if the general was arrested?" asked Annabelle.

"He has a large following, so Nancy and I are not really safe. Sandra Billingsley is known as her bodyguard, driver, and housemate to those people, but no one knows my role in the art bust. It is critical that it stay that way because Interpol is working on other art crimes. I'm helping with that."

"And I thought you were a coed at GWU," said Luke.

"Billingsley still is. After she graduates next spring, she'll disappear. Meanwhile, Sandra Bari won't be anywhere near the FBI until the Bureau is ready to bring her in – the way we did before."

While they absorbed the information in silence, Sandra looked around. Joe grinned with pride. Nancy looked a little alarmed until Luke squeezed her hand, and she relaxed. Mary smiled as if one of her pupils were presenting a great paper, and Nancy's parents looked surprised.

"Any questions?"

Luke asked, "Is Sandra Bari American or Italian?"

"Today, I'm American. The name allows us to create an Italian or an American cover easily, along with the necessary documents. The American was born and raised in Brooklyn. The hospital, the house, and the schools I attended were in buildings that have burned down. My birth certificate and driver's license are on file in Albany. And my background is growing in the Italian records offices."

"I assume your personnel file is classified," said Matthew.

"Yes, sir. The intern who worked for the FBI in Rome two years ago went back to GWU and only came back to Rome to take the summer course at the American Academy. That's when she ran into Nancy again, but it was an established friendship." She reached out for Joe's hand.

A ding from the kitchen made Annabelle stand. "*Bonne chance, alors.*" Good luck, then.

The others rose and followed her.

CHAPTER 6

CHRISTMAS BREAK

SANDRA'S FINGERS FLEW OVER THE KEYBOARD. She hit the period, smacked the ENTER key, and sat back.

"Whew! That's done."

Linda looked up from her desk. "You got all that put in?"

"Yep. Notes on every newspaper report to the fifteenth of December. I am ready for a holiday!"

"Do you really want to wait until next year to analyze this?"

"Mary said I could run a full set of queries tomorrow. Do you have time to check my input today?"

"Sure. I'm not going home until the weekend. Harrisonburg is a ghost town between semesters at JMU. Where are you going for Christmas?" Her expression reminded Sandra that Bari did not have a home to go to.

"Some friends invited me to spend the holidays with them."

"I'm happy for you. I think being alone at Christmas would be terrible."

"Even without plans, the holiday makes friends magically appear. I've never spent Christmas truly alone."

"That's a nice thought."

Sandra let Linda sit at her place, with the pages of her input data before her. She had highlighted the relevant material in the newspapers, so Linda could easily check that Sandra had not made a mistake typing in the text fields.

The next morning, Mary was waiting on the porch when Sandra parked the car at the farm. They both wore coveralls and boots.

"This is like having a regular job," Sandra said. She had been commuting every day since the semester ended. Joe had given her a key to his apartment.

"And you have done a surprising amount of work too." Mary held the door. "Let's look at this material."

They broke for lunch when Mac asked them to let the machines cool down for a while.

"We've never run such large queries one right after the other." He smiled as he said it. "I'm glad these babies can handle it, but I don't want to push our luck."

"See why I was so hard on Jim?" Mary said with a smirk as they walked up to the conference room to unpack their lunches. "Anyway, what do you think?"

"I'm worried, Mary. Of the three hundred suspects, two-thirds have paths that are twice as short as they were the month before. Someone must notice soon. But pushing the nodes toward the four outcomes does not seem to be working very well."

"I agree. The machines are running the data properly – you did a great job with Linda setting up the queries. I'm concerned that we haven't visualized what we want in a way that we can program."

"These men golf at the same clubs, go to the same parties and art exhibits. Why haven't they noticed yet?"

"Failure in their company is a secret they would never reveal to anyone. Even their wives."

"Are we too close to this?" Sandra asked. "Who could we bring in for a fresh look?"

"Good idea. Who is cleared?"

"Jim, Joe, and David. That's it unless you know some others."

"Linda and Mac are smart cookies."

"I hate letting this go until after the holidays. Could we get them together quickly?"

"Let's try." Mary walked to her office to make a phone call on the secure line.

❦❦❦

Sandra picked Joe up in Richmond at dawn. They spoke in Italian as Sandra drove down Broad Street to take Interstate 95 North.

"You know, I don't think anyone in my family has been in this car."

"Let's keep it that way, darling."

"Right. Where are we going?"

"First to Union Station to meet someone. Then to the farm."

"The farm you work at?"

"Yes. Mary will already be there. We want to gather some people who have not been working on this as closely as we have."

"How many are cleared to do that?"

"Seven: Mary, you, me, her assistant, the computer tech, and two FBI agents."

"Computer tech? What kind of a place is this?"

"To give you an idea, I looked up the specs on the data systems computers in *Springfield* and *Point Defiance*. Ours can crunch more data five times faster. When you get there, you'll see why the whole place is classified."

"And who is Mary? You've never mentioned her."

"No, I haven't. Everyone will be introduced soon."

They switched to talking about the Bari family, partly to reinforce Sandra's comfort with the cover story and partly because it was fun. They also discussed accounting methods of valuating their respective fields: translation work in Joe's case and art consulting in Sandra's. Joe helped her with the accounting terms in Italian.

Joe had completed all the general requirements for his bachelor's degree and was looking forward to his graduate courses in Italian in the spring semester. He needed two of them to complete the hours for his degree. The others would count toward his master's degree this time next year.

With so many people gone for the holidays, traffic was light. Soon Sandra pulled up to the curb in the taxi rank outside Washington's main train station. The cabbies turned to swear at what they thought was a limo using their rank but swung their heads back when the blue lights under the grill flashed briefly.

A familiar figure walked from the station entrance and jumped in the back.

"Agent Vasari!" Joe turned around. "What a surprise." He smiled and put his hand back for a shake. Sandra moved quickly into traffic.

"*Ciao, Davide,*" said Sandra, and continued in Italian. "Did Jim brief you?"

"Only enough to know that it's what I don't know

that got me the invitation – and my security clearance."

"Same here," said Joe.

"We'll brief you at the farm, then you can ask questions."

On Constitution Avenue, she pulled into a bus stop outside the National Archives. Jim Redwood let himself in the back as David moved over.

"Hello, Jim. Are we holding the meeting in the car?" Dave shook hands with the senior agent.

"No, but this way, we won't attract attention at the farm with too many cars, and it's faster."

"It is that. Shall we continue in Italian? That was fun."

"*Perché no?*" said Jim. Why not?

ଚ୧ଚ୧ଚ୧

It took most of the morning to brief the data collection from the arrests, the database management system, how they had modified the Navy software, and what Sandra and Mary were trying to do. Mary summarized it as "figuring out what to ask this database that will keep us from reacting to new information. We need to get ahead of events."

"This is so far outside anything I have ever thought of that my head hurts," said David as he finished his fourth cup of coffee. "Just seeing the impact of our raids last summer terrifies me."

"We're asking for thoughts, ideas, questions – anything this may trigger," said Mary. "Sandra, Linda, and I can figure out the programming." She stood. "Let's break for lunch. We'll leave this material up so you can ruminate on it with your food."

ଷଷଷ

When the lunch boxes and leftovers were discarded in the indoor bin that was emptied off-site, the group gathered in the conference room.

"Part of this seems to be a hardware problem, in addition to what to ask the computer, which I guess is what you call software," said Joe. "You said that when you run the queries, the machines overheat, and you have to stop to let them cool."

"It's still faster than trying to run those comparisons manually," said Mary.

Joe looked at the nodes and arrows on the board.

"What if you ran the queries only on a subset of the three hundred names? Would that allow you to avoid stopping for the computers to cool down?"

"Which of the three hundred?" asked Jim.

"That's the software problem, isn't it, Mary?" Joe said.

"Yes. And it would help with the hardware problem. Sandra?"

"I would pick the current critical path, then maybe the fifty next shortest paths."

"Then run them until you can see if you can flex things for the different outcomes," said Joe.

They sat silently for a few minutes. David stared, trying to understand the arrows. Jim looked at the others as if evaluating their reactions to Joe's idea. Sandra and Mary both looked out the window, their brows creased in thought. Mary's head moved ever so slightly as if she were running permutations through her brain instead of a computer – which was close to what she was doing.

"Joe, I think we can do that. And it will allow us to keep moving.

"More important, I think we can improve on the idea. Sandra, let's work up a method for swapping out the suspects after we succeed in creating valid displays for the first set."

"And we can swap out any suspects we are not running if they develop a sudden critical path of sorts," said Sandra.

"Could you insert noncritical path players if you want to include them for some other reason?" asked Joe.

"Of course," said Mary. "Good idea."

Jim said, "How will this help us predict an attack?"

"It won't, not directly. But it helps us use our resources efficiently. You can't put a watch on all of them at once.

"Also, if, as Joe suggested, we pull in interesting parties for other reasons, we can work out what needs to happen for them to go critical and be ready for it."

Linda said, "We seem to have two tasks here. One is to run the small subset to see if we can make it work. The other is to run the larger group, using the endpoints we developed from the smaller group."

"All the while sliding people in and out," said Sandra. "I will keep reading the financial press."

More silence as each took notes and considered their reaction to them.

David spoke first. "We are ready to continue with the new investigation. I am not sure how this exercise will help us."

Jim answered. "When we pulled this data together,

I was thinking that three hundred art collectors and dealers would include some who will do it again. They can't help themselves; it's a passion or even an addiction."

"For what it's worth," said David, "only twenty-five of them are incarcerated. That's two hundred seventy-five angry rich men out free."

"An investigation increases the stress on them if their financial assets are threatened, as Sandra has discovered," said Jim, looking at her. "That increases the likelihood that they will act, maybe violently."

Mary stood and walked to the board. "I propose that we look for those parties in our database suffering more stress. When these arrows shorten or Sandra spots something relevant in the press, we'll send you their names, even though we don't know what, when, or where. Then you can at least pay attention to them and perhaps prevent something or limit the damage."

Jim said, "I agree, Mary. We'll issue a new codeword for those reports. Send the names to me. Bob Worthman, David, and I will work with the field offices and with Interpol." Worthman was the SAC in New York.

"Meanwhile, this gives me a new way to approach what we are doing," said David. "It may speed our work to be ready for return players. Thanks."

As they packed up their notes and the materials, Joe stood silently at the board, thinking. Occasionally, he would turn to the data pages and check the names on the bubble diagrams. Sandra came over to stand by him. Jim Redwood looked up as he snapped his briefcase shut.

"*Che vedi, caro?*" What do you see, dear?

Joe pointed to a name. "Did you say this was the original shortest path?"

"Yes."

"What art did he buy? I mean, who did he buy it from?" Redwood joined them.

Sandra paged through her data sheets. "General Arcibaldo. Joe, how did you guess that?"

"I didn't. I recognized him from a *Herald Tribune* article after you returned to GWU two years ago." He looked over their shoulders and lowered his voice. "He was one of the four men arrested after we stopped Arcibaldo the first time. The public charge was violation of currency laws, but we know they financed Arcibaldo's coup attempt."

The FBI agent and Joe had passed two tense days in the Presidential Palace while the Italian government thwarted the coup. The operation would remain classified for many years. Redwood blinked and straightened his back.

"Sandra, let's get David to his train. I'll get out the files on the four 'investors' from that affair." He switched back to English. "They may be the first names in our new system after the holidays."

Sandra reversed her drive, leaving David at Union Station in time to catch the four-p.m. train to New York.

Dinner was almost ready when they walked into the house in Richmond. Sandra drove back to Washington that night, so she could pack to go to Columbus.

⋈⋈⋈

Snowflakes melted on the windshield the next morning as Sandra drove the car to the Redwood home in Georgetown. By the time she saw Jim on the sidewalk outside the townhouse, the pavement was wet but not frozen. The flurries turned into a light drizzle as she moved over so he could drive.

"Any word on your brother?" he asked as he did a U-turn.

"No."

"I'm sorry."

In silence, they moved slowly along Massachusetts Avenue. Holiday travelers only added to the workday rush hour.

"Ready for this?" he asked when Union Station came into view.

"Being Sandra Billingsley is easy."

"Do you have the answer to 'what will you do after graduation?'"

"The cover we were working on before I became an NIS agent. I've applied to three museums in the New York area for a conservator apprenticeship. Interviews will be in April, so I won't know anything right away."

She frowned in thought. "Later, they will want to write to me and call me."

"By then, we'll have you covered. An answering service for the roommate in the apartment you are never in. An address where we intercept your mail and give it to you."

"My family will want to meet the roommate."

"They never stay long enough for that." He grinned. "Don't worry."

"It sounds exciting."

"Where is Sandra Bari?"

"Who?" She winked and smiled. "She is locked in the desk in my apartment. I have a ticket from Columbus with me in case I need to leave London suddenly."

"How do you get to Columbus?"

"There's a bus, or I can steal my old bicycle from the barn. It's not far to the station from there."

"Do you have the numbers for the field offices in Columbus and Springfield?"

Sandra recited them. "I hope I don't need them."

"If we have to pull you in, call Dale Peters in Columbus."

"Isn't he the SAC?"

"Yes. I've already briefed him and the SAC in Springfield. Use the codename Bari. They'll pick you up close to home. Leave the bike."

"Yes, sir."

Two hours later, Sandra watched the snow flurries turn into flakes again as the train crossed the Alleghenies and dropped into Ohio.

ಬಬಬ

The low-pressure cell over Lake Ontario blanketed Ohio with snow from Cleveland to Cincinnati and pulled southern air up to New York, quickly melting the white Christmas on the East Coast. By January, the cell had still not moved, causing scenes of tee-shirt-clad motorists from New Jersey trying to shovel their cars out of snowbanks along Interstate 70 in Ohio.

Manfredo Bonin stepped into the exit area of John F. Kennedy airport (which he still thought of as Idlewild), a Gucci briefcase in his left hand and a cashmere blend overcoat over his right arm. *If it stays this warm, I'll put this thing in a donation box.* He looked over the other passengers, almost all of whom had also come first class and been expedited through customs. His suitcase was already on its way to the hotel.

The chauffeur from the concierge service was standing by the door, thankfully with a more discrete sign than his colleagues. The service had remembered to send the same driver as last time. The man folded the sign into his pocket, tipped his hat to his passenger, and held the door to the outside.

The black limousine delivered Manny to the entrance of the Waldorf-Astoria. Normally, he would use the company apartment in Manhattan, but this time he did not want anyone to know about the meeting he would attend the next day.

In the suite, he shed his suit jacket, loosened his tie, and made himself a gin and tonic. Only then did he relax. From the armchair by the desk, he dialed from memory.

"Hello?"

"*Sono qui.*" I'm here.

"*Eccellente. Arrivederci a domani.*" Excellent. See you tomorrow.

The next morning, Bonin stepped into a black Land Rover that drove up to the entrance of the hotel just as he appeared at the door. Forty-five minutes later, he sat on the enclosed back porch of a mansion overlooking the Hudson River. No servants in the house, security men in the woods well out of earshot, and no sightlines to the porch from the neighbors on either side. Sandro Santis, as round and bald as ever, came out with drinks and sat in the Adirondack chair next to Manny's.

"Good trip?" Santis said in English.

"It's never good, but it was mercifully uneventful this time." Bonin sipped his drink. Knowing that Santis did not follow his British public school accent well, he switched to Italian. "I want to beat the jet lag by being home tomorrow morning."

"Then I won't keep you. I have a problem that I think you share."

"You did not need to hire those investigative accountants from Deloitte, Sandro. They already freelance for me, and I pay them better."

"Sorry, but due diligence is part of our business, isn't it?"

"Of course, which is why I told them to report back to you and to hold nothing back."

"It seems we both lost more than our contribution to the cause when Ettore's coup failed. You bought art from him last year too."

"A copy of a Rubens, and I knew it was a copy. But you, my friend, purchased an original Caravaggio."

"Still, we're out a considerable sum."

"No, Sandro, I am out a considerable sum of my own money, which I can afford. But you are out a considerable amount of your clients' investments."

"How—"

"Those auditors work for me, remember?" Bonin took another sip. "You did not cover your tracks very well, using your company accounts in the Caymans and Zurich for the transfers to Arcibaldo."

Santis twisted the heavy gold ring on his right hand. After a long silence, he looked up at his friend. "I need help, Manny."

"That's clear, but you are too risky. Look at it from my point of view: your clients are nervous, and you have spent all your cash and two overnight loans buying out the first ones to bail out."

"You know my financials better than my tax attorney,

so you know that we can replace their money and then some in under a year."

"Your firm's skill on the market is unrivaled, but what happens when you try to buy another piece of art? Interpol and the FBI are on to you – and maybe watching me, just in case. One more arrest and you will lose your job and your money, and your clients will sue you for what is left. Your firm will close overnight."

"Thank you for mentioning the FBI. I was not sure how to bring this up. You know who headed that operation?"

"Yes. An agent named David Vasari. Probably the best art investigator on the planet."

"But only because he has a secret weapon. He is not any sharper than the other cops on the case."

"What do you mean?"

"Did you ever check out the entire team of investigators?"

"How could I? The papers said some two hundred police and experts worked with Vasari."

"Yes, but I noticed a coincidence that made me curious. Do you remember the FBI agent who busted Ettore?"

"Yes. Redwood was the FBI liaison at the American Embassy."

"Did you notice that he was in the crowd in that picture on the front of the *Corriere della sera*?"

"The one with the president giving Vasari a commendation?"

"Yes. You probably recognized some of the art crime people from the Carabinieri and the Ministry of Cultural Assets."

"So?"

"Did you see Agent Redwood?"

"Not that I noticed. He was there?"

"Trying to stay out of the picture. Near the back row, moving away."

"What does another FBI agent have to do with it?"

"Not the agent directly, but his secretary." Santis stood. "Another drink?"

Bonin handed him his glass. "This better be a good story, Sandro."

"It is."

Santis came back in a few minutes and sat comfortably after handing Bonin a fresh gin and tonic.

"I was in Rome meeting with the American cultural attaché when Ettore was still organizing his coup. We went to that horrid American grill in the basement of the Embassy Annex because he wanted a hamburger."

Manny winced at the memory of the smells in the lobby of the Annex.

"As we stopped in the lobby, he nudged my elbow and tilted his head to a very pretty blonde with an armload of newspapers going upstairs. She really was delightful to look at, probably the youngest-looking woman I had ever seen at the Embassy.

"Morrison told me that she was Redwood's new secretary. His old one had been injured in a car crash and was repatriated. The young thing was an intern, but Redwood was happy with her and promoted her to the job."

"How happy was he?" The two men smirked and chuckled, then Bonin said, "Is there a point to this?"

"As Redwood's secretary, she had to be in on the FBI collaboration with the government when they put down the coup. So, imagine my surprise when I saw her again last summer."

"Where?"

"At the Cavalieri Hilton hotel, playing tennis with Nancy Lockhart."

"The Smithson executive?"

"That's the one. Ettore had been orchestrating a hate campaign against her because her son was apparently the one who tipped off Redwood and brought the whole coup crashing down."

"How?"

"He was translating the Smithson files for that executive who couldn't read Italian, and he stumbled across our coded messages."

"Damn! So that's how it happened."

"Pretty much. So why is the secretary hanging around now? And more than hanging around. My contacts in the police tell me that she was the one who pushed Lockhart down when the sniper tried to take her out and covered her during the car bombing at Fiumicino. They went back to the States together."

"Undercover bodyguard?"

"I had my people check on her. Sandra Billingsley. Grew up on a farm in Ohio. She's an art history major at the George Washington University and was taking a course in conservation and restoration at the American Academy."

"An undergraduate at the American Academy? Unusual."

"I thought so too. I had her followed, which turned into a challenge because she rides a bicycle in traffic. But they did learn that she goes to the Redwood home on Thursday evenings for dinner and chamber music."

"That seems harmless."

"That's what I thought, but Redwood was no longer the FBI liaison. For him to be in Rome for the art raids is too much of a coincidence."

"And where does the secretary fit in?"

"I don't know, but someone in all this has an uncanny ability to sort forgeries from originals. I got the list of the art taken in the recovery from the newspapers. Every one of them was the subject of a switch during a museum tour. I don't think Vasari, Redwood, or the present FBI man in Rome, Pietrowicz, has the eye to catch that. My guess is it's the secretary."

They stared at the river. A small sloop was running before the wind but not making that much progress against the current. The reflection of the sun on a pair of binoculars flashed. *Yachtsmen enjoying the water,* Bonin thought.

"What do you need, Sandro?"

"Three hundred thousand would cover all the outstanding liabilities."

"If all your clients ran at once?"

"Just barely, but yes."

"Just barely is not enough. You need to be in business to pay me back."

"I won't keep the money myself. I will put it in each account, so the performance would be completely above board. The clients won't be tempted to bail out on us if the accounts are making money again."

"That's better. I'll have my auditors checking on you."

"Of course. I'll send you copies of our books, but I expect you to check separately."

Bonin stood.

"Would a transfer to your Zurich office next week be convenient?"

"Mark it for 'services rendered.' That should be vague enough."

"Too vague. How about 'contribution to renovations' for this place?"

"Okay. I'll send you a description of the work we've had done in the last year for your files."

They walked out front, where the black Land Rover was waiting.

Bonin turned his back on the car and driver and leaned into his friend.

"Sandro, I can't tell you to stop collecting, but you need to find out more about how Interpol spotted the switches. Don't buy anything else until you do. Please."

"I promise, Manny. The breathing room you've given us will allow me to put resources on that."

They exchanged an Italian-style hug before Bonin turned and rode back to his hotel.

Chapter 7

Second Semester

SANDRA, MARY, AND JIM stared at the printouts taped to the blackboard in the conference room. They had not turned on the lights because the sunlight reflecting off the snowy fields outside made them unnecessary.

This was the final week of the semester break. Monday, Sandra would go back to twice-weekly trips to the farm and a double load in her class schedule.

"David's new investigation is getting in gear," said the FBI agent as he filled his coffee cup. "Will you be able to look at photos once in a while if he brings them here?"

"Yes. Want me to pick him up?"

"Let's play that by ear. We might take turns, with his renting a car every so often." He returned to the end of the table and sat.

"Our critical path has lengthened," said Mary, pointing to the relevant printout. "Could you explain that?"

Sandra consulted her notes. "According to RICO, the firm got an infusion of cash recently. The *Wall Street Journal* reported that three major investors who had announced their intention to back out changed their minds."

"Why RICO?"

Jim said, "That firm – All Saints Investments – uses accounts in the Cayman Islands and Zurich to move money, something that makes RICO's ears twitch. They were not targets of any investigation until Sandra had us compare money movements with art deliveries last summer.

"David called this morning. New York put a watch on Sandro Santis and the other Arcibaldo investors after Joe recognized his name. The authorities in Germany and Italy let New York know when Bonin or Kanter leave their country. Santis and Bonin had a secret meeting just after the New Year."

"How secret?"

"Very. If we had not been watching all four, we would never have known about Bonin flying to New York, then visiting Santis at his mansion on the Hudson before flying back to Rome that night. Must have been important. We may find that the cash in the All Saints account came from Bonin."

৪৪৪

As the days lengthened ever so slowly and the snow melted, Sandra fell into a familiar routine. Classes, library research, papers, and reports Monday through Friday kept her in class or her apartment. Tuesday afternoon at the dojo and Sunday on the tennis court with the Redwoods (or Joe, in Charlottesville). Thursday evenings at the Redwoods. Wednesday and Friday afternoons at the farm. And every Friday after work, she drove to Charlottesville, even if they only studied silently in Joe's apartment.

One evening as she dried her hair after a shower, she realized that she had not interacted socially with anyone at the university since her freshman year, three-and-a-half years ago. Her entire life revolved around her studies, her work for the Bureau, and an out-of-town lover. *By the time I graduate in May,* she thought, *no one will remember going to school with Sandra Billingsley.* She would miss her advisor, Maureen Andrews, but the invisibility of her previous life would help Alessandra Bari establish herself.

The telephone interrupted her musings. She wrapped the towel around herself and went to the instrument clamoring from its little table near the front door.

"*Ciao, bella.*" The familiar voice ran from her head to her toes with a thrill that she hungered for when she started thinking too much by herself. "I know you're coming this weekend, but I couldn't wait to tell you the news."

"Well?"

"The Academic Committee recommended giving me the BA this spring."

"We're classmates!"

"Yeah. Isn't that great?"

"Where will you go next year?"

"Nowhere. The unit still owns me for my naval training and agreed to keep me on as a graduate student. I'll have the coursework finished next semester, and I should be able to present my thesis and take the MA in January or February."

"But isn't the NROTC program a full four years?"

"Yes, but Captain Norwood and the major have figured out how to load me so that I could be commissioned after my first-class cruise."

"Wonderful. Commencement here is the last Saturday in May. What about there?"

"Same. I guess we won't be able to go to each other's graduation."

"It means less to me than it might now. If my family would not be disappointed, I would let the University mail my degree and go to your graduation."

"I never met your family."

"I know. Let's think about that. We could work out something."

"Gotta go. The pasta's al dente."

"See you Friday. Love ya."

"Love ya too."

They hung up.

ଟଟଟ

Mary stepped back from the collection of printouts. She turned her head to Sandra.

"This bothers me. What do you think?"

"All Saints merging with Borodin Financials just as Borodin lost its CEO? Santis has not exactly come out of the woods yet."

"What else?"

Sandra walked to the board and scanned the bubbles for a common item.

"Suicides."

"Yes. Six in the last week. A total of a dozen since Christmas."

"But not all the companies were becoming 'more desperate,' as Jim says."

"No. Let me call him. Maybe he or someone in New York can match this fatality rate with something happening at their end." She went to her office while Sandra sat and made some notes about which buyers and which sellers and art pieces connected with the suicides. Mary came back.

"Jim said that he thinks the Interpol investigation is adding to the stress. He'll be here Friday with more information."

"This may be relevant. All but two of them bought their art from Arcibaldo. The other two covered their tracks, but the pictures could have come from Arcibaldo via intermediaries."

"Curious. I hope this makes sense to Jim. Let's go home."

They packed up the papers and went their separate ways.

&&&

As Sandra transferred the omelet to her plate, the phone rang. She turned off the gas and walked to the phone.

"Miss Barry? Please call Mr. Redwood. He's at work." The secretary hung up before Sandra could say anything, but she had recognized the voice. *Probably not happy to be earning overtime tonight.* She glanced longingly at her supper, then washed her hands, donned her winter jacket, and walked to the coffee shop.

"You wanted to talk to me, sir?"

"Yes. Bad news. Arcibaldo is out on bail, which does not surprise me. Frankly, I can't believe it took so long."

"Didn't he lose the party leadership last fall?"

"Yes. He's holed up in his cousin's villa because he had to leave the party-owned apartment on Via della Scrofa. He's trying to piece his operation back together with his most loyal followers."

"Are we talking seriously desperate?"

"Yes. According to Italian intelligence sources in the party, he is going off the deep end. He has called markers from several known crime families and Fascist sympathizers. Some of them have connections here in the States.

"We think he wants to kill you and the Lockharts, in addition to Vasari and anyone involved in his fall from grace. He's in full revenge mode."

"He probably knows he'll never get his old position back."

"Right. I'm having the resident agent in Charlottesville brief Joe. The SAC in Richmond has already warned Nancy and scheduled a meeting with Smithson security. Be careful. You're possibly the hardest target for them, but that doesn't mean they won't try."

"Thanks, sir. Anything in particular?"

"I would say be careful everywhere."

"Any point in packing a weapon?"

"Whatever you feel comfortable with, that won't get Sandra Billingsley arrested."

"Got it. Will we see you Friday?"

"Yes. I have scheduled a secure call with New York tomorrow so we can tie up some loose ends. I'll have more answers when I see you."

"Anything else?"

"No. Just watch out."

"I will, sir. Thanks."

Back at the apartment, she heated up her dinner and reviewed her notes from the FBI Academy class on surveillance while she ate. In bed that night, she focused on Sergeant Moseley's advice before they went on their field training exercise after the Academy: *in combat, sleep and eat every chance; you never know when the next chance will be.*

Still, it took a while to doze off…

ⱅⱅⱅ

No one followed her to class on Thursday or to Georgetown that night. The Redwoods made a point of enjoying the dinner and the music and avoided talking about the case.

The next day, Sandra got off US-29 early as if going to Luray Caverns, then dropped onto Virginia Highway 231 to go to Madison. At the farm, she went straight to the collection of newspapers.

Two hours later, Sandra came up from the basement when she had keyed in the latest data from her newspaper reviews. She found Jim Redwood and Mary sitting in the conference room. It was dark outside.

"You could have called me."

"Jim and I were looking at the situation in Richmond in case there is anything I could do to help there."

"And?"

"Nothing, really. Pete Wembly and Nancy have a good handle on things. Her experience in Rome put her ahead of him and the SAC when it came to awareness, varying her commute, and such. The SAC thinks she'll be hard to target."

"Still, I wish she had Adriano to drive her in."

"She thought of that. Adele, Annabelle, Matthew, and François are taking turns, and at irregular times she drives herself. They are also rotating cars.

"François traded his old pickup truck for an Alfa Romeo."

They shared a chuckle over the image of the elderly gardener in a sporty car. They knew that the steel beneath the surface may be old, but it wasn't rusty. When Matthew served as a military attaché in Berlin and Paris, the Dampierre retainer had been his chauffeur. When the Ardwoods were called back to the US in 1939, François and Adele chose to go home to France. The two Resistance fighters worked for the OSS (Office of Strategic Services, precursor to the CIA) on missions that would not be declassified for many years.

Mary said, "Nancy is safer with them than I am on US-29 to Amherst."

Sandra poured herself a mug of coffee and joined them. "Another suicide, the CFO of the firm whose CEO died last week in a car crash: Borodin Financials." Chief Financial Officer.

"Wasn't he poised to be the new CEO with the All Saints takeover?" asked Mary.

"That leads to what I brought with me after talking to David and Bob. All three, Santis and the two Borodin men, were caught in the sweep. But the Borodin executives were also under investigation by David and Interpol concerning those pictures that you looked at back in the fall, Sandra."

"Was the car crash suspicious?"

"Not on the surface, but the SAC in LA met quietly with the police chief and the Highway Patrol to suggest they take a closer look. That will take time but should not expose David's investigation."

"And Borodin itself?"

"Busted. All Saints got it for twenty cents on the dollar. They could sell the real estate for the equity they put out." His gaze went to the printouts on the board. "Your predictions called that two weeks early. Good work."

"What about the other suicides?" asked Mary.

"I'm glad you two noticed this because it turns out that all twelve – thirteen now – were being investigated by the New York Field Office. Even with the connection these men have to the art bust and to the new investigation, I am having trouble seeing a coincidence in this many suicides."

"Maybe someone we haven't spotted who is threatened by their connection to the case?"

"That's a possibility, but there is another suspicious detail: the suicides began when David returned to work, and the investigation moved forward.

"There's a leak in New York."

"You told me that these collectors work hard to spy on the FBI."

"True, but this is too close. I called the IG for some discreet help. He said that David and Charley have done well. Bob and I are working on a diversionary case." Inspector General.

"A decoy?"

"If it works as designed, it will expose the leak quickly." He tapped his head. "Knock on wood."

Feeling more exposed than she had in months, Sandra opted not to drive directly to Charlottesville on US-29. Instead, she went back to Madison and drove through Orange and Gordonsville to approach Charlottesville from the east. She had studied more than a half dozen different ways to make that trip and planned to shuffle them.

Passing the turnoff for Wertland Street, she parked around the corner on Fourteenth Street and walked back to Joe's apartment.

CHAPTER 8

SPRING BREAK

THE CHERRY BLOSSOMS ON THE NATIONAL MALL seemed average this year, but they still attracted large crowds of tourists. Sandra and Joe dodged the tour buses, taxis, and rental cars as they navigated Constitution Avenue on their way back to her apartment. It was Tuesday of spring break, and they had chosen to leave the black battlewagon in the garage to ride downtown.

The visiting exhibit at the National Gallery of Art ("Miró and Modigliani") had been a special treat. Sandra could enjoy them without looking for inconsistencies or signs of forgery. She was building a reputation for Renaissance paintings, and she guessed that Interpol checked the modern pieces with others. *Until David shows up with one of these!* It was well-known that legions of forgers copied both artists, keeping Interpol busy.

Following Sandra by a car length, Joe shared her happy mood for many reasons. Last year, he had stormed out of her apartment in a jealous pique, slamming the door on their relationship. They tortured themselves with regrets for months but were unable to communicate until they were reunited in the FBI Office in Rome. By the time General Arcibaldo was arrested in July (for the second time) and the art recovery exploded in the headlines of the world press, Joe understood how deep their love was, and he learned to welcome David Vasari as her colleague and friend, not a rival.

The tourist traffic plus the normal rush hour made Pennsylvania Avenue impassable even for bicycles. Sandra led him up Virginia Avenue to New Hampshire Avenue and through Foggy Bottom to her apartment near GWU.

After their shower, Sandra sat in the bedroom to comb out her hair.

"Let me do that." Joe held out his hand. She shrugged and braced herself.

To her surprise, he started at the ends and worked his way to her scalp, gently teasing out the long, shiny hair. He smiled happily in the mirror as he combed. Then he expertly worked the hairbrush and dryer. She closed her eyes and reveled in the most sensuous experience her head had ever felt outside a salon.

He kissed her head and gave her the brush. She tied a ponytail as they went to the little kitchen.

"Where did you learn to do long hair?"

"Mom cracked her wrist my freshman year in high school. I did it every day for six weeks while her bone healed."

"She didn't have her hair done?"

"There wasn't time to go to a *parrucchiere* every day. She used one near work once a week."

"Jason Joseph Lockhart, you are a man of many talents. Laundry, cooking, and now hair? I think I'll keep you!"

They set about fixing Sandra's weekly Roman meal.

"This is so domestic," she said, "I wish we didn't have to go back to school."

"Me too, but—"

"I know, not until you come back from your first deployment." She put the knife on the cutting board and hugged her lover. "I agree. Neither of us is the person we will be for most of our lives." They kissed and turned back to the salad assembly. "But I'll be on the pier when the ship moors."

The pasta was al dente. They put out their supper.

"You have to go to the farm tomorrow, don't you?" Joe asked as he spilled his bucatini back into his plate. Sandra's toes were *very* distracting.

"Uh-huh. I was thinking of going in early. Want to come along?"

"Am I cleared?"

"I asked Mary and Jim about it. They said you just need to stay out of the basement."

"Okay. I can work on this translation I brought with me, but I could also take another look at those pages of data to see if something hits me."

"That might be helpful. Your picking out the investors was brilliant. David told me that Santis and Bonin had a secret meeting in January."

"Anything on the other two?"

"Quiet so far. Kanter's firm invested some in Wilder's oil drilling company, but he's done that several times over the years. Only Kanter bought art, but he had intermediaries, so only the museum director in Cologne took the fall for it. Kanter was all stunned innocence when he let the *Bundespolizei* confiscate his paintings."

Joe grunted at that.

🙰🙰🙰

The Italian novel and the draft translation sat under a cold mug of coffee as Joe pored over the data sheets and printouts at the conference table. Sandra was in the basement, entering the latest news reports into the system. Activity had been picking up: some of the target individuals' companies had begun to recover, others were merging with competitors, and still others were filing for bankruptcy.

He had noticed that one-third of the art collectors on the list were now divorced or separated, an unusually high number for their ages and social class. Almost all of them were dumped by their well-heeled wives for a wide range of reasons, and those one hundred men were on the "critical path" watchlist that Mary and Sandra had created.

The two women came into the room.

"Stand up, Joe!" said the professor. "You haven't moved since we left, have you?"

Joe felt his stiff back as he rose. "Er, no. Thanks." He stretched and walked around the table before carrying his cold coffee to the sideboard to exchange it.

"It must be more interesting than that novel. What have you found?"

"I haven't checked all three hundred collectors' data, but have you noticed that only one or two companies in each industry are buying out the ones that are merging? So far as I've seen, the other firms in trouble are simply going bankrupt."

"That sounds normal to me," said Mary.

"Yes, but those one or two buyers are all tied to the arrests in Rome – not the other cities – or to Arcibaldo in one of two ways."

"The art purchased or the four investors?" asked Sandra.

"Yes. Someone is moving very fast to take advantage of the fallout from the raids."

"That means that they noticed the impact quickly."

"Or they expected it."

"All Saints almost tanked."

"But not before Bonin could bail them out."

"I'm not sure what to make of that," said Mary, "but it smacks of more collusion than I am comfortable with among a limited number of players." She turned to Sandra. "Can you work up a sort on who is merging and who has bought whom? Linda is coming in late, so she can run them." JMU was not on the same spring break dates as UVA or GWU.

"Sure. I'm glad we made the company fields so flexible when we saw the first buyouts and mergers." She looked at Joe. "Want to come back tomorrow?"

"Let's remember to go back in time for your soirée with the Redwoods."

"I'll set up the queries before we leave, Mary. We should have the answers to work on in the morning."

Going back to Washington, Sandra turned off US-29 at Bealeton. She took US-28 to Manassas and US-50 into the District.

"Doesn't all this variety take longer?" asked Joe as they climbed up to her apartment.

"A little, but it allows me to take turns that expose a tail."

"I was followed last week to class, but there wasn't much I could do. I recognized him because twice he was outside my house."

"Guy with no neck in a green Ford?"

"That's the one." *She would have noticed,* he thought. "He was walking down the other side of the street when I came out. I called the resident agent because he asked me to report that sort of stuff when he came to my house to warn me."

"Who's the resident agent in Charlottesville?"

"Crunch McCall. What a name."

"Crunch in Charlottesville? He was in my cohort at the Academy. I only knew he was assigned to Richmond." She opened the door and motioned him in.

"I forget sometimes that you would have classmates from Quantico."

She slid into his arms for a long hug and a kiss. "Don't go all jealous on me now. I *was* the only girl in the class."

"Don't worry. I'm comfortable with it now." He picked up his bookbag and carried it into the bedroom….

CHAPTER 9

COMMENCEMENTS

FOR THE TENTH TIME IN AN HOUR, Sandra checked the academic gown hanging on the bedroom wall. No dust or stains had appeared since last she ran her hands over it. The white velvet on the hood blazed against the dark blue and buff of her school colors.

Am I really – finally – graduating? She had arrived at the George Washington University as a self-conscious but precocious sixteen-year-old. By staying in Rome to work in the FBI Liaison Office, she had dropped back by one year group. Adding the accounting major to art history required a fifth year. Meanwhile, Joe was getting his BA early, making up for the time he lost in elementary school after his father died.

It would be convenient for them to be in the same undergraduate class going forward.

Stepping to the front door of the apartment building, she checked carefully for people or cars that had not moved lately, then walked quickly to Dupont Circle. A quick bus ride up Connecticut Avenue took her to the rental agency by the Washington Hilton. Hertz was expensive, but they could get her the kind of vehicle she wanted and not make her go to the airport to pick it up. With her NIS income, she could afford it.

An hour later, she waited on the platform as the *Capitol Limited* eased into Union Station. She might have missed her family stepping off the train, but James and Arnie stood out in their service green Army uniforms. Both were in the ROTC at Ohio State University.

Her throat closed and she stopped breathing. Behind her brothers, she saw a flash of Walter in his Marine khaki shirt and green pants, a seabag on his shoulder. As she stared, he faded, but the reality of seeing him remained. She took a deep breath and pushed the tears back down.

They were past her when she shouted, "Over here!" from the side of the crowd. *My shadow skills are becoming ingrained.* They interrupted the hugging when they realized that they were blocking the others.

On the concourse level, Sandra led them to the parking garage and the big station wagon.

"Sandra, what is this?" her mother said.

"A rental. Easiest way to get you settled. Then everything will be in walking distance."

"Hertz. You can afford this?" Marcia worried about the cost of things, a habit from many years as the wife of a soldier and then a farmer.

"Yes, Mom. The scholarship covers my needs. I save the money from side gigs."

"What are those? You've never talked about anything but your classes."

"Mostly consulting on paintings. I do some work at the Corcoran since the conservator course in Rome. I'll tell you about it later."

"You have built your own community here," said her father as they drove to Georgetown.

"I have been at home here, though I'll have to start over after this weekend."

"Why is your boss from Rome hosting us?" asked Marcia.

"I met him again after he transferred here from Rome. We play music on Thursday nights and tennis on Sundays, so the routine is the same as it was there. With Doug away at Loyola, they enjoy having me over."

"I'm a little nervous staying with them the same day I meet them."

"Don't worry, Mom. They'll be great. It's Thursday, which is why I asked you to bring the violins."

"But she plays with the NSO."

"Jim doesn't." Sandra glanced at her quickly and smiled. "They will be delighted to have you on piano tonight. Seriously."

"It should be fun," said Arnie from the back. The brothers played violin. James preferred playing second, Arnie first.

There was a parking place open in front of the Redwood townhouse. Jim and Arlene came out as they opened the doors of the station wagon.

After introductions, Jim showed James and Arnie where to take the bags. Then the brothers took their instrument cases to Arlene's studio, where a borrowed bass waited for Martin.

While Sandra's brothers unpacked and changed out of their uniforms, Sandra put her viola case in the studio. They gathered in the living room. Jim poured Moselle for them.

"This is an enormous pleasure for me – for us," Redwood said with a glance at Arlene. "I have wanted to meet you since the day this amazing young woman answered the phone when I called to interview her in Rome."

"Why was that?" asked Martin.

"She had such a crisp, perfect Italian that I knew right there that she would make a *bella figura* for the office. You know what that means."

"Yes. Make the office look good."

"She was already the most qualified applicant for our little internship, but the musical quality of those simple words cinched it even before she came in."

"Please, sir. I just answered the phone." Sandra blushed fiercely.

The FBI agent laughed. "Anyway, you've done a fantastic job with this one."

"Thank you for taking her in the way you have," said Marcia. "We were worried when she was living alone."

"She is unbelievably resourceful. You should have seen how she stepped into the secretary's job. We missed her when she came back here."

Arlene rose to go to the kitchen. Marcia insisted on joining her.

Dinner involved helping oneself and carrying it to the dining room table. Music and musicians were the common areas of conversation. Arlene was surprised to learn that Martin had played on the same stage with her when the Field Band performed a Christmas benefit concert with the NSO.

Sandra and her brothers washed up while Arlene made coffee. They took it to the studio. After tuning and playing a few small pieces for each other, they played Mikhail Glinka's *Grand Sextet*.

"That was so much fun," said Marcia. "If I wanted to play chamber music, I shouldn't have married a bassist." She got up and kissed Martin.

"I'm glad I found something," said Arlene.

"Can we do it again?" asked Arnie.

They took a bathroom break, then played the Glinka again.

At the door, Sandra hugged her family and wished them goodnight.

"Come back for breakfast, Sandra," Arlene said.

"Okay. See you tomorrow."

Sandra knew that there would not be a parking place by her building, so she left the station wagon and walked home.

Back in her apartment, she called Joe in Charlottesville.

"Missed you. Are you busy?"

"Yes, but I wish I were there."

"Me too."

"Sunday, I can borrow a car from Mom or Grandpa. Someone will take me back to Charlottesville from Richmond after I return it."

"I wish I could come get you tonight."

"Me too. Hang in there, love."

ಜಜಜ

Friday morning, Sandra trotted to the Redwoods' house. The household was gathered around breakfast. Jim Redwood was finishing up. He took his plates to the sink and kissed his wife goodbye.

"I'll see you all this afternoon. Enjoy your day." And he was gone.

Sandra took a helping of scrambled eggs and bacon to the table. Then she came back with a mug of coffee.

"I don't have to turn in the wagon until noon. Is there anything you want to see that requires a car?"

They discussed it for a while, then decided to visit the Washington Cathedral, then come back through Georgetown. Sandra could return the car in time for lunch.

"Let us take you out, Arlene," said Martin.

"Thanks, but I have an NSO rehearsal at one and a student at four. Have lunch here, then walk to the National Mall for the afternoon."

Marcia got up quickly. "I wanted to share this with you yesterday. Wait." She went back to the guest bedroom and came back with a copy of the Madison *Messenger.* "This came out just as we were leaving for Columbus." She folded it and put it proudly on the table with the front page showing.

It was a full-page spread about Sandra, with photos of her in the *Messenger* newsroom, her yearbook photo, a photo of the family with the *Messenger* staff, and a few of the sketches she had done while she was the court artist for the newspaper.

The article described her rise from the farm on Route 38 to a full scholarship at GWU, her studies abroad at the American Academy, and an exciting year working for the FBI in Rome. And now, she would graduate with degrees in art history and accounting.

"Isn't it wonderful?" Marcia said. "We're so proud of you." She looked at her husband and sons, who grinned.

Sandra's heart sank, and she felt the terror build.

Arlene caught Sandra's eye and very slightly moved her head back and forth. Sandra pushed down her fear and smiled.

"Thanks, Mom. I get embarrassed by this kind of attention, you know."

Marcia patted her arm. "You deserve it. Once in a while, the world needs to know how amazing you are." She passed it to Arlene. "I got copies for Sandra and for you too."

"Thank you," said Arlene. "I'll make sure Jim sees it when he gets back."

Sandra rose. "Let's do the dishes and take that tour, shall we?" Her glance told Arlene how badly she needed to change the subject and move on.

ঠ঑ঠ঑ঠ঑

Marcia and Martin were taking a nap when Jim Redwood came home. The Billingsley boys had met a group of OSU students at the National Archives. They promised to be back for supper.

Sandra came up the street as he climbed the steps to the house. Arlene met him with a kiss. After he put his suit jacket away and returned, she handed him a glass of Riesling.

"You may want something stronger after you see this." She led them into the living room. The issue of the *Messenger* lay on the coffee table.

"So, this is the original story?" Sandra and Arlene stared with a questioning expression. "This was on the Associated Press wire service as a human-interest story. I have no idea who will pick it up and print it."

"You mean the evening papers?" Sandra asked.

"At least those. But it's a touching story, it's the weekend, and GWU graduation. It could be in the Sunday supplements or *Parade* nationwide."

"Oh no." Sandra sank into an armchair. "I might as well have a target—"

Jim held his finger to his lips. "Let's take a walk." He asked Arlene, "Need milk or something?"

"Get another half gallon and some ice cream." She tilted her head in the direction of the sleeping guests. "We'll be here."

Outside, they turned toward the corner grocery store.

"Quite a shock, isn't it?"

"Yes, sir. It scares the hell out of me."

"Well, you won't be the first agent to be in the spotlight, nor the last. You can get past this."

"I know, but it still scares me."

"Keep calm and it may help you."

"How?"

"For one, it reinforces the story of the undergraduate who went to GWU and Rome and then went home. Are you going to London after graduation?"

"I told them I would come visit after I moved out of my apartment and got settled."

"Where will you move?"

"I'll be at Joe's place until you send me to New York."

"Perfect. We need to let some time pass before Sandra Bari shows up in New York."

"Joe starts his second-class summer training on Tuesday. He'll be at Pensacola until the end of June. Then New London. We don't know if he'll come to Charlottesville on the way."

"I think your transfer to New York could happen by then. It will depend on the activity of our suspects. You and Mary will know about that as quickly as I will."

They chose two half gallons of ice cream and picked up the milk.

"What about the moveable roommates and the mail-drop?"

"Already set up. I'll call you at the farm. Then you can give the address and phone number to your family."

"I'll do that when I see them."

They walked up the steps to the townhouse.

"Feel better?"

"Yes, sir. Thanks."

Arlene met them in the hall. "Dinner is in the oven. Come join us."

ଉଉଉ

Saturday morning dawned clear, dry, and brilliant. Sandra hummed a happy tune as she walked to Dupont Circle. She carried her academic regalia on a covered hanger.

They had agreed to have breakfast under Darlene's care, so the Billingsleys could meet the woman who had provided wisdom, privacy, and solace to Sandra.

"Do we need a new sign for the branch office?" Darlene asked Jim Redwood as she poured coffee into their mugs. "Your meetings are getting crowded."

"Not yet," said Jim.

"I'm gonna miss this one."

"Not gone yet," said Sandra. "And I'll be back. Count on it."

"I will. What will you all have?"

An hour later, the two families walked to the University Yard. Sandra donned her gown and mortarboard hat before giving the hanger to her father. She saw them seated, then found her place in the second row of graduating students. The students on either side were deep in whispered conversation with classmates away from her. She welcomed the relative solitude in the crowded setting.

During her two years in Rome, the campus in DC boiled with civil rights and Vietnam War protests. Sandra read about the riots in the *Rome Daily American* and the *International Herald Tribune*. To her classmates, those events would be the most vivid memories of their undergraduate years, but they had seemed distant and strange to her. When she and Redwood found themselves helping the Italian government put down a coup attempt (discovered by Joe), events at GWU vanished from her radar screen.

When she thought of Joe, she knew that she had her priorities in order. She would never regret the adventures they had shared, regardless of what the future held for them.

She settled into a pleasant feeling as the crowd finished gathering, the orchestra and band played, and the official party marched onto the stage. It seemed too soon when she heard her name called.

At the reception for the fine arts students in Corcoran Gallery of Art nearby, Jim Redwood offered to take a family photo with Arnie's Instamatic camera. He also took pictures of them with his own camera and another with Arlene in it.

As he was shooting a final pose, a stranger stepped up next to him, took a photo with a reporter-style flash, then turned to move quickly away.

Sandra started after him, but her father grabbed her arm.

"Let him go, Sandra. What's the harm?" The man disappeared. "It's not as if you're a celebrity – yet."

She exchanged a quick glance with Jim Redwood, relaxed, and led the family to meet her advisor, who stood at the edges of the reception.

଼଼଼

Sunday morning, the Billingsleys slept in, the rarest of occurrences for a farming family that had commitments in church every weekend.

Sandra knocked on the door as they were organizing breakfast and refilling the coffee maker for another pot. She handed Jim the *Washington Post,* which she had collected on the stoop. The FBI agent took it to the kitchen, where seven place settings were laid.

"I need to check this. Please excuse me." He went into the living room with a coffee mug and the paper.

"Some things never take a day off," said Arlene as she carried a heaping bowl of scrambled eggs to the table. "Besides always being on call, he has to watch what the press has to say about everything – including crime and the Bureau."

"He read eight of them every day in Rome," said Sandra, "until my Italian got good enough to have a summary of the Italian press ready for him each morning."

Redwood came into the kitchen. He held a copy of *Parade* magazine, which had been wrapped in the Sunday issue of the *Washington Post*.

"You're famous, young lady." He handed the magazine to Sandra. The close-up shot of her from the Madison *Messenger* occupied the cover. The article appeared to be the same as the original, with a tie-in to the commencement ceremonies. "The coverage of graduation in the local news included a mention of you but not much else."

"They didn't need to." She gave *Parade* to her mother with a smile. "Good thing I don't have a fan club, or the phone would be ringing off the hook."

The phone in the hall rang, making Sandra start. She recovered as Arlene answered.

She came right back and said to Sandra, "Joe."

"*Ciao, amore, che c'è?*" Hello, love, what's up?

"Can you talk?" he asked in Italian. "We saw the *Parade* coverage this morning."

"Not really, but we can talk about it later. Just be extra careful now. Anyone looking for me now knows where to find me. When will you be here?"

"I promised to go to church because so many family friends want to see me. I was thinking of driving up after lunch. Mom's lending me her car."

"No racing, now. That's a hot car."

"Not as hot as the GT model François bought. About three."

"Come to my place first. I may be there with my family, or we can walk here together."

"Okay. See you at three. Love you."

"Love you too."

Coming back to the kitchen, Sandra was taken aback by the stares of her parents and brothers.

"Does he speak English?" asked Marcia.

Sandra laughed. "Of course, Mom. We got in the habit of speaking Italian when he had no privacy in the residence hall. Now we prefer it."

"That makes sense. It is more romantic sounding too."

"When will we meet this mystery man?" asked Martin.

"This afternoon. Parking is easier near my apartment, so he'll drive there. I want to show you the place anyway."

ജ്ഞ

Five Billingsleys made a crowd in Sandra's main room. They took turns checking everything out. She turned on the coffee maker and sliced up the Bundt cake on the kitchen counter.

"It feels like your room at home," said her mother. "Lovely."

"But this room is all studio," said James. "A piano, viola, and an easel with paints."

"What does the owner say about all those books?" asked Arnie, ever the engineer.

"He assured me that he is used to students and teachers, and the floors are rated for library stacks."

Her father paged through the music piled on the piano next to the viola. "I am glad that you could keep up your music. Thursday was beautiful."

"Thanks, Dad. The music keeps me sane."

"Anything we haven't heard?"

"Something I heard in Rome." She took her instrument from its case and tuned it.

As she finished playing Elliott Carter's *Elegy* for them, the doorbell rang. James reached back and opened it. Joe stepped in.

"I heard that. Beautiful." He leaned a gift-wrapped package on the side table by the telephone.

"Hi, Joe. Meet the family." Joe gave each a firm handshake, then excused himself.

"Nonstop drive from Richmond."

When he returned, they were sipping their coffee. Sandra handed him a dish with a slice of cake and a mug of coffee.

"Whatever it is has my name on it," she said.

"I could not come here without a graduation present. After all, you put more time into your degree than I did."

"Open it, Sandy." Arnie handed her his Swiss Army officer's knife, opened to the scissors. She unwrapped a high-quality photograph of Rome taken from the Vatican Observatory near sunset. Sandra caught her breath and held it up for them to see.

"The view from your home." She choked on the last word as the sight made her eyes well up.

"Well, nearby, but yes. I thought you'd appreciate the memory."

She gave the picture to her mother and turned to hug her lover. "Oh, thank you."

Martin and Marcia admired the photo while Sandra and Joe disengaged.

"This will be a memory for both of you, won't it?"

"Yes, sir," said Joe. "As long as she lets me come look at it." He squeezed her waist. "You've been to Rome, haven't you?"

"Oh yes, but we never went to the Monte Mario. Too bad. That is quite a view."

Conversation moved around shared memories of the Eternal City, commencement exercises on the Lawn in Charlottesville, James's and Arnie's studies at OSU, and the differences between wines in Italy and France.

"Speaking of that," said Sandra, as the sun dropped low enough to illuminate the wall behind her, "we have reservations at the Scoglio restaurant tonight, but I wanted to toast with something we can't get there. Joe, could you and James assemble a small *tagliere?* You know where everything is."

She went to the kitchen and came back with a bottle of 1967 Nero di Troia.

"No one has heard of this wine in North America. The secretary who relieved me sent two bottles for this occasion. I don't have enough crystal for everyone, but, Mom, there are four wineglasses behind you in that cabinet. Joe and I usually drink from jelly glasses, which is how they do it in Rome." She uncorked the wine and set it on the table to chamber.

When Joe came out with the cold cuts and cheeses on a cutting board, James passed around small dishes, and Sandra poured…

Jim Redwood and Martin Billingsley had already agreed (after some arguing) to split the cost of hosting dinner at the Scoglio restaurant near Dupont Circle.

The meal ran long and loud, then Joe drove back to Richmond.

Monday morning, Sandra picked up the station wagon at the rental agency. After hugs and best wishes from their new friends in Georgetown, the Billingsleys rode to Union Station for the trip back to London, Ohio. Sandra told them to expect her in a couple of weeks and that she would call as soon as she was settled.

🙐🙐🙐

Tuesday morning, Sandra had everything she owned in the black car. *A big car is a blessing for this,* she thought. Still, she was surprised that five years of her life fit into the back seat and what little room was left in the trunk among the emergency equipment. The moving company came on Monday afternoon and removed the piano and the bicycle.

The owner of the apartment was pleased with the condition of the space. Sandra signed the paper, scribbling *B—* for the surname.

She ate a final meal at the coffee shop on Dupont Circle, then drove to the lot of the moving company in Arlington. They took charge of everything except the suitcase in the front seat, and she drove away from her life in Washington, DC.

She fixed supper in the apartment on Wertland Street. Joe called while she was washing the dishes.

🙐🙐🙐

For the next two weeks, Sandra commuted to the farm. Her main task now was to work with the FBI program analyst who had been assigned to read the newspapers and input data. Linda and Mary would continue to design queries.

Jim Redwood stopped by the farm to give her an address on the Lower East Side and a phone number for her family. They stood on the porch before he drove back to Washington.

"When you get back from Ohio, we should be close to sending you to New York."

"Mary Ellen is doing well. Will she want to stay on if I don't come back?"

"Not your problem, Agent Bari, but yes, she says she enjoys this work."

"Do you want me to leave the car with Agent McCall or bring it back to you?"

"Put it in long-term parking at Union Station. That will make it easier for you to go back to Charlottesville."

"Thanks."

"Be careful, Sandra. If someone is gunning for you, they have one chance to find Billingsley."

He stepped down from the porch and drove home. Sandra took the black car back to Wertland Street.

The next day, she parked behind Union Station and boarded the *Capitol Limited* for Columbus. Arnie met her at the station and took her home.

CHAPTER 10

MADISON COUNTY, OHIO

SANDRA FACED OFF against Karen in the basement of the Monroe home not far from the Billingsley farm. Karen's father, a retired Green Beret, had outfitted a gym, and the two friends enjoyed practicing martial arts on the big mat.

An hour later, they emerged into the hall and went to the kitchen for orange juice. Both women were drenched in sweat and catching their breath. Karen's parents were at the table.

"From the noise, I couldn't tell who was winning," said Zeb Monroe.

"Now that we're the same size, it's close, Dad. But she does have some moves I've never seen." She chugged half her glass of juice. "Want to try her?"

"Maybe tomorrow." He smiled at Sandra. "Want to embarrass me again in the morning?"

Sandra shrugged. "Sure."

"Dinner's almost ready." Samara Monroe (née Majid, an acclaimed artist) tilted her head to the stairs. "You two get cleaned up."

They put their glasses in the dishwasher and ran upstairs.

Later that night, they lay in the bunk beds in Karen's room. She was an only child but had asked for a bunk bed when she was small. She enjoyed having a friend stay over. Sandra wondered when they would do this again. The day after tomorrow, they would go to Columbus together. Karen would take the westbound train to Chicago; Sandra would go the opposite way, to New York City (though she would get off in Washington, DC, and drive to Charlottesville).

They talked into the night about school, art, boys, and travel, then eased off to sleep. Karen dreamed of being in a room surrounded by the paintings she had studied. Sandra relived Vespa rides with Joe.

A gentle thump shook Sandra awake. It sounded as if something far away had gone through the sound barrier. *Why do I feel something terrible is happening?*

She slipped down the ladder to the floor. Karen slept soundly. She parted the drapes but could not see anything. Her watch told her it was three a.m. She eased into her clothes.

Then she heard the siren over the fire hall in London. The phone rang. Zeb answered it.

"Sandra, are you up?" he called softly.

"Yes, sir." She came down with her duffel bag. He was in his fireman's outfit, minus the helmet.

"It's your place. C'mon!"

Sergeant Monroe had his helmet, a red flashing light, and a siren in his pickup truck. In five minutes, they pulled up at the fire department. The pumper truck was just rolling out but stopped to let Sandra in. Zeb jumped on the back with the other fireman.

With her blood pounding in her ears and the adrenaline flowing, Sandra stared at the road ahead. The world flashed red and dark until she could see the flames as they turned into the driveway. The ladder truck was already there, its lights making the smoke glow eerily.

As the scene came closer, she shifted into the alert mode she had internalized since the FBI Academy and detached emotionally.

It was not the Billingsley farmhouse, not anymore. There was almost nothing left, but parts of the house were smoldering as much as a hundred yards away. While the firemen systematically worked their way from the center of the fire, Sandra walked to the barn and took the fire extinguisher bottle by the door. She moved from ember to ember, putting out tiny fires in a wide arc as she closed in on the teams working on the house. By the time the bottle ran out, there was nothing left to extinguish.

The fire marshal and the police chief detailed people into investigation mode. She knew the police officers and firemen in town from her days covering the crime beat for the local newspaper while in high school.

The police chief put his arm around her shoulder. "I'm so sorry, Sandra."

She stiffened and stood back. "Thank you, Chief." She said to the fire marshal, "Shaped charges on the south side of the building?"

The man suppressed his surprise quickly. "Maybe. How do you figure?"

"The pattern. Everything blew toward the barn. There's no wind tonight. More than a grenade to take out the whole house this way."

"Sandra, are you okay?" asked the police chief.

"Yes, Chief. I know who and what was in the house. I will do my grieving soon. Right now, I need to call Columbus. Is anyone there on your frequencies?"

He scratched his head. "Yes, CPD and the fire department. Who do you need?"

"FBI. They can bring in the ATF." Bureau of Alcohol, Tobacco and Firearms.

"Do you know something about this?"

"Not really, but I may have been the target. I only arranged to spend the night with the Monroes after I went there today."

"Come with me."

They raised the dispatcher in Columbus from the chief's car. Columbus was already aware of the fire and had units ready to deploy to the Billingsley farm. The chief gave Sandra the microphone.

"Dispatch, please call the FBI duty agent. Tell him to call Special Agent Peters. Codename Bari. I will wait here at the scene."

"SAC Peters. Barry. Ten-four."

Sandra returned the microphone to its holder.

"You know Dale Peters?"

"Not well. He was given to me as a point of contact, but we did not expect the emergency to be here." She got out of the car, breathing in steady, controlled repetitions. "I need to keep active. I hope you understand."

"Sure. Just remember I'm here if you need anything."

"Thanks, Chief."

They returned to the scene. It was clear that bodily remains were going to be few. Sandra told them who was supposed to be in the house: her parents, Marcia and Martin, and two of her four brothers, James and Arnold. Martin Jr. was in the Mediterranean with the Sixth Fleet Band, and Walter was MIA in Vietnam. The police chief promised to call the Red Cross to notify her older brother.

Occasionally a firefighter would approach her with debris to be identified. She was able to place most of the objects. Almost nothing organic survived the explosion and fire.

A man came out of the darkness near the barn with Sandra's suitcase in a clear plastic bag. She had left it in the window, so it had been thrown far from the house. The handle was gone, and the outside was black, but the suitcase had stayed shut.

Thirty minutes after the call to Columbus, two black sedans rolled up the driveway with blue lights flashing. Sandra walked to intercept the agents getting out of the car. The man who got out of the front passenger seat approached her first.

"Bari?" He looked surprised. "Aren't you Sandra Billingsley? I remember you."

She moved close to him. "Yes, sir. Let's not slip the codename around here. Did you talk to Agent Redwood?"

"Yes. He said to get you out of here but to follow your lead."

"You know the chief, so I'll let you tell him that you'll take me to a safe place. All he needs to know is that it's a federal case if I was the target. Why I'm the target is classified, but if they let it be known that the whole Billingsley family was wiped out, maybe the perpetrators will consider themselves successful."

Agent Peters signaled the FBI agent who had come with him and the ATF agent from the other car. Then he turned to Sandra. His expression was worried but businesslike.

"How are you?"

"I can hold it in until we get out of here. I'll have plenty of support back in DC."

"Put your duffel in the car. I'll make sure we get your suitcase as soon as CSI has all the evidence they can get from it. I'll be right back."

The FBI agent and the ATF inspector went to talk with the police chief and the fire marshal. Sandra carried her duffel to the FBI car and tossed it in the back. Zeb Monroe came over to her.

"You're leaving?"

"Yes. I'm the target." She took his arm, squeezing hard to control her boiling emotions. "Listen, Zeb. It's terribly important that whoever did this think that they killed the whole family. Can you explain to Samara and Karen? I went home after dinner, and you all went to bed."

"Got it. Don't worry." He stood back and considered the implications of what she had said. "We'll miss you, Sandra. Be safe out there."

He gave her a strong hug and went back to his crew.

When Dale Peters came back, she got in the front passenger seat.

"The ATF man will drive my agent back. Let's go."

He backed out, turned the car around, and took the driveway to Highway 38. Peters glanced at her only once. She felt grateful for his silence.

Sandra stared at the flashing lights in the rearview mirror until they disappeared below the horizon. She said a silent prayer for her family and let her tears fall.

Dale Peters parked behind the FBI Field Office in Columbus. At this hour, National Boulevard and Hanover Street were empty. The sky was light, but the sun had not risen yet.

"Let's get organized inside," he said. He opened the back door on his side and took out her duffel bag.

Sandra had silently cried herself dry. She wondered if dying felt this way. She had been someone for almost twenty-two years. Now she would never be that person again. The reality of leaving herself, her family, and her friends behind threatened to crush her. The grief was bad enough.

Among her emotions, guilt surprised her the most. She had pondered that for fifteen miles on Interstate 40, then realized that she had helped pick this new identity – enthusiastically.

She tried to imagine something good from the mess she was in.

Dale Peters leaned into the passenger's side, his hand on the roof.

"I've seen that face many times. Don't go there, Sandra. Come inside."

She took a breath and let him pull her from the car to face her new life.

ଙଙଙ

Dale's office was a welcoming place, unlike the sterile, government-issue offices they passed on the way up from the back door to the building. The walls were a pleasant peach cream, and the furniture was highly polished oak, including the file cabinet. The pictures included paintings and prints. The official portraits of J. Edgar Hoover and Lyndon Johnson were small and hidden by a vase of plastic flowers. A coffee maker sat on a sideboard near a conference table.

Sandra smiled. Jim's office in Rome had had a rich carpet on the floor, friezes and Rococo frescoes overhead, and no official photos of anyone.

She liked this man already.

"I can picture Agent Redwood in this office."

"Jim was one of my instructors at the Academy and my first SAC." He checked the coffee maker for water, added coffee from a canister next to it, and turned it on. "You worked for him too, didn't you?"

"Two years ago, in Rome."

"I saw the article in *The Columbus Dispatch*."

Sandra sighed. "That woman died last night."

"Right. Sorry." He took out two mugs from the cabinet under the coffee maker. "Coffee?"

"Yes, please. Black." He poured, then went to his desk.

"He should be getting ready to go to work now." He picked up the phone and looked around for his phone directory.

"202-351-6698."

He grinned. "You *do* know him, don't you?"

"And Arlene and Doug."

"Hello, Arlene, it's Dale. Sorry to disturb you … I was looking for Jim. … Okay, thanks. We'll do that." He hung up.

"He's on his way. Touchdown at eight thirty. She said that he expects us to meet him."

Sandra consulted her watch. "Let me wipe my face, and I'll be ready."

ᘍᘍᘍ

Two hours later, the two FBI agents and the NIS agent sat in Dale's office with the door closed. The sun streamed through the window overlooking Hanover Street. The SAC drew the sheer curtains.

They had met the Lear jet at the airport and driven back, with the two men catching up on common acquaintances. Sandra was content to sit in the back seat and listen to the two long-time friends.

No one mentioned the bombing until they were in the office with coffee.

"Sandra, you seem to be keeping this in too well," Jim said. "I remember it took a week for you to cry after Miranda's crash. How you deal with your grief will determine where we go in the case."

"I've had one good cry." She bent her head toward Dale. "I'll have more, I'm sure."

"You weren't coming back to work until Wednesday. Want more time?"

"No, please. The only people who know Sandra Bari are in Virginia. I might as well hang out with them."

"If you need a shoulder, see Mary or her family. You need never mention the old surname for them to understand."

"She asked me to come back to Amherst soon. I might take her up on it while Joe is in Pensacola."

"Do that." Jim asked Dale, "Her suitcase?"

"Sometime this morning. The fire marshal said that CSI just needs to scrape samples of the stuff on the outside."

"Sandra, I think some disguise might be in order. Have you ever colored your hair or cut it?"

"Not yet, but I've been thinking we may need both going forward."

"We've got people in Washington who can do that and teach you how to maintain it. What about here, Dale?"

"We have a stylist on retainer who works with theater groups in town. Let's ask her opinion about what to do. She prepares our agents for undercover work." He made a phone call.

While they waited for the suitcase and the stylist, Dale went downstairs for some Danishes and doughnuts. When he returned, they ate and discussed his role going forward.

"We want to be alert for any hint getting out that Sandra Billingsley did not die," said Jim. "We may not be able to do anything about it but knowing will be crucial to protecting Sandra Bari."

"I agree," said Dale. "I'll swing back to reinforce the cover story with everyone who was at the fire."

"And minimizing your presence in Washington will help, Sandra."

"That's easy. Billingsley graduated and went away."

"If we need to turn over the car from here on out, do it with Crunch McCall."

"Who's that?" asked Dale.

"The resident agent in Charlottesville. He was also in my cohort at the Academy."

"He would know your former surname."

Jim said to Sandra, "We're briefing your instructors and classmates. They already knew that your presence at the Academy was secret. Your class records have been changed."

"The speed of this gets to me sometimes."

"Sorry about that. Any other worries?"

"Only that I might slip with those who met me with Joe."

"He wouldn't be the first middie who picked up a new girl."

"Yes, sir. I guess you're right."

The stylist knocked on the door. She spent some time running her hands through Sandra's long blond hair and considering her face and head. She even pushed her ears back and forth and had her insert small forms in her cheeks.

"Do you think you could get used to those?" she asked.

"Yes. Will they stay put if I'm chewing?"

"Sure. You should take them out and wash them at night."

Sandra looked in the stylist's hand mirror. "I don't recognize myself. So subtle."

Jim and Dale looked pleased.

"All at once or is there a logical sequence for this?"

"I would say dye the hair first, then use the inserts if she is still too recognizable. A dark foundation and some creative eyebrow pencil work might be all she needs. Any good stylist can recommend a cut for either her natural or disguised face but make that decision later." She raised an eyebrow at Sandra. "Any more than that, you'll need plastic surgery."

Sandra looked at Jim in alarm.

"Let's color it this afternoon because doing it right will take time." He thanked the stylist. Dale walked her outside.

The suitcase arrived at ten thirty. Dale drove them to the airport. Jim and Sandra slipped into the townhouse in Georgetown in time for a late lunch.

The young woman with her dark auburn hair in a tight chignon let herself into the apartment on Wertland Street just before midnight.

Chapter 11

Grief on Grief

FOR THE NEXT TWO WEEKS, SANDRA commuted to the farm from Charlottesville. On Friday nights, Joe would use a pay phone near the barracks in Pensacola.

"Should I call more often?" he asked the first time before she went to Ohio.

"No. It's too expensive."

He had called anyway the night after she returned. They talked for an hour. After the second time she broke down, she had asked him how it felt all these years later.

He knew exactly what she meant. The blow in his chest was not disabling now, but he did take a breath before describing the feeling:

> - of watching his father die in a hospital bed ("He asked Mom and me to hug him. We did, and he said 'Thank you. I love you both' and closed his eyes. I'll never forget the squeal on the monitor as we hugged each other and watched the trace flatline.")
>
> - of seeing the church filled with strangers in uniform ("As we passed the casket draped with an

American flag, I ran my hand along it. Then I kissed my hand the way I saw pilgrims do to Saint Peter's toe in Rome. That was our last holiday with him before he took ill.")

- of wondering night after night what took him and why.

- of having the grief hit again when Joe's commanding officer said that Joe's father had saved his life and that he had been one of the strangers at the funeral.

- and of waking up suddenly at night – not often now – six years old and watching his father slip away.

"I go back to sleep, but it is as real each time as it was in the hospital until I wake up fully."

Sandra spoke into the silence. "Last night, I dreamed of the burning scraps of our house and walking from one ember to the next with the fire extinguisher. It took me an hour to go back to sleep. I feel as if I worked all day after an all-nighter."

"Talk to my mother. She and I went through a terrible period even with therapy. You know that's why we went to Rome."

"Yes. We might never have met if you hadn't."

"There is that, isn't there?"

She could sense his smile on the phone.

"Joe, I miss you so much."

"I miss you too. When this gets you down, remember that. I asked for time to travel to New London alone so I can see you."

"I would love that. Goodness! It's been an hour. Is there a number where I can phone you next Friday?"

"Not really. For an emergency, let Crunch McCall know. I'll call on Fridays."

"*Va bene. Ti voglio bene, amore mio. Ciao.*" Okay. I love you.

⊗⊗⊗

Mary and Sandra sipped iced tea on the back porch of the older woman's house in Amherst County. It was the second time that they had left the big, black car at the farm. Sandra loved having the breeze tangle her hair, which she never wore down in public now. Linda and Mac had both complimented her on the color, then ignored it as life went on. This close to the summer solstice, the warm sun felt good after the air conditioning at work.

"I keep wondering if there were any other way we could have handled this besides my dropping out so completely and so suddenly."

"Probably not, although losing your family is not how I would have wanted it to unfold."

"I feel cruel admitting that it simplifies my cover." Sandra inhaled sharply. "No! It's not a cover anymore, is it?"

"It's your life now."

"But how can Sandra Bari grieve a family that doesn't exist?" She felt tears coming again. Mary leaned forward and put her hand on the young woman's arm.

"You are not the first person to set up a whole new life and leave a happy one behind. The others had to watch their families move on in grief without them. After you learn to live with your loss, that aspect will not torture your future life. And you have something I have never seen before in this situation."

"What?"

"People in witness protection, especially individuals, rarely have anyone close to make the transition with them. You have me, Nancy, our parents, the Redwoods, and, of course, Joe. We share your past with you, and we'll be there to help you hold on to it in a healthy way."

Sandra's gaze followed a flock of small birds heading north. She put her hand on Mary's.

"Thank you. I will need to be reminded in the next few weeks or months."

"Or years. This may come back at odd intervals for the rest of your life. Grief never goes away; we just learn to live with it."

"You grieve?"

"Oh yes. Our parents vanished on us. Matthew was in the Pacific, and I was locked in a supersecret location in the Pentagon. Nancy and her mother were in Canada. They were buried before we found out about their deaths. My brother took it harder than I. Thank God he had Annabelle.

"I miss them every day, but it doesn't get in my way anymore. At night, I say a thanksgiving prayer to them for all they did to make me who I am. That's a lot of thank-you notes at my age."

"It keeps them present to you, doesn't it?"

"Indeed."

"That is helpful. Thank you."

The phone rang. Mary went in to answer it.

"Hello… she's here… I'll tell her… Bye."

When she came back, she stopped to consider her young friend.

"That was Jim. He guessed you were here after he called Charlottesville. Did you say that your brother was coming back for the funeral?"

"Yes. Dale Peters in Columbus is keeping an eye on things for us. Marty has thirty days emergency leave."

"This may give you some closure: Walter's body was found. It will be back in time to be buried with the others."

Sandra traced the Blue Ridge with her eyes, as she felt her heart beating. She had almost come to grips with Walter being missing in action. Now his death had become real. *He died before I did,* she thought. *This is a blessing, though it doesn't feel that way.*

"Thanks for telling me."

Mary reached down and pulled the younger woman up. After a pause, she embraced the grieving girl. Sandra let her tears roll again.

"Come. I'll give you a deadly weapon, and you can prep the potatoes for supper."

❦❦❦

The fourth Saturday in June, Sandra parked behind Nancy's white Alfa Romeo. The housekeeper opened the door.

"Hello, miss. Madame is—"

"Here, Adele." Nancy came down the stairs. She looked beyond the housekeeper. "Hello, Sandra. Oh, I *love* your hair! And I don't think I've ever seen that car. Joe told me you had one."

"I've been driving it since November. Thank you for inviting me over. It's lonely without him."

"I can imagine. He called here to tell us that they won't let him travel to New London on his own."

"He told me too."

Sandra left her duffel bag in the hall and followed Nancy through the living room to the veranda. "My parents are playing tennis. They should be home for lunch."

"That's another thing I miss with Joe gone and the Redwoods in Washington. I don't know anyone in Charlottesville."

"Why not?"

"I'm kind of hiding there, between one Sandra graduating and the other showing up in New York."

"I understand. Are you working for the Bureau again?" She arched an eyebrow.

"You might as well know, I never stopped. It's been awkward going to school, avoiding attention, and keeping my work secret. It's related to what I was doing when I was in Rome."

"I won't ask. You're not driving me to Smithson, so I think I know what it's about." Sandra shrugged. "It's only ten o'clock. Would you care to knock a few tennis balls around? Maybe doubles with my parents if they're not exhausted?"

"Sure." She ran upstairs with her duffel, changed, and retrieved her racket from the back of the car. They walked to the courts.

They played two sets of singles and one of doubles with the elder Ardwoods. The walk home allowed them to cool off. Adele had a cold lunch on the dining room table when they returned.

Sandra insisted that Nancy shower first. Meanwhile, she checked the mirror. She still worried that her roots would show and catch her by surprise, but the stylist in Washington had explained what to expect. *My worrying about it is not making the hair grow faster.*

Over sandwiches and Moselle, Sandra told them about her commencement weekend and Joe's whirlwind visit on that Sunday. Joe was letting her use the apartment in Charlottesville, so she moved out of Foggy Bottom.

"How are your family?" asked Matthew.

"Not good, sir. Has Jim Redwood or anyone else been in touch with you?"

"Not since the winter, when he introduced us to the SAC of the Richmond office. What's wrong, Sandra?"

"I'm going to need help to get this all out." She held out her glass.

After he poured, she told them about her visit to London, the bombing, and finding out that Walter was dead too. When she finished, they sat in silence for a while. He rose and refilled their glasses.

"So, what now?"

"Remember I said that Billingsley would vanish after graduation? Well, it happened. I didn't expect it to take everyone. Marty died in a car crash driving back from the closing on the sale of the farm. Of course, his sister is dead, so I can't act on that."

Nancy said, "I'm so sorry, S—"

"Please, I am trying to focus on my life ahead as Sandra Bari, who also lost her parents to a house fire. But I could use some help with one final step."

"Anything. What do you need?"

"After the publicity at graduation, the TV stations came to the Billingsley funeral. The SAC in Columbus is heading up the investigation of the bombing and watching out for a leak about me. The local NBC station gave him a duplicate of the broadcast, and he sent it to FBI headquarters. Jim Redwood brought it to me at work, along with a 16-millimeter projector. They're in the car. Could you sit with me to look at it?"

"Certainly. Whenever you're ready."

"Let's do it after supper, unless you'd rather do it another time."

"After dinner, then," said Matthew. "May we talk about this going forward?"

"What I said at Thanksgiving still holds, but I might as well let you know that even if whoever did this thinks they killed Sandra Billingsley, they could still be planning to kill anyone associated with Joe. We know how serious they can be."

"Is this that general?"

"At least him, yes. He was released late last year, but he has lost his pension and his place in the party. He is fully bent on revenge, according to the sources watching him in Rome." She sipped her wine. "But there are other players who would try to stop Sandra Bari if they knew about her."

"Who is cleared for this?"

"Only you, Joe, and Aunt Mary know that one of the graves is empty. To the rest of the world Sandra Billingsley must stay buried in London, Ohio. The firemen and police who responded to the fire know that it's a federal case, and they are helping to keep her dead."

They cleaned up lunch and washed the dishes. The elder Ardwoods changed to go to the University of Richmond, where Matthew had been invited to facilitate a colloquium on the Vietnam War. Nancy and Sandra took a walk around the grounds, then Nancy took a nap. Sandra tried, but her thoughts kept her from resting. She went to the bookshelves downstairs and found a copy of nineteenth century Romantic poetry and read that until she felt herself relaxing. She closed her eyes and set the book on her lap.

She heard Joe's mother come down the stairs. The sun was streaming into the room.

"I told Adele to go home with François. Want to help me fix something for supper?"

Sandra stood, replaced the book, and followed Joe's mother into the kitchen.

ଷଷଷ

Dishes dried and put away, the family gathered in the living room. They sat in silence, watching Matthew deploy the projector on the coffee table while Sandra put up the screen.

"This is the same model we used to show the movies after dinner when I was on active duty," he said, as he threaded the film through the projector.

Sandra sat and held herself. She breathed slowly, willing herself not to tremble. She dreaded this moment, the final step of her life (and death) with the world she had left behind.

"Let's do this." Matthew plugged in the projector. He flipped the switch, and the reels began moving. For a moment, a bright white stripe blinded everyone as the leader ran over the lamp of the projector.

The peacock logo came on, then the announcer's voice. "This is NBC, Channel Four in Columbus. Last month, the tragic fire in Madison County claimed the lives of the Billingsley family…"

Sandra watched transfixed as the images crossed the screen: the remains of the bombing, the investigation team (after Dale Peters had taken her away), photographs from the *Messenger*, and Walter's casket being unloaded at Wright-Patterson Air Force Base. The announcer reported the latest news of Marty's death.

He read a report taken mostly from the newspaper article, while images of her last orchestra concert and the school art show came and went. Those pictures vanished in the flames. Only the one of Alice Marshall in the snow, which she had brought back to Washington two years ago, survived from her past.

Nancy moved next to Sandra and put her arm around the grieving woman's shoulder. The two older women cried freely, and Matthew clenched his jaw.

The scene shifted to the cemetery. A large area with seven half-sized headstones, symmetrically arranged to fit. A stela at the end of the plot carried the word "Billingsley." The camera panned close-ups of each name on the smaller markers.

As the camera closed in on Sandra's grave, a young Black woman came into view. She walked to the headstone and knelt, crying as she bent over the grave of her best friend.

Sandra sobbed and leaned into Nancy. She could feel what Karen was feeling: they would never see one other again. She may or may not know whether Sandra's remains were there. Sandra had been gone when Karen got up the next morning.

The segment ended with a fade-out shot of the family photograph taken the last time they were all together on the farm. Matthew rewound the film.

"Ten minutes," he said. "That's surprisingly long for a news broadcast."

"Jim told me that schools around the state were asking for copies, but they're too expensive. The Columbus station is organizing a traveling presentation that the schools can request."

"I wouldn't be surprised if the Billingsley massacre becomes an annual remembrance, with that kind of reinforcement."

"I don't know if that is good or bad, but it should help keep me dead to whoever organized this." She dried her eyes. So did Annabelle and Nancy.

"Let's take a short walk," Nancy said, standing. "We need some distance between this and bedtime."

"Thank you, all. I needed not to look at that alone."

The Ardwoods hugged her.

The women instinctively scanned the outside before stepping out. Matthew turned on the porch light.

Crickets and frogs sang in the dark. Sandra and Nancy locked arms as they followed the Ardwoods into the night…

After the insects and animals had silenced, Sandra lay in bed, savoring the quiet.

Alessandra, she thought, *tutto andrà bene.* All will be well.

She recited the closing prayer from Compline, "…bless us and keep us this night and evermore. Amen.

"Thank you, Mom."

In the silence, she heard the voice from countless nights at the door to her room, "Good night, dear. Sleep tight."

And she did.

Chapter 12

The Brooklyn Museum

WHEN SANDRA REPORTED to the farm on Monday, Mary beckoned her into the office and closed the door. Motioning for Sandra to sit, she poured two mugs from a carafe and set one in front of the NIS agent.

"We knew this day would come. Jim just called. You have thirty days leave for your transfer. We've done all we can do here, and New York is ready for you to join the team."

"How soon do I have to go? Will I see him? I need to return the car at least."

Mary held up her hands.

"Sorry, Sandra. I didn't handle that well. He will be here later today. You'll be able to work everything out with him and everyone else. I just needed you to know that you don't have to do anything here. You are free to come and go while you arrange to move."

"How's Mary Ellen doing?"

"Fine. She can't design queries as quickly as you yet, but you were a good writer before, and her background did not prepare her for the creative side of programming. She'll catch up."

"With you as a teacher, I know she will."

"This is not your first move, is it?"

"No. I was old enough to help with the transfer to Ohio, and the longest I have lived anywhere since then was two years in Foggy Bottom. I don't have much to move."

"Will you be at the New York office?"

"No. The Brooklyn Museum has hired me as an apprentice. The head conservator apprenticed to David's father and became a family friend. He has worked with the FBI for years and agreed to wait until I was released here."

"Still undercover, then."

"Kind of, but it's a real job. Because it involves going to the other museums, I'll be expected to look at art around the area."

"Lots of that in New York. You'll be in your element."

"Yes. And my boss at the museum understands that I may disappear for short periods. During the interview, he joked about the Bureau owing the museum an agent after David joined the Marines and never came back. The SAC suggested paying me as an intern, which will put me on the museum's payroll without attracting attention."

Mary opened the drawer of her desk and took out a notebook. She transcribed some entries. "Here are some people who would probably be delighted to host you while you hunt for an apartment. I'll call them this week."

"Thank you." Sandra stood. "I'll check the rooms to make sure all my things are in the car. Until Jim gets here, I'll say goodbye to the others then start making phone calls."

"Well, Sandra Bari from Brooklyn, remember that you have family here in Virginia." They hugged. "Don't be a stranger."

"Never, Aunt Mary. Thank you for everything."

❧❧❧

Joe's cohort boarded the train in New London. While the others dozed or played cards, Joe looked at the scenery and daydreamed. He planned to call Sandra from the barracks at Little Creek. Just knowing he would be closer to her lifted his spirits.

Not that he was depressed. Primary Flight Training in Pensacola had been the most exciting thing he had ever done outside a bedroom, and the decompression and surface ascents in the tank at the Submarine School had felt very strange. He still intended to choose destroyers, but he had reinforced his choice with positive first-hand experiences. After two weeks of amphibious training at Camp Pendleton near Virginia Beach, they would be on leave until the academic year began.

"Richmond, Broad Street Station. Exit by the door at the end of the car. Richmond!" The conductor moved swiftly through the coach, leaving a jostling crowd of midshipmen pressing to the door with their seabags.

"Hey, it's USO girls!" the first men off the train shouted as they debarked. When Joe reached the door, his jaw dropped. He recognized his mother and grandparents, but who was the beautiful woman with the elegant auburn hair?

Sandra pulled him out of the line for a hug and long kiss.

"Sandra! What? How?"

"You forget who I work for, Mr. Lockhart. Call me when you get settled. I'll be in Richmond tonight." She slapped him on the back. "Go!"

The other midshipmen hooted and whistled as they walked past. Nancy, Annabelle, and Sandra waved. The men gathered around Joe with joking and friendly punches as they flowed to the parking lot. He did not stop grinning until the bus passed Williamsburg.

☙☙☙

The last Friday in July, Joe walked out of the barracks with his seabag. He was still in uniform.

"Hey, sailor, want a ride?" Sandra leaned on the black car under the "official vehicles only" sign. He hurried down the stairs and ran into her outstretched arms.

"Finally! I'm on leave too. You report on Monday?"

"Tuesday morning. I'll drive up on Monday. It will feel strange not to have this battlewagon all the time." She backed the car out and turned onto US-60 outside the Little Creek Amphibious Base.

"Didn't Jim Redwood give it to you?"

"Yes, but it will become part of the inventory in New York. Who knows? I may be driving it again."

"I should get one."

"Think about it. In Charlottesville, you only need it to leave town."

"True. It takes twice as long to take the train to New York as Washington, you know."

"But you don't have to drive. I just drove I-95 four times while you were at Little Creek. It gets old fast."

"You're all moved in?"

"Yup. I thought I'd still be looking, but it took less than a week."

They spent the night in Charlottesville so Joe could reorganize his stuff. For the next four weeks, Joe stayed with her in Brooklyn. His translation clients on Wall Street were delighted. He could pick up their third-quarter financial reports and hand-deliver them. He also made personal acquaintances that led to more referrals. When he took the train back to Virginia, he had earned enough to pay for a fax machine for his apartment on Wertland Street.

ଷଷଷ

Sandra climbed from the subway station on Center Street and donned her sunglasses. She walked two blocks north to Federal Plaza. The skyscraper had the bare look of a brand-new building. Tenant agencies were still moving in and had not made their mark on it yet.

In the two years since Quantico, she had never been to the field office to which she had been assigned. The one time she had come to New York to examine paintings, David had met her in a conference room at the Brooklyn Museum.

This was a milestone. She belonged here. David Vasari, and Bob Worthman, the SAC, had both been enthusiastic on the phone when she called.

Having everything come together so quickly was exciting. She exchanged smiles with the security guard and showed her credentials. He pulled the visitor log away from her and slid the sign-in book at her.

"Welcome aboard, Agent Bari. We've been expecting you. Twenty-third floor, then to the right."

Upstairs, she followed the signs to the FBI Field Office. She knew that David worked with a Charley Spears, but she did not know who else.

In a glassed-in reception area, she saw a forty-something woman at a desk. Her black hair was sprayed into a bouffant hairstyle, something Sandra hoped never to wear again. Olive skin, plain, black-framed glasses, and muted lipstick. Sandra pushed the door open and stepped in.

Sandra had just noticed the name plate when the woman looked up, smiled, and stood. "You must be Special Agent Bari. Welcome. I'm Charlene Angelilli."

"Pleased to meet you." They shook hands. "Is Agent Vasari in?"

"Of course. He said you should be reporting today." She started for the door.

"I know David. Let me surprise him."

Charlene winked, knocked on the door and held it open.

David and another agent were bent over a desk looking at some photographs. They stood back and turned to her.

"May I help you?" said David. Then shock passed across his face. "Sandra?"

"Special Agent Bari, reporting for duty, sir." She grinned. "Pull your jaw up, David. Introduce me."

Charley Spears was already walking toward her with his hand out. Firm grip, and he looked straight into her eyes. Late thirties, fit, slender, with a brown crew-cut and brown eyes.

"Wonderful hair," said David, "but you didn't warn me."

"It's very recent. You know what happened in Ohio. We're keeping that girl buried as deeply as possible for now. I may go back to my natural color and let it down later."

"Coffee?" Charley called from the coffee maker.

"Black, thanks."

"I'm glad you're here. Before we start orientation, could you look at some photos with us?"

"It's why I'm here."

David laid the pictures on a wall-length table by a wide window. "These just came in from Edinburgh. Paintings that moved from the Louvre last month. We have the insurance photos and the photos from the annual inventory documentation in Paris."

Sandra put her backpack on a chair, took a sip of her coffee and set the mug on the desk. She took a pair of white gloves from her pocket (which made Charley grunt approvingly) and arranged the pictures so she could look at them with the light behind her.

"Just the two pieces?" she asked.

"There are ten in the exhibition, but they only sent these initially. The exhibit is coming to the Metropolitan Museum after Christmas. The curator remembered us and asked us to have a look."

"Are you getting a lot of requests?"

"Yes, but we try to accept only ones related to the ongoing investigation."

"We'll get to that after orientation, right?"

"Of course. I only asked because you walked in. If you want to do this later—"

"No. Now is fine." She went to the desk, took another sip, then bent over the pictures.

After ten minutes, she straightened and stood back. She moved once over the set, then said, "These three were done by the same person, so that piece is either by the same forger or it's an original. The other trio has a copy in it: the one in the Louvre and the insurance photo are by the same hand, but the one in Edinburgh is not."

"Oh. My. God." Charley put his mug down and stared. "Are you sure?"

"No, never. But a lab analysis will give us more data." She waved them over and showed them the difference in the brush strokes on the back wall of the room, and the different hue of Christ's skin.

"I can't see the change in skin color, but now I see what you mean about the strokes. That is just about invisible. It's just a couple of places on the whole background."

David nudged his elbow. "See why we want her here?" He said to Sandra, "Thanks. I can't wait to show you the rest of the project."

"This time, I don't have to squeeze it between term papers and exams."

"Yes. Charley, do you want to write up the report for Edinburgh and Interpol, or take her around?"

"I'll do the message. We'll have plenty of time to get to know each other." He picked up the photos with his notes. "See you this afternoon."

ଧଧଧ

Special Agent Bari was already officially assigned, so there was very little paperwork. She asked to see her record and history, to catch any Billingsleys in the files. There were none, and she noticed that her record as Bari went all the way back to the FBI Academy graduation, when she had been detailed to New York for her field office indoctrination.

Anyone looking at the file would conclude that she had been coming to work in New York since leaving Quantico.

David gave her a tour of the building and introduced her to the special agent in charge. About the same age as Jim Redwood, Bob Worthman was built like the football player he had been in college, although about twenty pounds lighter. He sported the close haircut he had received at Marine Corps basic training, so there was no guessing what color it was. Gray-blue eyes, sun-tanned skin, and a strong chin. The ubiquitous gray suit almost all agents seemed to wear as a uniform.

The SAC had never seen her as Billingsley, but they knew each other's voice from her time in Rome. He seemed genuinely pleased to be meeting her.

After asking about her family and background (which matched the cover story), he asked, "Any questions as you get started?"

"No, sir. I'll come back if I think of one that Agent Vasari can't answer."

"Do that, although it's unlikely. He's been here longer than I. Come see me anytime."

David walked her back to their office.

"Do we use first names in the building?" she asked.

"Being new, titles and surnames outside our little world, and definitely with the SAC. You don't have to 'sir' me because we have worked together for a while. Follow Charley's lead on that, though."

"Are gray suits required?" They both grinned.

"I would say that as the only representative of the NIS, you decide what the Navy wears on the job."

"I can deal with that." She waved at her lightweight summer blazer, dark trousers, and eggshell blouse. "This feels right but give me a heads-up if I need a skirt."

"We don't have a women's locker room, but you could keep it in the office coat closet."

"What about my service pistol?"

"I hadn't thought about that. The armory would be inconvenient, and we keep our sidearms in the locker room."

"If this will be our permanent arrangement, I'll need a small gun drawer."

"Ask Charlene to set it up. We'll want you to carry a weapon when we make an arrest. If we call you at the museum, you'll want it with you, so ask her to coordinate with Mel. The contractor should be able to do both jobs."

Charley told her not to "sir" him. The other agents who shared that office were out. She would meet them later.

They had lunch in the canteen downstairs, then spent the afternoon going over the new investigation. Sandra came back for the rest of the week. By the weekend, she knew how to get everywhere she needed to be and had met all her colleagues.

The following Monday, she started working at the Brooklyn Museum.

ଷଷଷ

Every morning, she clocked in at the museum and went to the lab. Melvin Conti, the head conservator, had her work in each different area: cleaning, repair, estimating, and provenance verification. The latter involved insurance people, academics, and forensic specialists.

She enjoyed learning how to use the analysis equipment, which was more advanced than what she had used in Rome. On the other hand, her inquisitiveness and attention to detail made her ask about things no one had noticed before.

Afternoons, Mel would send her to other museums or art schools. She went to the field office if no one had asked for her, in effect working half-time at each place.

After Joe left, they took turns calling on Friday night. The telephone bills imposed no hardship because neither was eating out or socializing.

Her favorite person at the Brooklyn was Maria Michaelis, an X-ray technician from a Greek family, who lived nearby. She had brought her black eyes and hair, ready smile, and perkiness to the museum to tend the machines, but she had quickly fallen in love with the art. The two women were close in age and shared a mischievous attitude that included keeping the men properly humbled. They usually walked to work together, sometimes having breakfast on the way instead of their respective homes.

One afternoon in early October, David called Sandra to his desk when she arrived.

"Don't get comfy. We just got this in, and we're taking it to the Brooklyn." He held up a sturdy box, which she could tell contained a painting.

"So, I could have spent my lunch hour in the Central Library. It has better reading material than the ads on the subway."

He did not rise to her jab. "This one is right down your alley. You know the Ghirlandaio?"

"The forest scene from the Decameron? I was just looking at it yesterday."

"Got another one here." He set it on his desk. "It's been hanging in a museum in Nebraska, donated by a rich patron. The new director used to work at the Brooklyn, so this caught his eye."

"David only painted one of them." The artist was also named David. "Back to Brooklyn?"

"Yes. I already called Mel. He's having theirs taken to the room we used before. You want to drive?"

"Sure."

In the meeting room of the Conservation Department, she watched the conservator and David unwrap the painting from Nebraska and lay it next to the one that had been in the Renaissance wing that morning.

"What do you think?" David asked. Mel looked curious. He knew that she did something special for the FBI, but he did not know what.

Sandra took out her white gloves, looked at the windows, and adjusted the positions of the paintings on the table. She moved them again after looking closely at each one from all four sides.

After twenty minutes, she stood back and took off the gloves. "I can tell you that these two were not painted by the same person, but you knew that." She asked Mel, "Doctor Conti, could we get Maria Michaelis up here?"

"We had them x-rayed. She would have the plates on file."

"We'll need those, but this is for something else, something she and I have been discussing." She waved at the two pictures. "If one picture were done over an existing image and the other not, which one would you consider the forgery?"

David and Mel stared at each other in amazement.

"You can tell?"

"No. I'm not that good. But something Maria is working on might detect a hidden picture under that one." She pointed to the Brooklyn's painting.

The conservator walked to the phone on the sideboard and called the X-ray room.

The technician was a little out of breath after four sets of stairs across the two buildings. She saw Sandra with the two men and smiled with her eyes. "You making trouble for me again, Bari?"

"Not these two – yet. This is David Vasari." They shook hands.

"Do you think you could tease a hidden image from one of these?" Sandra asked.

"I know that Ghirlandaio didn't do two of them. Are you FBI, Mr. Vasari?"

"Yes, and it's David. You don't work for me."

"The extra one is also tempera on wood, or we wouldn't be here. Am I right?"

"Yes. Sandra hasn't explained your idea. Can you tell us about it?"

"Sure. It's basic X-ray physics. You know that different thicknesses affect the final image on the photographic plates, don't you?" The men nodded. "And we are taught how to read the image on the plate as it is affected by the density of the material. Bone blocks more than muscle –

that sort of thing." Sandra enjoyed the sight of the second-most-junior staffer at the museum holding a science lesson on the two experts.

She glanced at Sandra and continued, "I've been wondering about something that we had trained out of us in school. The frequency makes a difference. Very small, mind you, but we are taught to calibrate our instruments constantly.

"I've been thinking about what happens when the frequency slips. We get a different image. If I could exaggerate, I would say think of getting a better focus on one organ than another when they were both in line with the X-ray."

"You can spot an extra layer under a painting?"

"Well, we don't know, but it wouldn't hurt anything to find out."

"What about ultrasound?" asked Mel. "That's used in medicine too."

"Now, that *would* damage something: it's high-frequency vibration."

"I see. But X-rays would not."

"No. The radiation might affect the organic tissue in our bodies, but not the inert materials in a painting."

"Has anyone done this, Maria?"

"Every museum with a conservation department routinely x-rays their inventory. This is the same, except that now we are looking for specific differences between two pictures that appear to be identical."

"Let's try it. Any reason we can't do this now?"

"No, sir. Come down when you're ready. It won't take me long to set up the machine."

ଷଷଷ

Sandra watched the X-ray technician take the plates from their bath and hang them in front of the light boxes in the lab. The head conservator stood next to her. He gasped when Maria stepped back.

"Amazing," he said, moving a little closer. "We x-rayed these before, but we weren't looking for anything in particular. How did you know that another painting would be under there?"

"I didn't, sir. She told me about trying to tease different layers by changing the frequency of the X-rays. I thought I could see how the surface seemed ever so slightly raised, compared to the Nebraska picture, and we know that sometimes panels were reused, as canvases were later."

"We can't take a photo of it," said Maria, "but we can see that Ghirlandaio painted over an old image."

"The forger did everything right," said Sandra, "except paint something else on the wood first."

"This will rock the conservation world. Well done, both of you."

When *Forensic Sciences* published "Fine-tuning X-ray analysis to detect hidden art" by M. Michaelis and A. Bari three months later, Maria was suddenly in demand throughout the New York area to train lab technicians in the technique. To be able to adjust their frequencies, some museums needed to update their equipment, which triggered successful fund drives. Donors were excited to participate in something cutting edge.

Meanwhile, Sandra kept a low profile. Maria insisted on sharing authorship because A. Bari had written the paper.

"It passed peer review because of you. I never could have assembled that article." Mel had been enthusiastic about it and supported Maria's position.

When scholars and researchers came to the museum, she admitted only to being the "research assistant" and helping to write the article. She heaped praise on the X-ray expert for her generosity.

In labs around the country, technicians with untuned machines made jokes about the "Michaelis effect," but deliberately changing the frequency became part of the arsenal of conservators and art fraud investigators.

CHAPTER 13

THE PLAZA HOTEL

SANDRA PUSHED THE GLASS DOOR as a blast of sound shook the room. The door beyond Charlene's desk failed to muffle the deep, boisterous "hoo-rah!" from six male voices.

"The Marines have landed?" she asked the secretary.

Charlene rolled her eyes. "The ball is next month. They're on the organizing committee."

David had mentioned being Security Battalion as a Marine.

"Are they all Marines?"

"Every one of them. And fifty percent of the other agents in the building."

"So, do we shut down the field office on the tenth? It's a Monday."

"Almost. Have them explain it. You're included, by the way, being Navy and all."

Sandra walked into the office where the art investigators shoveled their paperwork, held their meetings, and goofed off sometimes. It resembled the squad room of a police TV show. Filing cabinets covered all four walls. The desks appeared haphazardly placed, but in fact had assumed their positions from their occupants' urgent moving to and from the door.

David was standing facing the others, who were lined up against the far wall. It resembled the first-year hazing in the NROTC unit, which Joe had described.

"Are we breaking in the new boot camps, Agent Vasari?"

He executed a sharp about-face. With an equally precise salute he barked, "Good afternoon, Special Agent Bari. Would you care to join the few and the proud?"

She crossed the room, took a position at the end, and clicked the heels on her pumps as she stood at attention. The others grinned.

"Squad, dismissed!"

They relaxed and went laughing to their desks, each slapping Sandra on the back first.

"I guess this has something to do with the birthday ball coming up," she asked David, "and everyone is going."

"Correct on both counts." He took a cup of coffee from Charley. "Thank you, Sergeant."

Shaughnessy gave her a mug. "Thanks, Mack." She set it on her desk and hung her jacket in the closet. Then she unlocked the lower drawer and stored her sidearm.

"So, what's the drill? I assume that a handful of Army veterans and I will share the duty that day."

"No way. The organizing committee has already decided to detail you to represent our Sister Service."

"No invitation? No handsome escort?"

The others had gathered around, some sitting on desks. They laughed and pointed at David.

"Nope. This is a command performance, although you could volunteer for duty if you don't want to go," David said. "We reserved two tables. Only the Reserve Center has more Marines than we do."

"As for the handsome escort, we're sorry about that." Dario Torino slapped Vasari on the back. "The only single guy we have is also our only ugly one."

"Is this a way of asking me to the ball?"

"Not really, but as luck would have it, there are only five unmarried agents in the field office, and I would be honored to offer my arm."

"You may need to give him yours," said Dario. "He's clumsy."

"Remember who writes the duty schedule." David mouthed an Italian curse at him.

"You should know better than to mouth *vaffanculo* around me, *fetente*!"

"I like her," said Dario. "Why didn't you tell us she was so cool?"

"No offense, but can I bring my own date?"

"Of course. Talk to Joe about it."

ଷଷଷ

The NROTC unit planned to honor Joe at the Charlottesville event. It would be his last ball as a midshipman. Over the phone, they agreed that the New York celebration would be memorable.

"You go. I'll take Mom to this one. They invited my grandparents too."

"Okay. I will miss you."

"I will miss you too. Who's taking you?"

"No one and everyone. The whole field office goes as a group because so many of them are Marines. And I'm Navy. The numbers balance because David and I don't have partners."

"You'll be with David, then?"

"He isn't bringing anyone because he's on the organizing committee. Are you going jealous on me again?"

"No. Should I?"

"No, silly. He may be tall, dark, and handsome, but I don't do office romance. He's also the senior art crime agent, so he's kind of my boss."

"Enjoy it. We can swap stories at Thanksgiving."

"You too. I'll bet Nancy is an awesome dancer. You look like siblings, you know."

"Yeah, I've heard that before. Ciao, amore."

Returning the handset to its cradle, she sighed and went to the kitchen to fix supper.

ཥཥཥ

Sandra stepped out as the doorman held the door of the cab. The wind tore at her coat, but she was up the stairs and into the lobby before it could tug her hair or freeze her ankles.

A Marine major in a Class A blue dress uniform approached her from the side. Two rows of gleaming medals on his chest. She noticed the Purple Heart with a star: twice wounded in combat.

He took her wrap and handed it to the attendant.

"Wow, you look amazing! I think I saw Claudia Cardinale in something close to that, but you wear it better."

"Thanks, David. This may have come from the same dressmaker on the Via del Corso."

"Of course, the sketch artist work in Rome. Jim told me about that."

"I couldn't afford a gown for an embassy dinner. Arlene took me on a tour of the shops, and the office paid for it."

"That makes it appropriate for this." He gave her the claim token, then offered his arm, and they walked to the ballroom.

Sandra was no stranger to sumptuous rooms, but the Plaza ballroom decked out for a Marine Corps Birthday Ball stunned her. Unit colors and campaign flags bedecked the walls. She estimated that the tables of two dozen each would seat hundreds of people, and there was still room on the dance floor.

More Marines than she had ever seen in her life. Of all ages and in all conditions. The men had the typical close-cut hair, but many showed gray and white. The few female Marines wore trousers with their Class A uniforms.

David guided her to a table convenient to the dance floor and the exit. She recognized the men, though she slapped herself mentally to see them in uniform. The women, fit and self-confident, reminded her of military wives, like – her mother.

Sandra gasped and caught herself before anyone could hear her choke on the memory. She shook hands with Mrs. Spears (Marcella), Lieutenant Colonel Worthman, and Mrs. Worthman (Patsy). David held her chair.

"I'm across the street," he said. "The boss pulled rank tonight."

"Damn right," said the SAC as she sat. "Vasari gets you the rest of the year."

She relaxed and answered questions from Charley and the SAC, while she looked around the room.

After the initial impression, she noticed how many men were in wheelchairs or using crutches. Some were missing arms or legs. They seemed to enjoy the natural interaction with their fellow Marines.

She snapped her gaze back to the exit where she – *no!* – saw a staff sergeant in the wrong uniform. He wore the green service jacket with the khaki shirt and tie.

Walter!

"Sandra, are you okay?" David's voice across the table called her back. She blinked and shook her head.

"Fine. I thought I saw someone."

"Everyone who is anyone is here tonight." He held his glass to her in a salute. "Maybe you did."

One might expect music to be playing as the guests arrived, but this was a military ceremonial occasion. When the tables were all occupied, a drum roll came from the exit next to the stage. The musicians marched out sharply to take their position.

Sandra recognized the US Army Field Band from Washington. Her head swam as she pictured her father at the conductor's stand. A half dozen of the gray heads looked familiar.

It was too much. The grief made her dizzy. She started to leave when the band played a march as the color guard paraded the colors. Everyone stood and saluted.

She pressed down her rising despair, forcing herself into the performance mode her parents had drilled into her. She sang the National Anthem as proudly as she could.

As she sat, Sandra saw that many of the women, and some of the men, had tears on their cheeks. Without shame they wiped their eyes with their napkins and engaged their neighbors in conversation.

Bob Worthman spoke into her ear. "I remember your old self. Most of us in this room have lost loved ones, so you will have company if you need to cry."

"Thank you, sir. The women remind me of my mother." She indicated the stage. "And this band was my father's twilight tour. It's a lot to take in."

He squeezed her hand. "If you want to step out, no one will think anything of it. Patsy can show you the ladies' parlor. She tells me that there is usually someone in there dealing with her grief."

"I'm afraid of saying something that will expose my past."

"Then seek out David or me."

Sandra resolved to stay, though the recurring memory of Walter and her father would often catch her unawares. The easiest times were when she danced with strangers. They were all handsome, and she could not tell the active Marines from the retired ones unless they were *very* old.

With some wine and food, she started to relax. The parading of the birthday cake and the singing of *The Halls of Montezuma* went without incident. She wished that Joe were there, but David kept an eye on her, even when he was dancing with someone else.

About ten p.m., the senior officer present, a lieutenant general from the Pentagon, went to the microphone.

"Let us observe silence and remember the Marines we have lost since our last birthday."

The guests rose and stood at silent attention with their heads bowed, as he read the names of those who had died in combat.

Sandra struggled to control the panic when she realized that half of the names were from the Third Marine Division. She felt a firm hand grip her arm and pull up, just as she heard "Staff Sergeant Walter Billingsley, Third Marine Division."

She held her breath. The moment passed. The hand released. She glanced across the table and saw two different couples holding hands and crying silently. One pair seemed old enough to be someone's parents; the other two were her age. Someone else had lost family.

Ten minutes later, she was breathing normally as the Marines and their guests sat.

"Thank you, sir," she whispered to the SAC.

"Don't mention it. If you come to my office, I have information that may give you some closure. Only you and I need to know, and David will understand."

"I'll do that. Thanks."

David appeared behind her. "Care for a dance?"

ଽଽଽ

The phone rang as she climbed into bed. She left the lights off and walked across the apartment to the instrument.

Speaking Italian in the dark helped Sandra detach the feelings that she had experienced during the ball. As was his habit, Joe was silent as she talked her way through the evening.

"After he read all the names, it was very quiet as we sat. The ladies' parlor was packed, and half of them were either crying or comforting someone."

"So, Worthman was right."

"Yes. It doesn't make the grief go away, but it's hard to feel sorry for yourself, when you have so much company."

"Would you go again, say, next year?"

"I think so. I found out that the Worthmans lost their son in Vietnam. I didn't think the SAC was old enough, but Peter was only eighteen."

"And yet, they go each year. Sounds healthy to me."

"He said he had some information about Walter. I don't know whether to go see him or not."

Joe was silent for a while. "Do it. One of the hardest parts of my father's death was not knowing what killed him. Maybe knowing what happened to your brother will help."

"Thanks. I'll see him tomorrow."

"Then in two weeks, I'll see you at the station."

"Yes. I can't wait. Ciao, amore."

It took another hour for Sandra's emotional state to settle enough to sleep.

ଓଓଓ

The next afternoon, Sandra walked to the SAC's office. He stood at his desk reading papers and talking with the phone caught in his shoulder. He pointed to the chair. She sat. He rang off, then came around the desk. With an inquiring arch of the eyebrows, he headed for the coffee maker.

"Yes, sir. Thanks." She joined him at the little coffee mess.

When they returned to the desk, he did not go behind it. Instead, he pulled up a chair on the same side, sitting a comfortable distance away.

"About Walter."

"Yes, sir."

"When I saw his name on a list this summer, I called Eighth and Eye for some details." Marine Corps headquarters was at the corner of Eighth Avenue and I Street in Southeast Washington.

Sandra looked steadily at him. He held her gaze. She resisted the urge to ask questions.

"He died with two other Marines. After eight months, the bodies had decomposed. The team responding to a farmer's report found their skeletons in their uniforms with their weapons and gear. They had been completely hidden for all that time.

"Are you okay so far?"

"Yes, sir."

"The recovery unit reconstructed their last moments, which is why I wanted to share this with you.

"All three men were wounded. One had a broken leg and could not walk. The other man must have been unconscious because they were on stretchers.

"Your brother was pulling both stretchers, trying to get to the LZ." Landing Zone. "Near as the investigators could determine, shrapnel from a nearby mortar or bomb killed them. The explosion buried them. The next round of monsoon rains washed enough dirt away for them to be discovered in the spring."

She gripped her mug with white knuckles.

"A quick death?"

"Yes, and he died a hero, Sandra. He could have gotten out, but he would never leave a Marine behind."

She felt equal parts of pride, grief, and love rise in her chest.

"My father taught us that growing up, only it was 'soldier' in our house."

They sat for a few minutes, sipping their coffee, imagining the final moments of Staff Sergeant Walter Billingsley.

"Thank you for telling me. It does give some closure."

"He has been awarded the Bronze Star and another Purple Heart posthumously. I suggested that the Corps present them to London Public Schools for the Billingsley exhibit in the lobby of the high school." Sandra raised her eyebrows. "Oh yes. I am told it's a lovely case, with photos and biographies of each of you, shadow boxes of the men's decorations, and some pictures by you and your mother, which were in the library and the art room."

"Someday when I have enough miles on this identity, maybe I could go see that. Thank you for dealing with the medals. But won't your asking expose me?"

"No. The entire FBI knows the Billingsley name from the bombing investigation, and I knew you as Jim Redwood's secretary. You were a hero in your former life, Sandra. Too bad only David and I can share that with you."

They stood. He extended his hand. "Call me if you need anything and keep up the good work. You are doing your talented family proud."

"Thank you, sir."

Outside the office, she thought she would hide in the ladies' room. On her way there, she noticed the stairs, and climbed twenty-four stories to the roof of the Federal Building.

The new skyscraper rose above most of its neighbors. Surrounded by the noise of the rooftop machinery,

Sandra hugged herself and breathed in the cold air. To the west, she looked beyond the Hudson River and Jersey City, and imagined the land all the way to London, Ohio.

She had expected to have a big cry, but instead she scanned the metropolis shining in the early afternoon sun and felt much as she had at her graduation: Accomplishment. Passage. Milestone. Her grief was tempered by the knowledge that Walter had met his end with his eyes open, fully conscious and engaged in what he knew was the right thing to do. Her love for her brother and her family swirled around her heart. Their presence stirred deep in her soul, and she said a prayer of thanks out loud to all of them.

At home that night, she called Joe and told him about her experience. They shared a cry over the phone, but the tears came from the intensity of the emotion, and from the new knowledge that it was a good thing to feel so deeply.

CHAPTER 14

THE GALLERY

WHEN SANDRA CAME BACK FROM THE COFFEE MESS at the museum, her boss waved her into his office.

"David called. He said to come in and pack, whatever that means."

"Got it. Thanks." The word "pack" meant to show up armed.

Mel had assigned her a corner desk hidden by filing cabinets. She unlocked the specially reinforced lower drawer and took out her service pistol, then pocketed some spare clips of ammunition. She transferred her brew to a paper cup and donned her winter coat. The snow had not finished melting on the shoulder. *A blizzard in late January. Thank God for subways.*

As she walked to the subway, she felt the presence of the sidearm more than ever. She had almost gotten used to it being there on her walks to work with Maria. Without the modification to her desk, she would not have been free to take off her jacket.

Sitting on the subway she reviewed the case and how it had come about...

Between Thanksgiving and Christmas, the SAC had gathered the art investigators in his office.

"The Postal Service investigation of the donor who gave the forged Ghirlandaio to the Nebraska museum led them to a gallery on Franklin Street. Tell them what you told me, Agent Vasari."

"This could be big enough to justify a raid even before we finish the trail on the Interpol case," said David. "If anything, it might trigger some reactions that will tip the hand of some of our suspects. Charley?"

"George Gorman lives in New York, though he was born in Omaha. His father made his fortune in beef and agribusiness, and young George has multiplied his inheritance playing the stock market and investing in other areas.

"The gallery moves the art for him, procures pieces that he wants, and generally handles the business end and the documentation. The donation to the museum was a tax write-off long ago."

"He must have known it was a forgery," said Sandra. "I can't imagine parting with an original Ghirlandaio before I had a foot in the grave."

"My thinking exactly," said David. He motioned for Charley to continue.

"It was the Interpol case last year that put this gallery on our radar. It was one of four places in the metro area that was involved in moving swapped art. The paper trail was squeaky clean, so we could never hang anything on them.

"Then we noticed that they have a very interesting clientele. The usual tourists and small buyers, but almost every buyer who spent more than ten thousand dollars is on the suspect list."

"Including Gorman?" asked the SAC.

"No. One of the few who wasn't."

"We don't have a formal request but look into it. If something ties into the Interpol case, we can move on it."

Back at their own office, Sandra asked David, "May I see the client list?"

"Of course. In fact, please read the whole file." He waved at Charley, who handed her a fat folder. "Let me know what you see."

Two hours later, she had walked to David's desk with the file and a sheet of handwritten notes. He beckoned Charley to join them.

"This is surprising. There are only two dozen men who were *not* caught up in the raids. But one of them is familiar." She pointed to the name she had circled. Tex Wilder. "I know that one."

He checked the entries in the file.

"Just one print of a Holgate. How do you know about him?"

"He is one of the 'investors.'" She put air quotes on "investors." David blinked slowly. "The only one of the four who was not on the list from the bust."

Charley looked puzzled but said nothing. David called across the room. "Frank."

The big Navajo agent moved slowly to David's desk. Something about Benally seemed to inject a little calm into every situation. It made her smile to herself.

"Does the name Tex Wilder mean anything to you?"

"Owns a bunch of West Texas. He shops all over the Four Corners area. We get rumors of stolen Anasazi artifacts, but no one has been able to connect him to them." He looked Sandra. "No forged art – as far as we know."

David showed him Sandra's notes. "Any reason for him to deal here?"

"Not that I can think of. He works mainly with galleries in Albuquerque and Santa Fe. He wouldn't normally buy things from that gallery."

She asked, "What if he were here for something else, and visited them because he is a collector?"

Frank shrugged.

David stood and looked at his watch. "Let me check this with the SAC. If he's on the list from the farm, someone may have information on him." He left the office.

"What farm?" asked Charley.

"Codeword project that I was on," said Sandra. "I'll ask how much I can say about it after he gets back."

A half hour later, David came back. He waved for the others to come closer.

"Good call, Sandra. Wilder's come to New York to meet several times with Santis and once with him and Bonin. He even met Arcibaldo when he honeymooned in Italy."

"What about the gallery?" asked Mack.

"And what's this farm?" asked Charley.

"Both good questions. The farm is handled by Special Projects in DC. I'll be meeting with them soon to examine how much overlap there is. Headquarters may open some of it to us.

"Meanwhile, let's focus on the gallery. Maybe there is an exhibit coming up that will attract a critical mass of our suspects or an unusual shipment."

When they had all returned from Christmas, nothing new had developed on the gallery. The agents in the room were brainstorming the case one morning.

"Could one of us swing by the place?" asked Sandra. "I enjoy visiting galleries and museums."

"No," said David. "The people in the gallery know us, because we have stopped by on various investigations."

"Do they know about me?"

David thought for a minute. "They should not have any reason to know you, but I worry about exposing you."

"We can't hide me forever, David. I can still be the art history graduate and conservator looking at art wherever I find it."

Dario pitched a crumpled paper ball at David.

"I say let her stop by. She doesn't have to identify herself. Just look."

David looked around. The others shrugged.

"Do it. As little contact as possible, but I would not be surprised if you notice something we could not have found out otherwise."

On her lunch break, Sandra had walked up Franklin Street with a hot dog and a Coke. She ate her lunch looking in the window of the gallery. After putting her cup and paper in a trashcan, she walked in.

The staff had seen her looking at the window and pegged her as a student or tourist. Clearly not a potential sales prospect. After greeting her walking in, they lost interest as she moved around, admiring the paintings on display.

She took a flyer from a display on the counter.

"Is this the Peter Glasson from England?" she asked the clerk. "I've only read about his work. I'd love to see it live."

"Yes. The largest exhibit of his work ever assembled."

"Just exhibit, or also sales?"

"Sales. We expect nothing to go back to England."

"So, this would be my first and last time to see those paintings."

"That's the idea."

"Something to come back for." She folded the flyer into her pocket. "May I continue looking?"

"Of course. If you have questions, just ask."

"Thank you."

Sandra walked around the entire sales floor. In the next room, she saw a variety of paintings of different eras, though mostly American and Canadian Impressionists. Staff were coming and going from the back room, carrying paperwork or art. She noticed that the door did not close unless pulled, so she positioned herself behind different pictures, where she could see into the room. *Omigod!* She carefully moved to different pictures, while trying to focus on the three paintings she saw leaning against the wall on a workbench. She made her way back to the front. After taking a card from the counter, she thanked the clerk and left.

Back in the field office, she went to David.

"Let's go see the SAC, so I only have to say this once." They walked to Bob Worthman's office.

"Judging from your face, I take it you saw something," said the SAC.

"Remember the pictures I looked at for the touring exhibition coming to the Frick this month?"

"Yes. You said the three pictures of each piece were done by the same person, so they were probably originals."

"So why are there three of those paintings on a workbench in the back of the gallery I just visited?" She explained what she had seen.

"I can only think of one reason, Sandra. Good work."

"I'll call the Frick," said David.

The rest had happened very quickly…

When Sandra entered the office, she sensed the excitement in the air. The five agents in the room were wearing their holsters and bulletproof vests. Each seemed very focused on whatever was on his desk, though they acknowledged her. The phone rang on three different desks while she crossed the room.

She hung her coat and removed the vest next to the emergency skirt she had not needed yet.

David walked in with the SAC as she was tightening the vest. He waved for them to gather around his desk.

"As you know, the Glasson exhibition starts this weekend. Between now and then, it's 'all hands on deck' for the gallery staff to get ready. Perfect cover for a large shipment.

"Scotland Yard called. Ten pieces are coming to the Frick from London. According to the plan, a Brinks truck will meet the aircraft late this afternoon. The gallery will take possession of the art and deliver it to the museum tomorrow."

"Swap tonight?" asked Charley.

"Probably," said the SAC.

"Why aren't they going straight to the Frick?" asked Sandra.

"The gallery belongs to the company that has the contract for the move. It was in the initial order to secure the art overnight. This also saves overtime pay at the Frick."

"Does Peter Glasson's exhibit have anything to do with the Frick delivery?"

"No. But having everyone working and the place open late allows the swap to be made almost in plain sight."

The SAC stayed for the briefing. NYPD would stand by to block all the exits. The gallery was only two blocks from the Federal Plaza. The agents would move into position after the shipment left the airport.

Sandra's job was to assist, but her principal role would be to examine the paintings if that became necessary. If the team seized multiple versions of the same art, the place would probably be roped off for a while.

"Frankly, Sandra, if no one knows you were there, it will be great."

"I understand. Not looking for a medal here."

They had lunch at their desks, using the waiting time to review the files on the case. She had been living with the ten pictures for a week: two by Caravaggio, two by Rubens and one each by Raffaello, Fra Angelico, da Vinci, Cherubino, Sarto, and Titian. Even this close to the event, she could not believe that such a collection would be moving in one shipment. She would have sent each picture on a separate aircraft.

At three p.m., word came that the art was on its way in a Brinks truck. They stood, put in their earbuds, and did their comm checks. David gave the "move forward" hand signal, and they filed out the office. Charlene looked grim as she nodded to each agent.

Sandra walked up Broadway with David, their vests hidden by their coats. She waited in a bodega on Franklin across from the gallery, where she could watch with a cup of coffee. He went around the block to check on the team. The delivery entrance was on the side of the building.

At five minutes to four, the Brinks truck turned off Church Street and stopped at the alley. She watched the crew exchange identification with the staff, comparing cards to their clipboards. They opened the back and stood guard while the gallery people carried ten sturdy boxes into the alley.

"All paintings inside." Charley's voice crackled in the comm circuit.

"Let Brinks clear," said David. "New York, close up."

Sandra put her empty cup in the trash and stepped outside. NYPD officers in pairs were rounding the corners from Broadway and Church Street. When they reached the door of the gallery and the alley entrance, David ordered the team to move. Sandra watched him and Frank push the front door of the gallery open and disappear.

The paddy wagon entered Franklin Street, and police cruisers moved to block either end, but not before a heavy engine roared. Sandra pulled her pistol out as the Ford Mustang exploded from the alley, turned with burning rubber onto Franklin, and headed for Broadway.

She stepped into the street, dropped to one knee, and blew out both rear tires of the car. The Mustang screamed as the wheels spun and tread flew off the rims. It came to a stop at the Broadway intersection, and two men jumped out – into the arms of NYPD officers.

Sandra holstered her weapon and finished crossing the street. From the door, she saw gallery personnel being gathered into one corner of the front room. David spotted her from the back wall and waved her in.

"The art is in the back, and we have everyone out here."

"How many pictures?"

"Ten from the Brinks truck, six not packaged."

"Oops! Let's see."

Accompanied by a police photographer and a cinematographer, Sandra followed David and the NYPD detective as they donned latex gloves and carefully set the paintings against the worktables.

Two by Caravaggio; one each by Raffaello, Titian, Sarto, and Cherubino.

"I know these pieces. Want me to look at them now?"

"Go ahead. From what they chose, I have a hunch about this."

Sandra moved the pictures to the worktable, so that she could look at them two at a time. While she worked, the police gathered the gallery personnel into the paddy wagon for processing at the precinct. The press arrived, but the police kept them away from the back room. David allowed the director of the Frick in.

"We think your pictures are in those boxes, which have not been opened since they came from the airport. Of course, they are now evidence, so we will keep custody of them until we sort out this"—he waved at the paintings on the workbench—"mess."

"What is she doing?"

Sandra carefully placed two pieces against the wall. She turned around.

"Hello, Doctor Messer."

"Miss Bari, from the Brooklyn."

"Yes, sir. Good to see you again."

"This seems very irregular. What *are* you doing, young lady?" Then he noticed her bulletproof vest and badge. "Are you FBI?"

"I'm working with them. Agent Vasari, this is an amazing collection. All were done by the same person. I can't tell you more than that, but this person is a world-class expert on sixteenth-century Italian art."

"That was my hunch why he skipped the Rubens and the older pieces."

"Doctor Messer could know better than I, but I think we have six top-notch forgeries without even opening the boxes."

"I agree. I'll call for the truck." He spoke into his mike. "Charley, do you have the files under control? … Roger that. Box everything. We'll work on it back in the office."

It was after ten p.m. when the agents gathered in the office. The art was in the vault. Messer promised to return in the afternoon with his experts for the unboxing. NYPD had processed the employees and jailed the owner and his assistant, who had been driving the Mustang.

That they would be out on bond in the morning was not Sandra's problem. The FBI had the art, and the case would move where it would. What was in the boxes on Charley's desk would probably prove more relevant to the investigation.

"Good job, everyone," said David when they had each reported their part of the raid. "Go home. We may need you all tomorrow to sort Charley's files." He pointed at Sandra. "Check your weapon with Charlene, Bari."

"Oh yes. Sorry about that." She took out her pistol and emptied the rounds from it.

"I'm not, but you did discharge your firearm."

Chapter 15

Threads Come Together

THE SNOW STOPPED FALLING and bright green shoots peeked out in Central Park by the time Internal Affairs (IA) ruled that Special Agent Bari had not improperly discharged her sidearm. Part of the delay was finding an NIS representative for the inquiry.

There were six men involved, evenly split between those who acted aghast at her firing a weapon at a moving car on a public street and those who seemed to accept Sandra's argument that she had chosen the minimum force needed to prevent a serious collision, if not also a shootout with the NYPD. The assistant carried a concealed .38 pistol.

None of the investigators believed that she could destroy two spinning tires with a pistol. It was a narrow shot even with the target not moving: twenty-two inches to the bottom of the bumper and less than a foot of tire width.

The SAC had observed most of the testimony, as her supervisor. When the IA men seemed bent on wrapping it up, he asked to speak.

"Not on her behalf. You've already deposed me. I

suggest you find some independent party who can vouch for her marksmanship. Obviously, being best in her cohort at the FBI Academy is not enough."

"Any suggestions, Agent Worthman?"

"Agent Bari?" he asked.

"You might ask Sergeant Moseley, our drill instructor. Also, you might note the pistol performance of the next three shots in our class: Special Agents Yu, Jefferson and McCall."

Sandra resisted the urge to wring her hands. Trying to look calm was making her heart race. This morning, she had even applied foundation and powder, which felt strange. She had not used that makeup since the stylist in Washington had convinced Jim Redwood that she did not need to alter her face after all.

"Good idea. Let's do it," said the NIS agent. "It should only take a day to make the calls."

They adjourned after deciding who would call whom.

The next day, the lead investigator put Sandra's weapon on the table and said, "Agent Bari, all four men from the Academy insisted that you could take that shot easily. Why did you not tell us that Yu, Jefferson, and McCall were on the US Olympic Team?"

"I thought they would be famous enough, sir. I was surprised that no one reacted."

"Why weren't you on the team?"

"My sex, sir."

The lead detective started to say something, then shut his mouth. The NIS agent tried and failed to suppress a grin.

"Let's adjourn to the range downstairs. I want to see this for myself."

The IA agents had designed a series of target situations, some fixed and some in motion. Twice, they thought she had only hit the center three times in five, until she pointed out that one hole was larger than the others. The bullets were in the padding behind the targets.

They were shocked when she dropped to one knee and fired under the table, putting a round in each target moving sideways. The two shapes approximated the tires on the Mustang.

She stood, emptied the pistol, and stepped back. Seeing their expressions, she said, "I can make that shot any time, sir, but it requires a prone or kneeling position."

That afternoon, IA issued their finding, adding a paragraph commending her for using the minimum force necessary.

The field office agents and Charlene were all smiles for the rest of the day, and life went back to normal.

♋♋♋

Two thousand miles away, USS *Semmes* (DDG-18) steamed at 21 knots north toward the island of Vieques, southeast of Puerto Rico. Off the port bow, USS *Newport News* (CA-148), flagship of the US Second Fleet, cut a wide swath of bioluminescence in the water. By the light of the full moon, the scene resembled the TV series, *Victory at Sea*. Midshipman First Class Jason J. Lockhart finished the turnover briefing with the JOOD (Junior Officer of the Deck). He made sure his eyes were completely adapted to the dark.

"Attention on the bridge! This is Ensign Schwartz. Midshipman Lockhart has the conn!"

"Midshipman Lockhart. I have the conn."

"Aye, aye, sir!" the four enlisted watch standers replied in hearty unison.

Centuries of mariners had established this ritual, and it never dulled. Joe was deeply aware that at all times, only one voice would maneuver the ship. If that 21,000-ton behemoth over there began turning, or a yacht or fishing vessel showed up unannounced, he would adjust *Semmes's* path to avoid collision. He had learned to stay away from wandering aircraft carriers (notorious for not warning their escorts when changing course). Dodging a heavy cruiser was equally serious.

More urgent were the reactions needed in emergencies. Every minute of his watch, he remained alert for the dread words, "Man overboard!", and hoped that he would have the ship turned and retracing its wake before the victim went down.

Assuming the conn always thrilled him and scared him at the same time. That was good.

Three hours later, the navigator came to the bridge with his quartermaster to shoot stars, another ritual established over centuries. LORAN (long range radar navigation) and other electronic wizardry notwithstanding, a sextant and chronometer provided the most reliable means of fixing one's position on the featureless expanse of water that covered three-quarters of the earth. No external power required.

This was Joe's favorite time of the day. The sky was never darker, the stars were never more brilliant, and the world was never more silent than in the hour before dawn. As the navigator moved to the bridge wing, Joe saw the horizon, and admired the quirk that made it appear in the west. In a little while, the sky would lighten in the east, and sunrise would follow thirty minutes or so later. The navigator would note the direction of the sun as it rose, but his "fix" of their position would be determined by the angles of five different stars, measured at nautical twilight, that narrow window in time when the horizon appeared but the stars had not begun to disappear.

The little task group changed course only once during the watch, and only one contact crossed their path, a cruise ship that almost blinded them as it traveled toward Miami, probably coming from the Lesser Antilles.

After the damage control assistant relieved him as JOOD and assumed the conn, Joe made his way to the wardroom. He grabbed some pastries and a doughnut, which he tossed in his stateroom before joining the Main Propulsion Division at morning quarters.

Attendance duly taken and reported, the day's notices were read. The crew would go to general quarters that afternoon. Gunfire exercises until midnight. The next day, antiaircraft training north of Vieques. Finally, a port visit at US Naval Station, Roosevelt Roads.

"Rosy Roads" was on the other side of Puerto Rico from the nightlife of San Juan, but the crew would be glad to go ashore, drink at the club, and stand down from the underway watchstanding. It took fewer men to keep one boiler going when they could plug into the pier for steam, electricity, water, and sewage.

Not that Joe expected to go ashore. The "snipes" used downtime to fix things, and the 1200-psi steam plant of the *Adams*-class destroyers demanded a lot of maintenance and repair. Since reporting aboard in late February, he had stepped off the ship only twice, once to go to the Naval Supply Center to back up his chief in an argument over the availability of spare parts, the other to claim a pair of his sailors from the shore patrol.

Joe's personalized first-class cruise should have consisted of two months of learning various junior officers' duties, much as he had rotated through different enlisted roles in USS *Point Defiance* for his third-class cruise. However, a surprise awaited him in Charleston, South Carolina, when he stepped on board.

"Welcome aboard, Mister Lockhart," said the officer of the deck after returning Joe's salute on the quarterdeck. "The captain wants to see you as soon as you can drop your seabag. Follow Seaman Santini."

The messenger showed Joe to a stateroom near the back of the superstructure, then led him to the commanding officer's stateroom below the bridge.

Commander John Covert. The only thing Joe knew about his new CO. He knocked on the door, paused, then opened it.

A man in the white shirt sleeves of the Service Dress Blue uniform sat at the fold-down shelf that served as a desk in the closet-drawer-storage-unit in every officer's stateroom. He looked up and stood. About five feet eleven, trim, with brown hair and brown eyes. Crow's feet and smile lines, but also a tan even in the middle of winter. A man who had spent years staring at open water.

"Midshipman Lockhart, reporting for duty, sir."

"Mister Lockhart, I am delighted to meet you." His handshake was firm. He waved to a chair and sat. "When we were asked to take on a midshipman in the off-season, so to speak, I spoke to Captain Norwood. He said some very nice things about you, but I still have some questions. Coffee?"

"Yes, sir. Thank you. Black, sir."

The skipper stood and slid the door on a small pass-through in the bulkhead behind Joe. "Two coffees, please."

He took the mugs from the messman's hands and set them on the desk. "Thank you, Morton."

They each sipped. Joe held his coffee in his lap and waited. The silence worried him. He had expected to be treated differently, but this personal encounter with the commanding officer was more than that. He forced himself to breathe carefully.

"Captain Norwood said that you earned your master's degree in Italian. As I understand it, you're about two years out of sync with your classmates."

"Yes, sir. I majored in Italian, but the university had me take graduate courses. After completing the requirements for the BA, I had only two courses and a thesis to present."

"So, you took your MA a few months after your second-class summer."

"Yes, sir. Captain Norwood said that having a grad student in the unit was unusual enough, but a PhD candidate would be over the top."

"Are you in a hurry, Mister Lockhart?"

"Not really, sir. The idea of putting me in graduate courses came from the faculty. The Naval Science Department is playing catch-up."

"He said that you were keen on engineering in *Point Defiance*."

"Yes, sir. I enjoyed all the departments, but especially engineering."

"Let's go to the wardroom. I want you to meet some of your messmates and put a proposal to you."

They rose and stepped next door to the wardroom. Three officers gathered by the coffee table at the end of the room rose to their feet and stood at attention. One lieutenant and two lieutenants junior grade.

"At ease, gentlemen. This is our one-man first-class cruise. Joe Lockhart, this is the chief engineer, Tom Dearborn, the MPA, Jerry Knudsen," Main Propulsion Assistant, "and the DCA, Matt Siemens." Damage Control Assistant. Handshakes all around. The skipper pulled one of the chairs from the dining table and motioned them to sit.

"Normally, we would rotate a firstie through all the departments, but we have a problem and an opportunity here." Firsties were first-class midshipmen in their last year. "This is a midshipman who actually wants to be a black shoe." Surface officers were called "black shoes" because aviators wore brown footwear.

"Why do you want to go surface?" asked the MPA.

"Better liberty."

"You're kidding, of course."

"No. I don't just want to go surface. I want destroyers. Something small enough to pull into the good ports that the carrier can't fit into."

"You must be pretty smart to be here with a master's degree," said the chief engineer.

"No, sir. I'm just dumb in two languages."

"I like you already."

"Anyway," said the captain, "he wants to be a black shoe, and his CO said he enjoys engineering."

"Not as smart as I thought," said the chief engineer. "So, Captain, is this going where I think it is?"

"Maybe." The skipper sat back. "Ask him."

"What do you know about the holes?" asked the MPA.

"Only what's in the training manuals," said Joe. "I did rebrick a boiler, pack a few feed pump valves and change the bearings on a forced draft blower. *Point Defiance* was in remote manual, so I have never seen a fully automatic plant operate."

"Neither have we," said the MPA. "The system is impossible to balance, but we keep working on it."

They quizzed Joe for another fifteen minutes, mostly about what he was familiar with. Then the captain asked, "Do you have any questions for us?"

"Two. Can I meet your chiefs, and what do you have in mind for me?"

"Get the senior chief up here," said the captain. Jerry Knudsen went to the phone. "What we have in mind, Mister Lockhart, is to let you be the division officer for two months. No rotating. You would be the Acting MPA while Mister Knudsen goes off to get married."

"When?"

"Sunday. Did you have plans for the weekend?"

"Not anymore, sir."

"You called for me, Captain?" At the door stood a rail-thin man in clean khakis, sporting the anchor and star of a senior chief. Leathery skin, deep-set eyes, short hair mostly gray.

"Come in, Senior Chief," said the skipper. "This is Mister Lockhart. He's supposed to be on his first-class midshipman cruise, but unlike the ones we've seen before, he does not aspire to be a flyboy or a grunt. Do you think you could put up with him while Mister Knudsen goes on his honeymoon?"

"We're already shorthanded, sir, but if you want, I can keep him busy."

"I was thinking of letting him be the MPA for two months."

The senior chief's face went dark. "He wants to be the division officer, sir?" He spoke to the commanding officer as he stared at Joe.

"Mister Lockhart?" said the captain.

Joe stood. He remembered what old Chief Burbank, his scoutmaster, told him back in Troop 236 in Rome. He held the senior chief's gaze just long enough to make the older man blink. "Yes, Chief, I do. Is your rating MM or BT?" Machinist Mate or Boiler Technician.

"MM, sir."

"Mine is people. I keep these fine gentlemen off your case"—he waved toward the officers behind him—"and you and the men keep the plant running. I'm Midshipman Lockhart, by the way." He shook the chief's hand. "Want to show me around?"

"Mackay, sir, pleased to meet you." He looked at the other officers.

Joe turned his head and saw the captain grinning broadly. "Carry on, Mister Lockhart. Come back and tell us what you think."

An hour later, Jerry Knudsen departed on leave. His fiancée was waiting on the pier. Joe took a two-foot stack of operating manuals and training guides into the wardroom and started studying…

଼଼଼

The week after Sandra was "packing" again, she and Mel were checking a new acquisition. She had explained what she learned in Rome about approximating the date of a paint chip by knowing when different ingredients were mixed. They had been working on it for two weeks, carefully testing the canvas and sending the tiniest piece of paint out for carbon dating.

The painting had been in a cache of art stolen by the Nazis during World War Two. The paperwork from the "Monuments Men," the officers of the MFAA (Monuments, Fine Arts and Archives), identified it as "unknown young man, attr. G. V." Sandra had noticed what might be an MFAA accession number on the frame. Mel wanted to be sure it was not a forgery.

"Any idea why this is coming out now?" she asked. "The Army got it in 1945. I thought everything stayed in Europe."

"Postwar snafu," he said. "Several hundred pieces were found in a warehouse at Fort Leavenworth, Kansas. No one knows how the shipment got there or where it was supposed to go. The Army is tracking down former Monuments Men to find someone who can shed some light on this."

"Why did we get this one?"

"The Army wants proper care and storage for the art while they figure out what happened. About two dozen museums are involved. We have five other pictures."

"I'd love to be on that case."

"I know, but then I'd lose you." He leaned over the pages that she had smeared with different compositions of paint. "Anything?"

"I see one that is closest to that background. What do you think?"

"I can't see it as sharply as you can, Sandra. These two swatches look identical even before I hold them by the painting."

"Compare each to the painting. See if you feel something."

Mel did so, moving the samples to change the light.

"This one is closer – I think."

"I agree." She looked at her notes. "Except for the restorer's touch-up, no ingredients newer than 1595. I'd say this picture was done in the sixteenth century."

"The others have already estimated it to be Italian in the decade after 1560."

"I hope the carbon dating can confirm it. It often doesn't. But canvas was still rare. We may be able to eliminate places and times."

The phone rang.

Mel answered it. "…Thanks. I'll tell her. … Bye." He cradled the handset. "That was David. He said to have lunch before you come this afternoon, and he may need you full-time for a few days."

"Is that alright with you?"

"Sure. We've gone as far as we can on this until the carbon dating results come back. Having your other job means I don't have to make work for you the way we would for a normal apprentice."

"There's that. But I am still learning a lot here, believe me."

As she packed up the portrait of the young man, Sandra paused to consider him. Late teens or early twenties, with thick black hair, but beginning to recede slightly on the sides. Dark eyes and an expression of strong confidence. He looked at the painter with unfeigned affection. *Not the usual gaze of a model,* she thought.

At one p.m., she walked into the field office.

"Go see the SAC," said Charlene. "David is already there."

Sandra stowed her gun and went to the SAC's room. She stopped at the door and looked at David. *Something? Naw.*

"You sent for me, sir?"

"Grab a mug and join us," said the SAC.

"The charts at the farm are wobbling again," said David, as Sandra sat with a fresh cup of coffee. "Bonin and All Saints both put out calls for more investment, and guess who stepped up among the usual small chips?"

"Tex Wilder?"

"The investors are tighter than we suspected. He has a two-percent stake in each of the others now."

"What I don't understand is how that unit in Redwood's office knew it last week," said Worthman. "If he had not tipped us, we would not have been looking when the equity call went out. I called him, but he said that you could explain it after you talk to Mary."

"I couldn't explain what you and she were doing," said David.

"Want me to get the details from her?" she asked.

"Sure. Then brief us."

She went to the small room with the secure phone. Joe's great-aunt answered on the second ring.

"Ardwood."

"Aunt Mary? Are you having fun down there?"

"I hope no one is listening to that, young lady."

Sandra chuckled. "No, but I am at work. David and the SAC are wondering how you predicted the equity calls from the two investors."

"I didn't. Your program did. As the two companies spent, their paths got shorter. Every run shows a change that way because income and expenditure are never static."

"And Wilder?"

"That was in the *Wall Street Journal.* We've added his company to the database, even though he wasn't a suspect before. He's too active with Bonin and All Saints to ignore."

"I've been so busy with art, I stopped following the financial press outside the *New York Times.* Maybe I should start reading again."

"It's an old adage, Sandra, 'follow the money.' Just scan to see what names pop up. You're good at that."

"Thanks for the tip. May I explain how our program works to the SAC?"

"Call Jim first. I think at least David and the SAC should understand what we're doing."

"Okay."

"Tell the SAC to send you down here for something. I miss our chats."

"Me too. Bye, Aunt Mary."

It was fine with Jim. "If you explain how the program works after you all modified it, I think Bob will understand. David may have to keep trusting you." She could feel him smiling on the line.

"Thanks, sir. I'll do that."

જ્ઞજ્ઞજ્ઞ

The SAC walked into their office the next morning. David, Charley, and Sandra were cross-checking the client list from the gallery against the suspects in the recovery last summer.

"How is it coming?" Worthman asked.

"Good," said David. "Not enough names for computer support"—he nudged Sandra's shoulder—"but we are getting a fair number of returning collectors." He turned the page around, so the boss could read it.

"Of the two hundred clients who bought art there this year, about fifty spent more than five thousand dollars on an individual painting. Thirty of those were on our watch list."

"How many are ours?" The New York Field Office had to investigate the suspects in its territory.

"What would you expect for the capital of the world?" said David. "Twenty-five of them."

The SAC considered that. "Thank you for the critical path sort, Sandra. We can't track that many at once."

She glanced at David, who waved for her to continue. "Something else." She reached for a notebook open on her desk. "I know that the other offices help us with the watchlist from the farm."

"Yes. Well?"

"This morning we were discussing the different industries, and Agent Vasari mentioned that HQ has a unit that keeps an eye on mercenaries in the country. I know the CIA watches them overseas. When I worked in Rome, Agent Redwood met regularly with the CIA station chief to coordinate their work.

"A half dozen men in the mercenary business had art that was confiscated. None are on the critical path sort, but I noticed that four of them bought something from the gallery.

"Do you think that the unit in Headquarters could check those four and their companies? It might not take any extra manpower to see if they connect to the art in our current investigation."

"I'll ask Redwood. He'll probably be happy to work on it."

xxx

Charlene pushed her head into their office. She frowned at David, who was swaying a zig-zag path through the odd layout of desks.

"Good thing I have the glass door and you all can hide back here."

David gave her a grin and put down the three files he was carrying to his desk. "What can we do for you?"

"Nothing, thanks, but the SAC wants to see you and Sandra." She closed the door and returned to her station.

On the way to Worthman's office, she asked, "David, do you have any pictures of your ancestors?"

"Some. Why?"

"Anything as far back as Beniamino?"

David thought for a moment. "Maybe. My mother had a charcoal sketch that she said was Beniamino. She said it was a study for a portrait, but we can't prove it. My grandmother told her that they had to leave everything in the house when they left Italy. They had no idea what the Gentile family did with the painting."

"Any chance I could see it? We have a sixteenth-century painting from the Monuments Men with a vague attribution and no history. We're still waiting on the carbon dating and other analyses."

"I'll ask my mother what happened to the sketch."

"Thanks. Maybe you'd could come out to see the picture too."

"Sure. Here we are."

In the SAC office, Bob Worthman looked up from his desk.

"You wanted to see us?" David said.

"Two things. Sandra, Patsy and I are having my fraternity brother Luke Arland over this weekend. Does he know you from before?"

"Yes, sir. He is one of the few people who know my new and old surnames."

"You were working for Agent Redwood when Luke tipped us to what I hear you and David call the investors."

"Yes, sir."

"Anything I should know?"

"Luke is very close to Nancy Lockhart."

"He mentioned her – and her son. Joe?"

"Joe and I have roughly the same relationship as Luke and his mother. Luke and I have been to her home in Richmond for Christmases and Thanksgivings. Luke and her family helped me make the transition to Bari.

"Give him my regards and tell him I haven't found a tennis partner yet."

"So, he knows you work here?"

"Not from me, sir. They know about the job at the Brooklyn, and they know that I continued to help you all after the art bust. They know that she and I may be targets.

"Only Joe knows that I am an agent. I won't tell them until you tell me. I keep expecting it to slip, but so far it hasn't."

"Agent Redwood and I want to stop hiding you too. The second thing may be related to that.

"Either of you come across a Trent Braxton?"

"He's on the client list at the gallery," said David.

"CEO of Impi, Inc.," said Sandra. "Mercenaries. He had an original Correggio that was swapped on its way to Chicago."

"See why I want her here?" David pointed at her.

"Agent Redwood had a connection for us in less than thirty minutes, and he expects more later.

"His company recruits and trains throughout the world, but also on a large stretch of the West Texas desert north of I-10. Guess who owns the land?"

"Tex Wilder?" Worthman nodded. She shivered slightly.

"Having a company such as Impi connected to the investors bears watching. I'll look up what we have, sir."

"Redwood agrees. We'll watch him and Impi along with the other four."

Back in the office, she went straight to the files. Twenty minutes later, she stood and walked to David's desk.

"Braxton convinced the investigators that he had no idea the Correggio was stolen. A museum director was arrested, but the case is weak against him." She frowned. "That is almost exactly what happened with Siegfried Kanter, the other investor in the art bust who was not charged."

"I did a little reading on Impi and similar companies," said David. "Scary. A couple hundred men out there angry at us, and one of them has a trained army of special forces."

She felt the blood rush from her head as the image of her home burning in little pieces in the night passed before her eyes. She leaned on the desk, gripping the edge.

"Sandra?" Hands on her arms. She shook her head and stood back.

"Sorry. Flashback to the night my family farm was bombed. The ATF is still trying to figure out who could have rigged incendiary bombs with the power to do what we saw."

"This may get personal. Will you be okay?"

"Yes. Do you know who we could tell to help ATF connect the dots if there is a connection? An outfit as big as Impi would know how to make the explosive lot untraceable from the explosion, but if the investigators knew where to look—"

"Hey, this is the FBI. Of course, we know someone." He reached for the Rolodex card file. "This is a guy I worked with on a couple of arson cases."

Sandra sat in the chair by the desk as he dialed. "This is Special Agent Vasari, FBI. Could I speak with Agent Hardmon? … Jack, David… yeah, me too. Listen, is there anyone there who is following the case of the farm that was bombed in Ohio last June?… Great. Could we come up to talk about it?… It may dovetail with one of ours … not on the phone. We're sweeping bugs all the time here… Tomorrow at three. See you then." He hung up and looked at Sandra.

"We're in luck. Jack Hardmon is the point of contact for New York, and their explosives guy is on the next desk. I want you to meet them."

"Thanks, David."

"You're welcome, but I would want to do this anyway. It's not every day that we bring them a tip. Usually, they're bailing us out on some detail."

"Where are they?"

"Just off the Hutchinson Parkway north of the Bronx. Ask Charlene to reserve a car."

ಒಒಒ

Midafternoon traffic was similar to Rome. Sandra was grateful for the Interceptor engine in the black sedan as she flowed among the tourists and taxis up the East Side. It took about forty-five minutes to reach the commercial building that housed the Bureau of Alcohol, Tobacco, and Firearms, and other tenants.

She lengthened her stride to keep up with David. He waved to secretaries and rounded corners until he pushed into an office at the far end of the floor. She paused as he crossed the room.

Corner room with sunny windows looking over the Hutchinson Parkway to Pelham Bay and Long Island Sound. Six desks, two unoccupied. Four agents along the wall: all in their late forties, except for the man with the best view. He rose and came to meet David: average height, fifties, gray hair cut short, blue eyes, and a dark scar down the left side of his face from the hairline to the jaw.

His hand was out. She stepped in and shook it.

"Jack Hardmon."

"Sandra Bari. Pleased to meet you, sir."

"Jack."

"Sandra, then."

"David, you could have brought her up any time. I hope I don't have to work for the pleasure of meeting her."

David laughed. "Actually, she is the reason for the trip."

Hardmon led them to the coffee mess hidden in an alcove. When they returned to his desk, David and Sandra took the guest chairs. Jack waved his colleagues over.

"The Three Musketeers: Wes Morton, Tray Hicks, and Buck Streeter." Handshakes all around. "Tray and Buck work with alcohol and tobacco, so you probably want Wes in on this."

"That's right. Good to see you again, Wes."

The other two went back to their desks, while Wes rolled his chair closer.

"Your nickel, David."

David took a sip and put the mug down. "How involved have you been with that case so far?"

"Not much." He tapped a file on his desk. "A pair of custom-made incendiary bombs with shaped charges. Designed to push into the middle of the structure and make sure it burned completely."

"Not foreign?"

"No, except for an Israeli timer and German detonators. But you can find those parts anywhere in the world."

"What about the explosive?"

"Lot numbers went to all offices, but the trail ended one wholesaler away from the manufacturer. The wholesaler had a fire in the office that destroyed all the records for the year of the sale. No one knows who bought the stuff or how much of it."

David exchanged glances with Sandra. "Convenient. So, how do you find who has or had material from that lot?"

"We don't until we get lucky, and it turns up somewhere else."

"Do the people who buy the explosive have to report it?"

"Not unless they use it in something they sell or export, for example, a bomb or a construction charge."

"We may have a lead, if you want to follow it."

Wes pulled a notepad from his desk and uncapped his pen. "Shoot."

"Sandra and I are working a case – two related cases, actually – that exposed a party that had the means, motive and opportunity to blow up the Billingsley farmhouse."

"Who is that?"

"A company called Impi, Inc."

"Soldiers of fortune. We see a lot of their work overseas," said Jack.

"And they buy from almost everyone, including the manufacturer of the lot in that bombing," added Wes.

"But you have to tie the lot numbers to someone, don't you?"

"Yes, but Impi moves so much material around, they are forced to report often. We might have a match if they are moving the explosive, or using it to make devices, which is common."

"They certainly have the means," said Jack. "What motive do they have to hit a farm in the middle of Ohio?"

David shot a look at Sandra and said, "Stolen and forged art. Last year, Interpol confiscated paintings from three hundred collectors and dealers."

"I heard about that. Congratulations."

"Thank you. Well, the CEO—"

"Trent Braxton."

"Yes. He bought one of the pieces. Sandra noticed that he also purchased art from a gallery on Franklin Street where we intercepted a swap."

"I read about that. Congratulations, again."

"Then she suggested that we watch Braxton and the three other men in the mercenary business on our list."

"And?"

"Braxton is chummy with three other men who were involved in an operation two years ago in Italy. One of them owns the chunk of the West Texas desert where Impi trains."

"Tex Wilder's place?"

"You know all the players already."

"Braxton is a charismatic leader, David, and a hero to the sorts to people who love things that go bang."

"Lot of those in Texas," said Wes.

"So, revenge?" asked Jack.

"Not for Braxton, but maybe for his three friends or the man who sold them the art. The seller was an Italian retired general who was arrested in the bust in Rome. That man is known to want revenge on everyone involved. He, or one or more of his customers, could have retained Impi to take out the Billingsley family."

"Why them?"

"Because the daughter was working with us. Frankly, she triggered the whole operation by noticing the first forgeries. She was also a friend and housemate of Nancy Lockhart, whom the general tried to assassinate in Italy."

"So, Braxton might not have a desire for revenge," said Jack, "but he might perceive this woman as a problem and be willing to help the general."

"Yes. And dozens of other collectors with illegal art or forgeries. Our current case involves a surprising number of repeat offenders."

"David was stabbed last fall," said Sandra, "and we still don't know who ordered the attempted hit."

"What do you think, Wes?"

"We're stuck tracing back from the bomb, but maybe we can find enough of that lot in the Impi reports to account for the production in those burned files. I'll get on it with the people who track professional shipments."

"This may not hang Braxton, or help your case directly," said Jack, "but they would feel the heat and perhaps do something stupid."

"We are working on the art, which is not related to the Ohio bombing, but I hope what we find helps you."

"I'll get back to you." They stood. "Pleased to meet you, Sandra. You come back anytime."

"Thanks, Jack, Wes."

Handshakes all around. Hardmon walked them to the main door, and they returned to the car.

ଷଷଷ

The second Friday in May, Sandra stepped from the *Southern Crescent* and moved quickly to the fence beyond the platform where Joe waited with open arms. The other passengers getting off in Charlottesville were halfway to the station when the two lovers disengaged.

"I haven't been here by train since your first year," she said as they walked to the street. She squeezed his arm. "I have missed you terribly, love."

"And I've missed you. We have a lot to catch up on."

"I know graduation was canceled."

"Yes. Things are tense here since Kent State. There was a sit-in at Maury Hall last night. Lots of angry students milling around. We're not wearing our uniforms, but some of the guys have been hit by bricks or beaten up."

"So, I don't get to put your shoulder boards on." She faked a pout.

"Maybe tomorrow morning. Captain Norwood will administer the oath in his office and give me my commission. I'm glad you were coming anyway. I was told not to invite anyone. A crowd would attract attention."

"You should have thirty days' leave. Did you find out what ship you're going to?"

"Orders came in yesterday. MPA in USS *Barry*. A *Forrest Sherman* class homeported in Newport."

"My place is on the way, if you want to stop there."

"I'd love to. How much time did you wrangle from the Bureau?"

"Two weeks. Starting Monday. I can help you move and spend some time in Richmond."

"Monday? Aren't you on leave now?"

"Nope. NIS recalled me yesterday. I'm your protection detail until you get out of town."

"I thought your agent status was secret."

"Jim Redwood and the SAC in New York were about to contact NIS about that, when Marty MacKenzie called and explained that the Navy brass watching what's going on want you to have your ceremony but not become grist for the press."

The next morning, Sandra walked with Joe to Maury Hall. He felt self-conscious at first, donning his Service Dress White uniform, but he need not have worried. At seven o'clock, there were few students out on Grounds. Thousands had been up late demonstrating the night before.

She wore her slacks and blazer. As the sun came out behind a cloud, she donned her sunglasses. A half dozen men stopped to gawk, then started toward them.

Sandra hooked her badge on her breast pocket. Then she pulled her blazer back to expose the service pistol on her belt. The students returned to their rooms.

"Jeez," Joe whispered, "you're not kidding, are you?"

Her expression was grim. "We plan to get Ensign Lockhart to his ship with a minimum of trouble."

Maury Hall still stank from the mattresses that protesters had burned that week, but the staff was moving around efficiently. Mrs. Blankenship stood when they entered the reception area.

"It will be crowded, but they're all here." She walked to the door, knocked, and held it for them.

Sandra paused at the door and removed her sunglasses. She saw a Navy captain at a lectern by the desk, a lieutenant commander at the far side, a Marine major on the near side, and a Marine gunnery sergeant near the door.

"Come in, Mister Lockhart. Stand right there." Captain Norwood pointed to Sandra. "Would you stand nearby? There." She moved in and stood just behind Joe. "Miss Bari, isn't it? I remember you from the Marine Ball two years ago."

"That's correct, sir. I think I've met everyone here."

"Any trouble getting here, Mister Lockhart? I thought you might have changed here."

"No, sir. Most of the students were sleeping, and Special Agent Bari discouraged the one group that approached us."

Norwood directed an inquiring glance at Sandra. She put her badge on her pocket. "NIS, Captain. They went back to their rooms."

The major coughed gently into the long silence.

"Let's do this, then," said the commanding officer. "Midshipman Lockhart, raise your right hand."

Captain Norwood administered the oath of office to Joe, then gave him the commission over the lectern.

"Special Agent Bari?" He handed her a pair of ensign shoulder boards. She removed his midshipman shoulder boards and snapped the larger ones in place.

"Congratulations, Ensign Lockhart, carry on."

Joe turned and gave her a long kiss and hug.

"It's not a wedding, Mister Lockhart," grumbled Sergeant Henry, smiling with his eyes.

"But it's an instant Navy family without one, isn't it?" said Major Jackson. "Congratulations, Ensign." He shook hands. The others took turns congratulating Joe. Mrs. Blankenship came up.

"Captain?" She arched an eyebrow at him.

"Of course. We can't have a big spread outside, but let's have some cake and coffee before we go our separate ways."

Sergeant Henry was standing to the right on the porch as Joe and Sandra stepped out the door of Maury Hall. The Marine snapped to attention and saluted. Joe returned the salute, reached into his trousers pocket, and handed him a crisp two-dollar bill. At the Naval Academy, the first man to salute a new ensign got a dollar. But this was Charlottesville, and the two-dollar bill with Monticello and Jefferson created a special variation on the tradition.

"Good luck, sir."

"Thank you, Sergeant." He looked out at the Grounds. There were more students about. "You too."

Ignoring some scowls, Joe and Sandra walked back to Wertland Street without incident. They spent the weekend cleaning the apartment.

CHAPTER 16

RICHMOND TO NEWPORT

MONDAY MORNING, MATTHEW ARDWOOD came to Charlottesville. In less than a half hour, they had Joe's belongings in the car and his bicycle lashed down under the trunk lid. Mrs. Garland was delighted with the condition of the apartment, so they rolled onto the driveway in Richmond in time for lunch.

In the afternoon, Joe's grandparents played some fast doubles with Joe and Sandra. Nancy came home from work while they were showering and changing.

Over supper, Nancy asked, "How was your commissioning ceremony? Things are tense in Charlottesville now."

"With graduation moved, the unit will be commissioned in June. Captain Lockwood hosted a small ceremony in his office."

"No uniforms or throwing hats in the air?"

"Actually, Sandra insisted that I walk from the apartment in my Service Dress White uniform. Almost everyone was asleep at that hour, and she scared off the one group that tried to approach us near the East Range."

"Undercover bodyguard again?" Nancy asked Sandra.

"No. I was on duty." She slipped her badge from her trousers pocket and passed it around.

"NIS?"

"Of course. He's Navy, isn't he?" She winked and took the badge back.

"When did this happen?" asked Matthew.

"Same time as the name change. NIS can recruit female agents, so they created Sandra Bari and commissioned me. I've been working with the FBI in New York, but both agencies wanted to let some time pass between the disappearance of one Sandra and the appearance of the next.

"NIS called me back for this detail, considering my history." She tipped her glass toward Nancy. "Now that my status is not a secret, I don't know if the FBI will let me stay at the Brooklyn. My bosses at the conservation lab and the field office want to keep the arrangement."

"Luke told me that your tennis is better," said Nancy.

"We both needed a partner, so this has forced us out of our apartments at least on the weekends. I've met some interesting people at Forest Hills."

Nancy's eyes gleamed. "Great memories of that club."

"I saw your photo in the hall. You haven't changed a bit."

"Thank you. How is Luke without me there?" The others grinned, knowing how different Nancy was with Luke.

"I only see him at tennis, but it's like hanging around with family. Like today. Being with him is– excuse me."

She pushed her chair back and ran to the bathroom off the hall. Joe jumped up, but Nancy reached out and put a hand on his arm.

"I have a hunch, Son. Let me go."

In the locked room, Sandra leaned over the wash basin and sobbed. Her heart ached with love for the firm and gentle man. His calloused hands stroking her head. His smile and wink when she wrestled her older brothers into the pigsty. Always, his insistence that they devote their all to their music. And his arms around her mother as he kissed her in a tender moment.

She could barely picture him, but the feeling was undimmed.

A soft knock on the door. "Sandra, it's Nancy. How are you doing now?"

"Just a minute." She rinsed and dried her face. Another day to be glad that she rarely wore mascara. As she opened the door, she knew that her eyes were still brimming. "I can talk now."

They returned to the table. Joe looked worried. His grandparents seemed to understand what was happening but kept silent.

Sandra sat, took a drink of water, then a deep breath. "As I was saying, being with him feels like being with my father – if Dad played tennis. Sorry about the scene. That night comes back to me sometimes, and I've never analyzed my feelings for Luke before."

Joe's expression cleared, and he blinked back his tears. "I was wondering on the morning watch last month why I never felt jealous when you wrote that you were playing tennis with him every weekend. You seemed so happy about it.

"Now I understand." He looked at his mother. "Mom?"

Nancy squeezed his hand. "Not at all the same feeling, Joe, but in addition to everything else, Luke 'gets it.' His empathy is incredible, and he relates to me the way that Jason did." She took Sandra's hand too. "You've done a fantastic job dealing with your loss, Sandra. It took us years."

Matthew said, "Feel free to cry or laugh around us. This is your family now."

They sat quietly for a while.

Annabelle spoke finally. "Dessert, anyone?"

ଷଷଷ

During breakfast, Nancy called her secretary to make sure no one needed her in the morning. As she returned to the kitchen, she noticed Joe's pensive expression.

"Something bothering you, Joe?"

"No, I've just been mulling something, and sometimes I get distracted thinking about it."

"Want to put more heads on the problem?" asked Sandra.

"A car." He gestured with his hands out. "I think I need one, then I wonder where the hell I would keep it and what would I do with it on deployment."

"Is cost an issue?" asked Annabelle.

"Not really. The accounting major taught me to charge appropriately for my translation work, and my clients haven't balked. As a result, I have enough in savings to pay cash if I had to. But I could take out a loan just to build my credit history."

"That's a nice place to be," said Nancy. "Congratulations, Joe." She raised her coffee cup in a salute.

"Sometimes I miss that battlewagon from the Bureau," said Sandra, "but living in New York, I can't justify owning a car. I know how you feel."

"For example," said Joe, "everything I own, including the bike, would fit in a medium sedan. But once I get it on board the ship, what do I do with the car? Store it after only one trip?"

"What about Diego?" she asked. "He'll be a firstie next year. They can have cars, and they have assigned parking. I bet he would not mind being able to pick up Serena easily, and neither of them can afford a car yet."

"You mean let him drive it while I'm deployed?"

"Sure. If you had a brother, that's what you would do, don't you think?"

"Great idea." Joe looked at his watch. "It's finals week, so he might be in his room."

He stopped at the door. "Can one or more of you help with this, getting it to Diego from Newport?"

"Of course, darling," said Sandra.

"And I could use an excuse to swing by Luke's place if she's busy," said Nancy. "Go call him."

When he came back from the phone, he was smiling.

"He's delighted. He'll have thirty days leave after his cruise, which will end in Norfolk. I told him I would buy something new that could go to California and back. He wants to introduce Serena to his folks."

"Love is in the air?" said Annabelle.

"They've been an item since before he went to Annapolis."

"Do you know what you want?"

"No, but with the combined expertise present, I think I can find the right car in time to drive to Newport."

"This will be fun," said Sandra.

ধ৶ধ৶ধ৶

It took a week for Joe and the family to choose a new Range Rover. Expensive, but it was a vehicle that would serve him for a long time. He had made "moving my stuff from one duty station to the next" the first criterion after durability and endurance. It had better visibility than the Jeep CJ and more passenger and cargo room than the muscle cars and sedans of American manufacturers.

Joe brought Sandra to Brooklyn when her leave ended. They played tennis and took in some shows. He did spring cleaning while she was out, which surprised her. The last three days were especially sweet, looking at nine months of separation ahead.

Sandra enjoyed driving the Range Rover. She had kissed him on the pier and gone back to New York. That weekend, she drove to Greenbelt, Maryland, where Diego was waiting at the Alquilar house. Serena's father had retired from the Air Force to work for NASA at the Robert Goddard laboratory.

Serena and Diego left Sandra at Union Station on their way to California. She shouldered the small backpack that had replaced her old duffel bag and caught the train to New York. For the first hour, she looked out the window at the familiar scenes, smiling as she relived the wonderful moments with Joe. As she reached the end of her daydream, she shared his excitement to be boarding ship for his first full, "real" deployment. For all he loved his languages and translating, and he obviously loved her, he had invested the best years of his life getting ready for this.

That feeling transformed into her own anticipation

of the work that lay ahead, and how her world might change now that she could live one life in the open. She took a sketchbook from her pack and drew portraits of Joe, Diego, Serena, and Joe's family until the train stopped in Philadelphia. From there to Penn Station in New York, she sketched David, Charley, Mel, Maria, and a page of connected bubbles representing the players in the case. A cluster of lines bound them tightly together.

Chapter 17

Mare Nostrum

JOE INITIALED THE LOG in Main Engineering Control ("Main Control" on the ship's phone circuits) and climbed the ladder to the main deck. It had been two months since he or Senior Chief Murray had needed to criticize anything about the watch standing. For the first six weeks after he reported aboard from ACC (automatic combustion controls) School on Coasters Harbor Island, the ship had either been on water hours because more than two of its four evaporators were out of commission or running on reduced power because one or more boilers was down.

The engine rooms always felt better than the firerooms because the latter each had two massive, oil-fired boilers generating superheated steam at more than 1500 degrees Fahrenheit around the clock. He walked forward to the hatch outside the number one fireroom ("Bravo-One"). Sucking a final breath of normal air, he clambered down the vertical ladder into the "hole."

To those who did not live there, the holes were a scene from Dante's *Inferno*. One never stripped, no matter how hot it seemed because touching any metal surface could raise blisters. A rupture in one of the 1500-psi water lines that fed the boilers or the 1200-psi steam lines going to the engine rooms meant instant death for anyone closer than ten feet. Thick asbestos insulation on all the pipes and the sides of the boilers brought the temperatures down to a livable one hundred degrees Fahrenheit on the upper level and ninety-eight degrees at the control station on the lower level.

It was so much worse, Joe thought as his foot touched the deck grating between two main feed pumps. After ACC School, he had found no one to relieve: the previous MPA was struggling for his life in the Naval Hospital. A gauge glass on the back of No. 1 boiler, used to see the water level in the steam drum, had failed, spewing superheated feed water and steam into the fireroom. The officer had run up the ladder instead of dashing across to the escape trunk, which would have allowed him to reach the main deck without breathing the steam. His lungs boiled in a flash, and he fell back to the lower level, on top of a young boilerman, who caught him and let him down to the deck plates.

The petty officer in charge had shut down the boiler and evacuated everyone through the escape trunk.

Although a freshly commissioned ensign, Joe was at least familiar with this propulsion plant, identical to the one in *Semmes.* That plant had been in about the same condition. The control system used pressurized air and it would not tolerate any humidity or oil in the line, a constant problem in a steamy fireroom full of Navy Special Fuel Oil (NSFO) and various lighter lubricating oils. He had spent most of his first-class cruise learning the systems and safety features, first with Senior Chief

Mackay looking over his shoulder, then on his own. He knew how to locate a blocked control line, bleed it, and calibrate the system.

It was no surprise that he was at the top of his class in ACC School. When *Barry* sailed from Newport to join the US Sixth Fleet in the Mediterranean, the boiler technicians were controlling the boilers from the control board, instead of standing by the fuel atomizers at each boiler front, and the valves controlling the steam to each forced draft blower. To Sandra, Joe described it as driving a train from the engineer's station in a diesel locomotive, compared to having a stoker shoveling coal and a man working a bellows to keep the fire going.

Each week, the boiler technicians cleaned and calibrated another section of the system. By the time they reached Gibraltar to turn over with the outgoing carrier task group, the ship had actually steamed in "full automatic" for the first time in anyone's memory. This was completely hands-off, with the boilers responding to the demand for steam from the engines without human intervention. The sweaty men watching the dials on the control boards move on their own felt that they were witnessing a miracle.

ཀཀཀ

Escorting USS *Enterprise* (CVN-65) from Greece to France, *Barry* steamed steadily into the night. The battle exercise had ended before the Athens visit. The task group was repositioning to patrol the Western Mediterranean. The carrier and the cruiser would dock in Toulon to be feted by the French Navy. The destroyers would pull into smaller ports along the Riviera. The destroyer squadron commander put his flagship into Nice. The next two senior captains selected Cannes and Saint Tropez. *Barry* was going to Genoa. In November, NATO Exercise Île d'Or would see the *Enterprise* battle group join the French and Italian navies in the sea between Corsica and the Balearic Islands for a week of at-sea training.

Joe inspected the logs in each fireroom and looked at the gauges on the control boards for a while, then went to his stateroom. After a shower, he took a nap before his watch on the bridge. He had qualified as a full officer of the deck during the battle exercise. This would be his third watch "alone," though he expected the captain to doze in his big chair on the bridge most of the time. Not that Bob Majella mistrusted his crew; it was simply quicker if everyone knew where to find the skipper when the ship was underway.

At 23:00 (eleven p.m.), Joe slipped from his bunk in the four-man "ensign locker" at the back of the superstructure. After padding softly to the head to relieve himself, he dressed in the dark and returned to the red-lit passageway outside the stateroom. Although red light in the internal passageways helped preserve his night vision, he always stepped onto the main deck as soon as he could. He never knew when an inexperienced or distracted shipmate would turn a corner with a white flashlight.

He made his way to the bridge using the outside ladders. A cold northeast wind, boosted by the ship's speed, whipped his trousers around his legs. The three-quarter moon was high in the sky, and a thick blanket of stars stretched in all directions. Plenty of light to see the six ships steaming in front of their white wakes. The stars would go out as the carrier and the cruiser USS *Columbus*

(CG-10) passed before them, providing an outline of the big warships if one knew how to look.

He almost impaled himself on the door between the bridge and the starboard bridge wing. With a mild oath, he found the piece of rope that had been jury-rigged to the door and tied it open.

"Sorry about that, Joe," said the JOOD. Pete Skouras, the DCA. "It's on the list to fix, first thing after Sea Detail tomorrow." The welders were in his Damage Control Division.

He tapped Pete's shoulder in acknowledgment and walked to the Combat Information Center behind the bridge, to see the tactical situation before assuming his watch. He always visited CIC well before assuming the watch because the space was not truly darkened. Too many radar repeaters, backlit status boards, and doors to the interior spaces being opened and closed. However, the lighting was low enough for Joe to recover his night vision quickly when he returned to the bridge.

The skipper stirred when Joe crossed the bridge to read the status board on the back bulkhead, then speak to the OOD on watch. The JOOD had just turned over. The OOD passed the conn to the oncoming JOOD. Buck Greenwald was a warrant officer, recently commissioned. He was the first lieutenant in charge of the exterior of the ship. He had been a boatswain's mate, so there was nothing his "deck apes" could pull that he could not anticipate. Pete went below.

"Good evening, Mr. Lockhart," said the captain in a voice intended to be heard by the entire bridge team. As if on cue, the light level on the radar repeaters and status boards dropped in half. Satisfied that no lights reflected on the inside of the windows, Joe commenced the turnover briefing.

Joe's reputation as a fanatic for night vision had earned him his early appointment as an OOD. It had also won the respect of the CIC team. Because his lookouts could see the loom of a ship's running lights before the ship itself appeared on the horizon, Joe's watchstanders consistently asked CIC about contacts that had not shown up on the radar yet.

"*Enterprise* at three-three-zero; *Belknap* on her port quarter; *Columbus* up ahead off the carrier's starboard bow; and *Lawrence* in plane guard position at two-seven-zero." The operations officer tapped the big radar repeater. "Mister Lockhart, I'm showing you."

"Yes, sir, I see them." He pointed to each one through the windows. "*Belknap, Lawrence, Enterprise, Columbus.*" Then Joe tapped a blip on the upper left of the screen. "And *Samspon* hauling ass to Barcelona."

"I wish."

"Me too, but I'll settle for Genova."

The ops officer whispered, "Can you really see them?"

"Yes, sir."

"Anyway, we're on three-three-five at twenty knots. Next planned course change at zero-three-fifteen, break formation at zero-four-hundred then direct to port."

"Why is *Lawrence* in plane guard? Flight operations at this hour?"

"A COD coming in from Naples with urgent parts," Carrier Onboard Delivery, "and a VIP who insisted on experiencing a night landing. Just came up an hour ago."

Joe walked out to the starboard bridge wing. He pointed up about forty-five degrees, at the blinking red and green lights floating toward them. "Should land just about the time I relieve you."

The two officers discussed what had happened in the past six hours, and who was on watch where. Joe made a round of the bridge team to see that his men were in place and the previous watch had gone to their bunks.

Joe saluted the OOD. "I relieve you, sir."

"This is Lieutenant Garson. Ensign Lockhart has the deck!"

"This is Ensign Lockhart. I have the deck!"

"Aye, aye, sir!"

"Three-three-zero, all ahead full!" the helmsman called out.

The ops officer reported to the captain and left by the starboard bridge wing. The door came loose from its rope and swung free. Joe motioned to the boatswain's mate, who went out and tied it back again.

ৡৡৡ

Commander Robert Majella was known throughout the fleet as a master shiphandler, which is why he could appear to doze in his chair, letting the younger officers make their mistakes and recover without a dangerous mishap. He had determined that Buck Greenwald was his best shiphandler, but he needed his first lieutenant on the main deck for Sea Detail. Greenwald's boatswain's mates handled the mooring lines. Thus, the captain was delighted when the new ensign from Virginia turned out to be an excellent conning officer too. After Athens, he made Joe the Sea Detail JOOD. The executive officer would have the deck but if anything happened, Joe could handle the ship.

Joe took a two-hour nap after the midwatch before dressing in his Service Dress Blue uniform. He swung by Main Control to check on his engineers. The chief engineer and Senior Chief Murray were already there. The senior chief gave Joe a smile and a thumbs-up as he climbed the ladder.

Sometimes, Joe thought that Murray had the look of a proud father. *Weird feeling.*

The sun was still working its way over the ridge of the Apennine Mountains when Joe stepped on deck and started to the bridge. He sighed to see the land taking shape in front of the growing light. This had been his home from his early memories until just three years ago.

He stopped in CIC. On the large radar repeater, he traced the Italian riviera and noted the blips following the shipping channels in and out of the harbor. *Barry* was still ten miles out.

As he stepped on the bridge, the boatswain blew his whistle into the 1MC public address system.

"Now set the Special Sea Detail!"

Most of the crew was already in position, but sailors who did not have a role in maneuvering the ship into port appeared on the main deck and lined up on both sides. As the rising sun warmed the land, the wind abated.

The pilot came aboard at the fantail and was escorted to the bridge. After shaking hands with the captain, he introduced himself to the XO and Joe. His accent was thick but understandable.

"*Piacere, capitano.*" Joe shook his hand. The pilot beamed with pleasure.

"Our understanding is that we will be alongside the pier near the commercial passenger terminal," said the skipper.

"Yes."

"We can do a Mediterranean moor if you need the space."

"No need, Captain."

"My first lieutenant tries to be prepared."

"He is smart. I hope we have no surprises."

Today, the XO kept the conn, though he simply relayed the orders from the pilot. Joe stood inside near the helmsman, making sure there were no misunderstandings.

He felt a thrumming excitement as the ship approached the pier. There were some family members of the crew at the end of the pier, away from the area where the ship would tie up. Some wives had organized a tour from Newport for this port visit. *Too bad Sandra could not be there.* He saw movement on the starboard bridge wing. *Damn door is swinging again.*

The pilot had the engines stopped. On his handheld radio, he ordered the tug to push *Barry* to the pier.

About fifteen feet from the pier, a bright flash outlined the pilot. Joe dropped to the deck.

The world went into slow motion.

As he heard the explosion, flames rose against the glass of the starboard bridge windows. The lookout who had been in the doorway was thrown into the bridge, his uniform burning around him. The door slammed shut. Everyone except the helmsman was on the deck. Glass sprayed across the bridge. Joe felt pain and sharp cuts on his back and right arm.

Then the shrapnel arrived through the broken window. The helmsman's head slammed into the port window, and his body fell lifeless at his station, blood spurting to the overhead. The pilot, the captain, the XO, and the messenger with his sound-powered telephone were incinerated against the side of the superstructure.

Joe rolled over on the flaming lookout, extinguishing the fire. The man lay still. Joe stood. The port lookout, the status board keeper, and the chief quartermaster and his assistant were getting to their feet. The pilot's radio had blown to the middle of the bridge.

As if to mock him, the door swung open. There was no bridge wing outside. He could see the pier engulfed in flames. Sea detail members who had not been killed were already unrolling firehoses on the starboard side. The lifeboats and the ship's whaleboat had vanished.

He swiped his left hand down his right upper arm, dislodging some glass that was sticking out of the thick wool sleeve.

"This is Ensign Lockhart. I have the deck and the conn!"

"Aye, aye, sir," came the reply from the four men on the bridge.

"You!" Joe pointed to the port lookout, "Helm!"

"You," he pointed to the status board keeper, "engines." The two men jumped to their new stations.

Then he detailed the assistant quartermaster to the phones and ordered him to have all stations report.

Engineering reported Bravo One shutting down, but watertight. The forecastle (where Greenwald was stationed) reported that the dead and wounded were being pulled from the deck. The fire was under control.

"Focs'le, fantail. Prepare for Med moor." The phone operator relayed the order.

Joe picked up the handheld radio and keyed it. *"Rimorchiatore indietro e state pronti. Attaccheremo a poppa al ponte Andrea Doria.*" Tug back up and stand by. We will moor the stern to the Andrea Doria pier.

"*Capito. D'accordo.*" Understood. Agreed.

Buck Greenwald appeared on the port bridge wing.

"I'll be on the fantail. The anchor detail is ready."

"Thank you, Mister Greenwald.

"Hard a starboard! Starboard engine back one-third, port engine ahead one-third!"

The helmsman and engine order telegraph operator repeated the orders and moved their controls.

As Buck went below, Joe stepped out onto the port side. At the right moment, he ordered the rudders centered, stopped the engines, and asked the tug to keep the stern from moving too far. The tug captain acknowledged and moved his vessel into position.

The ship stopped about twenty feet from the flaming pier. Joe glanced at the scene: a tanker truck on fire, burning fuel spilling onto the pier and igniting the asphalt. He could hear the sirens of the approaching fire trucks then tuned them out.

"Let go the port anchor!" The phone talker had barely finished the order when they heard the heavy chain roaring out the hawsepipe.

"All engines back slow!" Joe waited until he heard the machinery speeding up in the holes. "All engines, stop!"

The ship crept backward until the anchor chain stopped her, about six feet from the pier. The fantail party threw the mooring lines to the waiting line handlers.

Joe nodded to the boatswain. The man blew his whistle into the 1MC microphone. "Moored. Shift colors!"

Joe saw the jack go up on the flag staff at the bow and the American flag come down from the gaff behind the signal bridge. He knew that the flag now flew from the stern of the ship.

In an emergency, there was something affirming about traditions.

Joe keyed the radio, and told the tug in Italian, "Thanks for your help. The blast killed the pilot. We will send the body ashore with our casualties."

The corpsman appeared on the bridge while Joe was working with Buck on the fantail and his chief boatswain's mate on the forecastle to adjust the tension between the anchor chain and the mooring lines aft. A pair of ambulances came down the pier.

The operations officer came out of CIC and saw that Joe was the only officer. His eyes widened in alarm as his gaze passed the bloody men standing on the bridge. Then he spotted the remains of the conning party. He paled, turned, and threw up. The corpsman grabbed the towel attached to the status board and wiped him up. The ops officer returned inside to clean up.

The chief engineer came through the door.

"We're securing down below. What—"

"You're the senior officer on board, sir," said Joe. "I have the deck. We should stand down the Sea Detail, but do you want General Quarters or set the first watch?"

Michael Burton had not been selected early for lieutenant commander for his looks. He had seen combat in Vietnam as a gunfire spotter.

"Doc! What's the situation with casualties?" he asked the corpsman.

"Thirty-four wounded that we know of, not counting the bridge team here, sir. Twenty need a hospital, and we are moving them to the fantail now.

"The dead are another story. So far, I know of twenty"—he glanced at the bridge wing—"twenty-four."

"GQ, Mister Lockhart."

"Bos'n, General Quarters!" Joe turned to the phone talker. "Fantail, help the EMTs debark the wounded as soon as Mister Greenwald says it's safe."

The General Quarters alarm sounded, and the shrill notes of the boatswain's call echoed across the port. "General Quarters, General Quarters. All hands man your battle stations. General Quarters!"

The chief engineer called Main Control on the intercom circuit and ordered the senior chief to take charge, that he would be on the bridge. Then he went to the microphone for the 1MC, the ship wide announcing circuit. He watched Joe and the GQ status board keeper taking the ready reports from stations throughout the ship. He keyed the mike.

"This is Lieutenant Commander Burton. I am in command as Commander Majella and Lieutenant Commander Smithson are deceased. Lieutenant Garson is the acting executive officer. We will remain at General Quarters until all stations report in, and we can tend to any residual damage."

An hour later, all damage and casualties were accounted for. Besides the Sea Detail on the starboard side and the bridge, Bravo One had wounded men who had been thrown about by the blast. One had a broken leg, and another suffered a concussion.

The skin of the ship bulged inward but was not leaking. However, bent structural members would require careful inspection, and some of the piping looked precarious. The boiler technicians forward carefully shut down their boilers and depressurized the system. The two boilers in the after fireroom could provide all the steam they needed.

The pier was still burning. The section under the fuel truck was sagging. Police and other first responders were leading the wives and girlfriends away from the scene.

Barry stood down from General Quarters and set the first watch. The cooks started lunch. The damage control assistant became chief engineer.

Michael Burton, the new captain, ordered Joe and the bridge team to sick bay to have their burns and cuts checked.

The operations officer (now the executive officer) sent the required reports up the chain of command. COMSIXTHFLT (Commander US Sixth Fleet) ordered the shore commander in Naples to find NIS and ATF investigators as soon as possible.

They set a watch on the forecastle to keep an eye on the blazing pier. Pressurized firehoses were laid out in case the burning truck fell into the water or some other hazard brought the fire closer.

The new skipper and Joe met the port captain and the local *Vigili del Fuoco* (National Fire Service) commander on the quarterdeck set up by the stern. The port was a controlled access zone. No one was allowed in except emergency services. The police had escorted the dependents to the gate. All were safe, although distraught. The Vigili del Fuoco would begin investigating as soon as the fire was out, but with the support structure and the asphalt burning it would take a while.

The American consul general arrived after lunch. He received a briefing and promised to look after the dependents and to work with the local authorities to keep the press away. The Embassy in Rome would send the FBI liaison officer and an ATF investigator as soon as possible.

Back in his stateroom, Joe changed into his khakis. He trashed his bloody shirt and undershirt. He folded the service dress uniform and hoped that a tailor could repair it.

He sat on his bunk, closed his eyes, and hung his head between his knees.

When the shivering stopped, he went to Bravo One.

CHAPTER 18

MADRID

THE LEAVES WENT FROM GREEN TO BROWN as the train sped north. Some bright colors caught Sandra's eye in New Jersey. Autumn would be in full bloom soon. She reviewed her situation as she made the emotional transition to a life without Joe for months.

In the two weeks after she returned to work, nothing changed. Mel appreciated having her in the lab. Not only was it fun for all concerned, but she was a bargain: a trained conservator for the price of an intern. The FBI Field Office did not mind her spending mornings at the museum because she was instantly available with a phone call.

No one advertised her status as an agent, so Maria and maybe four other people in the building were aware of it. They could enjoy visiting each other at home now. The two friends enjoyed Roman and Greek cooking. They also took in a midweek movie now and again.

Tennis kept her from needing to buy a gym membership. Luke and Sandra played on Saturday mornings and went for lunch afterward. She had shared her emotional breakdown in Richmond with him.

He finished chewing his bite of spaghetti alle vongole and sipped his Trebbiano. He smiled with his eyes.

"And what did Nancy say?"

"We sat on the veranda after supper, and she said that I was a cross between a best girlfriend and the daughter she never had. That felt strange."

"Strange good or strange bad?"

"Strange good – and very right. She could never replace my mother, but she is more than an older friend."

"I think I can understand how she feels. She has told me how much she likes you. No, she loves you, but you two have a unique relationship. I can see that."

"How do you feel about being a father figure?" She sipped her wine while he thought.

"Some men would joke about that. I've never had kids, so I'm not sure.

"But if I had a daughter, I would want her to grow up like you. Strong and awesome, on the court and off. And I would want her to meet someone as special as Joe – and his mother." He tasted his wine. "How's that?"

"I can live with it. Just don't ask me to call you Old Man until I beat you five sets in a row."

"It's a deal. And, as Nancy said, I hope we'll be friends with or without Joe."

"I think he and I will be an item for a long time. We've been living in different cities for four years now."

"No wedding bells yet?"

"No. He has always been very clear that he would wait until after his first deployment. He wants his bride to marry the man he will be, not a midshipman or a student."

"He always was smarter than the average bear."

"Look at the changes in my life," she said. "I'm not ready to give up my career now that I have just gotten my badge and come out in the open with it."

Luke swiped his bread through the broth in the bottom of the bowl.

"With Joe, you'll never have to."

"I know, but how can you tell?"

"He has grown up being the man in a house with an active, working woman. I remember your telling us about the night you hid him in your apartment."

Sandra laughed. "Yeah, I pointed to the washing machine so he could wash his bloody clothes – and he washed and folded mine too.

"Thanks, Luke. I don't think I have been able to have this kind of a talk since —" She felt her chest stir.

He reached across the table and took her hands in his, knocking a fork to the floor. "Look at me. Hold your breath a moment. Let it out slowly. Breathe in. Out. There, better?"

Sandra sighed and took her hands back. She wiped her eyes with her napkin.

"Thank you again. I've never had anyone react so quickly. That worked."

"You're welcome. If you ever feel the grief taking you down, call me or Nancy – if Joe is at sea, of course. We can listen."

❖❖❖

Sandra hugged herself as she took the stairs to the subway station. The first flurries had danced during the Marine Ball when there were still colors in the Hudson Valley.

She knew it was not snowing in the Mediterranean, but Joe had reported that the annual rains had started. She was not sure that was better than this.

Excitement hummed in the FBI office when she pushed through the door. David and Charley were grinning so hard, she expected canary feathers to sprout from their mouths. Frank and Dario were taking turns throwing crumpled paper balls at them.

"You guys know we have a children's room at the Brooklyn if you want to trade jobs with me." She caught a paper ball. "What's going on?"

"Headquarters approved travel to the conference in Madrid, and we can send three agents." Interpol had been organizing a meeting of the police agencies assigned to the art-swapping case for months. Three dozen representatives would be there for a week, working out details for a joint operation to repeat the historic coordinated raids two summers ago.

"So, by the time you draw lots, and the losers take leave, will I be the senior agent in New York?"

"Don't be making plans, Bari," said David. "We already drew lots, and you were going regardless. Charley and I will escort you."

"Why me? I'm the junior person in this office."

Frank said, "It's not a seniority thing. After the last operation, we'd be crazy not to have you there again."

Sandra looked at the happy faces. *How did I luck into a bunch of such swell people to work with?*

જી

Jet lag did not belong in Sandra's vocabulary. Madrid was not Rome, but the ancient city humming with Romance languages and centuries of beautiful art on every block touched her deeply.

For security reasons, the participants had been asked to arrive by military aircraft. The C-130 from Naval Station Rota dropped its ramp at the Getafe air base south of the city just long enough for the three American agents to jump into the waiting *Guardia Civil* cruiser and follow the motorcycle to the Guardia Civil headquarters compound. They were shown rooms in the visiting officers' quarters, which were as big as a hotel in the USA.

The men shared a room with a pair of twin beds and a sink in the room. Sandra was assigned to a general officer suite at the end of the hall, with an ensuite bathroom and a minibar.

Major Lopez, the commander of the National Police Art Fraud Division, explained, "we don't have bathrooms for the ladies, so this was our solution. My apologies." He smiled at the irony. "If you want to go off the base, please remember to sign out at the gate. Otherwise, the sentries will detain you coming back until I can vouch for you."

While Charley napped and David made phone calls, Sandra went for a walk as soon as she unpacked. A lightweight trench coat proved more than enough layering after the temperatures in New York. Blue- and white-collar employees were already gathering in the tapa bars. She stepped into one and treated herself to a glass of Tempranillo and a slice of spinach and artichoke pie. She was surprised that she followed so much of the conversation around her. Her high school Spanish had not been wasted, and apparently it had been reinforced by the ubiquity of the language on the streets of Manhattan and Brooklyn.

Back at the officers' quarters, the desk gave her a note, "Call when you get back. 3526. DV." She called from her room.

"Charley is awake, come on over, so we can plan tonight."

David had been out, too, because there was wine in the refrigerator and a cutting board of cold cuts and cheese on the table.

"Here is the schedule for the week," said David, passing her a single page. "You'll notice that the meetings start at nine thirty every morning at the command building." He pointed out the window to a large, featureless block. "We'll walk over together at nine."

Sandra scanned the sheet. "No one plans to get any sleep."

"Only at lunch time. Dinner is early tonight, at ten p.m."

"Are these all plenary sessions? I thought there might be working groups."

"We'll be in one big room, at different tables. We can move between them and connect quickly. It's what we did last time."

"How are the tables broken down?"

"Since this operation is all about paintings, we're starting out by era on Tuesday and Wednesday. Thursday, we'll gather around a conference table to report what we found and decide whether to convene by countries or regions, or something else.

"We can't script this in detail because so much depends on what the different member agencies have learned. This is our first chance to share."

"I see the dinner is in the officers' mess downstairs. Are we all staying here?"

"Everyone except the Spanish participants from Madrid. You and the wives will be the only women."

"I'm used to that. Why is the 'tour' all day Monday?"

"The Heritage Protection Division of the Guardia Civil is taking us to El Prado and the Special Collection at the Royal Palace. They are both closed on Mondays, so we're getting a private tour."

"Wow! That's a lot of art for one day."

"Scotland Yard took us to the Tate, the Victoria and Albert, and the British Museum. I was exhausted."

Sandra nibbled some ham and cheese. "It says 'Service Dress' for tonight. What does that mean for us?"

"For investigators who don't have uniforms, it means a business suit. I guess you can wear anything but jeans and a tee shirt."

"I think I can cobble something together. Please don't tell me you two will don your FBI gray suits."

"Charley might, but I never wear gray unless there's a chance I might run into the director."

"I'm with him," said Charley.

Sandra left when they finished their glasses of wine. Even with the tapa earlier, she was glad they had a snack in the room. Supper was still more than three hours away.

જ્ઞજ્ઞજ્ઞ

There were only four dozen people in the private room next to the large dining room where officers of the Spanish armed services were eating. She walked into the room far enough from David and Charley to make it clear that she was unescorted. She wore a simple dark blue dinner dress and the pearls that Nancy had given her as a graduation present. She had chosen the dress with her blond hair, but it worked with auburn.

Not expecting to see anyone she knew, it came as a shock when Alcide Mancini materialized from the crowd at the end of the table.

David caught her eye and moved quickly between her and the Carabiniere major.

"*Maggiore Mancini, che piacere!*" He continued in Italian, "may I introduce my colleague, Special Agent Alessandra Bari?"

Pleasure at the sight of an attractive woman yielded to recognition then understanding, as the officer picked up the cue. He bent and kissed Sandra's hand.

"*Piacere, agente.*"

"*Il piacere è mio, maggiore. Mi chiami Sandra.*" The pleasure is mine, Major. Call me Sandra.

"Alcide, then."

The same words they had exchanged in the hangar at Ciampino airport before going out on the raid that would be Sandra's baptism of fire. Alcide's eyes crinkled in a conspiratorial smile. He had called her *signorina* last time.

The general commanding the Organized Crime Branch of the National Police called for the delegates to find their seats. He gave some brief welcoming remarks and gestured for the servers to start dinner.

Sandra found herself between a detective chief inspector from Scotland Yard named Michael Beardsley and Major Mancini. David and Charley flanked an elegant woman with the shoulders of a swimmer or tennis player. Her husband sat on David's other side. The inspector bent to read Sandra's place card, which showed that the female agent was not *Señora* anyone.

"You're with the FBI in New York?" he asked.

"Yes, I am. Do you know Major Mancini?" She leaned back to let the two men acknowledge each other.

"Good to see you again, Mancini. This may be as exciting as before, eh?"

"Indeed, Beardsley. Especially with Agent Bari here. She is Vasari's secret weapon, you know."

He looked more closely at Sandra. "I thought you were familiar. You were a blonde."

"A lady's secrets are best kept secret, Inspector."

"Yes, of course." He addressed the mussels that had just been set before him.

The conversation level in the room dropped off sharply as three dozen non-Spaniards tucked into their long-overdue nourishment. When the food began moving, the chatter slowly resumed.

"One of the great pleasures of these meetings is that we don't need to keep looking over our shoulders for eavesdroppers," said Beardsley.

"That is a strain, true," Sandra said. "Are you involved with the paintings from London, which we confiscated last winter?"

"I am now. We weren't notified until after the paintings were boxed and riding to the airport. Your people intercepted them before they could be swapped. Good job, that. Thanks."

"Was that the one that almost cost the Frick?" asked Mancini.

"Yes. Our part is investigating how it was set up in the first place."

"That gallery has a very interesting client list." Sandra took a sip of her wine. "Quite a few of the men we stopped last year were customers. Details tomorrow."

"I look forward to that."

They moved to small talk, and she encouraged the two men to chat across her. They seemed happy to engage in a three-way conversation, and it let her avoid answering questions about her changed appearance and name.

During the meat course, David raised his glass to her. Charley copied him. Beardsley noticed.

"I say, Vasari, where have you been hiding this jewel?"

"I tripped over a rock in Central Park, and there she was. Right, Bari?"

"Right. It was cozy under that rock. I still haven't forgiven him." Sandra raised her glass to her two colleagues.

While Beardsley was talking to the woman to his left, Mancini leaned over and said in Italian, "Sandra, did you get married? I thought you were a student at the American Academy."

"I was, Alcide, but that girl is gone now. I really am Alessandra Bari. For the security of our office and my safety, please never mention the other name."

"I understand. If anyone from before notices, I'll steer them to your real name."

"Thanks."

The dinner ended early by Spanish standards, but the guests were pleased to make so many old and new acquaintances. Some made dates to go clubbing with their local friends. The three Americans were happy to sneak upstairs to recover from being up for thirty hours.

಄಄಄

The docent, a professor of art history at the Complutense University of Madrid, led the investigators into the brightly lit rooms of the Renaissance Italian wing. Sandra knew that the collection at the Prado Museum was world-famous, but the sheer number of exquisite pieces on the walls took her breath away. They slowed down because no one wanted to rush this experience.

There were two halls devoted to the sixteenth century. As Sandra, David, Charley, and Alcide moved slowly past the pictures, she felt her heart move faster. The docent kept up a steady spiel, but when the Italian Carabiniere and his colleagues came to a stop, he waited while they gazed at the artwork. The others stopped to watch the four Italian art fans.

"I'm sorry," she said, stepping back from Titian's *Saint Margaret.* "I'm holding us up." She moved to the next picture, Tintoretto's *The washing of the feet.* She admired it quietly and then *The Israelites drinking the miraculous water* by Bassano.

She said to David, "I want to come back to these three. See how the blues work together?"

"Yes. Let's do that." The group began to move to the next room. The American agents brought up the rear.

Sandra stopped. "The blues!"

She walked quickly back to the three paintings. As she looked closely at them, then began comparing the Tintoretto to the Titian, David joined her.

"Please, Sandra, not here." She ignored him. "Have you spotted another forgery?"

"No, David, I can't do that. I can only compare details." She started walking slowly to catch up with the tour. "Did you recognize those three?"

"I took art history too. Of course, I remember them."

"So why are they on the sales records of the gallery we raided?" She lowered her voice. "Could we call New York to make sure?"

"Let's."

"Then maybe we'll come back. Something bothers me, but we mustn't hold the others."

It was lunch time in New York when they returned to their rooms, but Charlene was in the office.

Sandra paced while David was on the phone. "Sure, Charlene, we'll wait. Just come back if it takes more than a minute… yes… both of them?" David glanced at Sandra. "… What about the Bassano? …okay. Got it. Thanks, Charlene." He hung up.

"Damn it, how did you know?"

"I didn't, but something about the blues made me want to look closer. Then I remembered the entries from the gallery's records. I know who bought the Tintoretto and the Titian."

"She told me. Trent Braxton. She couldn't read the name of the client who bought the Bassano."

"Who do we tell now? I may be able to tell with another look if those three were done by the same person, in which case we have another embarrassing swap in front of us."

"It's only seven o'clock. Let me track down our host. General Garcia will not be happy. I hope he doesn't shoot the messenger."

David consulted the contact phone numbers on his schedule and called the duty officer. Fifteen minutes later, he put down the phone.

"He's on his way. Let's go downstairs."

"I didn't know your Spanish was so good."

"Brooklyn born and bred."

She stood, checked her hair in the mirror, and followed him.

General Garcia stormed into the lobby flanked by two hard-eyed Guardia Civil with machine guns and followed by Major Lopez and a serious man in a suit. A hush went over the room. Everyone except David and Sandra shrank against the walls.

"*Buenas—*"

The general hushed David with a swing of his arm and pointed to a meeting room to the side. "*Aquí.*"

The two armed men took positions outside the door. The general introduced the director of El Prado.

"You know Major Lopez," he said in English. "Tell us."

"We may have some swapped paintings at your museum, Director." He turned toward Sandra. "Just so you don't have to hear it twice, let me introduce Special Agent Alessandra Bari." The Spaniards looked at her with interest. "She will explain."

Sandra took a breath and gathered her thoughts.

"In addition to the operation that has brought us here this week, we have three separate high-stakes investigations in progress, which concern collectors of Renaissance art. Last winter, we raided a gallery that was about to swap out six paintings on their way to the Frick Collection in New York City."

"We know about that." The general made an impatient wave.

"We impounded their records. Another agent and I went over them.

"The gallery recorded selling three paintings that we saw today at the Prado."

"There are forgers for all our art," said the director.

"Yes, sir, but the three pictures hanging in your museum may have been painted by the same person. The tour hurried off, but I wish that I could go back to look more closely, perhaps with the sun at a different angle."

"Our art has been certified—"

"One moment, Director, please." David let the man settle down. "We are not making accusations, but this is how we discover art that is swapped. Agent Bari noticed the forged *Dama con Liocorno* on tour at our National Gallery of Art three years ago. That led to the biggest recovery of stolen art in history. Some of those paintings were yours."

"Major Lopez, what do you know about that?" asked the general.

"It is as Agent Vasari said, sir. I was directing the raids in Paris while he was in Rome, but the intelligence from New York was phenomenal throughout the investigation. Someone in America seemed able to detect differences the most experienced experts could not see."

"Is this that someone?" asked the general.

"Yes, sir," said David.

"I've heard enough. Director, work out a time for the American agents to have a close look at the three paintings, and take notes. You might want to go back through the provenance and travel history in case your pictures went on tour too."

"*Sí, señor general.*"

The general motioned for the major to stay and observe, then left. Sandra heard heels click as the two guards fell in behind the senior officer.

❧❧❧

The only open time was during the lunch hour, which did not bother David and Sandra as much as their hosts. Major Lopez arranged for sack lunches. An Army sedan drove the two Americans and the major from the headquarters to the museum.

The director had a half dozen of his conservation staff on hand. They had rigged long tables in the middle of the room where the sun would give the best light, and they had taken down the three paintings and placed them on padded tablecloths.

Sandra remembered not to wring her hands and hoped she would not break out in a sweat. She took out her white gloves and donned them.

"Do you carry those gloves everywhere?" David asked.

"Except when I play tennis, yes."

"I'm glad you do. This is the third time you've surprised me this way."

She smiled and looked down. Then she approached the pictures. Gasps came from the conservators and the director when she moved the pictures about thirty degrees to put the sun over her shoulder.

The silence was absolute. She thought maybe the staff were holding their breath. She leaned over the painting with her hands behind her back. After walking past them slowly, she stood back. Then she compared pairs of paintings several times.

Finally, she removed her gloves.

"I'm sorry, Director, but I am afraid that all three were executed by the same person. We know that the originals were painted over twenty years, so I recommend a full analysis. It's up to you, but there you have it." She turned to David.

He said, "Meanwhile, we have records showing who should have purchased the pictures in the USA. We will contact you with the results of our investigation."

"We must take these down?"

"I am only a conservator and an investigator, sir," said Sandra. "I cannot give a final judgment."

"While we pursue the case to the originals," said Major Lopez, "I would put everything back as it is and maintain secrecy on this." He passed a fierce gaze over the staff. "Very powerful and wealthy men bought them. No one must know that the Americans are investigating this until they locate the other pictures and bring them in for analysis and comparison."

"We understand. Thank you, Agent Vasari." The director turned to Sandra. "And thank you, Agent Bari. This is most embarrassing, but it is better to find out than to continue in ignorance.

"Please bring our art back to us."

The two agents shook hands with the staff and followed the major to the car.

❧❧❧

David, Sandra, and Major Lopez had not missed much because Charley was giving the American report to a plenary session. They slipped into the back in time to help answer questions.

The next three days unfolded in a blur. This operation involved about a hundred paintings, one-third of the number before, and the teams benefitted from the lessons learned earlier. The other countries were seeing a proportion of returning actors close to what the Americans had. People from many agencies came up to thank David for passing them that hint.

Sandra found herself pulled from table to table as various groups asked her to compare photos. This conference was the first time that the investigators working in different countries could look comprehensively at the trail of the pictures and compare the photos in their files with similar photos elsewhere. The effort was more efficient than the time-consuming process of telephone calls or sending mail with one question at a time.

Friday was the last day. In the morning, the group met in a plenary session so that each country team could ask the questions they still had. As the answers came together from around the world, the investigators hoped to assemble a coordinated operation sooner. The United States had the highest number of persons being investigated; Rome had topped the list last year. This year Paris was second, and London third.

When the conference broke at noon, the three Americans went to their rooms. The final event was a cocktail party in the hotel at eight, with groups expecting to go out to dinner afterward.

David knocked on her door before Sandra had even hung her coat in the closet.

"Phone call from Washington. The desk put it through to our room."

"Who is it?"

"Marty MacKenzie."

Sandra walked to their room and picked up the handset. "Hello, Marty?"

"New York told me you were here. You're being recalled. We need you to work the scene in Genova." She thought, *it must be dawn in Washington.*

"What happened?"

"That's for you to find out. A major explosion in the harbor. About zero-eight-hundred your time. USS *Barry* was the target. All I know is that the ship and its berth were burning, and the Italians were fighting the fire.

"We want NIS there. The Sixth Fleet flagship is off Cyprus. Our agent in Naples is on emergency leave in the States, and the one in Rota broke his leg yesterday. You may be the first American investigator on the scene. Take notes, help the local authorities, and do what you can."

"Shall I make arrangements?"

"Done. The C-130 is leaving Rota now. Go to the Getafe Air Base. Rota has already called for someone to take you there." He dictated the phone numbers for Rota, Naples, and the Italian Naval Command in La Spezia.

"I'm on my way." She hung up.

David and Charley were in her room, emptying drawers and closets, and placing things on the bed next to her suitcase. She packed while she explained the situation to them.

"Do you know who's on that ship?" she asked David.

"Who?"

"Joe."

"Oh my God, Sandra. You can't—"

"Don't worry, David. If I can watch my family get blown to bits, I can work the crime scene until the other agents get there. Besides, my Italian is better than my Spanish."

They followed her downstairs. As they reached the door, a Guardia Civil cruiser and a motorcycle pulled up.

Chapter 19

Genoa

THE C-130 WAS NOT A FIGHTER JET, but Sandra swore the lumbering cargo plane was so slow that it flew backward. She was the only passenger, and the load-master told her that they stopped loading when the orders came to fly out. The aircraft would return to Rota for the rest of their cargo as soon as they delivered Sandra to the airport in Genoa.

The noise made conversation impractical, for which she was grateful. For two hours, she reviewed what she had learned about establishing and maintaining a crime scene. It could be a mess; much would depend on how quickly the Italian authorities got things under control. Her crime scene was the ship; theirs was the pier.

A Carabinieri cruiser was waiting on the tarmac when Sandra walked down the ramp. A Carabiniere captain approached the plane, looking past her. She put her badge on her jacket. He stopped and saluted.

"You are the Agent Bari?" he asked in English. "Captain Morissetti." He clicked his heels. She reached out and shook his hand.

"*Piacere. Sono l'agente Bari. Mi spieghi la situazione mentre andiamo alla scena, La prego.*" Pleased to meet you. I'm Agent Bari. Please explain the situation on the way.

As the car sped through the busy docks of the port, the officer brought Sandra up to date. The ship was no longer in danger. It had been six meters from the pier when the devices exploded. The starboard wing of the bridge took the worst of the blast, killing the senior officers and the pilot, and blowing the boats off their davits. The bombs killed dozens of sailors formed up along the ship's side. There was a big dent in the side below the bridge, but the explosion pushed the ship away.

The three men wheeling the articulated ladder for the quarterdeck and the two of the four line handlers were killed instantly.

The present problem was the fuel truck near the bombs. It spewed burning diesel fuel on the ship and the pier. The asphalt caught fire and was running down over the pilings below.

The crew extinguished the fire on board while the ship maneuvered to attach its stern to the opposite pier. Sandra remembered Joe's explanation of the "Med moor" used in ports with limited space.

He finished as the car stopped at the shore end of the basin. She got out before he could open the door for her and viewed the scene.

The destroyer seemed as normal as could be, tied to the Ponte Andrea Doria. As Sandra stood there, the sun set. The ship's public address system played *Retreat* as the flags came down. The "Med lights" came on, a string of white lights from bow to stern over the highest mast and along the side. The bright triangle seemed to shout to the world, "Nice try. We're still here." Pride filled her chest for a moment.

She focused on the burning pier.

"I need to look at the scene before it gets too dark," she said to her escort. She started walking.

"But *signorina*—" Sandra heard the protective tone implied in the use of "miss". The appellation brought her nubile status into every situation. She choked back a caustic retort.

"It's *agente* or *signora*. This is not my first bomb scene." She waved for him to accompany her. "Let's do this together."

He took the chastisement graciously and followed her. She could tell from his face that he was relieved not to have to be gallant with her.

A *vigile del fuoco* approached them. Sandra identified herself. He went to the scene to get his officer.

The Vigili del Fuoco officer recognized the Carabiniere. "Ciao, Morissetti. This is a restricted area. Who is this?"

"Fire Chief Fortegna, this is Special Agent Bari of the American Naval Investigative Service. She has been sent to assist."

Sandra reached out and shook the fireman's hand. "We are involved in this incident because our investigations on board will depend on the same evidence as yours. May I approach the scene for a first impression before I go to the ship? It will be dark soon."

"Very well, but stay outside the taped line closest to the sagging part of the pier."

"Thank you, Chief." She walked slowly to the edge. The fireman stayed close.

Besides the smell of burning fuel, she recognized the acrid odor that had permeated the scene in Ohio. Pushing down the visual memory, she concentrated on the smell.

Crouching to sight along the sagging surface, she pointed. "See that depression, the one inside the bend of the pier?"

"Yes," said Fortegna. "That was the location of the devices. There were two, side by side."

"I have seen that particular hole before. The metal on the fuel tank is bent away from that depression, but mostly the truck is intact."

"Your point?"

"Your arson investigators would know better than I, but that appears to be from a shaped charge, aimed at where the ship should have been. Very focused."

Chief Fortegna considered what she had said. "You may be right, Agent Bari. We need to finish here and set a flashback watch, but the full arson team will be here in the morning. Could you join us?"

"Certainly. I'll make sure the ship knows where I am. I haven't taken a room yet." Sandra thanked the fire chief and walked back to the car with the Carabiniere.

"We reserved a room at the *foresteria* for you, signora," said Morissetti. The Army visiting officers' quarters. "It's right over there." He pointed to a large building beyond the gate to the port. "I'll escort you."

"I have another idea. Let me check in with the ship. I don't know how long it will take, so why don't we meet there after supper? Say, ten o'clock?"

"Excellent. I'll be there to get you checked in." He wrote down a phone number on a business card. "Call there if you are delayed or if you want me to pick you up."

He held the door of the car.

"Thanks, but I can walk that far."

"May we drop your suitcase off?"

"Thank you. See you this evening."

❧❧❧

Sandra climbed the gangplank leading to the fantail of the ship. Standing at attention, she requested permission to come aboard. The officer of the deck saluted, and she stepped onto Joe's home.

The OOD was a lieutenant junior grade, who seemed about the same age as Joe. She showed her credential pack.

"Special Agent Bari. May I see the commanding officer, please?"

"Certainly, ma'am. We were briefed to expect you tomorrow or the next day. You're from the flagship?"

"No, but I was the closest agent available."

"The chief engineer is the CO now." He looked at the clock. "Probably at supper." He called the wardroom.

"He's there. Please follow the messenger. Not that way, Smith." The sailor pivoted from the starboard side and headed away from the damage.

"Hold it, Smith," she said. She turned to the OOD. "If you don't mind, I should go past the exterior damage on the way. It might not look the same in the morning."

"I understand. Go ahead, Smith."

Sandra walked along the outside, stepping around the chalk circles on the deck. She imagined how the davits looked before the blast pushed them into the side of the superstructure. Melted cabinets partially blocked the way, and rope had been rigged to replace the steel lifelines that had been there. She used one of her white gloves to take a swipe of the black residue, smelled it: the same explosive she had detected on the pier. She folded the smudge inside the glove and pocketed it.

Looking up, she saw the sheer, black side, where the starboard bridge wing and the outside ladder had been. The deck was buckled below the bridge and roped off. The messenger led her inside.

With one side off-limits, the chow line crammed into the passageways leading to the mess decks where the crew ate. The sailors pressed up against the bulkhead to let her pass. She wanted to return their smiles but was afraid of her emotions overtaking her. Following the messenger, she turned into the passageway to the wardroom.

A dozen men sat around a long table. The contrast of the white tablecloth and napkins with the haggard faces slapped her hard. The lieutenant commander at the head of the table stood. His khaki uniform was wrinkled and covered with black stains. His eyes had the look of a man who had stared at death and had yet to recover.

Eyes that Sandra had seen in the mirror twice already.

"Please don't get up, gentlemen." She looked at the man standing at the head of the table. "Special Agent Bari, Naval Investigative Service. My condolences, and my congratulations on your response. The Carabinieri briefed me on the way here."

The captain indicated an empty chair next to him. "Have you dined, Agent Bari? If not, please join us." A mess man stepped forward to pull the chair back.

"I'm Michael Burton, until this morning the chief engineer." The officer on his other side was the new executive officer, Dale Garson. He pointed out the new chief engineer, the new operations officer (former CIC Officer), the weapons officer, the supply officer, the first lieutenant and the ASW officer (Antisubmarine Warfare). She exchanged nods with each. "Nothing will change in the time it takes to eat. Let's relax."

"Just one thing, Captain," said Sandra, looking at Buck Greenwald. "I saw the roped-off area. I hope no one is planning on cleaning it, or the sides, until we can collect evidence. It's a crime scene."

"We told the crew not to deal with it today, but we will reinforce that," said the skipper. Buck was already up and heading for the phone. "Pete, make sure we don't start fixing things in the spaces yet."

The chief engineer got up and took the phone when Buck returned to the table.

"You're the first agent here. The consul told us to expect the FBI and ATF tomorrow or the next day. Are you from Naples?"

"No. I'm stationed in New York. I happened to be at a conference in Madrid when NIS in Washington called to send me here."

"Well, I'm glad you made it before we wiped out your crime scene, although I had the bodies removed. We chalked their locations first.

"The destroyer tender in Naples is putting together a team to analyze the damage, especially in the holes. We'll be here until they tell us we are seaworthy."

Peter Skouras came back from the phone. "By the time they get here, Skipper, we may not need the tender. Joe says that the ship fitters and marine engineers the Italian Navy sent over can help us with the evaluation and the repairs – except for the superheated piping.

"We won't get to that before the team from Naples arrives."

As she finished her soup, Sandra forced herself to keep calm.

"Joe?"

"Our MPA. He's in the holes with the Italians now."

The messman placed platters of steaks, potatoes, and spinach on the table. The officers passed the food around.

"Will he be coming to dinner?"

"Probably not."

Sandra refilled her iced tea.

"Captain, could we have a small meeting after supper with the people most involved? I could form a first impression of today's events. I'll be back tomorrow after I meet the Italian arson team, and we can move more deliberately."

"Of course. You would provide our first opportunity to look at this with an outside observer.

"Pete, find out when the Italians intend to quit for the night. XO, let's set up a meeting here after that. Joe can brief us then. You and I can go over the message traffic between now and then."

"Yes, sir," said Dale Garson. He said to the acting ops officer, "Bill, have the message boards sent down here. And some message forms for Agent Bari. She will want to file an initial report, I'm sure."

"Thank you, XO."

They finished their supper mostly in silence. The loss of one quarter of the crew weighed heavily on them. Bravo One called to report that the Italian shipyard experts would wrap up about seven thirty.

After dessert, the CO took Sandra to the bridge, while the mess men cleared the table. The XO followed them up the steep ladders. She thought, *never wear a skirt on a ship.*

Black residue coated the furnishings and bulkheads. From the exposed starboard bridge wing, the wind blew through the opening. The door had seized as it cooled and now held its open position. She peered out at the water and the buckled deck below. The stains on the bridge wing included the dried blood of four men, she knew. As she felt another reaction to her family tragedy, she scolded herself: *Not the time to relive things. Live with the experience and use it!*

"Thank you, Captain. Do you want to go back to the wardroom?"

"Yes, let's. You'll probably need to read most of the messages too."

⊠⊠⊠

At seven thirty, Sandra was sitting at the wardroom table, reading the captain's message board. She had sent a short report to NIS Washington and CINCUSNAVEUR in London (Commander, Naval Forces, Europe), copy to COMSIXTHFLT and COMFAIRMED (Commander, Fleet Air Mediterranean, based in Naples) confirming the casualty count, the watertight integrity of the ship, and that the crime scenes on the pier and the ship were being preserved for analysis in the morning.

She looked up when Joe pushed through the door. He seemed thinner, his face drawn and pale. His khaki uniform had even more black stains on it than the former chief engineer's.

"Captain, the shipyard people will be—" He stopped, and his jaw dropped. Sandra stood.

"Special Agent Bari," said the skipper, "this is Ensign Joe—"

"What are you doing here?" Joe asked Sandra.

"I *am* Navy, you know. I happened to be the closest agent available." She looked at the captain. "Excuse us."

She spread her arms and let Joe fall into them. The other four officers watched in surprise and then grinned as the two lovers hung on to each other. Joe whispered. "*Oddio, stamattina pensavo di non vederti mai più.*" Oh God, this morning I thought I would never see you again.

She hugged him sharply. He winced and stood back.

"Sorry, Captain. This is a shock. I thought she was in New York."

"We won't be sailing soon, so you two can catch up. Agent Bari, is this personal for you?"

"Only to the extent that I know Mister Lockhart here. I really was sent because I was closest."

"Okay, then, let's gather round, folks." The officers who had been working from the couch came to the table. As they passed the coffee carafe around, a messman placed a tray in front of Joe.

"Thank you, Morgan. I needed this."

The skipper reviewed the message traffic that had come in and gone out. The FBI liaison would arrive in the afternoon. The team from the destroyer tender the next day.

"Joe, what can you tell us?"

"It helps that we have Fincantieri, the big commercial shipyard, and the Italian naval shipyard nearby. A lot of experience and all the right skills.

"As Pete and I were afraid, the bent beams in Bravo One should be straightened or reinforced. The team agreed that they might not support motion in the open sea. The engineers need to take more measurements tomorrow, but the first impression is that we should move to the Fincantieri docks – that's next door – where they can insert reinforcing beams for us to steam safely to a dockyard to have that part of the side replaced.

"Lighting off the boilers is out of the question until we straighten the side. After that, we can replace bent or stressed lines. While we do the structural work, we can do the testing and analysis, and manufacture the replacement piping."

The XO said, "COMFAIRMED is collecting expressions of interest already, but won't issue an RFP until we determine what repairs we need." Request for Proposals.

"Where are we with notifications, XO?" asked the skipper.

"We sent the messages to CINCLANTFLT and COMSURFLANT. The day after tomorrow, the reports should be back confirming notification of next of kin." Commanders of the Atlantic Fleet and the Atlantic Surface Forces. "COMSIXTHFLT is sending his public information officer to meet with the press."

"Thank goodness the whole port area is restricted. That's the dead. What about the wounded?"

"Of the thirty-eight, fifteen are still in the hospital, seven in intensive care. Nine should be back tomorrow. Petty Officer Jones will be escorted to the Naval Hospital in Naples. He had a nervous breakdown even though he wasn't physically injured in the fireroom."

"That brings us to you, Agent Bari. The families will want closure."

"ATF and the Italian Vigili del Fuoco are the experts, but based on what I've seen, we are probably dealing with two incendiary bombs set on the pier. They had shaped charges, probably aimed to go through the side of the ship. Whether a timer went off early or a remote operator made a mistake, it was lucky for you that the ship had not gotten close enough for that.

"I recognized the explosive used. There is enough residue at the crime scenes that we should be able to trace the manufacturer. Then we connect the dots."

"How can you tell what explosive was used?" asked Bill Meadows, who was now the ops officer.

"The smell. The same explosive was used at the last bomb scene I was at." Joe looked up in alarm. She pursed her lips and shook her head. He settled down. "The arson investigators should be able to trace the lot number."

"Thank you. Agent Bari," said the skipper. "Let us know if you need anything at all."

"I should visit Bravo One tomorrow. Could someone lend me a set of coveralls? I left mine in New York."

"We can handle that." His expression darkened. "Tomorrow at quarters there will be holes in the formations. Get with your chiefs and look out for anyone taking this hard enough to hurt themselves. The squadron chaplain will be on the first morning train from Nice.

"Also, we don't have enough people to man a three-section watch, so normal operations will be impossible until replacements get here. BUPERS is working on that." Bureau of Personnel. "Meanwhile, look for opportunities to train junior sailors to step in. Ask your chiefs and senior petty officers to help with that."

The XO added, "Tomorrow, we will draw up new watch sections, so we can send the first liberty party ashore in the afternoon."

"Any other questions?" asked the captain. "Good. Let's get some sleep. Thank you, Agent Bari. We'll be here when you come back."

They rose. Sandra moved next to Joe. "*Domani, amore?*" Tomorrow, my love?

"*Sì, buona notte, cara.*" They exchanged a brief hug. To the skipper, he said, "I'll walk her aft. Be right back."

Sandra walked out the gates with her senses on full alert. At five minutes to ten, she walked up the steps to the visiting officers' quarters. Morissetti was waiting.

By ten thirty she was checked in, showered, and sound asleep.

Less than a quarter mile away, Joe eased his aching body into his bunk. The cuts from the glass in his back did not hurt as much now. He fell instantly asleep, to dream of explosions that resolved into Sandra's face, smiling. He did not wake.

Chapter 20

Pulling the Threads Tighter

THE SUN CLEARED THE RIDGE LINE to the east as Sandra walked from her billet to the gates of the *Stazione Marittima,* the passenger piers. She carried her small backpack over one shoulder. The sentry checked her credential pack then saluted sharply.

As she reached the burned-out pier, three cars pulled up behind her. She recognized Captain Morissetti and went to greet him. He introduced the others: two arson specialists from the Vigili del Fuoco, an Army EOD (bomb disposal) sergeant, and a *commissario* from the State Police. They seemed relieved that Sandra spoke Italian because only the Carabiniere officer spoke English.

An arson investigator passed out evidence bags and latex gloves to everyone. "Let's get to work."

She watched the careful way the team collected and bagged samples. She walked around the pier buildings, coming back with some debris from the blast. They were discussing the placement of the shaped charges.

"We need to see the ship to understand where the impact was," said the bomb disposal man.

"I have been onboard," said Sandra. She described the damage and helped them draw imaginary lines from the depressions to the main deck and the side of the fireroom, six meters away. "We can take exact measurements later, but that's the picture."

A Finance Guard sergeant arrived with copies of bills of lading. They identified two large boxes, allegedly containing urgent parts for USS *Barry*, which were positioned yesterday on the pier for the ship to pick up after arrival.

After an hour, Sandra accompanied the two arson specialists and the EOD man around the basin to *Barry's* quarterdeck. The OOD called Joe to meet them. While they waited, the mess man from the wardroom, approached her with a plastic bag.

"Your khakis, ma'am. The captain said to use his sea cabin."

Joe said, "I'll start them outside. Morgan can show you the way. You can go to the bridge or catch up with us."

She followed the sailor up the main deck, then three sets of ladders. At the top, he opened a door to the little stateroom that the CO used when underway.

"There's a john too. I'll wait here."

"Thank you, Morgan."

The bag contained a brand-new long-sleeved khaki shirt and trousers, and a handwritten note. *Wear your badge with these so people won't be confused about your lack of rank markings. XXOO, Joe.*

The uniform fit perfectly. *Luke was right*, she thought. Joe had picked men's sizes to fit a woman. She changed, threaded the khaki belt around her waist and checked herself. After using the john, she put her other clothes on a hanger in the little closet and transferred her sidearm to her backpack.

She opened the door to the passageway and stepped out.

"Is this room normally locked?"

"Yes, ma'am." He jingled the ring at his waist. "Only the captain and I have the key. Just come get me or send for me."

"Thank you, Morgan. I'll wait for the others on the bridge. Do you need to escort me?"

"Not if you don't want me to."

"You go back to whatever you were doing. I know where the wardroom is."

Morgan went down the ladder. Sandra opened the door to the bridge. She noticed how the black residue collected on the right side of all the items in the space. Clear "shadows" showed where the men had dropped to the deck. The glass from the last window to the right was scattered throughout the space, except where bodies or furniture had blocked it. The next two windows were crazed, but the panes had held.

Chalk outlined where the helmsman had been: a large shape near the helm and a smaller circle on the port side, with the word "head" in it. The blood across the overhead and down the bulkhead to the chalk circle had dried but stood out sharply against the light green paint.

Sandra did not feel anything until she visualized the scene from the clues in front of her. Swallowing hard, she took a breath and extracted her sketchbook from the backpack.

Ten minutes later, she had a detailed picture from three angles. She walked to the starboard bridge wing and stepped carefully to the section of deck that still had lifelines and stanchions. She drew the destroyed structure, with its twisted pelorus and folded skirting.

After putting away her sketchbook, she scraped blood samples from the bulkheads inside and out and noted the locations with reference to her drawings.

She heard the arson team and went to meet them.

In Italian, Joe asked her, "Have you taken what you need, or should we come back?" He motioned for the men to line up against the back bulkhead.

"Finished here. I want to show the FBI agent what I have before we clean this." She spoke to the others, "Be careful stepping outside." She saw how they were carefully staying where her footprints were.

In English, she said, "Joe, do you have a photocopier for my drawings and notes?"

"Sure, we can take care of that after we see these gentlemen off."

By eleven o'clock, the visitors stood on the quarterdeck with the skipper, Joe, and Sandra, having demurred on the offer of coffee in the wardroom. "We want to combine the evidence from the pier with this as soon as possible," said Morissetti. "We'll be back the day after tomorrow."

As they watched the Italians walk away, he asked Sandra in Italian, "What do you want to do now, dear, photocopies or boiler room tour?"

"What I want, Ensign Lockhart, is to drag you back to my room and ravage your body." They chuckled. "Let's tour first, then the copies."

❖❖❖

In the midafternoon, they sat in the wardroom. Joe was doing division paperwork. Sandra was writing a report of her initial findings. She had stapled her drawings and notes into six packets, hoping it was enough for now. COMFAIRMED had sent a message asking her to copy the NIS agent at Rota, who would take over from the Sixth Fleet agent afloat later. The 1MC announcing system interrupted them.

"Ensign Lockhart, Warrant Officer Greenwald to the quarterdeck."

Joe stood.

"Probably your colleagues from Naples, Sandra."

"Coming."

An Italian Navy sedan was parked at the end of the gangplank. Two Americans in their mid-forties stood with the watch, shaking hands with Buck. Sandra recognized the FBI liaison officer. She nudged Joe and whispered in Italian, "Introduce me before they say anything."

Joe stepped forward with his hand out. "Special Agent Pietrowicz, good to see you again, sir." He spun around. "This is Special Agent Bari, NIS. She arrived yesterday."

Mark looked puzzled, then recognition dawned, and he noticed the serious expressions of the two young people who had played a crucial role in Rome during his first year there.

"This is ATF Special Agent Winslow. Ensign Lockhart and Special Agent B–Bari." They shook hands. "Agent Winslow is teaching a course for Italian bomb investigators, so we were lucky to have him here."

Michael Burton came out from the port side. Joe introduced him.

"Let's take this to the wardroom," the skipper said. "Agent Bari is in charge of the scene. Let her brief you, then take a look for yourselves."

After coffee and a short explanation of how the ship was recovering from the loss of the officers and men, the captain left them alone.

The two agents were pleased that Joe and Sandra had so much detail on the work by the Italians. Sandra gave the ATF agent one of her bags of scrapings.

"I'm waiting for COMFAIRMED to tell us who gets the rest of the samples, but I collected enough for ATF to run an independent analysis. It couldn't hurt."

"The Italians will have the lead on that," said Winslow.

"They have the explosion on the pier, but NIS has a murder investigation on board, tied to the same evidence." She glanced around the wardroom to make sure that Joe and the agents were the only ones in the room. "Do you know Wes Morton and Jack Hardmon in the Hudson Valley office?"

"Jack was in my cohort. Wes worked for me in Texas."

"I recognized the smell of the explosive while the scene was fresh. That and the depressions left by the shaped charges in the bombs resemble those from a case in Columbus, Ohio. You may want to share the lot numbers or other data you get from that bag with Jack and Wes directly. They should not have to wait on the system for the information. Mention my name. If this is from a different lot, we haven't lost anything, but if it's the same, this will speed up their investigation and ours." She sat back. "Any questions?"

"No," said Pietrowicz. Winslow shook his head. "Let's have a look while there is still plenty of daylight."

On the way out, Mark leaned toward Sandra and whispered, "Weren't you FBI last year?"

"Yes, but I am an NIS agent, seconded to the New York Field Office. NIS called me out of a conference in Madrid because I was the closest agent."

"But—"

She squeezed his forearm. "That girl is gone. I really am Sandra Bari, and what you knew about me is still true – including Joe up there. Just never mention the other surname, please. Jim Redwood can give you the details."

"Thank you, Agent Bari. It's a pleasure to see you again."

The two agents compared the scenes on the bridge and the ship's sides to Sandra's drawings. In the forward fireroom, she had drawn the locations where the two boiler technicians had been wounded, choosing a perspective that would have been impossible for a camera, but illustrated the gap into which the sailor fell and broke his leg.

"These are amazing sketches," said Winslow.

"Agent Redwood told me about your work. I never appreciated how useful it could be."

"She can shoot straight too," said Joe.

"I've seen enough here. Mark, I say we go rescue our driver and make an appointment to meet the Italian investigators."

They walked the two agents to the quarterdeck.

Despite his responsibilities, Joe was still the newest junior officer on board: he had the midwatch (from midnight until four a.m.). Sandra and he dined in the officer's mess of the visiting officers' quarters because it was nearby. They found some private time in her room after supper....

ଷଷଷ

"As long as we're in port, I won't use the sea cabin," the skipper said. Sandra had joined them for breakfast. "Consider it your office and the ship's ladies' room while you're here." He gave her his key. "Morgan can help if I need something."

"Thank you, Captain. The Sixth Fleet agent afloat arrives tomorrow, so I should be out of your way no later than the next day."

"He'll miss the show. This afternoon, we'll move around the corner. This will make it easier for everyone going forward."

"You can watch Joe's shiphandling," said the XO. "Although it will be hard to top watching him switch from mooring alongside to a Med moor without a pilot while being bombed."

As an NIS agent, Sandra had free run of the ship. Joe had taught her the compartment numbering system, so she could find her way to someplace new if given the "address."

"It works on any ship, from tugboat to aircraft carrier," he told her as he showed her the labels. "I need to check the spaces. See you for lunch in the wardroom?"

"Sure."

He left her to explore.

Wearing her khakis with her backpack slung over one shoulder, Sandra spent the morning visiting the rest of the ship. She marveled at the ingenious use of very small spaces, from the personal lockers to the control stations and displays. The cooks in the galley could feed hundreds of men in an hour in no more room than Charlene's reception area.

She learned firsthand about the heat and noise in the holes when she climbed into the after fireroom and the two engine rooms. The heads, showers, and berthing compartments were clearly identified, and the doors were always closed. She skipped those. The electronics in CIC made her think of a science fiction movie, with men writing backward behind plexiglass status boards, so the watch standers could read what they wrote without anyone standing in the way.

After lunch, she sat in a corner of Damage Control Central to look at her notes. She took out her sketchbook and recorded her impressions of the different people and places she had just seen. She heard someone come in. A seat cushion hissed.

Two sailors chatted in front of the control console, unaware that she was on the other side.

"Hey, man, got any weed?" Nasal voice. Teenager.

"Nah." Deeper, but also a teenager. "My stash is tight. Double Ziplocs."

"Why? You always have some." Nasal whining. "C'mon, give."

"Shut up, dummy. You seen that hot broad in khakis?"

"Yeah. I could jump on that!"

"You stupid shit, she's NIS."

"Bullshit. Ain't no woman agents."

"Next time you see her, you look at what's ON her tits. A big-ass badge, man."

"So, she could get us?"

"That's what the NIS does, ain't it? If I was you, I stay off the stuff until they's no more fuzz around. And if you got some in your locker, you better double bag it.

Monroe says she's tight with the Italians, so she might bring one of them damn dogs. Remember Naples?"

"Shit, man. I gotta check my locker…"

Sandra heard the two men walk out and turn toward the forward berthing compartments. Only when she was sure she was alone, did she lean over and laugh till she cried.

After climbing to the sea cabin, she used the john, then went down to the wardroom. After lunch, she and Joe climbed to the bridge together. He coughed, then cleared phlegm into his handkerchief. It was black.

"Are you okay? That looks terrible."

"Strange. I don't feel anything." He coughed again. "Here we are." He held the door for her.

Sandra found a corner where she was not in the way and settled in to watch.

Everyone was in khakis or dungarees. No dressing up for this sea detail. Joe walked around, checking repeaters, chatting with the sea detail personnel as they arrived.

At 13:45, Dale Garson came to the bridge from CIC. He went to the intercom box and called the fantail. "Quarterdeck, bridge. This is the XO. Set the Sea Detail."

Sandra felt spikes through her skull as the boatswain's pipe squealed into the public address system. "Now set the Special Sea Detail. Do not man the rails. Set the Special Sea Detail!"

She took her hands away from her ears and let the ringing subside.

"Sorry, Agent Bari," said Joe. "I should have warned you."

"It means I fit in, so thanks."

Lieutenant Commander Burton stepped through the door on the port side.

"Captain on the bridge!" shouted the quartermaster.

"Carry on!" The skipper hoisted himself into the chair, which allowed him to see in all directions and out the windows. He noticed Sandra in the corner. "This gets me out of the way." He smiled.

In five minutes, the bridge was fully manned with men on sound-powered phones, others at the status board, the quartermaster and his navigation team assembled around their charts.

Buck Greenwald had been the OOD on the quarterdeck. He introduced the pilot to the CO, who slid down from his chair and shook the pilot's hand, then dismissed Buck to go to his line handlers on the main deck.

"XO, Mister Lockhart." He beckoned them to the starboard doorway. Sandra was in that corner. "This is exceptional, but I want you to take the conn, Joe. XO, you take the deck. Joe here can work faster with the pilot than either of us and he handles the ship better. Any questions?"

"Let's do it, skipper," said the XO.

"No questions, sir."

"Carry on, then."

"Attention on the bridge! This is Lieutenant Garson. I have the deck!"

"This is Ensign Lockhart. I have the conn!"

"Aye, aye, sir!" Sandra started at the sound of a dozen men shouting at once. Then she noticed the grins on some of them. *They like Joe,* she thought.

Joe and the pilot discussed the operation and agreed on when the tug would apply pressure to the starboard quarter (*Right side, near the stern,* Sandra remembered).

"Ready, Captain?" Joe asked the pilot.

"Yes."

Joe moved to the port bridge wing. The pilot stayed by the damaged side.

"Fantail, bring in the lines!" The phone operator relayed the order.

Just as Joe waved at the pilot, Sandra heard the phone talker report, "ship clear of the pier" and the pilot call the tug to hold the starboard quarter.

The pilot waved to Joe with his free hand.

"Hoist anchor!" Sandra heard the sailor relay that order, then the rhythmic clanking of the heavy chain slinking into the hawsepipe by the bow. For the longest time, she could not see anything happening.

Then the phone talker reported, "Anchors aweigh!"

The XO pointed at the boatswain's mate. This time, she plugged her ears. A loud whistle preceded the announcement, "Underway! Shift colors!"

Joe crossed the bridge and joined the pilot.

"Hard a starboard. Starboard engine back one-third. Port engine ahead one-third." The two sailors in the center of the bridge repeated the orders and moved the steering wheel and engine order telegraph levers into position.

Sandra had just noticed the empty jackstaff on the bow begin to swing when Joe shouted "Starboard engine stop! Steer one eight zero!" Again, the helmsman and the engine telegraph operator repeated the orders and moved levers. Meanwhile, the pilot was ordering the tug to stop and follow alongside. Then Joe ordered the starboard engine ahead one-third.

And so it went. The pilot spoke quietly to Joe. She had been told that pilots conned the ship directly, but these two seemed to confer instead. Joe gave orders well before anything happened, but the timing was perfect. Four thousand tons of steel ship floated with the grace of a swan. With the lag between commands, it felt as if the ship were moving on her own. *No wonder sailors think their ships are alive.*

Forty-five minutes later, *Barry* had made a graceful U from one basin to the next, spun around in place and let the tug push her sideways to the pier. Six mooring lines went over together. The whistle blew and the colors shifted.

Reports came through the intercom and sound-powered phones as CIC and other stations stood down.

A team of men pulled a rolling gangplank to the side of the ship. The quarterdeck reported to the bridge on the intercom.

The XO pointed at the boatswain's mate. Sandra held her hands to her ears in time for the piercing boatswain's call.

"Now secure the Special Sea Detail. Set the watch. On deck Section Two."

Barry was in her new home.

ଓଓଓ

The sun set behind threatening clouds as Sandra changed in the sea cabin. The skipper asked her to join them for dinner because message traffic was coming in rapidly, as commands all the way to the White House responded to the bombing in Genoa. She had intended to go ashore instead, but after changing, she saw reporters and TV cameras deployed outside the gates, and journalists from different national networks pressing against a police cordon.

The Sixth Fleet public information officer, Lieutenant Commander Masters, came aboard as soon as the ship moored. The captain gave him the chief engineer's stateroom. The acting captain and the acting XO had moved into the staterooms of the two dead officers.

After interviewing the skipper, Sandra, and Joe, the PIO held a press conference at the gate, which was broadcast on AFN, the American Armed Forces radio network, and TV networks in Europe and North America. He was a Hollywood-handsome specialist with a sharp mind and the ability to field questions off the cuff with the appearance of careful research. The officers in the wardroom watched the *Telegiornale* coverage from Italian state television, with help from Joe and Sandra. After the press conference, he returned to the ship.

Masters spent a half hour alone with Michael Burton in the captain's cabin. Then he went up to CIC, where he called COMSIXTHFLT on the secure phone from the radio room. No one was allowed to listen to that call.

Sandra walked back to her room about ten p.m., slipping past the journalists outside the gate. The press mobbed anyone who they thought might be an American officer or sailor. Joe stayed aboard.

The next morning, Sandra accompanied Morissetti to meet the NIS agent flying in from Naples. The Carabinieri car met her at nine, and they rode to the airport at the edge of the port area. A light rain had cleaned the street and piers and washed away most of the evidence.

Special Agent Xavier Palumbo paused at the top of the ladder from the aircraft and spotted Sandra and the

Carabiniere captain immediately. Palumbo's grandfather had immigrated from Sicily, but his mother was Norwegian. He took after his mother. He carried a small suitcase and wore a trench coat against the rain.

The two agents and the Carabiniere introduced themselves, ignoring the gawking passengers who watched them board the navy-blue police cruiser and vanish toward the port area.

Sandra gave him a summary of events since he had left the flagship. Mortimer Winslow and Mark Pietrowicz were waiting at *Barry*.

"Marty MacKenzie told me about you," Palumbo said. "Didn't you work for Pietrowicz?"

"No. I worked for Jim Redwood, the liaison officer before him. But I did work with Agent Pietrowicz on the art recovery two years ago."

"Will you be staying here?"

"My understanding was that you would take over and I would return to New York, but I won't leave until you are satisfied."

"Fair enough. Here we are, I take it."

The skipper, the two American agents, Joe and the XO were waiting to greet the NIS agent. Morgan took Palumbo's suitcase to the captain's sea cabin, which would become the NIS agent's office and home.

Joe's cough was worse, but she could only cast a worried glance at him as the investigators gathered with the ship's officers around the wardroom table.

She and Morissetti led the turnover briefing, folding the findings of the Italian and American investigations together. Sandra went through her notes and drawings in detail.

The rain stopped just before lunch. She gave Xavier a tour of the scenes. Xavier made some secure phone calls while she went to the wardroom. Joe was there, waiting with the others. He insisted that he felt fine, but the coughing was inconvenient.

"Plenty of expectoration," he said. "My mother taught me that clearing the lungs is what a cough should do."

"Okay but promise me you'll get the corpsman to have you checked if it doesn't ease up."

"Promise."

Xavier came down from the radio room.

"Do you have your kit with you?" he asked Sandra.

"Yes. I expected to be flying to Milano or Rome after we finished."

"Slight detour, but you'll get back almost as fast. A C-130 will pick you up at fifteen hundred at the airport. Brief the NIS agent at Rota, so he can take the case over later. Catch the red-eye charter flight to McGuire. You'll be in the office in time to fall asleep at your desk."

"Who set that up?"

"Marty. Apparently, your teammates in New York are desperate to have you back. Something about things coming together."

"Let's make more copies of my notes and drawings."

Three hours later, Sandra met with the NIS agent in the terminal at the US Naval Station Rota, Spain. Buddy Weschler was cheerful despite the obvious pain his broken leg still gave him. The fracture was such that he still needed a wheelchair to get around. He would shift to crutches in a few weeks.

It took an hour to bring Buddy up to speed. As the sun set, the TWA Boeing 707 lifted off, taking Special Agent Alessandra Bari back to the FBI.

CHAPTER 21

THINGS GET BETTER AND WORSE

THOUGH SHE GREW UP with lake effect snows, Sandra hated the white stuff. In the flat farmland of Madison County, Ohio, she had never learned skiing, snowboarding, or other winter sports. However, the harsh winters had given her extra time from farm chores, time that she had devoted to her art, her music, and her studies.

Looking out the window at McGuire Air Force Base, she called the FBI Field Office.

"David went out to get you himself," said Charlene. "Something about helping you get through customs."

"You may get a call soon. The MP's have me at the base police station because they did not expect an armed agent on this flight. I hope he can find me, but I'm fine for now. They're all being very nice about it."

"Sorry about that. Next time, I'll give you some paperwork to carry in case you are detoured again."

"Thanks, Charlene."

"McGuire base police station. I'll tell him if he calls."

An hour later, David pushed through the door of the station and identified himself to the desk sergeant. Sandra came from the office in the back, claimed her sidearm and backpack, and thanked the air policemen for their hospitality.

"Terribly sorry about this," David said as he maneuvered the Ford Vic through the slush onto the street.

"Could be worse. They spoke English; the coffee was fresh; and lots of handsome policemen in their snug blue uniforms to keep me company." She smirked at him. "I wonder if anyone was out on patrol."

He frowned. "This has happened before. I should have thought of it before you left Madrid."

"Charlene said she'd make sure I have the right forms next time."

The traffic into Manhattan kept the highway clear of snow, but then, the crush of the cars themselves slowed everything down.

"Marty said you were desperate without your naval support. You could have called for a destroyer from Newport."

He grinned to acknowledge the joke. "The Interpol case is coming together quickly. We may have a joint operation scheduled and planned by Christmas, to be carried out early in the new year."

" Considering how many subjects are in the USA, that's a lot of work for us."

"Speaking of destroyers from Newport, Wes and Jack were very excited about the samples their man in Rome sent them."

"Same lot?"

"Yes. We should hear soon about how that helps if it does."

"Are we going to the office?"

"Yes. After you're up to speed, you can go home to get organized and sleep off your jet lag. I just don't want to lose a day for orientation."

"I'm out of the Brooklyn then?"

"No. We'll keep it up at least until we are ready to strike. Your status may not be secret, but the SAC and I still prefer you as a conservator at the Brooklyn for now. We have swept three new bugs and caught four trespassers in the last two weeks."

"Let me call Mel from the office."

⅒⅒⅒

Wes Morton called the next day. David phoned Sandra at the Brooklyn, and she went to the Hudson Valley Field Office after lunch. Jack and Wes stood when she walked in.

"My favorite FBI agent!" said Jack as he shook her hand. Sandra rolled her eyes but smiled.

"David said we couldn't handle this on the phone, but I didn't know it would take two hours to get here."

"Oops. We're so used to using our cars that we forget you city dwellers don't."

Wes said, "I'll drive you back on my way to the courthouse."

"So, David told me the lot numbers from the bombing in Italy matched. What's new?"

"The amount that should have been in those two bombs completed the inventory of known reports from Impi. It also allowed us to account for all the material in the sales records that were lost."

"That's great! What now?"

"As for your Navy case, we have narrowed down the explosive to a pair of training devices that Impi sent to Algeria two years ago. The export licenses were in order, but I guess they didn't use them for training."

"Perhaps they did," said Sandra. "They detonated the devices too early. We were lucky there. What about Ohio?"

"Tracing to a specific person or group will take a while, but now that we have accounted for the whole lot sold that year, we can work our way through the retail sales. We may solve some cases we haven't even heard of yet."

"It was a long shot that it was Impi, wasn't it?"

"They did buy most of it. We'll eliminate the others first. It will keep Braxton from worrying about us."

"If we bring him in on the swapped art, we'll distract him even more."

"Let's stay in touch. I'll let you, Columbus and the Navy know how we're doing. Columbus may need to time their arrests with you."

"Let's. Anything else for us?"

"Yes. Merry Christmas, from our office to yours."

"Thanks, Jack. Happy New Year to you all."

"Let's go," said Wes.

An hour later, Sandra briefed the SAC and the others.

ВВВ

Joe reached the top of the ladder barely in time for a heavy attack of coughing. His head spun as he spit the black mass into the stained cleaning rag he carried instead of a handkerchief now.

"That sounds like hell," said Buck, coming down the passageway past the hatch to Bravo One.

"It sounds worse than it is. No fever or anything, and I keep expecting it to clear at some point, with all this stuff I'm coughing up."

"Well, you don't run up and down as fast as you used to, in my humble opinion. You should see the corpsman again."

"You're probably right. The skipper called. He wants to meet me on the bridge." Joe coughed again, just a little. He held the phlegm until he was at the foot of the first ladder to the bridge, away from the first lieutenant. Then he cleared it into the rag and ran up the three ladders.

He hurried onto the bridge. The captain was in his chair. The XO next to him, with the Fincantieri project manager.

"Captain, you called…"

It must have been a dream because he could feel himself waking up. A bright light pressed on his eyelids, so he did not open his eyes. He twisted his head and opened the eye closest to the mattress.

"*È sveglio, dottore!*" He's awake, Doctor.

A shadow blocked the overhead neon lamp. Joe turned back. A man with a black mustache and brown eyes, and salt-and-pepper hair, wearing a lab coat, leaned over the bed.

"Mister Lockhart, good to have you back." Italian accent.

"*Dove sono?*" Where am I?

"I thought you were American, sorry. In the Villa Scassi Hospital. The ambulance brought you from the American destroyer."

"I am American. What happened?"

"The short answer is you fainted. However, you did not wake up quickly, so they called an ambulance. So far, we have only determined that you have a serious pulmonary insufficiency. We are still testing to find out why. It is similar to pneumonia, but you lack the other symptoms."

"The black phlegm?"

"It is probably related. We'll know more later."

"How long was I out?"

The doctor looked at his watch. "About two hours. How do you feel now?"

"Fine, really. I don't even feel a cough coming on."

"We gave you an intravenous cough suppressant, but your lungs may fill up while it works. We won't release you until we can take X-rays to check you under various conditions."

"Is anyone else having these symptoms?"

"Now that you mention it, yes. Four sailors from your ship. Two are here, the other two we sent back."

"Could I know who they are? This could be related to the explosion if they were on the bridge with me."

"Thanks for the idea. We'll find out and let you know. We may need surveillance on the two we released."

The next day, he was taken to the X-ray room for a full set of lung scans. Then the team had him on a treadmill, measuring his air volume and oxygen intake. Six hours later, they did it again.

Joe could walk and move normally, and, except for the cough, he felt fine – until he had to climb or run quickly.

"Mr. Lockhart," said the doctor, "I'm afraid your lungs are only about twenty-five percent efficient. If you keep working above that, you could have a myocardial infarction, even at your age."

"*Un infarto?*" A heart attack?

"Yes. We will recommend that the Navy send you to the hospital in Naples. Whatever this is, it will take a long time to figure it out and then to recover. You can't work in this condition."

"What about the other four men?"

"The same. They are all back, and one of them had a heart attack on the way here."

❦❦❦

New Yorkers shuffled through two blizzards in December. Only a city with a well-developed subway system could have kept moving. Most of the country between Boston and Washington was stuck.

As the advertising increased and office party invitations arrived, Sandra found herself missing Joe terribly. Last year, she went to Richmond for the holiday. Being with him and the Ardwoods helped her deal with the depression that might have crushed her after losing her family the summer before. Nancy had invited her again. Joe would not be home until May.

Not that she could sit around moping. Mel kept her busy working on the six paintings from the MFAA, and the field office received packs of high-quality photographs every week. After Madrid, almost everyone involved in the Interpol case wanted her opinion. Then there were the usual tedious tasks: following subjects to verify that they lived and worked where they were supposed to, cross-checking files, records – even card catalogs and phone books in the New York Public Library.

David had not had time to come to the Brooklyn to look at the MFAA portrait "attributed to G.V.," and his mother said that his aunt took the sketch when she moved to Houston. The Army located the file from the accession number Sandra gave them, which led to a major discovery. The pictures in Fort Leavenworth were not identified as art stolen from Jewish families. They were in a cache in northern Italy, apparently plundered by Nazi officers from Christian homes. Cities known to have been carefully "sacked" included Arezzo, Pisa, Florence, Lucca, and Parma.

"Have you figured out what you want to do about the holiday?" David asked about the middle of the month. Sandra was packing up for the day.

"Go to Italy. Joe will still be in Genova."

"Get your request in. The task force wants to hold a meeting of stateside agents on the fifth of January. You should be here for it."

"Okay. First thing tomorrow."

The wind picked up as she trudged up Washington Avenue from the subway station. She blew out a breath of relief as she closed the outside door on the growing storm. She swung past the mailboxes to the stairs, then stopped and went back. She almost never got mail except from Joe, and his latest letter had come just yesterday.

It was a letter from Joe, but from a different Fleet Post Office number than the ship. She carried it up to her apartment. Inside, she sat in the armchair in her living room and slit open the envelope.

US Naval Hospital Naples
FPO, NY 09618
Carissima —
You were right to be worried about that cough. I'm in the extended care ward at the Naval Hospital in Agnano. I passed out running up to the bridge the other day and ended up in the hospital in Genova.

Although I feel fine, I have severely limited lung capacity. I'm still coughing up that black stuff.

The four men on the bridge with me have the same condition, so we're sure it's related to the explosive from the bombs. One of them had a heart attack, and all four are worse off than I.

The medical people have me here until they can see if it's getting better and also to determine what to do. I'll be here at least through the holidays. If they can't figure something out by then, the doctors say they will recommend repatriation and ordering in a new MPA.

There is a phone in our room. +39-0771-628-6868. AUTOVON 225-6868 (if you can use that).

I don't know what's happening back at the ship, but I guess that's not my problem anymore.

The doctors here say that I can go out. "Walk, don't run" is the rule. It's sudden exertion that my lungs can't support right now. I plan to walk a lot. The base library is just down the hill from here. It's not as big as the USIS Library in Rome, but I intend to read everything they have.

Of course, what I'd rather do is stay in bed, preferably with you…

I hope you're keeping busy and doing well. I miss you.

Ti amo e ti voglio bene.

Joe

Sandra stood, then sat, then paced. The wind lashed the dark windows outside. She wanted to race to an airline office to book a flight to Naples. She wanted to cry and run and fight at the same time. Everything was closed, and she had heard the evening red-eye flights take off from JFK Airport.

Fixing supper would postpone any need to react to something over which she had no control. She thought about it as she chopped lettuce and vegetables for a salad. She put two small potatoes on to boil and a steak in the pan.

What bothered her most, she realized, was not being able to do anything. Above all, she hated not having control, whether by fate (this) or at the hands of others (men, mostly). She sighed as she poured a glass of Montepulciano d'Abruzzo and set it on the kitchen table. She could do nothing until tomorrow. At least she knew where she would spend Christmas.

After she turned off the heat on the food, the phone rang.

"Hello, Sandra, it's Marty."

"About Joe?"

"Yes. Xavier told me Joe was in Naples."

"I just got his letter."

"Is there anything I can do?"

"If I have trouble getting a flight reservation, can you help?"

"As an NIS agent, you can board any military aircraft going anywhere, but orders would give you a higher priority. See what you can do. I'll call Walt Brennan in Naples. He's back from emergency leave now. You should check in with him anyway when you get there.

"By the way, Xavier said you did a great job setting up the crime scene and smoothing the relations with the Italians. Well done."

"Thanks, Marty. I enjoyed being NIS for a while, you know."

"We'll have more of that for you. Merry Christmas to you and Joe."

"Same to you. Bye."

ℜℜℜ

Joe came out of the base library and blinked. It had been raining two hours earlier when he walked in.

"Need help carrying those, sailor?"

He whirled about. "Sandra!" Reaching around his load, they embraced as best they could. "Why didn't you tell me?"

"My leave was approved just yesterday and then I had to rush to the airport to catch the only plane with a free seat going to Rome." She took the books from him. "They told me that you had gone for a walk, and where you probably would go."

"Do you have a place to stay?"

"Yes. That pensione across the street."

"It's Christmas Eve. Everything will be closed until Monday."

"I know. I didn't come to shop or see the sights but let me rent a car so we can go somewhere while all the public transit is stopped."

"It's right over there in the Navy Exchange compound."

An hour later, she parked outside the hospital, a horseshoe-shaped white building on the side of the

Solfatara volcano. From the parking lot, she looked down on the neighborhood that comprised the US Navy's "base" in Naples. Physically, it was a civilian neighborhood, mostly leased apartment buildings and industrial property, used to house the services that supported the Sixth Fleet. Forrest Sherman High School stood out because it could have been a brick school anywhere in the Midwest.

The sulfurous smell from the volcano overlooking the base abated when the wind was not from the north. Today it was from the southwest, blowing off the Gulf of Naples.

From the hospital room, Sandra called Walt Brennan to let him know she was in town. The doctors ran Joe through another battery of tests and told him that he could ride in a car in addition to walking.

"Just don't go to Capri or Ischia. We want you to get back quickly if anything happens."

She drove him to the Vigil service at Christ Church downtown. They shared Christmas dinner with the Brennan family on the Posillipo promontory where many foreign families lived. They toured the cameo factories south of the city. Joe bought her a necklace. Each afternoon, she parked at the pensione, where they enjoyed some time alone before she walked back to the hospital with him.

Monday after Christmas, she went to the travel agency in the Navy Exchange compound to collect her return ticket.

"I'm sorry, Miss Bari, but the airline overbooked the flight. Unless enough passengers back out, I can only give you a standby ticket."

"Not much chance of getting on the plane, is there?"

"Please check every day. As soon as I issue your ticket, you'll be locked in."

The attending physician absolutely forbade going into town on New Year's Eve. "Any pulmonary irritation from fireworks could be deadly, Mister Lockhart." They could hardly argue, seeing how he coughed more when the north wind blew Solfatara's fumes over the hospital.

Hanging over their heads was the unspoken reality that they did not know how much time they would have together going forward. Joe's condition seemed stubbornly static. The four sailors were bedridden. Another had a heart attack walking to the bathroom, so two of them were under special surveillance.

"Why am I not worse?" he asked one day after the treadmill test.

"My opinion?" said the doctor. "Smoking. Their lungs were compromised before the black gunk gummed them up. Your fitness meant you were not drawing in air as deeply as they were for the same amount of work.

"Whether that means you can clear the air sacs in your lungs remains to be seen."

Joe and Sandra discussed that when they were alone. They both clung to the hope that he would recover, however long it might take.

Every day, she checked with the travel agency in the Navy Exchange compound. On Thursday morning, she met Walt Brennan and his wife coming out of the commissary with a shopping cart. She helped them load groceries into their car.

"Any luck?"

"No, sir. And she says that this late, it won't change."

"There's a flight to McGuire on Saturday, your last chance to get back to New York by Monday. Let's cut courier orders for you. That will get you a seat."

"Thanks. I can turn in the car at the NAF at Capodichino." Naval Air Facility.

"Come to my office Saturday morning for your orders. Stop at the courier station at NAF to pick up a packet of classified papers to deliver to the courier service at McGuire."

The next two mornings, Sandra and Joe walked along the Riviera di Chiaia. The mile-long promenade by the waterfront downtown resembled an amusement park with an open-air Christmas market. Couples and families of all sizes and ages mingled, shopped, and ate.

They spent the afternoons in Sandra's room. Much of the time, they stared at the sunlight on the wall, then on the ceiling, holding each other, sharing the silence....

CHAPTER 22

MANHATTAN

IN HIS MANSION ON THE HUDSON, Sandro Santis paced in the living room. His guest sat in Sandro's favorite armchair by the fireplace, swirling the Scotch around in his glass. The white wonderland on the cliffs leading down to the river did not impress either man.

"Trent, how could this have failed so spectacularly?"

"Relying on humans in a high stress situation calls for highly trained humans or stupid machinery that won't overthink the problem. I suggested a proximity detonation device."

"True, but now we have more publicity, and the ship is still there, taunting us."

"Don't be so personal, Sandro. The ship isn't taunting anyone, and no one knows who ordered or set the explosion."

"Won't the police be able to find out? They can trace bullets. Why not bombs?"

"You should worry about what you're good at: making money."

"But—"

"No buts. If you want the job done right, retain me to do it. The investigators will never figure out what happened at the farm in Ohio. But don't try to buy pieces and do it yourselves on the cheap. You're a financial whiz; Ettore is a politician. I like you both. Learn from your mistake and move on."

"I thought your people made those devices."

"I told Arcibaldo who had them, but I also emphasized what he needed to pull off an attack on a warship. Sixth Fleet ships aren't crewed by amateurs. They're trained to take on the Soviet Navy. And Sandro –" He stood and fixed his gaze on the investment manager.

"Yes?"

"Don't you ever think or say, even in your dreams, that I or my people had anything to do with those bombs. Am I clear?"

Sandro swallowed whatever he was going to say and nodded slowly.

"Good. Thanks for the drink."

Trent let himself out.

ଧ୧୧

David met Sandra at McGuire Air Force Base, this time at the passenger terminal. The Air Force courier station was in the terminal. She delivered the package, and they drove to Brooklyn.

They rode in silence. She was grateful he did not quiz her about Joe. She had dozed fitfully on the flight. Now she felt crushed by a sense that the happiness she and Joe had hoped to share might never come to pass. She stared at the cars ahead as the tears slid down her cheeks, matching the cold rain on the car windows.

Traffic backed up on the Verrazzano Narrows Bridge.

She glanced at David, and her grief stopped dead. Anger, sadness, and resignation flowed over his face like the shadows of a tree on a windy day.

"What's wrong?"

"Everything. Nothing. Something."

"What happened while I was gone?"

He sighed and his face cleared. "Nothing to report here. The case is coming together very quickly and no snags yet. But I am angry, impatient, and helpless.

"You, and by extension Joe, are the two people not in my family that I care most about in this world. What happened to you, in Ohio and in Italy, makes me furious."

"They may not be related."

"This has Impi stamped all over it. Braxton and his friends."

"That doesn't sound very professional, David."

"No, it doesn't. But investigators are people too. Being dispassionate is not easy sometimes. And this is the hardest challenge I have ever faced."

"Why? You've been an agent for, what, thirteen years or more? And Security Battalion before."

He smiled at her, and his eyes had a gentle depth.

"With all that training and experience, I can't help you and Joe. I'm not in Columbus, I'm not ATF, I'm not in Rome working with the Carabinieri." He slammed his hand on the steering wheel. "I want to be tracing explosives records, staking out factories in West Texas, or trailing Braxton. Instead, I'm collecting forged Renaissance art."

Sandra considered the angry, frustrated man near her. *But the art...* she thought.

"David?"

"What?" He started at his own brusqueness and

followed the bark with a blink. "Sorry. Yes?"

"The art is what connects them, isn't it?"

He thought about that as the brake lights went off ahead. They inched over the top of the bridge and stopped again, pointing down at Brooklyn.

"Yes, it is. But it's a long way from paying a fine and losing some pictures to blowing up an innocent family and bombing a ship of your own Navy."

"And yet, these men are into the bombings through the art. It's what connects them all to General Arcibaldo."

"Let me follow you. Arcibaldo wanted revenge last year. He knew the four investors and Braxton. When the general needed a job done, he would reach out to Braxton, wouldn't he?"

"It would have been a business deal for Impi. It must have cost a fortune. Arcibaldo couldn't have hired the hit in Ohio."

"But Arcibaldo wasn't the only one threatened by our secret weapon, was he?" He glanced at her. "The others could have put up the money to hire Braxton."

"And Braxton has art to hide too. He might not have taken the job otherwise."

"So why target the ship? Just because Joe was on it?"

"There is a lot of anti-American sentiment floating around. Perhaps the people who tried to sink the ship turned to a source we don't even know and obtained bombs that were supposed to be in Algeria."

"Is that coincidence creeping in, Sandra?"

She backed up on her thought and considered how Arcibaldo used his enemies.

"Yes. But it would not be a coincidence for the general to blow up a ship just to get close to Joe. Look at how elaborate the campaign against Nancy was."

"Jesus, what did Joe do to attract that level of hatred?"

"I can't tell you, David, but believe me, it was big, very big."

ᚱᚱᚱ

They finally reached the end of the bridge. David took the first exit, driving along Fort Hamilton Parkway to Parkside and Washington Avenue. Outside Sandra's apartment building, they sat in the car for a while.

"Will you be okay?"

"Yes, thanks. I'm still processing everything that has happened." She got out and took her suitcase and backpack from the back seat.

"Thank you, David. See you Monday."

"Call me if you need anything. *Arrivederci a lunedì.*"

He put the car in gear and fed into traffic. Sandra let herself in.

In the apartment, she set a kettle on the stove and carried her luggage to her room. She no longer had tears to cry, so she sat at the kitchen table with her hot tea and stared at the photo of Rome that Joe had given her.

She wanted to kill someone. She wanted to break something. She wanted her mother. She wanted her – father.

She stood and realized how stiff she was from sitting for twenty-four hours. She picked up the phone by the front door and dialed.

"Luke, I know the court's wet, but would you mind knocking a few tennis balls around? I need to get things out of my system."

Two sets later, they had ruined six balls and the sun had set. They walked to the Italian restaurant nearby, where they usually ate lunch.

"Thanks. I needed that."

"I could tell."

Over *bucatini all'arrabbiata*, Sandra took him through her time in Naples and Joe's condition.

"So, he might be discharged?"

"It's too early to tell. Some of the doctors want to do that, but his attending physician seems impressed that he is not getting worse, while the other four sailors are in intensive care."

"How will they figure it out?"

"Right now, they're putting him on a treadmill twice a day, taking measurements and X-rays and hoping he starts clearing his lungs."

"It could take a long time."

"Yes. Longer than the Navy wants to wait, I'm afraid."

"How is he taking it?"

"Better than I am. He said that he enjoys being a translator, and he can type with only a quarter of his lungs working."

"I know how much he wanted to go to sea – and how he loves tennis."

"That's why I'm so tormented. I can't get over how much this could cost him."

"Cost him or cost you?"

Sandra looked up sharply and lowered her bucatini to the plate. His eyes seemed kind, which contrasted with the shock of what he said.

"What do you mean?"

"Is he beating himself up about this?"

"He seemed sad, sort of wistful when we were sitting in silence together, but no, I wouldn't say he's beating himself up."

"Then why are you beating yourself up?"

"But—" She sat back and considered what he had said. "It's not about me."

"It *is* about you. But is it about your expectations or your fears?"

She thought, *fears for what?*

"I would care for him."

"Are you expecting to do that? Does he seem to need it?"

She felt comforted by his steady, deep gaze. It made her clamp down on whatever she was going to say about Joe needing a caretaker.

"No, he doesn't. He has already mapped out what he can do if the Navy lets him go."

"So, why are you beating yourself up?" He smiled over his glass and took a sip.

"Thank you, Luke. I needed that too."

"Anytime."

He drove her back to her apartment. At seven thirty, she crawled into bed and slept until noon Sunday.

ଧଧଧ

Monday morning, Sandra went straight to the Federal Building. She would be full-time at the FBI this week. The agents reviewed all the material they had on the art-swapping case, both in the USA and abroad. Charlene and Sandra helped David review the paper slides of the presentation for the meeting on Tuesday. In the afternoon, Charlene created transparencies from the pages, while Sandra double-checked the reservations at the Reade Hotel and other details that agents had requested.

Meanwhile, Frank, Charley, and Mack drove to La Guardia and JFK airports. Dario went with the SAC to Penn Station.

Agents from almost every city with an art-collecting millionaire were expected: Seattle, San Francisco, Los Angeles (representing the offices in southern California), Albuquerque (for the Southwest), Omaha, Chicago, Houston, Dallas, Columbus (also for Cincinnati and Springfield), Atlanta, Miami, Philadelphia, Richmond, Boston, and Washington, DC.

"That's all of them," Sandra said, hanging up the phone. She and David were alone in the office.

"I've done all I can for tomorrow. How about you?"

"I'm not the one with a presentation, and I've studied everything I can about the paintings and the collectors. Anything else?"

"Yes. Some of that detail magic of yours before and while our visitors arrive. Let's go to the Reade."

"What do you need me to do?"

"Check out the lobby, and some street-facing rooms above it. Pick the one with the best view. Frank should be there about three with the first guests.

"Watch the street and tell me if anyone seems to be staking out the entrance."

"Rocks in the stream?"

"Exactly. Tomorrow, I want you to do the same thing above the entrance to this building. The Treasury Department on the second floor will let you use the Secret Service office. You can see the entire Federal Plaza."

Sandra went to her desk, checked and holstered her sidearm, stuffed a fresh sketchbook and a box of pencils into her backpack, and followed David out the door.

ଧଧଧ

Less than a mile away, Trent Braxton twiddled a No. 2 pencil in his hands as he looked across the street at the façade of the New York Stock Exchange. He seemed relaxed sitting in his large leather armchair, the desk on his left, the window to his right, ankles crossed on a small, padded stool.

Inside, he stormed. *This is more trouble than a couple of damn pictures are worth.* He had considered selling the two paintings from Madrid that he still had. Then he could cut off Santis, Bonin, and the rest of the artsy people. He had thought he was done with them, after he and Siegfried Kanter had lost one painting each, confiscated with bowing apologies by the investigators.

Then he got wind of another major Interpol investigation, also focused on art swapped on tour. That was all he could find out before the man he had planted in the FBI Field Office got himself busted over something unrelated to Braxton. He could not move the Tintoretto and the Titian until the operation ended, and no one was looking for his pictures.

He paid people good money to tell him what the FBI was doing. Special Agent in Charge Robert Worthman and his field office were not his only worry — or even his biggest concern. That honor belonged to Special Agent James Redwood and his Special Projects Office. The senior officer had created a Domestic Threat

Unit in Special Projects that, among other things, tracked companies such as Impi. From the ex-CIA men in his company, Braxton knew Redwood had learned more about the mercenary business while he was in Rome than any FBI agent should know.

When Santis introduced him to Arcibaldo, Braxton had sensed a kindred spirit, one who had been wronged by the Corps that each had devoted himself to: the Marines and the Carabinieri. The Italian Carabiniere would have been a worthy adversary had Major Braxton been sent to Italy instead of the Pacific in World War Two. Arcibaldo was an old-fashioned patriot, fiercely loyal to his king and his duce, yet smart enough to adapt to the messy politics of the postwar Italian Republic. That he had retired as the commander of the Carabinieri Corps spoke to his ability. Trent was not sure what happened to the Italian officer, but it had to be very serious.

A kindred feeling did not extend to Arcibaldo's three friends: Kanter, Bonin, and Santis. Only Kanter seemed to understand the ramifications of his actions, so when they arranged to buy a piece of art each to help out Arcibaldo, it was no surprise to Braxton that only the two Italians got arrested.

Tex Wilder had supported the general too, but as far as Trent could tell, his involvement had been strictly an investment that didn't work out. Impi's West Texas landlord collected Southwest American art.

The blue phone on his desk rang.

"Speak."

"I told you the entire office except Vasari emptied out after lunch."

"Well?"

"With only three men, I could not tail them all, so I staked out the Federal Building and the Reade Hotel."

"The field office has a contract with them."

"True. They all returned in two hours, escorting at least fifteen men who must be FBI agents. As soon as the film is developed, I'll let you know who."

"Meet me at my apartment with the photos."

"Yes, sir." They hung up.

Braxton swung his feet off the stool, stood and looked again at the building that had allowed him to buy two floors of a Wall Street skyscraper and three apartments at another Wall Street address. Within a four-block area, it would be impossible to find him if he wished not to be found.

"Taking it home, Mrs. Dempsey," he said to the woman at the desk outside his office. "You may switch to the answering service. I'll be back tomorrow."

"Yes, sir. Have a nice evening."

"Thanks. You too." He exchanged a smile with the woman who graced his public space. And who for ten years had been his secret weapon in two dozen countries.

ଷଷଷ

Sandra checked the spy hole before opening the door of the room over the portico of the Reade Hotel. It was David.

"Anything?"

"They weren't very subtle about it." She took out her sketchbook. "This man stayed out there the whole afternoon. He moved to a different store window every twenty minutes or so, but never left the block. He was taking pictures too. He tried to make it appear that he was photographing everything around, but he zeroed in on our visitors and their escorts."

"Have you seen him before?"

"No, but I have seen this one." She turned to the next sheet. "He came by twice and they talked while watching the hotel."

David looked at the picture. "One of the two outside headquarters back when I was coming to the Special Projects conference room. Jim will know who he is."

"About ten minutes ago, the stakeout made a call from that pay phone." She moved to the window and pointed to the corner. "Then he walked south on Broadway."

"Good work, Sandra. We'll get an ID on this guy. Whoever he reported to knows there's a meeting of FBI agents from across the country. They'll be outside the Federal Building tomorrow."

"Should I be early?"

"Early enough to pick out rocks in the stream. Our guests should walk over about nine."

"Do I check out or something?" She held up the key. He took it.

"I'll take care of it. Do you need to go back to the office?"

"Not unless you have something for me."

"Go home, then. Use the side entrance through the kitchen.

"Be careful out there."

☙☙☙

The next morning, Sandra was up before dawn, to allow time to exercise, shower, eat, and catch the subway to the Federal Building. She picked up fresh coffee on her way to the Secret Service office.

By nine thirty, she had counted all fifteen visitors. She watched the stakeout man call on the phone, then walk toward Lafayette Street. She packed up and rode to the twenty-third floor.

She paused after stepping off the elevator. David and the SAC were talking in the hallway. Beyond them, a janitor was pushing a long broom near them.

At nine thirty in the morning? She recognized the face under the beard. Slipping her backpack off her shoulder, she ran past the two agents. The janitor's eyes flashed in surprise for only a second, then narrowed as his training took over.

He brought up his broom as a spear. Sandra dodged ever so slightly and grabbed it as she felt it glance off her ribs and catch inside her jacket. He let go, but by then she had clasped his wrists and pulled him in for a fierce head-butt on the nose. Her momentum pushed them both over. As they fell, she wrapped her arms around his head. They crashed to the floor; her arms protecting his head, his body breaking her fall.

She hissed into his ear. "Move and I'll break your neck." They could see the two FBI agents standing close with their weapons drawn. "If they don't shoot you first."

Sandra lifted back on her knees and rolled the man on his stomach. She pulled the zip-tie cuffs from her jacket, tied his wrists, then stood. Pulling him to his feet, she stayed behind him and patted him down. A small pistol in his right pocket, a stiletto in the other. Using a handkerchief, she handed the weapons to the SAC.

"Let's see some ID," she said, flicking the badge on his chest pocket. "You don't look like Manny Rodriguez."

The man glared at them. David recognized him. "The other one."

Sandra said, "Agent Redwood will have his name."

David walked quickly to the conference room. The noise of the socializing echoed down the hall while the door was open.

He came out with Jim, pointed to the others, then went to Charlene's desk to call the Federal Protective Police downstairs. Redwood approached the "janitor" and the two agents.

"Look familiar, sir?" said Sandra.

"This is *very* interesting. George Montoya, who at least two years ago, worked for Impi."

"The police are on their way," said David.

Ten minutes later, the police took Montoya away and promised to keep him hidden until the FBI could deal with him. "We need to get the meeting started," Jim said.

Sandra picked up her backpack and went to the ladies' room. Charlene came in with a first aid kit. The bloody blouse was torn on the right side. The secretary confirmed that the skin was not broken. Sandra would have a glorious bruise. Her knuckles had torn on the floor, but the wounds had already clotted. Sandra washed her face and hands, while Charlene wiped as much of Montoya's nose blood off the jacket as she could. The blazer would hide the tear until Sandra could change.

Even so, Bob Worthman stopped his remarks when she walked in. Every head in the room turned.

"Gentlemen, this is Special Agent Alessandra Bari of the Naval Investigative Service. She has been seconded to this operation from the beginning. In case any of you still wonder why we have such tight security on it, she has just disabled the fifth trespasser in the last two weeks. She also spotted the stakeouts who photographed you arriving at the hotel yesterday and here today."

Dale Peters, sitting across the room, smiled and gave a little wave as Sandra took a seat near the door. She did not recognize the others, except the New York team.

By the time the visitors left on Wednesday, each FBI agent had a clear assignment in terms of art to be confiscated, where it should be, who to arrest on which charges, and the justification for the local warrants. One phone call would let them know the date of the coordinated move. They agreed that socializing outside the meeting would not be wise. Agents from the New York Field Office ensured everyone made their flight or their train out of town safely.

Montoya got out on bail, escorted by a lawyer no janitor could ever have afforded. The SAC knew the weapons charge and the trespassing would stick, but they would probably not get much else from him. NYPD was looking for Manny Rodriguez, who had not returned from his night shift Tuesday morning. Redwood had Special Projects trace where Montoya had been since staking out FBI headquarters two years earlier. Social Security showed that he was still employed by Impi, Inc. His Texas driver's license and his passport had been routinely renewed this year.

Over the first weekend of January, a series of classified message exchanges confirmed that the coordinated raid would take place at 16:00 hours London time on Wednesday the third of February. Agents would be knocking on doors at eight a.m. in San Francisco, eleven a.m. in New York, and five p.m. in Madrid, Paris, and Rome. All one hundred suspects were expected to be on site.

❦❦❦

Monday morning, Sandra walked with Maria to work at the museum. The streets were wet, and the dirty snow piled on the sidewalks was melting fast. Both women wore sunglasses. They stopped at their favorite pancake house on the way.

"So, how's Joe?"

"Not good, but better than the others on the bridge. He can't do anything close to exertion, not even stairs, but he's not getting worse."

"Did that cramp the holiday?" Her eyes sparkled mischievously.

"Not at all," Sandra said with a straight face. "Did you know you can't have a heart attack for at least forty-five minutes after laughing or sex?"

"So, you're what the doctor ordered."

"Guess so. How are your folks?" …

When they got to the museum, Maria went down to the X-ray room. Sandra picked up a mug of coffee and went into the conservation lab. Mel waved at her to come into his office.

"Did you see the *Post* this morning?"

"No, sir. I read the *New York Times* and *Wall Street Journal* at my other job."

He shoved the paper across his desk. The front page screamed, WONDER WOMAN THE FBI SECRET

AGENT? A photo of the Federal Building and a photo of Montoya trying to hide his face as he was ushered into a limousine. They had enlarged and cropped the picture to feature his bruised and broken nose. The article reported that a female agent took down an enforcer of the mob who had infiltrated the New York Field Office of the FBI. Disclaimers by the FBI in New York (photo of Bob Worthman) and Washington (photo of the head of Personnel) that the FBI did not have female agents. "No comment" about the alleged incident.

Well, so much for hiding any longer.

"You?" Mel asked.

"You know I couldn't say one way or the other, sir."

"True. I'll ask David." He pulled the paper back. "The director at the Frick called to ask you to do a workshop on paint swatch matching. He has some students from Columbia in the lab."

"I'm probably their age."

"But they haven't spent years in Rome or gone to the American Academy twice. He was very impressed the way you foiled the swap."

"I didn't—"

"Stop right there, Miss Bari, and don't go all modest on me. 'You' means the whole field office, but your report triggered the lab analysis that convinced the prosecution. Doctor Messer wants his students to meet you, and to learn about the low-tech methods you used in Rome."

"Well, okay, I guess."

"And because he is grateful, this isn't a freebie. The Frick Foundation will pay you a consultant fee for the three afternoons."

"Wait a minute. Won't this break some rule?"

"Only if we pay you too, but you won't clock on here. They could pay us, but this is cleaner."

"I'll still explain it to David in case there is a memo that I didn't get."

Back at her desk, Sandra reviewed the list of tasks she was expected to complete this week. She looked forward to a morning restoring beautiful artwork.

The phone rang. It was David.

"Don't come in this week."

"The article in the *New York Post*?"

"Yes. There are journalists and paparazzi staked out front."

"The raid is in three weeks."

"We're still figuring this out. Could you meet me near here in the afternoon?"

"Doctor Messer has asked me to do a three-day workshop with some Columbia students at the Frick. I was going to see him this morning, but I could do it later. Would that work?"

"Perfect. You let me know what time. Your favorite black sedan will be near the back door on Seventy-First Street. We can take the side entrance to the garage before they react. After you collect the stuff you were going to work on this week, I'll drive you home. One of us will come to the Brooklyn if we need to meet."

"Got it. I'll call you."

Sandra jotted down the steps she wanted to show the students, inventoried the ingredients she would need, and checked the stocks in the Brooklyn's lab. Then she phoned Doctor Messer and agreed to come there at two p.m. She called the Frick conservation lab to review what chemicals they had and which she would bring.

The morning mail included a fat envelope from the Army Military History Center at Fort McNair in DC, one of a dozen commands that Mel and Sandra had contacted concerning the MFAA paintings they were holding. The Center had no information on five of the pieces, but the one attributed to G.V. was linked to an Italian family in Arezzo. The SS major who had stolen it had written down the address, but the name of the family was illegible. Enclosed was a photocopy of what they had on file. Sandra smirked to herself. What the Army employee had called illegible was cursive handwriting from the days when people still dipped pens in inkwells. She could read it. She took out the Michelin map of Arezzo from the collection in her desk and noted the address.

After lunch, she took the subway to the Frick, which took just under an hour. At three p.m., she paused at the back gate of the Frick Estate, then walked quickly across the sidewalk and got into the black sedan waiting by a fire hydrant.

"Ciao, Davide," she said and continued in Italian. "Does the name Mastroianni on Via delle Paniere mean anything to you?"

"I don't recognize the name, but Nonna said they lived on Via delle Paniere. We have a photo of the family in front of the building, number six."

"You never came to see the painting we have from the Monuments Men, but you should check on that name before you do. The Army still doesn't know why the paintings ended up in Fort Leavenworth, but they were stolen from Christian Italian families as the Nazis moved north. The cache was near the Austrian border. The archivist I talked to said that many of the houses were empty; the people left either to join the partisans or to hide from the Germans."

"Now I'm excited. I'll call you as soon as I talk to Mom. It was Pop's family who emigrated. I hope he mentioned it."

He slowed long enough to check the street, then turned sharply into the garage. An hour later, Sandra alighted outside her apartment building with a large file box and went inside.

ℛℛℛ

Montoya's arraignment would not be for another month. Without sightings of a female agent, the paparazzi wandered off, and a trio of UFOs in New Mexico took over the front page of the *New York Post*. Sandra resumed her double commute the following Monday.

For the rest of January, the investigators studied the art they expected to find, the men they would arrest, and photos and maps of the target areas. They would split up: David to London, Charley to Cologne. Sandra would stay with the New York Field Office.

By the first of February, one could squeeze the excitement from the air with a rag. It would take most of the field office staff, NYPD officers, and Connecticut, New Jersey, New York State troopers to confront, arrest and bring in the collectors, their illegal art, and the middlemen involved. The agents had memorized what they needed to find, as much to be sure of finding it as not to confiscate something not part of the investigation.

Sandra was assigned to the Trent Braxton arrest. Knowing that the mercenary kept several addresses, Bob Worthman had arranged to surround his buildings and made an appointment to meet him. The SAC himself would make this raid with Sandra and two very large agents who had been Green Berets in the Army. Surveillance over two years had narrowed down the places the art could be: the apartment that he seemed to sleep in, and the building between there and his office.

Knowing what she did about Impi and its owner, she spent hours at night studying the weapons used by poor nations, organized crime, and dictators. She studied diagrams and photos of hundreds of devices and reviewed how to identify types of shaped-charge munitions by the damage they did. Impi built and sold powerful bombs that could be carried and handled easily by one man (against a tank or warehouse), a forklift (against a concrete wall), or a small truck (against a ship). Uncomfortable would be an understatement, but the effort trained her to work past the fear, grief, disgust, and intense, burning anger that would have consumed her a year ago.

ಿ ಿ ಿ

Wednesday dawned as it had all week: freezing, cloudy, but no precipitation. The northeast winds promised to keep the air below thirty degrees, but the breezes were brisk, not stormy.

Sandra turned on the coffee maker and went to her bedroom. She had no idea how much Trent Braxton knew about her, but she might come across Sandro Santis before the day was over.

She inserted the soft cylinders to alter the shape of her face. She used dark foundation to change her skin tone, applied mascara and lipstick. When she finished, she felt disoriented looking at the stranger in the mirror. She dressed in comfortable shoes, a new wool blazer, and gray trousers.

The coffee was ready. She pocketed her inserts, poured a cup, and assembled a breakfast of oatmeal with fruit and honey.

Before leaving the house, she checked her sidearm and inventoried her pockets: keys, plastic handcuffs, extra ammunition, latex and white cotton gloves, badge, credentials, handkerchief, and a Swiss Army officer's knife.

At eight thirty, she cased the area between the subway station and the Federal Building. No one seemed interested in her or the building.

The field office was a humming beehive. In addition to the agents, analysts and secretaries, there were police officers and detectives from the City and the neighboring states. The conference room had been set up as a command center, with status boards and batteries of telephones. Communications checks were squawking on a dozen radio circuits.

At the end of the table stood Jim Redwood, cradling a mug of coffee. He and Bob Worthman were talking and pointing to various displays. A rush of pleasure and reassurance rose in Sandra's chest.

"Special Agent Redwood, good to see you again!"

The SAC recognized her only after she spoke. "Agent Bari? You look different today. Are you okay?"

Jim grinned.

"I'm fine," she said. "Someone went through a lot of trouble to kill Sandra Billingsley. We need to make sure she stays dead."

"We should switch you."

"No, Bob," said Jim. "It's too late. She'll be fine." He took a clipboard from Charlene. "Good luck today, Sandra, and good hunting. Braxton has the only cache whose exact location is unknown."

"But we have the list, sir. He'll produce it."

She put in her earbud and turned away to check her communications with the Wall Street team. Her stomach twisted inside. She consoled herself that others may feel the same. Enough of them had told her that the anxiety never went away.

At ten thirty all units were one block away from their assigned targets. Around Wall Street, NYPD had erected barriers as if preparing for another demonstration. They even had permits taped to the fencing and phone poles.

The SAC and his team walked to the headquarters of Impi, Inc. Sandra paused in the lobby to study the display cases with various products Impi sold globally, then trailed the three agents into the spacious reception area outside Braxton's office. A large desk commanded the room with a single word on the nameplate, "Dempsey."

The most fearsome woman she had ever seen greeted them: tall, broad shoulders, slim figure, muscular arms, and big hands with long fingers. Late thirties or early forties. She was not just Black: she was African and reminded Sandra of the queens in Samara Majid's paintings. *This is no secretary.*

The other agents did not seem to notice. "Special Agent Worthman for Mr. Braxton," said the SAC.

"Of course." Clipped. Precise. In two words, Sandra pegged her for an Abyssinian. Joe had some high school classmates who talked that way.

Mrs. Dempsey stepped away from her desk, knocked and opened the door. "Your eleven o'clock, Mr. Braxton."

The men walked in. Sandra stopped at the door and held it open. The woman started to enter. Sandra put her arm across the door.

"Please stay here, ma'am," she said. Anger flashed briefly over Dempsey's face, but then she smiled and waited quietly. The two women watched the SAC present the warrants to search the four apartments listed and the premises of Impi, Inc.

Braxton glanced past the SAC at Dempsey, who gestured almost invisibly: a slight shrug and an arched eyebrow toward Sandra. With a gracious bow, he accepted the SAC's invitation to accompany them.

"Mrs. Dempsey, get Abe."

"Yes, Mr. Braxton."

It was all over in an hour. They recognized the Tintoretto in the second apartment, which had been furnished to show off the collection and to entertain. Sandra spotted the Titian in the next room and pointed out three other paintings from the list of missing art in the case files. Two in the apartment and one in the reception area of Braxton's office.

Having located the art in the warrants, there was no point in looking in the other apartments. The SAC arrested Braxton, and the four agents escorted him to a waiting cruiser. Dempsey appeared on the sidewalk with a balding man who had to be the lawyer. Sandra put herself in front of the pair, conscious of the way Dempsey seemed protective of her employer. The older woman nodded her understanding and turned to the man.

"Let's go to the courthouse." She walked with him to the garage of the building.

Outside the federal courthouse, Sandra helped the two ex-Green Berets push through a crowd of reporters.

As the flashes popped and journalists shouted questions, she was glad that she looked as little like herself as she did.

The New York state police were already there, escorting Sandro Santis into the building. She put her group between the Italian investor and herself. The team from Connecticut drove up as the SAC and Braxton went into the building.

With the twenty-five men and two women booked and waiting for their lawyers to arrange bail, the air seemed to go still.

"Nothing more to do here," said Worthman. "Go to the vault, Bari. Well done today."

"What did I do?"

"Probably the most important thing to disable Braxton. You fended off Dempsey. She couldn't help him. Thanks."

"You noticed she wasn't really a secretary?"

"I might not have, but Redwood warned me about her." He started for the door. "Stay at the Brooklyn tomorrow."

"Yes, sir."

Sandra walked across Thomas Paine Park to the Federal Building. By midnight, she and the other agents had inventoried the art in the vault, secured the room, and gone home.

Sandra had a nightmare about an incendiary bomb destroying the paintings. She fixed a mug of hot milk and went back to bed.

CHAPTER 23

PCS

IN EARLY FEBRUARY, Joe sat at the table under the window of his hospital room. Piles of dictionaries and books rose on either side of him. He typed on an ancient Underwood borrowed from the library. The corpsmen and nurses seemed to compete to carry things for him, and his doctors agreed that moving around and working was better than lying in bed.

Every day, he walked to the library and the Navy Exchange compound. He had promised to take the elevator, but in the past two weeks he had carefully climbed to his room. At first, the lack of air on the stairs scared him, but he learned to slow down until his lungs felt normal. Though the X-rays and oxygen testing showed no more lung capacity than before, he was getting stronger. *Something* was improving.

He heard a knock and turned around. His attending physician came in.

"Good morning, Mister Lockhart."

"Hello, Doctor Gersheim. Is it time for the treadmill again?"

"No. I came to chat – and to discuss your situation." Joe motioned to the chair. The physician sat. "Are you related to Nancy Lockhart of Smithson Global?"

"My mother."

"And former national tennis champion. You have great genes."

"Do you know my mother?"

"No, but I read a profile article on her in an academic journal, and I remembered your mentioning that you were from Richmond. Yesterday I was talking to my father, who retired from MCV." Medical College of Virginia. "He was her dissertation advisor."

"Small world, sir."

"And this may tie into your case. The medical board here wants to transfer you to a bigger hospital stateside. Better support, more specialists, and more room."

"PCS?" Permanent Change of Station.

"Yes. A new MPA has been ordered in, and your things, which are already boxed up, will be shipped."

"Where?"

"Bethesda. It's the biggest facility in the Navy, with the National Institutes of Health nearby. It's also not far from Richmond."

"My bicycle is in the number two forward forced draft blower chamber. It should be included. Can my stuff go to Richmond? Obviously I can get along without it." He waved at the cluttered table. "My family can bring me anything I need."

"Yes. Any other questions?"

"How soon? And how do I get back?"

"The board will issue its recommendation tomorrow. After they check on handicapped facilities between here and DC, they'll order you returned in a medevac status or commercial air."

"Handicapped?"

"Stairs, or long walks."

"Oh. Now that you mention it, I'm not using the elevator."

"I suspected as much." Gersheim smiled. "You don't have a poker face. Any problems?"

"It took a week to work up to it because I always slow down depending on what my lungs tell me."

"Good. Listen to your body."

"Always."

Monday, Joe flew to Andrews Air Force Base via McGuire AFB. A military shuttle bus took him to Bethesda. He called his family from his new hospital room overlooking the Maryland suburbs. After leaving a message on Sandra's answering machine, he slept for fifteen hours.

ଥଥଥ

Charlene called the conservation lab the morning after the arrests of Braxton, Santis, and the others.

"Stay there today."

"The SAC told me. Is everything okay?"

"Here, yes. You haven't seen the papers yet, have you?"

"No. They're at your office."

"You're on the front page again. This time it's not about you, but you're in photos among the other agents. There are journalists hanging around outside."

"David gets back tomorrow. Want me to meet him?"

"He can find his way in. You lie low for a few days."

"I can do that. Would you tell him I have something that may affect the bombing case?"

On Friday afternoon, Vasari walked into the conservation lab.

"Hello, Sandra. I love seeing you in your natural environment."

"Hi, David. I take it I can't come in yet."

"You could sneak in the side entrance, but Charlene said you have something for me."

"Yes. The display cases in the lobby of the Impi building had two incendiary devices that would fit the holes in Ohio and Genova. Who do I pass the information to?"

"Me. Could you identify them from a catalog?"

"A mercenary catalog? You're kidding."

"Not the mail-order type, but it could be. Jim Redwood had it drawn up from research by his Domestic Terrorism Unit, working with ATF. He started it when you worked for him."

"I remember a file of bomb scene photographs. It was quite thick by the time I left."

"Well, they're in a book now, maintained by the DTU. It has pictures of an incredible variety of devices, matched to the scenes they leave behind."

"Mug shots for bombs."

"Something along those lines. This might help the Ohio investigation because you are the only detective who can compare those depressions to the ones in Genova."

"How do we do this?"

"I'll tell ATF. Jack or Wes would probably be happy to bring it here for you." He glanced out the window and back. "Meanwhile, the SAC and Marty have been talking."

"NIS wants me?"

"Mainly. We can't detail you within the FBI because you're seconded to New York specifically for this project."

"I guess I'd be overpaid to stay here."

"Marty will call you at home tomorrow."

"Let's go tell Mel." She waved at the picture she was restoring and carefully set it in its storage stand for the weekend. "I hope I'll be here Monday."

"By the way, Mom doesn't think Pop ever told her the name of the Gentile family that bought their house, but the deed of sale was in his safe deposit box at the bank. It was Mastroianni."

In Mel's office, she said, "Doctor Conti, could we see the portrait from the Monuments Men?"

"Of course." He looked at David. "About time."

In the vault, she led David to the back part of the room. "Cover your eyes."

She put the picture on a table, leaning against the wall.

"It may take years to get this back in your family's living room, but it will be worth it. Look." He took his hands down. "Meet Beniamino Vasari. I'd bet anything on it."

David gasped. He stared. He took a deep breath and held it. Then his shoulders relaxed, and he stood there with tears streaming down his cheeks.

"Oh my God, Sandra. How did you know?"

"Apart from it being a younger you, I have never, ever, seen a model look at the painter that way.

"He is obviously looking at his father, and they love each other very much."

She moved up and hugged him. He laid his chin on her shoulder and continued to look at his ancestor as his tears fell.

Behind David, she saw Mel take out his handkerchief.

☙☙☙

Saturday morning, the phone rang while Sandra was washing the breakfast dishes. It was Marty.

"Do you usually work weekends?"

"More often than I wish, but talking with you makes it worthwhile." She felt him grin on the phone.

"David said you were working on something."

"NIS is reassigning you."

"What about my work here?"

"We're pulling you until the Bureau begs for you to come back. You'll need to return to testify for the handful that go to trial."

"Where are you sending me?"

"Washington Navy Yard."

"How long?"

"It's PCS. Your orders will have the accounting codes to set up the move." Silence. "Sandra?"

"Sorry, Marty. It's a shock, that's all."

He waited for a moment. "Remember the badge you wanted?"

"Yes?"

"NIS and FBI tours are two to four years. Neither agency would let a junior agent remain forever in the same assignment.

"Someday, the Bureau will start commissioning women, and you will need to choose one agency or the other. Talk to David and Bob about their careers before they ended up in New York."

"Jim told me about some of his."

"That's the life. You have to say goodbye every couple of years. The true friends will stay in touch."

Sandra looked at the rain sliding down the window. "Do you send Christmas cards?"

"Yes, with a letter catching up the events of the year."

"How many?"

"About two hundred now. And almost all of those write back."

"Collecting friends all over the world."

"You got it. Not a bad thing for someone in your situation."

"Thanks, Marty. How do the orders come in?"

"By telex to the field office."

"I know where the machine is."

"Take care, Sandra. Call me if you need anything."

When she got back from the Brooklyn Museum on Monday afternoon, she had a message from Joe on her answering machine.

Going to Washington would not be so bad after all.

ଧଧଧ

Abe Armstrong had never visited his client at Impi headquarters because his law offices were around the corner. Being summoned made him very uncomfortable.

Mrs. Dempsey rose when he walked in. The smile did not include her eyes, which he suspected could scan for weapons from across the room. Bad enough that she stood a head taller than he.

"Good morning, Mr. Armstrong. He is on the telephone." She indicated the comfortable divan against the wall. A new picture of a war scene from Biafra occupied the place of a Vermeyen the FBI had confiscated.

The CEO of Impi opened the door almost as soon as Abe sat. He waved the lawyer in. "Hold all calls, please, Mrs. Dempsey." She pressed a button on her phone, forwarding it to the answering service on the next floor down.

After closing the door, Braxton motioned to a sofa and two armchairs around a low table across from his desk. Abe turned right and took a seat.

"Help yourself." A tea set held silver carafes of coffee and hot water, and a selection of teas. The mercenary brought a large mug to the table. The lawyer poured himself some coffee.

"You called this meeting, Trent, although you could come see me anytime."

"I know, but I want to have a free-ranging conversation. We are still covered by attorney-client privilege, aren't we?"

"Of course."

"Good. Let's review exactly what must happen for this to go away. Evidence, testimony, timing – the whole thing."

"We can win—"

"Not winning. I'm talking about there being no case, no trial, nothing."

"You can't make seven paintings, the paper trail for them, and the agents just go away."

"Why not?"

Abe felt a chill press him into the cushion of the divan. His mouth sagged.

Trent sipped his coffee. "Pull your jaw up, friend. You won't be involved. The art is a loss. When the experts compare the pictures to the forgeries, the originals will be returned to the museums. Let's determine exactly what the prosecutors need to indict me or Impi, Inc. Then we'll agree on the minimum needed for them to give up. Let's start with the charges, then the potential witnesses and physical evidence…"

☙☙☙

Sandro Santis looked nervously up and down the street before entering the building. He would not have spotted a tail anyway.

He stepped onto the twenty-fifth floor into a living room gleaming with marble in the light from a full picture window. Braxton came from the far wall where he had been looking at the miserable weather. He held a glass of wine.

"Thank you for coming. Something to drink?"

"Coffee? I skipped that after lunch." He looked around. "I've never been here. I thought my secretary got the wrong address."

"I keep this place for special meetings. This apartment can't be traced to me. Have a seat." He brought a cup to the coffee table. Sandro scanned the newspapers spread on it: *New York Times, New York Post, Wall Street Journal, Financial Times, Washington Post, Figaro, Le Monde,* and the major dailies from London, Cologne, and Rome.

"I've never seen so many pictures of myself."

"Neither have I. We have a lot of company, so this won't go away soon. And you were in the same crowd two and a half years ago. This bothers me."

"I don't like it either. My lawyer says I could be deported even before this goes to trial."

"That's a personal problem. Two years ago, you and your friends hired me to take out the FBI's secret weapon. Do you remember?"

"Yes." Sandro hung his head.

"So, who is this?" Trent reached for a Sharpie and circled Sandra on the front-page photos of the dailies.

"I don't know. An FBI agent? She has a badge."

"Don't be stupid. There aren't any female FBI agents. She came to my office. She's NIS."

"What's that?"

"US Naval Investigative Service." He threw the papers and pen on the table. "Did you hit the wrong family?"

"No! I saw Billingsley myself in the Embassy Annex in Rome and again when – when we were arrested. I don't know who this is."

"I do. She's Special Agent Alessandra Bari, assigned to the New York Field Office about three years ago. What are the chances of two secret weapons, huh?"

"Are you sure? The Navy would not have art experts."

"Oh, she's NIS alright. After Arcibaldo's clowns screwed up their attempt to sink the American destroyer, I sent my people to watch. Guess who showed up to take charge of the crime scene while the pier was still burning?" Santis pointed to Sandra's picture with an inquiring arch of the eyebrows. "Very good, Sandro. Nowhere near New York or the FBI. The embassy detailed the FBI and ATF the next day, but she was in charge until the NIS agent from the Sixth Fleet flagship came to take over."

"Where did she come from to be in Genova?"

"Hell, I don't know! She's not always at the FBI office, just shows up most afternoons and some mornings. She hasn't been back since the raids."

"Haven't you tailed her?"

"Of course, but she dropped every tail we've set on her. Honestly, though, we did not think she was important enough to follow until the other day."

"You think the NIS called her back?"

"Probably."

"That's good, no?"

"Makes no difference to me. I won't be indicted, but your friends in Italy have a problem. What if she was pulled off to investigate the bombing in Genova? The ship is still there, you know."

"I'll let Ettore and Manny know. They can find out whether she's in Italy or not."

"Meanwhile, you should let your lovely wife know that you may be spending more time with her on Lake Garda."

"She would be pleased, but I wouldn't."

Chapter 24

Washington Navy Yard

ON HER FIRST WEEKEND IN WASHINGTON, Sandra took the bus to the Naval Hospital in Bethesda. She entered the fourth-floor room quietly and stood in the doorway, admiring Joe's silhouette. He sat erect, unlike so many typists who slouched over their work. The light from the window passed through his tousled hair, turning it into a halo. His focus was absolute, as he looked at a thick manuscript and typed furiously on the IBM Selectric typewriter. He was sight-translating: reading in Italian and touch-typing in English.

After about three minutes, Joe spoke to the clear glass in front of him, "*So che sei lì. Ciao, amore.*" I know you're there. Hi, love.

"How could you tell?" She walked across the room and kissed his head.

"The draft on my ankles. If it had been the staff, they would have said something by now."

"Sometimes I love watching you work. You're so focused."

"Well, it takes focus to do this." He stood. They embraced and shared a long kiss. "Tell me about your first week."

Sandra hung her outer garments on the door and sat in the chair near the desk. He listened to her describe getting oriented and meeting the agents. She had been to the Housing Office, where she learned that she was on her own; the office only worked with active-duty military families.

"I haven't had time to look for an apartment yet. How about you?"

"The hospital seems resigned to putting me up for a long time. The phone came in yesterday, and the doctors are no longer surprised that I am up working when they come by. They're not used to a patient who isn't bedridden."

"And the medical board?"

"The first meeting is next week. Doctor Gladwick said he would recommend letting me come and go, if I don't climb more than two sets of stairs at a time. They want me here for the treadmill and oxygen tests twice a day."

"Still unchanged?"

"The X-rays look the same, but my VO2 max is up, which has everyone scratching their heads."

"Did you call your mother?"

"Yes. They plan to come tomorrow after church. Will you be here?"

"Of course. What about Diego?"

"My lucky day. He was in but had to leave for the evening meal formation. He'll come over with Serena for Spring Break the second week in March."

"If he plans to return the car, I'll drive him back."

"I'll tell him. Thanks."

They kissed again. She gathered her jacket and coat.

"*A domani, amore.*" See you tomorrow, love.

***

The next afternoon, Joe hosted a family reunion. The head nurse suggested that they move to the conference room one floor down. It was rarely used on Sunday.

Nancy asked many questions about what the doctors in Naples and Bethesda had asked and not asked. She even brought out a stethoscope and listened to Joe's lungs from several new points.

"Mom, I thought you were a pharmacologist."

"I was a physician first, dear, and remember whom I married. What do you think our pillow talk was about?"

The others started giggling.

"Get a grip, you four, really!"

"Sorry, Nancy," said Matthew, wiping his eyes. "Good thing one of you wasn't a proctologist."

"Mom, you're weird, you know." Joe tried to keep a straight face but couldn't do it. "Please don't ever become normal."

"Your father saw a lot of what you have. He couldn't do much about the burned-out lungs, but we did discuss it – and not just in bed." She scowled at the smirking. "Jason's observations are why Smithson funds research into pulmonary therapies for smoke and explosives. Some of them are in use at Hunter McGuire." The Veterans Administration hospital in Richmond. "Do you mind if I have a word with— what's his name?"

"Gladwick. Morton Gladwick."

"I may be back in midweek, Joe. I know some of the doctors here. Now that you have a phone, Angela or I will let you know."

***

On Monday, Nancy walked into her office after a meeting down the hall. The sun was coming through the trees to bounce off the rich colors she and Angela had chosen when she had returned from Rome. Her secretary was hanging up the phone.

"Good morning, Doctor Lockhart. That was the Naval Hospital. Doctor Southwood came back. Shall I call him now?"

"Give me about five minutes to grab some coffee and my notes."

As she set her mug on the desk, the phone rang.

"Captain Southwood on line one."

"Thank you, Angela." She pressed the blinking button.

"Hello, Josh. It's been too long…"

The next day, Nancy drove to Bethesda, where she visited Joe, his attending physician, and Jason's former shipmate and their long-time friend, now commanding officer of the National Naval Medical Center.

On Wednesday, the medical board released Joe to come and go, but he needed to remain overnight at the hospital and report for morning and afternoon testing. Doctor Gladwick began listening to the same places Nancy had and reported an improvement on the back of his lungs, which was obscured on the X-rays.

Over the weekend, Sandra signed the lease for a two-bedroom apartment in Bethesda off Rockville Pike. It cost half what her apartment in Brooklyn had. She took two weeks off to move, which hardly scratched her leave balance.

The following week was spring break at the Naval Academy. Diego and Serena brought the Range Rover and stayed with Sandra for two nights. She drove them back after they helped set up her apartment and spent time with Joe. She left Serena at home, then Diego at the dealership where his new car was waiting, purchased with the zero-interest loan that Marine Midland Bank offered first-class midshipmen.

Sandra usually picked up Joe with the car on her days off. They could not go far, with only six hours or so between treadmill tests.

ଧଧଧ

The week after she took Diego and Serena home, Sandra had Thursday and Friday off. Doctor Gladwick had called on Wednesday to ask if she could be in Joe's room at ten a.m. She wondered what that was about as she climbed to the fourth floor.

At the nurses' station, she saw Nancy, Matthew, and Annabelle.

"Something special?"

"Yes," said Lieutenant Commander Simpson, the head nurse. "Come with me, please." She led them to the conference room they had used before. Many of the shift nurses and corpsmen were there. Doctor Gladwick and the four members of the medical board flanked Joe against the wall, all wearing Service Dress Blue. Joe looked as curious as the others.

"Attention on deck!" someone called. Captain Southwood walked in, followed by his executive officer. Those who had been sitting at the conference table rose.

"Good morning, everyone. XO?"

"Attention to orders!" They stood at attention. The XO opened a folder and read aloud.

"The Secretary of the Navy takes pleasure in presenting the Navy and Marine Corps Medal for Heroism to Ensign Jason Joseph Lockhart Junior, United States Navy, while serving as officer of the deck in USS *Barry*…"

Oh my God! thought Sandra. *That's the highest noncombat award in the Navy.*

Her eyes welled and her heart pounded as the XO read through the dry description of that morning. She recalled the blackened bridge, the blood on the bulkheads, and the chalk circles of the scene. She looked at the others.

Nancy seemed stiff and pale, her eyes bright. Matthew stood proudly, with the kind of smile she had seen on senior agents when they watched one of their men doing something exceptionally well. David and Jim had both worn that expression sometimes. Annabelle seemed calm, though pale, but more resigned. *Grateful.*

When the executive officer finished, the petty officer holding a box next to the CO opened it. Captain Southwood pinned the medal below Joe's lonely National Defense Ribbon. *I'll buy a new ribbon bar for him,* Sandra thought.

"Congratulations, Mister Lockhart. Do you have anything to say to us?"

"Only that the four men who stepped up to save the ship are not here. Two died, and the other two may not make it. I will never forget them."

"Thank you. At ease and carry on." He shook Joe's hand and accompanied him to the other side of the room, where some refreshments awaited.

಑಑಑

Sandra sat in the office she shared with Sherry and the other NIS agents. The unseasonably cold rain outside made her glad once again that Joe insisted she use the Range Rover. Everyone seemed focused.

She asked Sherry, "Is it my imagination or is something different in here today?"

"The SAC is back." She gave a little jiggle in her chair. "The SAC is back, the SAC is back, so watch out, Mack!"

"Get serious, Twopeak," grumbled Sid, but his eyes smiled. He tossed a crumpled paper ball at her. "One of these days, he'll catch you making up jingles about him."

"I got so used to working for the ASAC I forgot about him." Sandra glanced at the door to the SAC's office. "Anything I should know?"

"Not really. Be patient. He's buried in paperwork and catching up. He may not even know you're here for a couple of days."

As if he were listening, the SAC opened the door and waited there. Average height, a little overweight, round face with very short, receding hair, deep-set eyes, and a full mouth. He looked at each agent in turn, until his gaze rested on Sandra.

"Bari?" She stood. "Welcome aboard. Come in."

While she crossed the room followed by the gazes of the entire team, the SAC turned and sat at his desk.

She paused at the door: plain office with more gray steel file cabinets than usual; USCGS charts of the Mediterranean, the Atlantic and the Gulf of Mexico; street map of the District of Columbia and its suburbs; gray steel desk; gun cabinet in the corner behind the desk.

"Close the door and have a seat. Coffee?"

"Yes, sir."

He pointed a shoulder at the coffee maker on the filing cabinet behind the door. She drew a mug and sat in the visitor chair. She waited in silence while he reviewed the folder in front of him. Sandra recognized her classified service record. Fixing her face in a neutral expression, she breathed very slowly to quell her heart.

He pushed back, then took a sip.

"Kenneth Strong."

"Yes, sir. Sandra Bari."

"For a twenty-three-year-old agent you have a very strange record."

"Sir?"

"You went to the FBI Academy but were not commissioned. Instead, they sent you to the FBI Field Office in New York as a typist. Suddenly you're an NIS agent, but still in the FBI Office."

"Yes, sir."

"You've never worked for NIS?"

"Only the *Barry* bombing because I was the closest agent."

The SAC sipped in silence.

"When I went to West Virginia, we were down one agent. I come back and we have a new agent. I shouldn't complain, but can you explain this?"

"NIS was doing the FBI a favor, sir." Strong rolled his hand. "I've worked with the Bureau for six and a half years. Some officers in FBI headquarters could see that one day they would need to diversify, so they recruited some minority men and me, and put us through the Academy. The others were sent to field offices away from Washington, but I could not be given a badge and a commission."

"Because of your sex."

"Yes, sir. I was quietly sent to the New York Field Office to continue the work I was doing while I was at GWU."

"Which was?"

"Investigating art crimes, mainly theft and forgery."

"I won't ask for a tutorial right here, but it doesn't sound much like what we do here."

"You could think of drug dealing or smuggling, with millionaire players and very high stakes. I've dealt with bomb scenes, done personal protection, thwarted several assassination attempts, been bombed and shot at, and I killed one man."

"Who can vouch for all this?"

"Special Agent Marty MacKenzie here at the Navy Yard, and Special Agent Jim Redwood at FBI Headquarters. He heads up Special Projects."

"MacKenzie had this job earlier."

"Yes, sir. He can explain better than I."

Strong took another sip of coffee.

"Meanwhile, the ASAC says you have been performing well, better than he expected. He was pleased with the leads you developed in the Seventh Fleet contracts case."

"I hope to carry my weight."

"It seems that you are off to a good start. You're not a complete rookie, but there is no track record on you in here." He patted the service record. "We may talk again after I see Agent MacKenzie."

⸿⸿⸿

Joe and Sandra were doing the dishes one evening when the phone rang. He answered it.

"Yes…How are you doing?… Fine. Still go in twice a day… Sure. Here." He put the handset down. "It's David. He said you left a message."

She went to the phone. "Hi! I was going to call you again tomorrow. I went to the Army Center for Military History the day before yesterday, and I looked at the original documentation. What the archivist thought was an 'S' on the end of Via delle Paniere was a six. It was too faint to show up on the photocopy… Sure. … Mostly regular police work, but I've had fun tracking down some fraud cases… You too. Ciao."

Joe looked up. "I take it that the Mastroianni family got the house and its contents."

"Yup. David is the heir to a picture of his many-times-great-grandfather."

"Omigod. I knew it was a sixteenth century painting, but Beniamino Vasari painted by his father? "Why didn't he know about it?"

"He said his family never talked about what they left behind, so he never knew about the painting. If his father had not kept the sketch, they would have never known."

ଷଷଷ

In late April, the medical board at the hospital met to review the case of Ensign Lockhart. The consensus was that his lungs were ever so slowly beginning to recover, but it would take a year or more before he could return to full duty.

"In his present condition, we could not even offer him a transfer to the restricted line," said the commander chairing the board. "When could we?" he asked Doctor Gladwick.

"Not before Christmas."

"How about this?" said Lieutenant Commander Simpson, the head nurse of the extended care section. "We agree he doesn't need daily treatment or supervision. Let's send him on medical leave. We could give him a medical discharge or even retire him on disability, but I have a hunch about him.

"Require him to come back for evaluation in, say, six months. That would be September."

"That's a good idea," said Gladwick. "He clearly knows how to listen to his body, and he pushes it safely."

"Then we will recommend a transfer to the restricted line or even a return to full duty after another evaluation. How does that sit?" They agreed.

Joe had his back to the door when the commanding officer of the hospital walked in.

"Mister Lockhart, don't jump up. I have a surprise for you."

Joe stood and turned around. "Sorry, sir. I wasn't expecting anyone this early." Nurse Simpson and Doctor Gladwick came in behind the CO.

"Relax. The board just adjourned, but I wanted to be the one to let you know the results."

"Sir?"

"We're sending you on medical leave pending evaluation in September. Then, we will see how much you have improved. We don't need to keep you here while you heal."

Joe's elation bordered on dizziness.

"Regular leave, free to go anywhere?"

"Yes, but you must stay in touch so we can call you back, and you must report here in time for your evaluation."

"I could do what I do here, but at home?" Joe waved at the table with his translation work.

"That's right. We trust you to listen to your body, and, even more important, your mother. She may have some surprising things to show you." He winked. "Frankly, I think we're releasing you to a more advanced care environment."

"Thank you, sir. What do I do now, and when can I pack out?"

"Nurse Simpson can send you to the right places. Good luck, Mister Lockhart, and remember, you're still stationed here."

The two doctors shook his hand and left.

Nurse Simpson explained the procedures. He packed, then walked to the discharge desk downstairs to collect his orders. He signed some additional paperwork to establish his address (Richmond) and where his pay should be sent (Navy Federal Credit Union). His housing allowance would be based on being stationed at Bethesda.

When Sandra arrived that evening from work, she helped move his things to the Range Rover and took him to her apartment....

CHAPTER 25

PCS, AGAIN

SANDRA'S MOUTH WATERED as she unlocked the door of her apartment. The exhaustion of an annoying day of small things vanished beneath the aromas of risotto and roast pork.

"Ciao, bella," Joe came out and leaned in to keep the grease from his apron off her blazer.

She embraced him and pulled him in for a long kiss.

"How did I get so lucky?" She looked at the front of her jacket. "It's going to the cleaners anyway. I've been battling toddlers on a playground, teenagers in a parking lot, and a slobbering Great Pyrenees."

"So, average day for Special Agent Bari of the fearsome Naval Investigative Service?" Joe reached back into the kitchen while she shed the dirty garment. He handed her a glass of Montepulciano d'Abruzzo. "Dinner in forty-five. Take a load off."

Sandra eased into the armchair and put her feet on the ottoman. "You know, as detectives, we do a lot of day-to-day police work."

"Don't the masters-at-arms and the base police do that?"

"Yes but take today. There was a child-snatching at the day care center. The police responded, but we had to interrogate the people who were there. While Sid took statements from the daycare attendants, I crouched down with the toddlers and preschoolers. It turned out the snatcher left a sibling behind, and the little girl told me it was their uncle, not their dad."

"So, case solved by an abandoned little girl."

"Just about. We drove to his address and brought in him and the child."

"And the teenagers?"

"The usual. When you see them outside during school hours, the alarm bells go off. Sid and I were on our way back from the housing area and we went past four of them buying marijuana in the McDonald's parking lot. The seller tried to run, but he didn't get far."

"I've seen you in action. You're a cheetah." He grinned and continued stirring the risotto. "So, I take it the dog was smarter than those four?"

"Oh, definitely. You've heard me mention 'Mrs. Colonel' Smythe, haven't you?"

"The one who wears her husband's rank around. Her dog?"

"Actually, her daughter's. Anyway, 'Mrs. Colonel' Smythe came into the office and lambasted the SAC that it was our responsibility to find the pooch. It was almost the end of the school day, and I knew the youngster. I gave the SAC a high-sign and left him to tranquilize the irate mother."

"And?"

"The dog was waiting for the girl at school. I walked them home and went back to the car. She's a bright one."

"The girl or the canine?"

"Both." She carried her empty glass to the kitchen. "I'll be back in a flash."

With a shower, fresh clothes and some food, Sandra felt much restored. She played with his leg as they ate, something he never tired of, but still made him spill food.

"Let's not get rich," she said.

"Why? We're doing well with two Navy salaries and my translating."

"Because I never want to have a table too big for me to reach your leg." She whacked his shin playfully.

❧❧❧

The next day, Sandra started her "weekend," a Tuesday and Wednesday. They slept in and made love before breakfast.

The phone rang. Joe got up to answer it. When he came back, he was smiling.

"I've been promoted. The list came out yesterday. I am now a lieutenant, junior grade."

"Congratulations, Lieutenant. Can we go shopping for shoulder boards and silver bars today?"

"That and stop by the Pass Office for a new ID card."

While they were out, they left his blue uniforms with the tailor near the hospital to be restriped. The Washington Naval District had shifted to summer uniforms, so he would not need them soon.

Sandra went back to work on Thursday. The SAC called her into his office about midmorning. "Bring your coffee."

He waved at the chair. She sat. He eased behind his desk.

"Finally talked with MacKenzie. For a guy in a desk job, he spends a lot of time on the road."

"I found that, too, sir."

"Anyway, your record said nothing about protection experience, but he said you excelled at it."

"I spent two months protecting an executive in Rome."

"Nancy Lockhart. I read up on it."

"Yes, sir."

"We're the only NIS office that does personnel protection. Usually for the Secretary of the Navy, VIP visitors, and sometimes to augment Secret Service and the District police. Tomorrow, we'll bring you into our training program."

ଧଧଧ

That evening after supper at the Redwoods, Joe enjoyed listening to Sandra, Arlene, Jim, and Amanda play chamber music. After Amanda left, Jim said, "I thought you could use an update on the bombing investigations."

"Sure," they said.

"ATF finally accounted for all the explosive in the lot. They raided the Impi facility in West Texas, which was where they manufactured custom devices and weaponry for special projects. They found the rest of the material in storage."

"How does the trail look?"

"It's close. Columbus, Rome, and Interpol are building the evidence chain, but they know who assembled and deployed both devices. The four men who were arrested in Ohio are in Witness Protection until we arrest the right people: six Impi employees. As you might expect, Arcibaldo sympathizers bought the Algerian bombs through a Libyan warlord and smuggled them into Italy. When *Barry* didn't sink and life went on, they decided not to turn it into a propaganda opportunity. As soon as the Carabinieri and the Polizia line up the evidence, they will take out what's left of Arcibaldo's more violent supporters."

"I can't wait to know it's resolved."

"Your spotting those displays in New York cinched it because ATF had an Impi paper trail on those. Good job, Sandra.

"How's NIS?"

"Much like the FBI, I guess, without the fine art. Some interesting work investigating fraud and bribery. The accounting major helps. In general, the players aren't millionaires with paid armies. Lots of stupidity, more than anything."

"I remember it well."

"I just got assigned to the Protection Detail. Training for the first few weeks, then accompanying someone else. It will keep my profile down."

"I love your versatility."

Jim and Joe chatted for about two minutes.

As they left, Jim said, "Keep an eye on the financial press, especially the *Wall Street Journal.*"

"We get that and the *Washington Post* already," said Joe, "I'll cover for her."

ৡৡৡ

Riding with the protection team to speeches, ribbon-cuttings, and other events became routine. She was never alone on these assignments, so she was well back from the cameras and the attention of the press. The subject was usually the Secretary of the Navy, but sometimes the Chief of Naval Operations or the Commandant of the Marine Corps.

The *Wall Street Journal* reported that Impi, Inc. lost its export license and was under investigation for violating sanctions imposed by the federal government.

"Braxton will stress out," Sandra said when Joe read her the notice. "I hope he doesn't become vengeful the way Arcibaldo did."

"From what you told me, he doesn't seem the type. I worry about the trial, though. The press has been strangely quiet since the original arrests back in February."

"It takes time to see the cases through the courts. Some of these men have better lawyers, and Braxton's lawyer, Abe Armstrong, is one of the best."

"It might just be me thinking *all'italiana*, but he should be eliminating people the prosecution needs to indict him. Braxton can't do anything about the art, but the agents will need to testify at some point, won't they?"

"Yes, they – omigod, Joe, are you serious?"

"Taking out witnesses is a time-honored tradition, you know."

Sandra went to the phone and called Vasari at home. She hung up in less than a minute.

"He said you were dead on. Bob Worthman was injured in a drive-by shooting this afternoon and is in intensive care. David had not thought of what you said, but he'll call the ASAC, so they can move the other two agents somewhere."

"Then Braxton will be looking for you. He knows you're NIS, and you were pulled out of New York. What if he finds out you were the agent in charge of the scene in Genova?"

"Oh, shit, Joe." He always wanted to grin when she cursed because it was so rare, but also so natural and appropriate. "Who would know?"

"Jim Redwood has a unit watching Impi."

She went to the phone. When she came back, she said, "He agreed that it's a credible threat. He'll put out feelers to see if Braxton has been snooping around. He'll talk to Marty too."

ЄЄЄ

He does cut a fine figure, Sandra thought, as the Secretary walked to the lectern. Some two thousand people sat in rows of folding chairs on the University Lawn. She stood off to the right where she would be out of the view of photographers and TV cameras, but able to reach the Secretary with a leap. It was only her second trip as the closest agent.

The press would report this as a beautiful day. Scanning behind her sunglasses, Sandra would have welcomed a little cloud cover. Still, her position gave her a clear view. Her eyes were constantly snapping back to something glinting. The sun shone off the windows to the right, but that reflection did not move.

Or did it? The sun bounced off a long, thin — *gun barrel!*

She leaped and tackled the Secretary. Splinters from the lectern exploded as the bullet blasted through the spot where he had been standing and went through the foot of the university rector in the front row of dignitaries.

Then she heard the shot. She rolled off and rose to one knee, her weapon drawn. The rifle moved slightly. She aimed and fired.

Her left arm flew backward, wrenching her shoulder. Then she felt the burning and pain up her forearm. Her body spun to the left.

A policeman tried to drag her off the stage.

"Let me get up!" she shouted. She stood to check on her charge. The Secretary was already going down the stairs, flanked by his aide and followed by panicking attendees.

Sandra looked at the window. It was open, but there was no movement. The sniper was either going to be caught or was gone. She scanned the running crowd as she holstered her pistol, then went down the stairs, holding her left arm with her right hand.

In the shade of a tree behind the stage, they stopped to assess the situation and to wait for the Secretary's car and escort cruiser. He seemed calm, more concerned about the dirt on his suit than anything else. A typical reaction in combat.

"Thank you, Agent Bari," he said. "That was — you're wounded."

"Not a problem, sir. Let's get you to your car. Then I'll go see the paramedics over there." She pointed to the ambulance. The limo arrived. The aide held the door for the Secretary, while Sandra scanned their surroundings.

She watched them drive off, then wondered why she could not see the ambulance...

ଢଢଢ

White light behind her eyelids. Sandra turned her head to open her eyes. Her left side hurt terribly but subsided if she didn't try to move her arm.

Joe sat in the visitor chair. He came over to her bed and kissed her head.

"*Ben tornata.*" Welcome back.

"Where am I and how long?"

He stepped back for the nurse coming through the door with a bag of saline.

"GWU Hospital and just a few hours. It's eight p.m." said Joe.

"You were in surgery for two hours," said the nurse, a thirty-something Asian. "The rest was sleeping off the sedation."

"I passed out?"

"Blood loss. You owe the Red Cross a couple of pints."

Sandra tilted her head toward the massive cast. "What about my arm?"

"Doctor Meyers is on his way."

As if on cue, a man in a lab coat, about late thirties, walked in.

"Hello, Agent Bari. You're looking much better."

She introduced Joe. The two men shook hands. "Can you tell me what happened?"

"Your forearm was flayed as the bullet went up the ulna before glancing off your elbow. It will take longer than most bones to heal, but the surgeons put all the pieces back where they belong. That's amazing because with this kind of injury, there is almost always some chip that goes

351

missing, and the joint is never the same again. You should be able to rehab those torn muscles and the joint."

"How long?"

"A week here for the transfusion and because we don't want you to move the joint at all. Then home for another week or so. We'll transfer your care to the Naval Medical Center in Bethesda. They'll check it regularly. Light duty by the end of the month."

She looked at Joe.

"Ken Strong was here. He'll be back after he tucks the kids in. The photo of you taking down the Secretary of the Navy is on the front pages of the evening papers. The lectern blowing up made it even more dramatic.

"I turned off the TV because you were sleeping, but it was at the top of the news on all channels."

"So much for hiding from Braxton."

"There's more. The shooter is dead."

"The police got there that fast?"

"No. Your shot was that good. According to Ken, the round blew his head off."

"Omigod. I aimed for where the barrel went into the shade, hoping to keep him from shooting again."

"You must have pulled your triggers simultaneously. He was aiming for you, at least on the second shot."

"Wait a minute. How did you find out?"

"Sherry in the office called me. She said I'm your emergency point of contact."

She reached with her right hand and squeezed his. "My only point of contact, love. Thank you."

☙☙☙

Ken Strong did come back, about nine. He told Sandra that she was something of a hero, but now the office was down an agent again.

"Any details on the attack?"

"The weapon was a modified Kalashnikov. Scope and fancy shoulder stock, but not a proper sniper rifle."

"No spotter?"

"No, and we figure he planned on shooting two people, so he needed a semiautomatic."

"Any ID?"

"Nothing on the body. Still waiting on NCIC." National Crime Information Center.

"Soviet weapon. Trying to mislead us?"

"We haven't released that detail to the press because we want to see how this plays out. The ID and past history will be more relevant."

"Thanks, sir. Sorry about this."

"Don't be. You did your job, better than most." He put his hand on her right shoulder. "Take it easy and get well."

He shook hands with Joe on the way out.

જાજાજા

Sandra slept more than she remembered sleeping in her whole life. The nurse said it was only partly the pain-killers; she was down to a very small dose. On the other hand, the deflation after the trauma would make her sleep – and her body needed to heal.

On the third day after the SAC came by, she woke to find her lover sleeping on a couch across the room. He had bedding and a pillow and seemed quite comfortable.

She worked her bed into a sitting position and enjoyed watching his breathing and his face at rest.

The door moved. Joe snapped awake and swung out so fast that he was crouched to leap before the nurse entered the room.

The nurse ignored him and approached Sandra to take her vital signs. "Good. No fever and everything is normal. Doctor Meyer will be pleased."

"Thank you." Sandra looked past her. "Joe, what are you doing here at this hour?"

He stood. "Back in a moment; you two have a chat." He picked up a toilet kit from the chair near the couch and let himself out.

The nurse wound up her stethoscope and put it in her pocket. "He made a deal with security. While he is in here, our ward nurses don't have to maintain continuous surveillance of your door. It's helping everyone on the floor."

"But why?"

"Ask him. Something about developments in the case. Breakfast will be here soon." She left.

When Joe came back in, Sandra tried to cross her arms. "Ouch!"

He leaped to the side of the bed, held her cast and lowered it slowly before kissing it.

"Well? The nurse said something about a deal with security."

"Marty and Ken Strong both called at home. Everyone is worried about you, from New York to Norfolk. The shooter was a professional hit man, active in the New Orleans area. Law enforcement was never able to nail him, but he had a quite a reputation."

"Not a sniper normally, then."

"No. Always worked alone, and usually arranged 'accidents' for his victims. But guess what his day job was, at least until last year."

"Impi, Incorporated?"

"Right in one. Fought in Chad and Niger until three years ago. No record of his assignments after coming back to the States, but the Impi association was enough for Marty, Jim, Ken, and David to want protection for you. I came over and joined the argument between hospital security and the police. By volunteering to sleep here with a trip wire on the door, I convinced them to go away and to check in during the day to see if I needed to go anywhere."

"So, you're my bodyguard? What if you need to fight?"

"I'm mostly an early warning system. A policeman on your door would be like a neon sign. If anything happens here, the nurse at the ward station hits the alarm. An intruder wouldn't get far."

"My hero," Sandra cooed and batted her eyelashes theatrically. "A disabled sailor guarding a crippled agent. This is hilarious."

The next day, she was discharged. Joe drove her to the National Naval Medical Center, where they admitted her and promptly discharged her with orders to come back every week for evaluation.

Unable to go anywhere, they missed Diego's graduation from the Naval Academy. They were delighted when Diego and Serena came over on two different days before driving to Camp LeJeune, which would be the Marine second lieutenant's first duty station. Diego was impressed at how well Joe got around, especially running errands. Everything they needed was in walking distance in the neighborhood, and Joe had bought a small supermarket shopping cart to carry things.

"Will you ever play tennis again?" Diego asked over dinner the second night. He and Joe had been the strongest players on the Virginia junior varsity team. They had led the varsities at the Naval Academy and Virginia after Diego went to Annapolis.

"Saving tennis for Richmond because I want my mother there when I start. At first, just returning serves that don't need sprinting, but I expect to beat you some day."

Sandra returned to the office two weeks after Diego and Serena drove away. By the Fourth of July holiday, she was back to full duty, although she went to the physical therapy clinic twice a week. That was expected to continue through the summer.

❦❦❦

On the fifteenth of September, Joe drove himself to the Naval Medical Center after leaving Sandra at the Washington Navy Yard. She had been following paper trails in a suspected bribery case involving an Italian ship chandler and supply contracts to Sixth Fleet ships.

While Joe ran on the treadmill, did calisthenics, and stood still for X-rays, SAC Ken Strong called Sandra into his office.

"Bring your coffee and close the door." She grabbed her mug and joined the SAC. "Are you still in physical therapy?"

"No, sir. The final session was last week. Now I just need to get my tennis game back up to snuff."

"You're amazing, Bari. I'm glad you've come out of this so well."

"Me too."

"I hope you haven't put roots down too deep."

"I haven't bought a house or a car, if that's what you mean."

"Good because we're transferring you out."

"PCS?"

"Yes. Problem?"

"Not at all; I couldn't break my lease for anything else."

"You'll get orders to NAS Miramar, California, this week. Use those to arrange for the movers and break your lease. We'll hold the usual farewell party. We might even do a small press release."

He pointed to an envelope on his desk, marked CONFIDENTIAL – FOUO. For Official Use Only. "Your real orders are here. COMFAIRMED Naples, Italy. The Navy wants you to work with the Finance Guard and the Carabinieri on several different cases, including the one we had you reviewing. The confidentiality of the mission fits nicely with getting you out of sight for a while.

"Let me know if we can help with anything. Some of the guys would be happy to move furniture or boxes."

"No need, sir. The apartment was furnished. The pros will move the piano."

The SAC stood and shook her hand. "Good luck. I'd be happy to cross paths with you again."

"Thank you, sir. Me too."

When Joe picked her up in the afternoon, he told her that X-rays detected thirty-five percent clear area, and the oxygen testing showed forty percent capacity.

"Finally, some physical evidence to confirm my feelings."

Sandra squealed in delight and gave him a bear hug. After a long kiss, she stood back.

"Are you ready to haul moving boxes?"

"Huh?"

She told him about the transfer.

While they were packing out, Marty MacKenzie knocked on the door. "This is too confidential for the telephone."

When they were seated with cups of coffee, he said "Sorry about all the secrecy. Jim is in on this. NIS wants to protect its assets, and the Bureau wants to take Braxton to trial."

"What about the other two agents?" asked Sandra.

"They're okay, but the prosecutor is afraid their testimony won't be enough, especially since only you and the SAC were privy to the details. Besides, you spotted the three extra paintings."

"With the SAC still out of commission, she is the last prosecution witness?" asked Joe.

"Against Braxton, yes."

"Any word what he's up to now?" She sipped her coffee.

"Thanks to your eliminating his hitman, he's been easier to follow."

"Like Arcibaldo?" Joe asked.

"Revenge is not his style, but he must move around to meet his people. He doesn't have time for them to visit him to set up something else."

"So you can track him," said Sandra.

"Right. He is at the training camp in West Texas now.

"Wilder lost art too. He can't play dumb this time."

"I don't know all the players in the art investigation. For now, you're both on leave. Enjoy it. Let's stay in touch."

Chapter 26

In harm's way

THE NIS OFFICE THREW A FAREWELL PARTY at which the Secretary of the Navy showed up, so Sandra's assignment to California appeared in the news. While the reporters were filing their dispatches, Joe and Sandra packed his Range Rover and left town.

Settling into the house on Richmond's West End, they went to the tennis courts every day. Joe played normally now, but they stopped after a few volleys so he could recover. After playing, they would shower. Joe would comb out her hair, then brush it.

Nancy checked her son every third day. His lungs were clearing.

"We have a nebulizer therapy in clinical trials, which will be ready before your next medical board. I might have you try it."

"Guinea pig?"

"No. It's close to final approval, but you won't have to wait for the global manufacturing system to gear up."

Sandra's transfer included commercial tickets, one way. Joe bought his own. They flew to Rome and stayed with Aldo, Joe's classmate and tennis partner from high school. While there, they called at the FBI Liaison Office. Mark Pietrowicz was turning over to Special Agent Arthur Gladdins. Maria Williams, who had relieved Sandra as Jim Redwood's secretary, welcomed them enthusiastically. The four gathered in the office.

"Jim Redwood came a week ago to brief Art here," said Mark. "Knowing you would be in the country, he included the art investigations and the problems with the general."

"Did he mention Trent Braxton?"

"Yes. And you should know that Braxton and Wilder came to Rome and met with Arcibaldo, Bonin, Santis, and Kanter for two days at the Cavalieri Hilton."

"Any reason for them to know I'm here?"

"Redwood expected the 'investors' to get together at some point, so this doesn't tell us they know you are here. They are all vulnerable to indictment in the USA and Italy, but Arcibaldo's desire for revenge fits with Braxton's apparent plan to eliminate witnesses."

"They'll find out soon enough. So, Joe and I stay on the hit lists for now."

"I'm afraid so. If it's any consolation, we have a lot of support from the Italian agencies."

The second week in October, they checked into the hotel in Agnano across from the base library. She reported to Walter Brennan and got up to speed on the cases. In addition to the investigation of several ship chandlers, the Carabinieri were keeping the office informed on the *Barry* bombing case. Joe had his translation work.

Joe took the tours with the Housing Office van. He rented a scooter and went back to the more promising buildings. After he negotiated a rental contract for a two-bedroom apartment overlooking the postcard view of the Bay of Naples, Sandra signed the lease. They got the place for half what the Housing Office published. Joe's success came partly from not paying an agent's commission, partly from his bargaining skill, and partly from the fact the landlord and Joe both rooted for whoever was playing against Juventus, a northern soccer team disliked by many Southerners.

They bought a used Fiat 124 and drove to Gaeta to meet Special Agent Xavier Palumbo. Joe had spent part of his third-class midshipman cruise in the Sixth Fleet flagship, homeported in Gaeta, but all the people he knew had moved on.

Back in Naples, Joe showed Sandra four different ways out of their neighborhood, three of which only locals knew about. He also showed her the nasty neighborhoods surrounding the Stazione Marittima, where to set up surveillance of the Fleet Landing, and how to get in and out of the area unobserved.

They played tennis at the naval station and the NATO base nearby, shopped in the market, cooked at home, and visited museums and the San Carlo opera house. Neither let their guard down, but they did not allow the threat to keep them from enjoying the gleaming old jewel that was Naples. Because of the air pollution, he could not ride his bicycle around the city, so he bought a Vespa 125 scooter.

By the time he returned for his medical board in December, she was well-settled, and he was able to play a full set if he caught his breath before serves.

❧❧❧

From a bar on the corner, Sandra watched the foot traffic in and out of the Stazione Marittima, the passenger terminal of the Port of Naples. Inside the gates was the Fleet Landing, where the launches from the carriers, amphibious ships, and other large vessels picked up and discharged personnel and small cargo. The rest of the pier accommodated passenger liners, cruise ships, and the big ferries to Sardinia and Sicily. The next pier over was the Italian submarine base. Allied destroyers Med-moored beyond the line of submarines and used small boats to the Fleet Landing.

Working with the Finance Guard and the State Police, the NIS office in Naples had built a solid dossier on three Italian contractors and an American expatriate who were inflating charges to supply the fleet with food and parts and pocketing the difference. Compared to the sums in the art world, this was small potatoes, but the cases had taken many months of painstaking, careful research to get to this point.

The streetlights came on. Christmas lights reflecting off the wet streets flashed in a distracting manner, making it difficult for someone outside to see Sandra from where she watched. It had stopped raining only a half hour ago, but now the temperature was hovering just above freezing and the wind was picking up.

The American was expected to come off the ferry from Palermo and meet the three Italians in the lobby of the Londres Hotel nearby. Finance Guard officers were following the Italian suspects.

She saw her man among the ferry passengers flowing out the gates. He was a second-generation New Yorker but Sicilian on both sides. If he had chosen to wear an

Italian suit, he might have vanished into the crowd. She left a tip at the table and walked to the door.

And stopped.

Four people behind him was Mrs. Dempsey, scanning over the heads of the people around her as she walked across the piazza. She did not seem to be following anyone, but Sandra pulled back.

She slipped into the crowd as it passed in front of the bar, keeping Dempsey ahead of her. Sandra's target turned right into the Londres Hotel, while the Impi woman kept walking toward the Hotel Mediterranean at the far end of the Piazza Municipio. Sandra followed the suspect into the hotel. Two of the Carabinieri and the Finance Guard officer working the case were already there.

The four targets shook hands and started for the bar. The Finance Guard officer stopped them at the door. Sandra and the two Finance Guard officers tailing the Italians moved up behind them and handcuffed them, while the Carabinieri blocked them from the sides before they could move.

"What—"

"Alfonso Parisi, you are under arrest…"

An hour later, Sandra returned to the NIS office in Agnano. Parisi had been booked as an accomplice of the three Italians. Other people would decide whether the US authorities would get him immediately or after extradition proceedings.

After debriefing Walter, she called the FBI Office in Rome.

"Maria, it's Sandra. I have some news for Agent Gladdins to pass on, and I need some help…"

⁕⁕⁕

The next morning, Sandra sat at her desk with a fresh cup of coffee and opened the file on Parisi. One more report on the arrest, and she could turn the case over to Walter, who would send the package to the Department of Justice representative in Rome. A familiar male voice in Italian made her look up.

"Special Agent Bari?"

"*Maggiore Mascagni! Che piacere.*" What a pleasure. She rose and put her hand out to shake, but he kissed it with a bow.

"But you are—" She cut him off with a finger to her lips.

"I'll explain my identity crisis in a moment," she said in Italian. "What brings you here?"

He looked at the Americans in the office and took her hint to keep speaking in Italian. "The Genova bombing and the woman you reported yesterday."

Sandra came around the desk and snagged an umbrella by the door. "You never came back for that *caffè*. Let's do it now. The bar across the street serves Kimbo brand coffee."

As they walked, she explained that after the adventures in Rome six years ago, she had trained at the FBI Academy and been recruited by the NIS.

"Please never mention the name I had back then. I really am Sandra Bari."

"You are still in contact with Agent Redwood?"

"Yes, he is the reason I am involved with Mrs. Dempsey. What are you working on? Obviously not court security."

"No. Since then, I have been investigating international arms trafficking, which involves Mrs. Dempsey's employer."

"Impi, Incorporated."

"Yes. What is your part in this?"

"I arrested Trent Braxton in February, and now I am a target because the prosecution will need my testimony at his trial."

"Is this the art theft arrest?"

"Yes. Do you have something else?"

"My unit is following the trail from the bombing in Genova. You were the initial agent in charge of the scene, weren't you?"

They gave their orders at the cash register. Sandra insisted on paying. "Remember I offered you coffee in the office when you brought those beautiful flowers? You said 'later' and here we are."

"Well, alright then."

She ordered two coffees and paid. "By the way, I still have the Murano glass vase. It makes any bouquet explode with color."

"I am happy to know that."

They tossed off their espressos in the Neapolitan fashion then left the bar.

Outside, she said, "To answer your question, yes, I established the scene on board *Barry* in Genova. I was the closest NIS agent at the time."

"Agent Gladdins suggested we exchange notes. Your ATF determined the devices came from Impi."

"Training devices sent to Algeria, smuggled through Libya. Did you find out who?"

"Impi employees, but we have not ascertained whether the company was retained to provide the bombs or if they were acting on their own, being Fascist supporters of their now-disgraced party leader."

"General Arcibaldo."

"*Caspita!* You seem to know a lot about this."

"Between Braxton needing me dead and his association with the general, the same players keep cropping up. Seeing Mrs. Dempsey was a shock. I know only that she has been an Impi operative for ten years. What can you tell me about her?"

"Her real name is Ambessa Daniat Zula."

"I thought she might be Abyssinian."

"Eritrean. Her parents were well-off Italian Eritreans who moved to Rome when she was very small. Young Ambessa went to that American Catholic school on the via Cassia."

"Marymount."

"That's the one. Her mother's family had the money and the status, which is why she has her mother's and grandmother's names instead of her father's. The father died when she was young."

"Interesting."

"Anyway, she has been on the radar of European secret services for a long time. She had a falling out with her mother. She did not want to be a proper lady and marry well, as they say."

"I could read that the instant I walked into her office."

"She went to Eritrea and disappeared into the bush. We suspect she joined the Eritrean Liberation Front. She turned up in Algeria in time for the Algerian revolution, where Trent Braxton heard about her."

"Is she famous among mercenaries?"

"Quite the opposite. She is a ghost. After a mission, the survivors argue about who killed the victims and half of them won't believe she exists. The French Foreign Legion is the only one that actually wants to talk to her by name."

"Wow."

"Braxton hired her, and she disappeared again. My guess is that he provided the advanced training that made her one of the most effective assassins in the business."

"*Oddio!* I got in her way twice, blocking her from getting close to him."

"A professional picks her battles. How did she react?"

"Both times with a cold smile, a nod and then she just watched. She also signaled to him not to fight."

"She probably sized you up as fast as you did her."

"Any idea why she is here, and coming off the ferry from Palermo?"

"No. With her Italian citizenship she can come and go. Her mother died two years ago and willed her the apartment in Rome. She stays close to Braxton, so having her pop up here is a surprise to us too."

"Is there a Mister Dempsey?"

"We don't know. She has used the name since she left the USA. She has an American passport, so your people would know more than we would."

"I know the people to ask."

"Be careful. We have never had any whiff of her doing anything illegal here in Italy, but she is the type who does not leave whiffs."

"Does she have a modus operandi?

"If she does, no one has figured it out. She is consistent about one thing. Unless showing the death is part of the deal – say a political assassination – her victims disappear and are presumed dead years later."

The chill that made Sandra shiver had nothing to do with the weather.

ଊଊଊ

"Agent Bari," Walter Brennan called from his office as Sandra walked in after bidding farewell to Mascagni outside. "Grab a cup and come in."

When she was seated, the door closed, her boss looked at her sternly for about thirty seconds before saying anything.

"Well done on Parisi. That was so clean and complete that he will go down for any of the five different warrants. And I don't care if the Italian taxpayers support him for the next ten years."

"Thank you, sir."

"Now, what else is going on? Who is Mrs. Dempsey? What is a Carabinieri major doing in here, whisking you away and then disappearing? Who is he?"

"I met Major Mascagni when I was interning with the FBI in Rome. He works on international arms trafficking now, specifically finding out how the bombs used against *Barry* were moved and by whom. I mentioned Mrs. Dempsey when I briefed you last night, and I said I would report her presence to Rome. I wasn't trying to hide her, but we were talking about Parisi."

"Who is she?"

"She is an Impi operative, personal bodyguard of the CEO, Trent Braxton, whom we arrested in February in New York. After I called last night, Major Mascagni was sent to exchange information with me. Her presence here is a shock to the Italian authorities too."

Sandra explained the background on Ambessa Daniat Zula, Impi, the bombs used in Ohio and Genova, and why Braxton needed Sandra dead.

"Any questions, sir?"

"Is she here to kill you?"

"I don't know. Having an Italian passport, she could be here on her own business just as easily as a mission for Impi or Braxton personally."

They sipped their coffee as they thought.

"I don't have extra agents. It's just you and me."

"I know, sir. Do you mind if I reach out for as much information on her as I can find? You or I could ask up the line, but my contacts in the FBI and ATF are actively tracking everything to do with Impi. What they learn bears on both the *Barry* bombing and the threat to me."

"Go for it. Have you ever used the secure phones?"

"Not here, but we had them in Rome, New York and Washington."

"Before you go, start the clearance paperwork for the spaces upstairs." The intelligence offices of COMFAIRMED. "I'll sign it."

"Thank you, sir. Anything else?"

"Watch your back. I like having another agent here."

CHAPTER 27

PALACE COUP

THREE DAYS LATER, Sandra hung up the secure phone and considered her notes. Jim Redwood's Special Projects Office had the most information, but she had also talked to the former first minister to Italy, whom she and Joe had known in Rome and who was now a deputy assistant Secretary of State. David Vasari and Bob Worthman had called the New York State Police. Mrs. Dempsey had a remarkable biography.

While little Sandra played with Selena Menendez during recess at Foggy Bottom Elementary School, Ambessa Daniat Zula married Gerald Dempsey of Yonkers. She was a junior at Sarah Lawrence College; he a shy senior at nearby Iona College. The marriage ended the week after her American naturalization ceremony when Gerald's car plowed into a construction zone on the Cross County Parkway. He died at the scene. The new widow took her grief to her mother in Italy, according to the news reports at the time.

The US Consulate in Cairo had a record from 1961 of a Mrs. Gerald Dempsey registering as was customary for expatriates, but nothing after that. Sandra knew that the Eritrean Liberation Front was founded there that year. From the beginning, young Ambessa worked behind the scenes. The war for Eritrean liberation was still going on, so Sandra figured that the ELF freedom fighter must have gone freelance.

A Berber chief fighting at the fringes of the Algerian revolution retained Braxton's company, Impi, Inc., to fight the French Foreign Legion and the tribe that controlled the land between the Atlas Mountains and Algiers. Braxton found himself kidnapped from his own tent at night by a lone woman who had been hired to kill him. In the desert far from anyone else, the charismatic *condottiere* and the Amazon reached an understanding. The French commander received a refund check in the mail, and the assassin vanished.

The Italian authorities did not have a reason to trail Mrs. Dempsey except when they were watching Braxton come and go from their country. Official records showed that Ambessa still lived at the address in Rome. The housekeeper from the cleaning service said she came by a couple of times each year.

The court in New York confiscated Braxton's passport when he was released on bail.

Special Agent Gladdins contacted Major Mascagni and confirmed that Signora Zula had not returned to her apartment in Rome. The Carabiniere captain that Sandra worked with on the Navy contractor case was happy to check around the hotels in Naples. Signora Zula had checked into the Hotel Mediterranean for two days. The Polizia were looking through the identity reports from the other hotels.

What the hell was she doing here if not to kill me?

A partial answer came the next day, when she came back to the office after spending her lunch break buying a Christmas present for Joe. She had mailed presents to Richmond long ago.

"Agent Bari, it's for you." The master-at-arms handed her the phone.

"*Pronto, Bari.*" It was Mascagni.

"*Salve Mascagni.*" They continued in Italian.

"Are you still trying to find Zula?"

"Yes."

"I may have some relevant information, but not on the phone."

"Either we can meet, or you can tell Agent Gladdins. He can call me from Rome."

"Or you could go to the Comando Carabinieri at the NATO base."

"The Italian Army Element?"

"Yes. Let's say in thirty minutes?"

When Sandra arrived at the Italian Army building, the Carabiniere sergeant at the front desk was expecting her. He escorted her to the command center deep in the building. Another Carabiniere dialed when she walked in, then handed to phone to her.

"Ciao, Bari. This is better. I will leave instructions to let you use this anytime you need to contact me – or other law enforcement."

"Thanks. Is this normal?"

"No, but nothing is normal about you." She could hear him smile on the line. "Anyway, the two Impi employees who brought the bombs into Italy are dead."

"Homicide?"

"It would not have appeared so had we not been watching them. One had what was thought to be a heart attack in Barletta, but it turned out to be air injected into his blood. The other was run off the autostrada and plunged thirty meters into a valley in the Cilento National Park. It will be tomorrow before they even reach what is left of his car."

"Did you ever determine whether they were working for Impi or not?"

"Unfortunately, no. Now it's a moot point because we can only show that they imported the bombs, but not who they were working for or why."

"So, both the general and Braxton are safe for now."

"For now. We have issued a nationwide request to detain Zula-Dempsey if we find her, but we don't have any way to connect her to the deaths."

"She couldn't make these two disappear, could she?"

"Well, no, but they would not have been suspected as homicides if the two victims had not been under investigation."

"The local police are looking through the hotel registries for me. I guess they'll report it to you if you have an APB out on her."

"Yes. I'm glad you have friends. Be careful."

"I will. Thanks."

৪৫৪

Walter took his family to the US to see his parents and in-laws, so Sandra was the only NIS agent for the last two weeks of the year. The day after the medical board, Joe flew to Fiumicino and took the *rapido* nonstop train to Naples. She was waiting on the platform.

"Don't keep me guessing, love. What did the board

say?"

"They gave me a choice. Full duty with some restrictions or restricted line. Either way, no discharge."

"Considering what we were looking at last summer, that sounds good. Why are you not more excited?"

"Now I—"

"*Fetente juventino!*" Sandra braked and downshifted to skid around the Fiat 600 running a stop sign.

"You know, I've never heard you use the horn," he said after they straightened out on the Corso Umberto.

"It doesn't do anything. A hand on the horn can't pull the emergency brake or steer."

"What good is it, then?"

"Warning pedestrians not to step in front of the car. Not much else." She stopped for a red light. "So, you were saying?"

"Oh yes. Now I must decide what I want to do going forward. My lungs are at eighty-five percent, and the X-rays show only a twenty percent dark area, not even as black as it was."

"The exercise helped, eh?"

"And the nebulizer from Smithson. Mom started me on it as soon as I got back, and I brought it with me. It's amazing, although I cough up crud as if I'm going to die for about a quarter hour after I use it."

"What kind of restrictions are they talking about? And which specialty of restricted line?"

"If I want to stay unrestricted line, I can't go back to sea, at least not until my lungs clear completely and I can pass a full physical exam."

"And that could take a while."

"Next summer unless the nebulizer makes a

difference. I could miss a whole year of sea duty."

"And the restricted line options?"

"I simply apply now for one of them. Since most line officers transition after their first sea tour, I would be ahead of my peers in the new specialty."

"Here we are. Let's continue this indoors."

Sandra carried the nebulizer, Joe his suitcase. The nebulizer case resembled a lady's cosmetics valise. Almost as heavy.

Inside, they paused for a long kiss. With his luggage in the bedroom, they took glasses of Aglianico to the living room. The Gulf of Naples stretched out beyond the French doors to the balcony. They sat to admire the view.

"I will help any way I can, dear, but I am delighted you are so much better and there is an end in sight."

"Me, too, but I need to make up my mind soon. The board agreed to wait six weeks – the end of January – before issuing their decision."

"What specialties of restricted line?"

"With a little additional training, I could go Intelligence, Cryptology, or Public Affairs. With my accounting degree, I could also be fast-tracked to the Supply Corps. I'd have to go back to college for anything else."

"And the unrestricted line without sea duty?"

"Shore staff, Pentagon, NROTC, teaching at the Academy, since I have my master's, lots of things. Almost no potential for future promotion, until I qualify for sea duty." He smiled. Sandra had made three PCS moves in less than two years. He had moved twice. "If they put me in something I really enjoy, I would have to resign and try to get the job as a civilian."

"If all you need is a sounding board I will be happy to do that. I don't see any bad choices, which is probably what makes it harder, eh?"

"Right." He sipped his wine. "So, what's happening here?"

She told him about the contractors and stumbling across Mrs. Dempsey.

ജ്ജ

Sandra kissed Joe goodbye and drove to work. It seemed weird to know that he no longer needed help with normal physical tasks. With the Vespa he had his own transportation too.

The phone rang about four p.m. The duty master-at-arms was answering a call of nature.

"*Polizia militare americana, pronto?*" American military police, hello?

"You still make the office sound good, Sandra." Jim Redwood.

"Thank you sir. Is everything okay?"

"I don't know. Call me secure."

"Give me five minutes to go upstairs. Are you at work?"

"Yes."

In the Intelligence Division spaces, Sandra dialed the secure phone at FBI headquarters.

"Mary called me. Big movement in Impi. Not sure what it means, but the *Wall Street Journal* reported that an obscure investor has bought enough shares to have a controlling interest in the company. You may remember that after you arrested Braxton, Impi stock fell slightly."

"Doesn't he own the company?"

"He held the traditional fifty-one percent, but Mary

noticed that two months ago, Impi issued an equity call. Braxton didn't buy more stock, so his share slipped. Then yesterday, this investor bought up the shares needed to achieve fifty-one percent."

"Who is it?"

"Never heard of them. Daniat LLC."

She gasped then held her breath.

"Sandra?"

"Sorry, sir. I know who it is. I'm stunned."

"Well?"

"Mrs. Dempsey. Her full name is Ambessa Daniat Zula. Daniat is her mother."

"The one you saw in Naples? Braxton's secretary?"

"Hardly a secretary, but yes." She gave him a quick summary of what she had learned about the Eritrean assassin.

"What do you make of it?"

"A palace coup? Braxton is going down, and she does not plan to be a rat abandoning a sinking ship."

"Instead, she has taken over the ship."

"The Italian authorities are looking for her, but I don't expect them to find her. She just needs to sit tight until whatever happens to Braxton unfolds." She paused. "She could still be here to kill me. Protecting Braxton was her primary job for ten years, and the Impi men who imported the bombs from Libya are dead."

"Who are you working with?"

"Remember Major Mascagni? He commands the unit that investigates international arms trafficking, so he's on the *Barry* bombing case. He issued an APB on her after I reported seeing her. If she is picked up here, he'll let me know."

"Be careful, Sandra. This is big enough to crush you."

ଽଽଽ

While Joe put dinner in the oven, Sandra bent over a detailed map of Naples on the dining room table. She tried to imagine herself in Ambessa Daniat's position and what she would do. However, that required knowing what the Eritrean woman wanted to achieve. After the fourth trail through different scenarios, she gave out a frustrated sigh and leaned back on the wall, staring at the map from about the height of an aircraft approaching the runway at Capodichino.

"I thought I was burning dinner, but that's you I smell. What is making your brain smoke?"

"Where Mrs. Dempsey-Zula could have gone after she checked out of the Mediterranean Hotel."

"How many names does she have?"

"Two, but — Joe! You're a genius!" She ran to the phone. She made three calls. When she came back, she folded up the map.

"She booked a suite as Mrs. Gerald Dempsey, so she never went anywhere. The police are looking for Ambessa Daniat Zula, and the hotel registry has her recorded as Gerald."

"Of course! Always the surname first in this country."

"I called Mascagni and Gladdins, but I asked them not to move on it. Tomorrow, I'll have a full conversation on secure with them. I have a hunch about this."

"You think she may not be here to kill you."

"I will have to marry you some day, Joe. I can't have

you running around with a direct channel to my brain."

He grinned briefly. "So, what do you think?"

"Assume that Braxton did not send her to eliminate me. Why else would she be here?"

"Most obvious to me? Cut a deal with you to make sure Braxton goes down. Wouldn't he still have almost half the company?"

"No. If he is convicted, he would not be allowed to have a major interest in a firm such as Impi. She would control the company, and others would snap up his shares. It's still a very successful firm."

"Then she could simply step into the leadership role."

"A woman-owned modern mercenary company. What a concept."

"In the finest tradition of Boudicca, Joan, Gudit, and Ana Zinga."

"Show-off. You're the only guy I know who can name four famous female warriors without looking it up." He made a mock bow.

The oven timer dinged. They went into the kitchen.

"What else?" she asked.

"Again, talk to you. Show you enough to let you – and by extension the US government – know that she controls Impi and intends to run it. She probably has proof the art was Braxton's hobby, and he never used Impi assets. She might also prove he ignored her advice not to get involved in the art swapping."

"Let's work on this while we eat. I'm famished." ….

ജ ജ ജ

"Signora Gerald" let herself into her room. In one movement, she hung the trench coat on a hook and tore off her wig. She tossed it in the sink as she walked toward the drinks cabinet.

"*Buona sera, signora Zula,* or should I say good evening, Mrs. Dempsey?"

Ambessa whirled around as Sandra stepped from the door to the adjoining room.

"Agent Bari, what a surprise. How are you this evening?" Her body language, however, conveyed no surprise at all. Sandra noted that the smile included her eyes, which answered Sandra's most important question.

"I'm well, thank you." Sandra twisted her sidearm ninety degrees and arched an eyebrow. "May I assume that neither of us is here to kill the other? If so, shall we sheathe our weapons?" She paused the weapon over its holster.

Ambessa grinned broadly. "By all means." Slowly, she drew the throwing knife from behind her back and turned her body sideways, so Sandra could see her slide it into the sheath built into her belt. "I was about to pour a drink. What's your pleasure?"

"Something white. I think the hotel stocks Moselle and Trebbiano. Either."

Ambessa uncorked the half bottle of Moselle and handed a generous glass to Sandra. Then she poured herself a single malt whisky and motioned to the sitting area.

"I am glad you found me. I have been trying to talk to you since I arrived."

"The NIS office is a public space."

"And your skill at shaking me every time you leave the place is remarkable."

"Sorry about that. Mr. Braxton is not the only reason I have developed that habit."

"Did you make me?"

"No." Sandra sipped some wine. "Wouldn't you have a team on me if you wanted to find me?"

"That leads me to why I want to see you. I'm here alone, not at Mr. Braxton's behest. And I need not to have anyone at Impi know about this meeting." She motioned with her glass. "How long have you known I was here?"

"I watched you come from the Palermo ferry. I was following someone else, so I had to let you go."

"Impressive. You seem young for someone so skilled."

"Weren't you this age when you learned, ma'am?"

"So I was. Since we seem to be matched, let's not be so formal. Call me Ambessa, please."

"Sandra, then." She stared long enough for the older woman to blink. Ambessa nodded very slightly: Sandra was not setting her badge aside for this meeting. "What do you need from me?"

"I want to let you know what I am doing, but also to understand each other better. When you showed up to arrest Mr. Braxton, I was shocked. It was the first I had heard of the Naval Investigative Service. After some research, I gathered the NIS recruited you at the request of the FBI, specifically to work on art crime. Knowing the attitude of the FBI toward women and people with permanent suntans, I was not surprised. The unit that wanted you, Special Projects, watches us and we watch them.

"You may have participated in a dramatic art recovery in Rome three and a half years ago, using a cover name, Billingsley. Some of the collectors asked Impi to eliminate Billingsley, to ensure that whoever was helping Interpol and the FBI would not be able to catch their newer art thefts. I thought that these men were not reliable, but Mr. Braxton lost some art in the recovery, so he accepted the job. It was the first time that he went against my advice. I insisted that he set it up himself and not run their money through Impi. We don't operate inside the United States.

"How am I doing?"

Sandra nodded and sipped her wine. She felt grateful that she had spent so much time on this case, or she could not have held in her emotions. "Please continue."

"Does anyone ever take you for granted, Sandra?"

"Not for long. Why?"

"In my country, it is the fate of women every day, all the time. Rarely are women recognized at all."

"And yet you have your mother's and grandmother's names, which is exceptional in both Italy and Eritrea."

"You have done your research. *Complimenti.*"

"Once I learned the naming convention, it only took a baby names dictionary."

Ambessa gave a little snort.

"I grew up hating being taken for granted. It was useful during the war, but afterward every male around thought he was special, a rooster among hens. That is why my mother sent me to girls' schools as soon as she could. My late husband expected me, a Sarah Lawrence graduate, to be a housewife. My mother wasn't a housewife even in Fascist Italy!

"After Gerald died, I returned to Italy. All hell was breaking loose in Eritrea with the liberation movement. I thought the fight for a free country would be more important than my sex."

"Did you join the ELF?"

"Yes."

"How was it?"

"Same bullshit. They resented my ability to shoot and fight and expected me to fill support roles. After the third attempted rape, I decided to freelance. The Sudanese were fighting the English; the Libyans were fighting the Italians; the Algerians were fighting the French. As a mercenary I was paid to fight, not spread my legs or do the laundry."

Ambessa rose and refilled their glasses.

"Weren't the mercenaries a rough bunch?"

"After the first broken arm or kneed groin in each camp, they learned to respect me for what we were there for. And as I always delivered more than my clients asked, word got around."

"Specialized work?"

Ambessa grinned. "You probably guessed it. By the time I got to Algeria, I was working solo."

"I know about Trent Braxton and the French Foreign Legion. I take it you have had an equal relationship with him since then."

"Yes, until recently, but what do you do when you are not taken seriously?"

"Usually, I ignore it. Also, being taken for granted can be an asset in this field. The men I actually work with don't make the mistake."

"I envy you. After everything I put into Impi, I never expected this from Trent."

"I didn't sense that in your office. What is different?"

"He has a terrible temper, but he never made the mistake of venting his anger on me. However, since he got involved with these art collectors, he has been making decisions that hurt the company. I won't stand for it, but he forgets that secretary is only my cover. He has forgotten how we brought this company up."

"Why are you sharing this with me? You don't need

to betray him. Just don't kill the last witness. He'll go down."

"Because it's not about my anger with him. If I were simply annoyed with him, I would have eliminated him or left the company – or both."

"So, you don't want him taking Impi down with him?"

"You're smart for a G-man."

"I'm not FBI and I'm not a man." Sandra tilted her glass and smiled. "And I know who controls Impi, Incorporated." Ambessa's surprise lasted only a moment. "Are you trying to assure me that you won't get in our way when we take Mr. Braxton to trial, or are you asking for something?"

"A little of both. The next shareholders' meeting is in May. If he is indicted before then, the company won't suffer because others will buy his shares. I may not have the cachet of a World War Two hero, but his generation is starting to retire, and I have something of a reputation myself."

"But if he still owns his shares in May, it will be muddier."

"Right. Investors could be dumping their shares. The deepest pockets shy away from exposure or risk."

"I can't speed up the trial, you know."

"I know, but I want you to know that the prosecutors don't need to worry about Abe Armstrong. I want to protect Impi from the fallout of this trial and give you whatever you need to indict him and try him. To his credit, Trent always and only used his own money to buy art. I will provide proof to show that, so no one comes after Impi.

"Without Braxton, Impi will improve. Much of our reputation was built on my management. I don't have his temper and I don't collect art or people. I won't involve the company in stupid affairs."

They sat silently for a while. Sandra tried to picture where this case was headed now.

"Two questions."

"Ask."

"Did you know that the two men who imported the bombs for the *Barry* attack are dead?"

"Yes. Do you know who General Arcibaldo is?" Sandra nodded. "He ordered them killed to keep the trail from leading to him. The 'Ndrangheta did it for him. A boss in Cosenza owed him a favor."

"They were Impi employees."

"We fired them as soon as we found out who moved the devices from Algeria. They were acting on their own. Another question?"

"I will be going back to New York for the trial at some point."

"I can't control the art collectors, but Impi wants you to testify and survive."

"Thank you."

They rose and shook hands. Sandra walked back into the adjoining room and closed the door. The Carabinieri and the recording technician stood down after they were sure that Ambessa had turned in for the night.

CHAPTER 28

NEW YORK CITY

A FREEZING NOR'EASTER made ghostly spirals of snow rise from the grass and dance across the tarmac. Sandra and Joe wrapped their coats around themselves and sprinted for the warmth of the airport terminal.

"Next time I complain about the cold rain in Naples, slap me!" he said as they slowed inside and walked to baggage claim. An hour later, they had cleared customs and taken the subway to Federal Plaza. The prosecutor's office had booked her into the Reade Hotel, convenient to both the court and the FBI Field Office. When they had moved in and unpacked, she reassembled and checked her sidearm, then called the field office. After just a moment, she covered the mouthpiece.

"It's Jim Redwood. The prosecution is hosting a meeting in the conference room after lunch. Do you think we could stand one of the Italian restaurants near here? Jim will meet us in the lobby."

The owner of the Saltimbocca restaurant welcomed Sandra as a long-lost friend and guided them to a booth in the back of the room. They chatted about Arlene, Doug, Nancy, and tennis while the servers brought water and took their orders.

"I can't believe we're finally here for the trial," she said. "What do you need to know, sir?"

"We're caught up, thanks to the secure phone. Have you noticed anything recently?"

She nudged Joe.

"Someone tried to follow us from the apartment," he said. "That's a first because we have always been able to drop tails going home."

"Two men are watching this place," she said. "One is Impi. I don't know the other one."

"How do you know he's Impi?" Redwood looked beyond her at the door but shifted his gaze back quickly.

"He was stationed outside the field office during our coordination meeting, then at the Impi office when we arrested Braxton."

"Is Impi so shorthanded?"

"It fits with what Mrs. Dempsey told me. She won't let him use the company for personal problems. He is using men who have been with him all along."

"She seems to have been working herself into a position of control for a long time."

"Daniat LLC started buying shares more than eight years ago, which shows her commitment to Impi."

"They're good," said the FBI agent. "I only spotted one of them."

"From almost the beginning, she has managed the recruiting. Considering the client list and her contacts among African and Middle Eastern mercenaries, she could do that better than he."

"I hope they don't herd us into an ambush," said Joe.

The waiter came with their first course, spaghetti alle vongole.

After he left, Sandra asked, "Is there anything I should know before the meeting?"

"Some of the prosecutor's people and the agents you haven't met will be curious about your information. I myself wonder how you knew the history of Impi investments and tracked Dempsey's fighting between Cairo and Algeria."

"I have my secret weapon too." She patted Joe on the shoulder. "A nearly full-time research assistant."

"Very little of it is classified." He shrugged. "It's tedious, but I'm on medical leave, and research is research."

Jim finished chewing his mouthful and sipped some wine. "Come to the meeting, Joe. You'll be an asset."

"Yes, sir. Happy to help."

As they left the restaurant later, Sandra waved at the two stalkers across the street. They frowned and quickly turned in opposite directions.

"What was that about?" asked Jim.

"I wanted them to know we made them. They may or may not report it, but if we see either one again, we'll know for sure that whoever sent them is shorthanded."

෨෨෨

The conference room in the FBI Field Office was crowded, but it was bigger than the Department of Justice room several floors down. Most of the people in the room were lawyers. Sandra introduced Joe to Charlene, David, Charley, Jim, and Bob Worthman. It pained her to see the SAC so thin and pale. Occasionally she caught him suppressing a grimace. For him to be here to testify against Braxton was a major victory.

"Thank you, everyone," said the man at the head of the table. He had distinguished silver at the temples, piercing dark eyes, a thin mouth, strong chin, and a suit that would have cost Sandra two months' pay before taxes. "I'm Dexter Whitestone, US Attorney for the Southern District of New York. I see only a few new faces, but I hope to meet you all on the breaks."

He explained that this meeting would focus on the trial of Trent Braxton, although the others arrested on the third of February would stand trial later. Braxton had been arrested on state charges of harboring stolen goods and on federal charges of mail fraud, transportation of stolen goods and forgery. An Interpol Red Notice would be served to respond to Spanish and Italian charges of art theft.

The meeting ran for three hours, with breaks every hour. The prosecutors had many questions for the FBI agents but spent almost half the time questioning David, Sandra, and Joe. Most had trouble believing the extent of Joe's research and Sandra's ability to spot the forgeries in Madrid. The lab analyses from the paintings that she had identified were crucial, but they wanted to be sure that her testimony would not shift under cross-examination.

They had similar questions for Bob Worthman but seemed to accept the answers from a special agent in charge more readily than from Sandra (*pretty young thing,* Joe imagined them thinking). On the first break, Joe overheard two of the younger lawyers admitting they had never heard of NIS.

By the end of the day, Joe and Sandra were feeling the stress of the long day and the grilling. They begged off dinner invitations from David and Jim, and promised to catch up the next day. By nine p.m., they were sound asleep in their room.

ૹૹૹ

The next day individual participants worked in their offices on the questions that came out of the meeting. David asked Joe to join them.

About ten a.m., Sandra went to the SAC's office to see him.

"I wanted to see you alone a moment, sir. How are you doing?"

"Much better, but there is still one bullet in there. The surgeons want the rest of me to heal before they take it out."

"How long have you been back?"

"Only two weeks. It feels like a whole new duty station." He put down the folder he had been holding. "I'm grateful to Joe for your warning us in time to get the others out of town. Agent Vasari told me. I was delighted to meet Joe. How is he doing?"

"He has a final medical board next month. He has completely recovered, although he hasn't beaten me in tennis yet."

"What happens then?"

"Probably orders to another destroyer to catch up his sea duty."

"He'd be great in the FBI."

"Agent Redwood tried to recruit him in high school."

"I guess one cop in the family is enough."

"Yes, sir."

Joe and David were matching evidence files from the earlier arrests with the ones from this one. She walked over and squeezed his arm.

"The SAC wants to recruit you."

"He'll have to take a number. The Navy has me for three more years."

She looked at the papers and pictures laid out on the desk. "I was supposed to do that."

"I saved you some time, then." He pointed to the pile of matched documents. "While you finish, I'll go downstairs to check on our surveillance." Sandra arched her eyebrows. "I'll let you know who's there before we go out."

She kissed him on the cheek, and he left.

ʚʚʚ

The sun was setting when Sandra came off the elevator into the lobby. Joe appeared from the side.

"Same guy as yesterday until about a half hour ago." He pointed out the two men trying not to be obvious about looking at the building.

"That's one of the two watching FBI headquarters last year."

"So, one of these guys at least is working directly for Braxton. You think the other one is from Dempsey?"

"Could be."

Bob Worthman stepped off the elevator. As he neared the doors, the man that she recognized raised his arm as if hailing a taxi. Sandra threw herself on the SAC. A large, black car blocked her view of the two stalkers. Joe dropped to the floor.

Glass splintered into the lobby; screaming mingled with the popping sound of automatic rifle fire. The car accelerated away.

Joe picked himself up. Sandra got off the SAC. The two Impi men had disappeared.

After helping Worthman to his feet, she waved at Joe. They walked to the three people on the floor. One man was dead. Two women were unconscious and bleeding. Sirens were coming down the street.

"First aid kit!" Joe shouted at the reception policeman. While the guard and Sandra tended the two women, Joe went out to the street. One body on the sidewalk. Everyone else had fled.

The emergency medical technicians came in as the two women regained consciousness. Sandra stood and stepped back for the paramedics. She looked for the SAC.

Bob Worthman was sitting on the couch. His face was pale, and his teeth clenched. She sat next to him.

"Sorry, sir. Are you hit?"

"No. It's the old bullet."

"Joe! See if the ambulance has room for Agent Worthman."

He came back with two EMTs and a stretcher. As they picked up the SAC, the senior agent reached out to her.

"Thanks, Bari. I'll be okay now, but I would not have survived another bullet."

"See you in court, sir. He's going down."

They stood away from the open entrance and watched the ambulance leave.

The lobby filled with NYPD officers, detectives, and crime scene technicians. NYPD blocked off the entrance to preserve the scene and keep crowds away.

Sandra, Joe, and the guard had the most information for the detectives, but only Sandra and Joe had noticed the stakeout pair and the signal for the attack.

When the precinct detectives understood who Sandra was, and that she and Agent Worthman were the likely targets, they paid close attention to the details. They also left their cards and agreed that Sandra and Joe could make their statements the next day at the precinct.

"Let's go back to the hotel," said Joe. "I don't want to do a pub crawl tonight." He put his arm over her shoulders.

"Me, neither. Ouch!" She winced. "My back!"

He took his arm away.

"You've been hit."

"Let's look at it."

In the hotel room, he examined the streak across her back.

"I think the bullet scorched the blazer going across your shoulder blades, but the skin is not broken. You need a new blouse and jacket."

"And I'll have a doozy of a bruise soon." She folded the clothes carefully. "Bag these, please, they'll be evidence someday."

While he found a dry cleaner's bag in the closet and wrapped the clothes, she called the NYPD precinct and left a message for the detective in charge of investigating the attack.

They sat at the table in the room and considered the situation.

"I want to talk to Ambessa about the two guys we did not recognize." She dialed an outside line. Joe admired her ability to remember countless phone numbers.

"Hello, Ambessa. I expected the answering service, but I need to ask you some questions… Yes… Sure. See you then." She hung up.

"She knew what happened, and she will meet us downstairs in a half hour."

Joe was waiting in the hotel lobby when Ambessa walked in. He approached her with his hand out.

"Mrs. Dempsey, I'm Joe Lockhart."

"Sandra's friend." She shook the hand and looked around.

"Yes, ma'am. Very pleased to meet you. Sandra has spoken highly of you." He motioned to the hotel bar. "Let's find a booth."

"I expected to meet her."

"Right behind you, Ambessa." Sandra smiled. "Joe is a good guy. Come."

The Impi owner shook her head. "I need to retire. That's the second time."

They took a booth in the back of the bar where they could watch the kitchen door and the main entrance. They sat in silence until the server brought their drinks and went away.

"Two Impi men watched the attack from across the street," said Sandra. "Joe was watching them."

"Two more watched us go to lunch yesterday," he said.

Ambessa said, "Only one Impi operative was watching you. He ran from the scene and called me immediately."

"So, who was the other one? I recognized the one yesterday from January, and one today from surveillance in Washington last year."

"Part of the original crew loyal to Braxton."

"Where is your boss in all this?"

"He's not my boss. He has not been to work for a week. As soon as I learned of the unauthorized surveillance yesterday, I called an emergency meeting of the board. They will be here tomorrow."

"But Braxton is the CEO, and he is due in court," said Sandra. "He can't be two places at once."

Ambessa looked at her glass for a while, then fixed her gaze on the NIS agent.

"He won't be in either place, I'm afraid. He is taking matters into his own hands.

"You won't be safe until he is found and stopped."

ﬧﬧﬧ

The next day, Sandra and Joe sat in Federal Court. The bailiff consulted with the judge for a long time. Then the judge called a recess until after lunch.

They walked to the precinct to make their statements, and to turn in the damaged clothing. The detective thanked them.

"How sure are you about suspecting Trent Braxton?"

She explained what she had learned from Ambessa and how Braxton was at that moment absent from court and being fired from his job at Impi. She identified the four operatives, and gave him Mrs. Dempsey's contact information at Impi, Inc.

They ate lunch in the dining room of the hotel. Everywhere else felt too exposed.

ﬧﬧﬧ

As they approached the steps of the courthouse after lunch, Sandra grabbed Joe arm and pulled him to the lawn. She crouched next to a tree.

Sandra pointed to a bushy area on the other side of the path they had been using. Trent Braxton was crouching out of sight of the steps, watching the people coming and going. "Can you get to his other side?" Joe nodded. "Go! Jump him when you see me move."

He disappeared well behind Braxton. Sandra moved carefully behind the mercenary, who seemed focused on the pedestrian traffic.

She could see a radio device of some kind in his hands. She leaned to the left and saw Joe in position. With a glance at him, she started running silently. Joe was in her peripheral vision.

Braxton sensed her presence and turned halfway. She leaped, knocking the radio away. She felt a sharp pain in her side, then nothing…

ଷଷଷ

Clouds. White and puffy. An oak, its limbs bare.

Sandra rolled over. Joe was lying on a motionless Braxton.

"Joe!"

"I don't trust him to stay down. Help me."

She stood too quickly and paused to let her head settle. She knelt on Braxton's back and took the handcuffs from her jacket. She asked Joe, "Where's the detonator?"

Joe looked around. "There." He walked to the device.

"Don't touch it! Get the police." She pointed to the steps with her head. Joe ran. She finished cuffing Braxton's wrists. He stirred, then lay there when he realized that the NIS agent with a knee in his back was not going to move.

After the police took Braxton away, she felt a sharp pain when she tried to stand. Looking down, she saw the blood soaking her jacket and the top of her trousers. A short blade dangled from her side. Joe caught her as she collapsed…

Two hours later, the emergency evacuation of the Federal Courthouse ended, and the building went back to work. The bomb squad found a pair of antipersonnel mines positioned to kill everyone on the stairs with the press of a button from Braxton's radio.

Sandra woke up in the hospital. The small blade had not done much damage, but she had bled enough to faint. She was released the next day.

The photo of the bleeding NIS agent kneeling on the bomber led the newspaper and TV coverage for two days.

Abe Armstrong withdrew as Braxton's attorney, citing a conflict of interest because he was retained by Impi, Inc. The court ordered Braxton held without bail. The Impi Board of Directors fired him and elected Ambessa Daniat Zula-Dempsey as the new CEO.

Sandra and the SAC testified in the trial. Braxton was found guilty of all charges from the international theft of the five pictures. He was remanded to custody pending sentencing. Then the state trials for murder-for-hire and mass murder, and another federal trial for explosives violations and attempted mass murder could go ahead. Impi, Inc., filed an intention to sue in civil court for misuse of corporate assets, just in case.

Special Agent Bari returned to her duty station at COMFAIRMED in Naples. Lieutenant Junior Grade Lockhart reported to the National Naval Medical Center for his final medical evaluation. He was returned to full duty and reported to a guided missile destroyer undergoing overhaul in the Norfolk Naval Shipyard in Portsmouth, Virginia. The ship deployed to the Mediterranean Sea in September.

Joe's ship spent Christmas in Naples and came back for three more visits during the deployment. The apartment overlooking the Bay of Naples became the setting for passionate loving, but also long hours of conversation about their lives going forward.

In March, Sandra had orders again, this time to NIS Field Office, Norfolk, Virginia.

CHAPTER 29

NORFOLK, VIRGINIA

USS *CONYNGHAM* (DDG-17) STEAMED THROUGH THE NIGHT at twenty knots, the "bone in her teeth" as she cut through the Atlantic. After nine months on deployment, excitement hummed in the chest of every man on board. Tomorrow, they would be home.

"Attention on deck. This is Lieutenant Borne. Lieutenant Lockhart has the deck!"

"Aye, aye sir!"

Joe could see a few grins in the glow of the radar repeaters. He grinned, too, then looked out to make sure he could still see stars through the windows, and not any reflections…

Twelve hours later, he returned in his Tropical White Long uniform, just as the boatswain's pipe squealed on the public address system, "Now set the Special Sea Detail!"

Hardly anyone moved on deck. Almost every man on board was already at his sea detail station, eagerly looking west to spot the Chesapeake Bay Bridge-Tunnel. White uniforms lined the sides and the lifelines of the upper decks. No one who could be outside wanted to wait inside.

In the midmorning, the twenty-first sea detail since Joe had conned his damaged ship into a Med moor ended with a squeal on the speakers, "Now secure the Special Sea Detail!"

Civilians packed the pier: wives, fiancées, parents, and children of the men of Destroyer Squadron Twenty-Six. Joe scanned for the familiar figure in a blazer and an auburn chignon. *With my luck, she has duty for someone who got hurt.*

He went to the wardroom. The quarterdeck and gangway would be impassable for a while.

"Ciao, amore." Sandra wrapped her arms around him. The kiss was long and deep.

He stepped back. "Your hair!"

"You like it?" She twirled the blond ponytail.

"It's you again. I got used to the auburn bun."

"I hope you're not disappointed. Hair color is not healthy, you know. No one should notice this dye job as my hair grows out."

"It looks great. How come you were not on the pier?"

"I was. The OOD recognized the NIS agent from Naples and waved me aboard while they were setting up the quarterdeck." She took his hand. "Let's go. I can't wait to show you our new apartment."....

ଈଈଈ

Sandra let herself in and wrestled the shopping bags to the kitchen counter. Her blouse was soaked, and even without air conditioning, their apartment felt blessedly cool. Joe would be back from the Caribbean tomorrow, and she wanted something special for their first meal together since June. She had already arranged to have the next three days off.

The phone rang.

"Hello. I'm glad you're home." Jim Redwood.

"Great to hear from you. What can I do for you, sir?"

"I wanted to get to you before Marty did. Tomorrow morning, the Bureau will send email to all agencies with federal law enforcement officers offering transfers to women who want to join the FBI."

"We knew this would happen. The papers ran articles on two women going through Quantico already."

"Are you still interested?"

She paused, then took a deep breath.

"Short answer, yes. Still interested."

"But…?"

"Joe gets back tomorrow, and this is part of a larger conversation. Let me make some phone calls and talk to some people who may be affected."

"I understand."

"Would this be regular service, with PCS moves every so often? The full range of investigations?"

"Yes."

"I'll look for the announcement, but do you want me to contact you directly?"

"Please. You have a record with the Bureau already."

ଷଷଷ

The next morning, Sandra stood on the pier with the wives and children. None of the other women worked outside the home. The school-age children were in their classrooms.

There were not as many as after a full deployment, but the emotions running through the little crowd ran from the giddy excitement of new brides and little children for whom a three-month cruise seemed forever to the easy familiarity of older wives who enjoyed hanging out with their friends on the pier almost as much as seeing their husbands.

Sandra's own feelings whirled somewhere in the middle. She was chatting with Dot Hennessey, the XO's wife, and Margie Buchwald, the CO's spouse. They were old hands by comparison, having married during graduation week at the Naval Academy. When they met Sandra in Naples last Christmas as an experienced NIS agent whose military rank matched that of the XO, they had welcomed her among the senior wives in a way that the junior wives could not. On the other hand, Sandra shared the girlish anticipation of those younger wives, both because of her age and because she had never lived with Joe for more than a few months at a time.

When the gangplank was ready, the three women smiled as a half dozen preschoolers broke from their mothers to run ahead. Sandra and Dot reached out quickly. Each grabbed a small wrist, which blocked the stampede before the first step. Margie held out a hand and beckoned the young families to go first. The embarrassed mothers took charge of their children, except for one who had three; Sandra escorted the six-year-old and followed the others aboard.

Forty-five minutes later, Joe came to the wardroom, and they could go home....

ෂෂෂ

As she returned the phone handset to its cradle, Sandra heard the key in the front door. She held it open so Joe could wheel his bicycle into the apartment. They had converted the small dressing area near the entrance into parking for the bicycles. He left his things in the bicycle panniers and turned around with his arms out.

"I'm still sorry I had duty when you took time off," he said after the passionate kiss.

"Don't worry about it. I made more phone calls about Jim's offer."

They walked into the kitchen, where he extracted a beer from the refrigerator and held it up with an inquiring look. Sandra demurred. She had been comfortable in the apartment for hours, while he was still sweating from the ride down Hampton Boulevard. They sat in the living room.

"Well?"

"I talked to Marty at ONI, Mel at the Brooklyn, and David." The Office of Naval Intelligence operated the NIS.

"How are they?"

"Fine. And Bob Worthman has completely recovered. I talked to him too. He is thinking of retiring next year, though I think he'd make a great liaison officer in Rome. I told him so. He had not thought about that."

"So would David. Anyway, are you any closer to a decision? NIS, FBI or something else?"

"Something else does not include housewife, you know. I like your cooking better than mine. However, what if I took a job at the Brooklyn or another museum? The Frick, the Met, and the National Gallery of Art have openings. So does the Chrysler here in Norfolk. None pay as well as a special agent, but enough to get by.

"The decision depends on what you want to do."

"Why me?" Joe took a swig of his beer.

"Because everyone is being so damn helpful. Marty even said the NIS would be willing to second me to New York to help with Interpol cases. He said it's no more inconvenient to a field office than sending me to be a special agent afloat for a year, and the FBI would reimburse NIS for my pay.

"I need to know whether you want to stay in or not before I commit myself."

"That's easy. If you want to be a special agent, I'll go into the Naval Reserve and become a full-time translator. I enjoy translating more than anything else – even my work in the Navy has involved more translating than I expected; it has been what I enjoyed most.

"I can translate anywhere, so if you get transferred, I can pack up my fax machine, dictionaries and typewriter, and move with you. The translating makes more per hour than my Navy salary."

"But you had your heart set on going to sea."

"I've done that. I owe the Navy eighteen more months of active service and another year in the Naval Reserve. If I stay in the reserves, I would be available if the Navy needs me. So, which do you want to do?"

"I want to work the art cases in New York. Bob Worthman said he would love to have me full-time because he's shorthanded. But he would not mind sharing me with the Brooklyn. He and Mel liked the arrangement because it was so flexible."

"Could you work full-time at the Brooklyn, consulting to the FBI?"

"Yes. And consulting for the Bureau would pay better per hour than my agent salary, as you well know.

Also, I would not risk a transfer to New Mexico or Tampa. No badge and gun, though."

"You like that, don't you?"

"It's exciting, but we're sitting here having a rational discussion about it. The art collectors are scary enough, but it would be a shame to take a bullet busting pushers in a parking lot."

"What if you take no action?"

"I stay here in Norfolk at the NIS Field Office until the next set of PCS orders."

"When do you need to tell someone?"

"I promised Jim an answer this week."

Joe finished his beer and thought for a while. "Unless I missed something, it seems that you should stay with the NIS but arrange for the FBI to request you for specific art cases, at least until my obligated service expires. You won't get NIS orders before that because you only reported here last spring. Before you have to move, we'll know whether you want to stay with NIS, go to a museum or transfer to the FBI." He paused. "What do you think?"

"I think I love you." She moved into his arms. "Grazie, amore. This sort of choosing drives me nuts. Now we have a plan."

"Shall we have dinner and a movie to celebrate?"

"A movie would be fun, but let's eat here. What movie?"

"*La Dolce Vita* at the Naro Cinema. I never saw it when it came out."

"I wanted to see it, too, but the theater in Ohio would not let us in. Let's see how many places we recognize."

The end

Author's Notes

This completes the original *Lockhart* trilogy, but Joe, Sandra, and the supporting characters will step into other adventures. Look for them.

The *Lockhart* books are not historical novels, but the stories unfold in a particular time. In the United States, art theft was not a crime. Constance Lowenthal, arguably one of the preeminent experts on art theft and forgery, was still in graduate school. The FBI would not establish the Art Crime Division until 2004. However, the USA was always a major market, so the FBI helped Interpol pursue criminals on foreign warrants, using existing American laws, for example, transporting stolen goods, deceit, forgery, theft, grand larceny, and mail fraud.

All characters are fictional and any resemblance to real persons is coincidental.

There is some science fiction in the story. Today, X-ray analysis can display hidden images under paintings, but it was not even a dream then. I also made up the Smithson nebulizer and the black goo from the bombs that damaged *Barry*.

On the other hand, Sandra's skill in comparing paintings and her marksmanship are not superpowers. Think of a super-recognizer with very sharp vision. She also has the exceptional hearing, smell, and hand-eye coordination of a superior athlete, but she isn't about to fly anywhere.

For the seagoing parts of the tale, I followed the English maritime usage of the era: a friendly ship is "she," an enemy ship is "he," and an unidentified ship is "it."

Characters who have lived in Italy tend to call Italian cities by their local names except for the big three (Rome, Venice, Naples). They do this even when not speaking in Italian. Thus, you may see Genova, Livorno, Firenze, etc. in dialog.

I hope you have enjoyed reading this book as much as I enjoyed writing it. If so, please leave a review with the retailer of your choice (Amazon, Barnes & Noble, Draft2Digital, Feltrinelli, Goodreads, Google, Kobo, Smashwords, etc.). Recommend it to your local library, or post something on social media. The hashtag #jthinenovels will lead people to my books.

Any writer worth the name is grateful for the criticism of careful readers. Write to jt@jthine.com. My thanks in advance.

Dramatis Personae

Recurring characters in the *Lockhart* series, in alphabetical order within each book. Major characters in bold. An asterisk (*) indicates a real person.

Volume One. Lockhart:

Adriano – Smithson Italia driver.

Ettore Arcibaldo, General, Carabinieri Corps, Italian Army (retired) – neofascist politician and former head of the Italian military police.

Lucius J. Arland (Luke) – Vice President for Strategy and Investment, Smithson Global Group.

Beatrice (Bea) – Luke's sister.

Elly – Luke's niece, Bea's daughter.

Signor Barbera – manager at the Mayflower warehouse.

Sandra Billingsley – GWU student, secretary in the FBI Liaison Office.

Manfredo Bonin (Manny) – investor, art collector and Arcibaldo supporter.

Marcantonio Borghese – Lanzera family friend.

Angela Ceccarelli née Rossi – housekeeper and cook for the Lockharts.

Claudia, secretary to the First Minister, American Embassy, Rome.

Klaus Durst – Chief Financial Officer, Smithson
Deutschland GmbH.

Maryse Durst – Klaus' wife.

Matt Fisher – Joe's classmate, the only one with a car.
Lives in Vigna Clara.

Giacomo – Luke Arland's secretary.

Maria Grazia – Executive secretary to Nancy Lockhart.

Hans – Joe's classmate, newly arrived from Germany.

Helmut Gottlieb – President of Smithson Deutschland
GmbH.

Maria Gottlieb – Helmut's wife.

Greg – Joe's classmate, a passenger in Matt's car.

Kurt Hansen – CEO of Bayer GmbH.

Mathilde Hansen (Matty) – Kurt's wife.

Siegfried Kanter –investor, art collector and Arcibaldo
supporter.

Count Otto von Kracken – Chief Operating Officer,
Bayer GmbH.

Leonora Coburg von Kracken – Otto's wife.

Aldo Lanzera – Joe's classmate, who lives downtown.

Conte di Lanzera – Aldo's father.

Benjamin Liu (Benny) – Joe's best friend and classmate.

**Jason Joseph Lockhart, Jr. (Joe) – student and
translator.**

Jason Joseph Lockhart, MD (Jace) – Joe's father and
Nancy's late husband.

**Nancy Ardwood Lockhart, MD, PhD – Vice
President for Operations, Smithson Italia
SpA. Joe's mother.**

Brother Mark – history teacher at Notre Dame
International School (NDI).

Sandro Moretti – President of Smithson Italia SpA.

Brother Peter – biology teacher at NDI.

Mario Perla, Commander, Italian Navy – assigned to SIFAR (Military Intelligence Service).

Giuseppe del Piave (Pino) – owner of the del Piave Group.

Maurizio Proietti – motocycle officer with the *Polizia di Stato.*

James Redwood, Special Agent, FBI (Jim) – FBI Liaison Office, Rome.

Douglas Redwood (Doug) – Jim's son, Joe's classmate, captain of the basketball team. Passenger in Matt's car.

Brother Roger – headmaster of NDI.

Mario Rossi – Angela Ceccarelli's brother, killed in a terrorist bombing in Milan.

Vittoria Rossi – Angela Ceccarelli's sister.

Sonia Rossi– Angela Ceccarelli's sister.

Giuseppe – Sonia's husband.

Signor Sacchi – Director of Personnel, Smithson Italia SpA.

Sonja Sankar – Sandra's classmate and friend from the George Washington University.

Sandro Santis – investor, art collector and Arcibaldo supporter.

Siegfried Scherer – Operations Plans, Bayer GmbH.

Hans Schmidt – Vice President for Operations, Smithson Deutschland GmbH.

Ulrike Bessemer Schmidt (Rikki) – former German national tennis champion, Hans' wife.

Hans Ulsdorf – General manager, Grand Hotel Cologne.

Vittoria – the Redwood's maid in Vigna Clara.

Betty Walker – former girlfriend of Joe, who returned to
the USA.
Tex Wilder – oilman, art collector and Arcibaldo
supporter.
Steven Wolcowski (Steve) – First Minister, American
Embassy, Rome.
Robert Worthman, Special Agent in Charge (Bob), FBI
Field Office, New York City.
Patricia Worthman (Patsy) – his wife.

Volume Two. Enemies:

Those in *Lockhart,* plus:

Professor Alberini – conservation instructor at the
American Academy, Rome.
Serena Alquilar – Diego's friend from Greenbelt,
Maryland.
Matthew J. Ardwood, Brigadier General, US Army (ret)
– Joe's maternal grandfather.
Annabelle Dampierre Ardwood – Joe's maternal
grandmother.
**Mary Ardwood – Professor at Sweet Briar College.
Nancy's aunt. Matthew's sister.**
Arnold Billingsley (Arnie) – Sandra's youngest brother.
ROTC at Ohio State University.
James Billingsley (Jim) – Sandra's younger brother.
ROTC at OSU.
Martin Billingsley, CWO, USA (retired) – Sandra's
father.
Marcia Billingsley – Sandra's mother. Art teacher at
London (OH) High School.
Martin Billingsley, Jr., MU2, USN (Marty) – Sandra's
eldest brother.

Walter Billingsley, Staff Sergeant, USMC – Sandra's older brother.

Elaine Blankenship – Commanding Officer's secretary, NROTC Unit, UVA.

Lieutenant Briggs, USN – Intelligence Officer (N-2), Amphibious Squadron Two.

Darlene – waitress at the diner/coffee shop on Dupont Circle.

Steven Dixon – legacy student who resented rooming with Diego and started a fight.

Matthew Ford – legacy student who resented rooming with Diego and started a fight.

Nunzio Giraldi – Professor of Italian, UVA.

Professor Gonzalez – Chairman, Department of Spanish, Italian and Portuguese, UVA.

Madeleine Grimaldi, MD – incoming Vice President for Operations, Smithson Italia SpA.

Gunnery Sergeant James Henry, USMC – instructor at NROTC Unit, UVA.

Jack – Resident Assistant, McCormick Hall, UVA.

Major Jackson, USMC – Executive Officer, NROTC Unit, UVA.

Leroy Jefferson – Sandra's classmate at the FBI Academy.

Lucy – Sandra's roommate at the American Academy conservation course.

Martin MacKenzie, Special Agent, NIS (Marty) – Special Agent Afloat (SAA), US Sixth Fleet.

Anthony Madison (Tony) – in Spanish class with Joe. Martial arts instructor and friend.

Alvin and Thelma Madison – Tony's parents.

Alcide Mancini, Major, Carabinieri Corps, Italian Army – leading the raid at Arcibaldo's villa.

Professor Mattei – conservation instructor at the American Academy, Rome.

Melanie – Sandra's roommate at the American Academy conservation course.

Lieutenant Commander Masters, USN – Instructor, NROTC Unit, UVA.

Karen Monroe – Sandra's friend from high school.

Samara Majid Monroe – acclaimed artist, Karen's mother.

Zebadiah Monroe, Master Sergeant, USA (retired) (Zeb) – Karen's father.

Cornelia Moretti – Sandro Moretti's wife.

Doctor Morgen – curator at the National Gallery of Art.

Gunnery Sergeant Mosely, USMC (ret) (Sarge) – combat instructor, FBI Academy.

L. Michael Norwood, Captain, USN – Commanding Officer, NROTC Unit, UVA.

Eleanor Page – operator of a boarding house, friend of Matt and Annabelle Ardwood.

Officer Payne – Richmond Police Department.

Mark Pietrowicz, Special Agent, FBI – FBI Liaison Officer, Rome.

Nelson Portague, Vice Admiral, USN – Commander, US Sixth Fleet (COMSIXTHFLT).

Arlene Redwood – Jim Redwood's wife and Doug's mother. Cellist.

Dottor Ricci – Editor of Il Secolo d'Italia, the MSI party newspaper.

Marcantonio Rispoli, RD3, USN – radar operator in CIC, USS Point Defiance.

Sergeant Robinson, USMC (ret) – friend of Sgt. Mosely. Owns a dojo in Georgetown.

(*) Pierre Paul Saunier – Assistant to President Shannon.

Ed Schlesinger, Cadet, USAFR – Air Force ROTC, Diego and Joe's neighbor.

Dietrich Schulz – Professor of German, UVA.

(*) Edgar Shannon – President of the University of Virginia.

Charles Spears, Special Agent, FBI (Charley) – art crimes investigator, NY Field Office.

Bubba Taylor, BT3, USN – Petty Officer in forward fireroom, USS Point Defiance.

Officer Tomkins – Richmond Police Department.

Diego de la Torre y Alcina – Joe's roommate in McCormick Hall, UVA.

Don Carlos de la Torre – Diego's father.

David Vasari, Special Agent, FBI – art crimes investigator, NY Field Office.

Beniamino Vasari – David's ancestor, son of Giorgio.

William White – Professor at the George Washington University.

Maria Williams – FBI Liaison Office secretary who replaced Sandra.

Roy Yu – friend and classmate of Sandra at the FBI Academy.

Millie Yu – Roy's wife.

Annie Yu – Roy and Millie's daughter.

Volume Three. Art to Die for:

Those in *Lockhart* and *Enemies,* plus:

Maureen Andrews – Professor of Fine Art, GWU, Sandra's advisor.

Charlene Angelilli – Secretary in the FBI Field Office, New York City.

Abraham Armstrong (Abe) – Impi, Inc. attorney.

Alessandra Bari, Special Agent, NIS (Sandra) – Sandra Billingsley's new identity.

Frank Benally, Special Agent, FBI – art crimes investigator, NY Field Office.

Dale Berken – Facilities Management at Smithson Global.

Trent Braxton – CEO, Impi, Inc., mercenary.

Walter Brennan, Special Agent, NIS (Walt) –NIS Agent, COMFAIRMED Naples.

Michael Burton, LCDR, USN – Chief Engineer, Barry, then acting CO.

Maria Chavez – Secretary of Department of Spanish, Italian and Portuguese, UVA.

Mary Ellen – Sandra's replacement at the "farm."

Melvin Conti – Head conservator, the Brooklyn Museum.

John Covert, CDR, USN – Commanding Officer, USS Semmes.

Amanda Curtis – violinist at the National Symphony Orchestra.

François and Adele – Dampierre family retainers, now working for the Ardwoods.

Ambessa Daniat Zula Dempsey – Impi, Inc. "secretary" and operative.

General Garcia, Guardia Civil – Commander of the Heritage Protection Division.

Mrs. Garland – Joe's landlady on Wertland Street in Charlottesville.

Dale Garson, LT, USN – Operations Officer, Barry, then acting XO.

Ari Gersheim, Jr., MD – attending physician at Naval
       Hospital Naples, and son of Nancy's dissertation
       advisor.
Arthur Gladdins, Special Agent, FBI (Art) – FBI
       Liaison Officer, Rome.
Morton Gladwick, MD – attending physician at
       National Naval Medical Center, Bethesda,
George Gorman – Nebraska-born art collector with a
       forged Ghirlandaio.
Buck Greenwald, CWO, USN – First Lieutenant,
       Barry.
Jack Hardmon, Special Agent, Bureau of Alcohol,
       Tobacco, and Firearms (ATF) – Hudson Valley
       Office.
Major Lopez, Spanish Guardia Civil – Heritage
       Protection Division.
Mac – FBI computer technician.
Senior Chief Machinist Mate MacKay, USN – Main
       Engineering Control, USS Semmes (DDG-18).
Commander Robert Majella, USN (Bob) –
       Commanding Officer, Barry.
Linda Martinez – graduate student at James Madison
       University and FBI programmer.
Major Mascagni, Carabinieri Corps, Italian Army –
       international arms trafficking unit.
Selena Menendez – violinist and Sandra's childhood
       friend.
Crunch McCall, Special Agent, FBI – FBI Resident
       Agent, Charlottesville, Virginia.
LT (j.g.) William Meadows, USN (Bill) – CIC Officer,
       Barry, then acting Operations Officer.
Doctor Messer – Director of the Frick Collection, New
       York City.

Maria Michaelis – X-ray technician at the Brooklyn
Museum.
George Montoya – Impi, Inc. operative.
Seaman Morgan – wardroom messman in Barry.
Seaman Morton – wardroom messman in Semmes.
Captain Morissetti, Carabinieri Corps – directing the
local interagency team responding to the Barry
bombing.
Wesley Morton, Special Agent, ATF (Wes) – Hudson
Valley Office explosives investigator.
Senior Chief Machinist Mate Murray, USN – Main
Engineering Control, USS Barry (DD-933)
Xavier Palumbo, Special Agent, NIS –SAA US Sixth
Fleet.
Dale Peters, Special Agent in Charge, FBI – Field
Office, Columbus, Ohio.
(*) General Louis "Chesty" Puller, US Marine Corps –
eulogist at Jason Lockhart's funeral.
Mack Shaughnessy, Special Agent, FBI – art crimes
investigator, NY Field Office.
Sidney (Sid) – Special Agent, NIS Washington, DC.
LT (j.g.) Peter Skouras, USN (Pete) – Damage Control
Assistant, Barry, then acting Chief Engineer.
Captain Joshua Southwood, MC, USN (Josh) –
Commanding Officer, National Naval Medical
Center, Bethesda.
Kenneth Strong, Special Agent in Charge, NIS (Ken) –
Washington, DC.
Dario Torino, Special Agent, FBI – art crimes
investigator, NY Field Office.
Sherry Twopeak, Special Agent, NIS –NIS Washington,
DC.

Peter Wembly (Major Pete) – Security at Smithson
    Global.
Barry Weschler, Special Agent, NIS – Resident Agent,
    Naval Station Rota, Spain.
Dexter Whitestone – US Attorney, SDNY.
Mortimer Winslow, Special Agent, ATF – teaching a
    course in Rome, called to the scene of the Barry
    bombing.